AIMÉE—the voluptuous flaming-haired, green-eyed spy who becomes a legend in New Orleans.

BRYAN—brooding, clever, handsome, and very much in love with the wife who spurns him.

VICKIE—an unscrupulous trouble-maker who does her best to ruin Aimée.

JUDD—Bryan's jealous brother, who will stop at nothing to gain his own ends.

JOHN RUNEFELT—the spy who loves Aimée and puts her life in danger.

Flame of New Orleans

—a towering novel of love, adventure, and intrigue in the Old South.

ABOUT THE AUTHOR

FRANCES PATTON STATHAM, a musician and artist, is
a native South Carolinian now living in Atlanta, Georgia.
She is a graduate of Winthrop College and the University
of Georgia. Mrs. Statham has recently completed three
years as a director and vice-president of a national
volunteer organization and is now president of her county
hospital auxiliary. She has three children, and includes
in the family an English setter. Mrs. Statham is currently
working on a new novel.

Flame Of New Orleans

Frances Patton Statham

A FAWCETT GOLD MEDAL BOOK

Fawcett Publications, Inc., Greenwich, Connecticut

$\mathcal{T}$o my sons—
George and Tim

Prologue

"They're coming!" a childish high-pitched voice shouted. "They're coming from the levee!"

The belfry from Christ Church on Canal Street began to toll the alarm and the news rapidly spread to every corner of New Orleans.

The sky was still black with smoke. Flaming ghost ships sailed unattended down the river and the sickening odor of burning cotton and sugar permeated the air.

Frantic, shrill voices of mothers calling to their children added to the din of the bells and the drubbing of feet against the cobblestones. Children were snatched from open doorways, doors were barred, and suddenly the only signs of life in the Vieux Carré were the enormously wide frightened eyes staring from behind tatted lace curtains—eyes watching warily for the approach of the enemy.

At the noise and uneasiness along the levee, an old brown pelican extended his six-foot wing span, and hoisting his awkward body from the wooden pile, flew to a deserted lagoon where he could watch in peace for the mullet and menhaden to fill his empty pouch.

Aimée, hearing the alarm, hurried from the shelter of the walled garden onto the banquette, anxious to see these Yankees who had come to take over her city. Her foot slipped and splashed in the gutter, where molasses flowed in a sluggish torrent. Not waiting to rescue the slipper caught in the sticky morass, she walked quickly on, pressing her hooded cape close to her in an attempt to

5

keep the rain from her face.

A newspaper caught against a lamp post fluttered in the breeze, its headlines streaked by the rain. Only the date, April 25, 1862, was readable in the top right-hand corner. But Aimée had no need to scan the paper. She knew the news by heart. . . .

The two lonely forts at Plaquemind Bend, guarding the seventy-odd miles of river, had not been sufficient defense, as Beauregard had warned, to repel the enemy. And so, the flotilla of ships, gunboats, and smaller vessels had sailed from the Gulf, breaking the chain across the river channel, hurrying past the ineffective guns of the forts, in its unceasing drive to the very doors of New Orleans.

And now, the general in charge of defending the city was evacuating his troops farther upriver, since the city was lost.

Still, Aimée could not believe that this was actually happening. When the war first started, her brother, Etienne, had teasingly pinched her cheek and said, "Do not worry, *ma petite*—we will have the Yankees whipped in no time. Have the gumbo waiting on the stove . . . I like it hot, you know." But despite his attempt at lightness, he had left with a heavy heart.

Never again would he taste the hot gumbo he loved, or dip the hard crusts of bread into the thick black coffee. Never again would he tease her, pulling her curls or pinching her cheek—for Etienne had fallen at Shiloh.

Aimée's tears of silent, frustrated anger mingled with the drops of rain falling on her cheeks.

Closer to the square, the people crowded the banquettes and spilled over into the streets, but they made little noise; for they were listening for the tramping of feet.

Aimée stood on tiptoe, but she was too far back to see anything.

"*Mon Dieu*, they are fierce looking," someone whispered.

Just then she found a small opening and quickly pressed through to see the sailors and marines marching up the street. Their bayonets were fixed and their faces alert to the hostile expressions of the people lining the streets.

There was no military authority present to answer the

formal demands of surrender. The only civil official on hand, the town mayor, took no part in the ceremony, but walked down the steps and stood with arms crossed, directly in front of one of the howitzers, in an attitude of protection for his people.

Aimée clenched her fists as the pelican flag was replaced by another flag . . . but there was nothing she could do, nothing anyone could do, with the howitzers pointing at them, ready to fire at the first sign of disorder.

As quickly as it had begun, the ceremony was over. The uniformed squads moved across the square, taking their weapons with them. The city now belonged to the enemy.

Dejectedly, Aimée drifted from the square with the other spectators surrounding her. The rain had slackened and Aimée, now conscious of the eyes turning in her direction, watching her furtively, and the elbows jostling her with an occasional jab as she picked her way through the debris of the streets, felt a tremor of alarm. What would Grand-père say if he should discover that she had gone to the square alone?

She had tried so hard to please Grand-père and Tante Dee Dee ever since she and Etienne had come from Thornfell to live with them, but she had constantly been in trouble because of her impulsive, exuberant behavior. Today there would be only one person to reprimand her for her actions. The fever had carried Tante Dee Dee away, and only Grand-père remained—kind, sweet Grand-père who was at a loss to oversee an impetuous virgin of marriageable age, without Tante Dee Dee's firm hand.

Up Royal Street Aimée went, until the three-storied old pink stucco and brick house, with its black shuttered windows and wrought-iron balcony covered with bougainvillea, came into view.

She opened the gate and walked down the passageway into the walled courtyard, until she faced the door framed by leaded fan-shaped glass. The dull reflection of her movements brought the glass to life as she stepped out of the one remaining slipper and shook the water from her cape before opening the heavy oak door.

"Aimée child, where have you been?" the frail old man's voice demanded from the edge of the stairs.

"To . . . to the square, Grand-père." Aimée quickly swallowed and nervously pushed back the wet red-gold hair that hung limply in her face.

"The square?" Grand-père questioned. "You went to the square—with *canaille* crowding the streets today?" The blue eyes were piercing and Aimée hastily explained.

"I . . . I had to see for myself these enemies—these Yankees . . ."

Grand-père clucked his tongue in disapproval. "That was not wise, *ma chère*. But I suppose I shall have to be satisfied that you came to no harm with Lisette accompanying you."

At her sudden start, Grand-père's eyes narrowed. "Lisette *did* go with you, did she not?"

Aimée hesitated but knew she must tell the truth. "No, Grand-père. Lisette was busy."

"So you went alone," he said, shaking his head sadly and sighing. "So headstrong. In my day, a young girl's reputation was ruined if she appeared on the street without a maid or chaperone. If you had only taken Lisette . . ." Again he sighed. "What would Dee Dee say, if she knew?"

"I am sorry, Grand-père. I . . . I hope you are not too angry with me."

But Grand-père made no reply. His eyes had become hazy and his thoughts were seemingly lost in the past. Aimée gazed at him, her face showing her love for the white-haired old man.

His elegant way of life had disappeared and there was little left of the society he knew, with all the young men away at war. As the days passed, even the servants had become more insolent, sensing the change in the air. But Grand-père, so attuned to the tradition of the world he knew, refused to face the change, and perhaps for him it was best. He would not understand alien things.

Let him remain happy a little longer, Amiée prayed, lost in his world of what used to be—what used to be before the enemy came. . . .

Chapter 1

"**A**imée! Aimée! Stop your dancing and settle
down. If you want to be at your prettiest tonight, you
must rest the entire afternoon . . . and do put your dress
back before you spoil it."

"But Tante Dee Dee, I am too excited to rest—and
isn't it the most beautiful dress in the whole world?"

Aimée, whirling about the room, hugged the white
debutante dress to her slim body until her dizziness forced
her to release it to Tante Dee Dee's outstretched hands
before collapsing on the high tester bed whose mosquito
netting had been pushed out of the way.

"Just think," Aimée said, bouncing up immediately, "I
am sixteen today, and in a few hours I shall be sitting
in the opera box, like any other grownup, wearing a Paris
gown and waiting to be presented to society."

The turquoise eyes clouded momentarily. "Do you . . .
think I shall be ignored, Tante Dee Dee? I will die if none
of the young gentlemen come to our box during intermission."

Tante Dee Dee's voice rang through the room in an
amusing ripple of laughter as she hung up the dress.

"You? Ignored? *Ma chérie*, that is an impossibility.
Have I not seen how Etienne's friends have watched you
with covetous looks? I only feel sorry for the other *jeunes
filles* who do not have your bewitching turquoise eyes and
flaming hair. And I should not be surprised, Aimée, if
several young gentlemen were to ask your *grand-père* this
very night for his permission to call upon you tomorrow."

9

"Do you actually think so, Tante Dee Dee, or are you only determined to make me feel better?"

"I am *determined* to get you to rest, Aimée. It would be embarrassing, would it not, to go to sleep in the opera box like some *enfant* kept up beyond her bedtime?"

"Oh, Tante Dee Dee!" Aimée responded in an exasperated voice. Immediately she curled up on her bed and shut her eyes. The door closed softly and the footsteps of her aunt vanished down the hallway.

When Aimée awoke, a shiver of excitement ran through her body. She stretched a long, lazy stretch, lifting her arms high over her head and touching her toes to the carved footboard.

Her eyes, sweeping over the room, focused on the pale pink chair tied with bowknots of ribbons, on the armoire carved in the rococo manner with cupids and flowers, and finally latched onto the shelves near the window. The row of dolls sat on the top shelf and stared at her with their painted eyes—one doll for each year she had lived with Tante Dee Dee and Grand-père.

Suddenly Aimée frowned as the realization struck her. It was a little girl's room. Why had she not noticed before? The dolls should have been relegated to the attic long ago, with Etienne's toy soldiers and the other amusements that she and her brother had outgrown.

The noise of the rattling tray brought her back to the present and Aimée sprang to her feet, her nose wrinkling at the aroma of food nearby.

"Supper will be quite late tonight, Aimée, so I had Lisette fix you a tray," Tante Dee Dee explained, carrying the food into her room and setting the tray by the bedside.

"You are spoiling me, Tante Dee Dee, bringing food up to my room. I could have come downstairs for it myself."

The gray-haired plump little woman smiled. "It is not every day that the Saint-Moreau family has a daughter come of age," she said, walking back toward the door. "A little cosseting will not harm you after so many years of being forced to conform to our strict ways." Tante Dee Dee held to the knob, while glancing over her shoulder at Aimée. "But it was for your own good, *ma petite*, even if the lessons were hard to take."

"All for '*le nom de la famille*,'" Aimée said softly when the door had closed. And then she blushed, remembering the day Tante Dee Dee had caught her swinging on the gate to the street with Etienne. How ashamed she had felt to be reprimanded not only by Grand-père in his study, but later upstairs in her bedroom by Tante Dee Dee.

"The honor of the family is in your hands, Aimée, and you must never betray it."

That lesson had been branded on her mind by Grand-père's quiet, sober words. His soft syllables had seared the message far deeper into her Creole heart than any sterner tone could have.

"It is not appropriate for a Saint-Moreau to be seen flagrantly showing her petticoats to passersby," Tante Dee Dee had added in the privacy of the bedroom. "If one breath of *scandale* were even whispered about you, Aimée, no Creole gentleman of any standing whatever would offer marriage. And such disgrace to the family—you might even be forced to marry one of those *Americains*," her aunt said disparagingly. "That is, of course, if you did not wish to remain a spinster. Do you understand, Aimée?"

Aimée nodded and the slow, burning blush of remorse crept up from her neck to spread over her cheeks.

Aimée's fingers touched her cheeks as she remembered. "I was only a child then," she said aloud. "Today I am a grown-up." She smiled to herself and picked up the piece of chicken—picked it up and daintily stripped the meat to press it into her mouth.

The house was soon filled with the rush of getting dressed for the opera. Lisette ran from one room to the other, helping first Tante Dee Dee and then Aimée, using the curling tongs to make several last-minute repairs on Aimée's curls after she had slipped the shimmering white satin gown over her many crinolines.

"I think I shall faint, Lisette—if not from excitement, at least from this tight corset," Aimée complained.

"Now, Miss Aimée, I did jes' what Miss Dee Dee tol' me to. You cain't go to the opera house without a corset

11

on. You's a lady now and you jes' has to get used to feelin' like a lady."

"What is my niece complaining about, Lisette?" Tante Dee Dee asked, appearing at the door and patting her salt-and-pepper curls that had been darkened by the coffee rinse.

"Miss Aimée don't like the feelin' of her corset nippin' at her waist. I tol' her all the ladies wears 'em. Ain't no use to complain."

Tante Dee Dee scrutinized Aimée's appearance from the top of her head to the dainty white satin slippers that matched her dress ordered from Paris months before in anticipation of her debut into Creole society.

"My dear, you should be happy that you have so little to worry about," Tante Dee Dee admonished. "Now, get your bouquet. It's time to go, I can hear your brother Etienne and Papa downstairs. They won't wait forever for us. . . . Do you have your lace fan?"

"Yes, Tante Dee Dee."

Aimée made her way downstairs—walking behind her aunt, since her white dress and crinolines took up the entire width of the stairs.

"The horses are getting restless, Grand-père," Etienne's voice complained. "I wish they would hurry." Etienne's voice stopped and he stared at the two who had come into the hall.

"Tante Dee Dee, you look *très élégante* tonight."

"Thank you, Etienne."

Then he turned to stare at Aimée. "But I don't recognize the young lady with you. She looks as if she has just stepped out of the chinoiserie wallpaper—all white and gold." His eyes opened wide and mockingly, as if he had made an important discovery.

"Can it be my little snippet of a sister who had jam on her face this morning? How did you perform the miracle, Tante Dee Dee?"

"Etienne, if you don't stop your teasing, I'll . . . I'll . . ." Aimée headed toward her dark-haired brother, handsomely attired in evening clothes, and he quickly stepped aside.

"Yes, it's my little sister all right. I recognize her temper."

"Now, Etienne," Grand-père said in an amused voice, "do not disturb Aimée. This is an important night for her." Grand-père walked to Aimée's side and offered his arm. "Come, my dear, and make an old man happy to attend the opera with the most beautiful young lady of all by his side."

"Thank you, Grand-père," Aimée said gratefully, reaching up to kiss him on the cheek.

"Well, Tante Dee Dee, shall we show these two what true elegance is?" Etienne bowed low before his aunt and placed her cape over her shoulders with a flourish before holding out his arm for her plump hand.

Raoul drove the carriage down the drive and onto the street. He headed for the corner of Bourbon and Toulouse streets, where the French Opera House waited with its chandeliers of thousands of twinkling crystal prisms that put to shame the meager light of the street.

Grand-père, Aimée, Tante Dee Dee, and Etienne stepped down from the carriage and onto the carpeting that had been spread at the entrance to save the beautiful gowns from being ruined by the mud.

Other carriages were lined up to deposit their passengers and Aimée gave a startled gasp at the beauty of the woman being helped from the next carriage. But Tante Dee Dee quickly diverted Aimée's attention to the chandeliers as they climbed the flight of carpeted stairs to the horseshoe-shaped boxes of the opera house.

Their box was filled with flowers, as were many others that contained young girls now at an age to be launched into society. Aimée took her seat and her turquoise eyes showed her excitement at being treated as a grown-up, while her fingers worried the streamers to her bouquet.

"I am so excited," Aimée whispered to Grand-père, "that I have forgotten which opera is being given tonight."

"It is *La Fille du Régiment* by Donizetti," he replied. "The new soprano who has just arrived to sing the leading role has been widely acclaimed in Europe. I am anxious to hear her sing—to compare her with La Belle Marie, who sang the role last year."

13

Grand-père's eyes twinkled and he leaned closer in a more intimate pose. "But I will keep the comparison to myself, lest Pierre Marin challenge me to a duel if I should think her better than La Belle Marie."

"Oh, Grand-père, would he really do that?"

"You must not talk, Aimée," Tante Dee Dee scolded. "The opera is to begin."

Aimée, happy to have the lights dim, straightened in her chair. At least for a little while she was safe from the indignity of being ignored. But at intermission—oh, how she wished that intermission would never come. . . .

As the conductor walked to the orchestra pit to the applause of the audience, Aimée turned her head slightly and gazed upward to the balconies. Raoul was seated in the top balcony with the other blacks who had come to the opera, but Aimée could not see him. And the young gentlemen, including Etienne's friends who she was so afraid would ignore her, were scattered throughout the boxes as well as the orchestra section. No woman would dare sit in the orchestra section, for that was reserved for men alone.

Aimée heard very little of the music after the overture. The soprano was too plump and the tenor was squat and solid, not at all the type for a hero. But much too soon they had stopped singing and the audience was applauding.

There was nothing Aimée could do but wait miserably for her humiliation. As soon as the house lights brightened, she turned to Tante Dee Dee at her side and whispered, "I . . . I don't feel well, Tante Dee Dee. May we . . . may we leave now?"

"Etienne, old fellow," the voice called out from the back of the box, interrupting Tante Dee Dee's answer. "I missed you today at the Metairie races."

"Prosper," Etienne's voice replied, "what a surprise to see you here. I was not aware that you enjoyed opera."

"Well, you know how it is," he answered smoothly. "A little culture is not a bad thing to have."

"Tante Dee Dee," Etienne began, "may I present my friend, Prosper Gautier."

Aimée glanced up and saw the interested look in the tall, handsome, fair-haired man's eyes. She immediately

14

brightened as she was introduced to him, but there was no chance for conversation, for two others had made their appearances at Etienne's side.

There was a telltale look of triumph in Tante Dee Dee's eyes when the three young men cornered Grand-père for conversation before leaving the box.

Aimée nervously fluttered her lace fan while the male eyes continued to scrutinize her appearance much more thoroughly than Tante Dee Dee's had before they left home.

I wonder if they would like to look in my mouth to see the state of my teeth, mused Aimée, feeling like a filly they were considering purchasing. The thought made her giggle, and at Tante Dee Dee's stern frown in her direction, Aimée quickly lifted her fan and hid the smile lurking at the corners of her mouth.

With the steady coming and going of young men anxious to be presented to the flaming-haired girl, Etienne had disappeared . . . probably to do a little close-up investigation of his own, thought Aimée. She saw him in the next box as he talked with the parents of her best friend, Michele.

Michele also had admirers surrounding her and her dark beauty was emphasized by the beautiful white dress decorated with pale pink rosebuds at the sleeves and neck. Michele lifted her head, and turning in Aimée's direction, smiled at her, acknowledging their friendship and the success of their first night at the opera. Of course, it was no surprise to Aimée that Michele was a success. For two years she had been practicing the pretty pout and the sudden lowering of eyelashes that so devastated a man. But it was Etienne she was determined to bring to quarry, and now he had disappeared from her box.

Michele suddenly flipped her fan shut, indicating her annoyance at the conversation around her.

As the lights lowered for the second half of the opera, Etienne slipped into his seat behind Tante Dee Dee.

"Etienne," Grand-père said beside him in a low, disapproving voice, "did I see you with Madame Calti a moment ago?"

Aimée watched while Etienne's face colored and his

15

voice stammered. "I . . . I went to speak with her . . . escort about the race."

"It would be better for you if you did not seek out such questionable company, especially with all the *jeunes filles'* mothers watching you. Your timing is off, my son."

"At least the man had the grace to hide her in one of the *loges grilles*," Tante Dee Dee added.

"Who is Madame Calti?" a curious Aimée asked.

"You are not to speak her name, Aimée," the woman replied. "For you, such creatures do not exist." And that was the end of the conversation.

The singers began, and for the first time that evening Aimée relaxed to listen to the music. Forgotten were the incongruous appearances of the singers. The music was all that mattered—the spinning of golden threads of sound throughout the French Opera House. No wonder the performances were discussed for days in the coffee-houses and barber shops, with tempers sometimes flaring into a duel at The Oaks because of some imagined slur on a favorite singer.

Aimée's heart responded to the music, and with the response came a new understanding of her *grand-père's* world of pride, elegance, and beauty. She joined in the enthusiasm, applauding the singers for their performances as the curtain fell. Red roses were carried onto the stage and the soprano graciously accepted them and acknowledged the applause with a kiss nimbly conveyed from her lips to her outswept fingers.

"She is far better than La Belle Marie," Grand-père whispered to Aimée, "but I shall never mention this to Monsieur Marin."

"Where do we go now, Grand-père?" Aimée asked, leaving the opera box under his guidance.

"I have a small supper arranged at the St. Louis Hotel —and I have asked Prosper Gautier to join us there."

So Prosper Gautier was the one Grand-père had given his approval to as Aimée's suitor. Aimée clung to her *grand-père's* arm, not sure that she wanted to enter the grown-up world after all.

The next day Aimée sat in the formal salon of the

pink stucco and brick townhouse with her aunt, tensely waiting for the three men who had asked permission to call on her. One was Prosper, who had gone to supper with them the evening before, but she could not remember the other two.

Prosper Gautier was nineteen, the same age as her brother Etienne, and already Tante Dee Dee had started extolling his wealth.

"He will have a fine inheritance one day, with the magnificent plantation up the river, as well as the house in town. And you are very lucky, Aimée, to be singled out by him, especially since your *papa* gambled away Thornfell and most of his other assets before he died."

"Then I will know that he is interested in me and not my money," Aimée answered haughtily, miffed that Tante Dee Dee should speak of her *papa* in such a way. "At least I have been spared the insult of having my name listed in that horrible book with the amount of my inheritance opposite it."

"Only the initials were used," Tante Dee Dee corrected her. "It wouldn't have done for a lady's name to be spelled out. But although Prosper Gautier does not need a rich wife, Etienne should purchase a copy of the book. To marry an heiress is the only way he can continue being a gentleman of leisure."

Grand-père walked into the room, and taking his place in the chair by the window, opened the newspaper to read. He usually left it where Aimée could find it, although Tante Dee Dee subscribed to the old-fashioned idea that no young girl had any business reading a newspaper.

"I do hope that Etienne will find something else to do," Aimée ventured aloud, "before Monsieur Gautier and the others come. I am nervous enough as it is."

"You should not feel that way, Aimée." Tante Dee Dee frowned at her over her needlework. "After all, Etienne is your family, too, and has a responsibility toward you."

"But he teases me so, Tante Dee Dee. And I am sure he will do something to embarrass me before his friends."

"Well, you can hardly be left alone with these gentlemen. And at your age, you are not expected to carry on

17

an intelligent conversation with men. It will be much easier to have Etienne present."

"Did I hear myself being discussed?" Etienne sauntered into the salon and draped himself over one end of the high-backed sofa.

"Dee Dee was only reassuring Aimée that you would help the time pass pleasantly this afternoon, Etienne," Grand-père's voice explained.

Etienne grinned at Aimée and asked, "Are you afraid that I shall tease you in front of your suitors, little one?"

She stuck her tongue out at him, but at the sound of voices in the hallway, Aimée quickly assumed a more demure pose, punching halfheartedly at the needlework Tante Dee Dee had insisted she work on.

Prosper, dressed in a dark suit, high cravat, and gloves, and carrying a walking cane, changed the tenor of the room immediately.

"You are quite lovely this afternoon, mam'selle," Prosper said, stopping before Aimée.

"*Merci*, monsieur," she answered shyly and then looked down again at her needlework.

He continued watching her, while he conversed on the other side of the room with Grand-père and Etienne.

Again voices sounded in the hall, and within a short time Lisette was showing the other two young men into the salon. Both men were dark, in contrast to Prosper's fairness—one tall, the other shorter and much more muscular.

For a while, upon finding Prosper Gautier already ensconced with the family, their dark scowls were duel sharp. But with glasses of madeira in their hands, the men drifted into a polite conversation of politics and the national election. Aimée, interested in their comments, forgot her needlework.

"They say the election is to be between Breckinridge and Bell," Prosper stated.

"Yes, it was too bad Douglas was nominated. That was bound to split the Democrats," Grand-père said.

"But what about Lincoln?" asked Etienne. "Is he not someone to be reckoned with?"

The tall dark man, Jean Brisot, laughed and said, "I

daresay he won't get a single vote in Louisiana."

Aimée without realizing the enormity of breaking into the men's conversation, said, "That would not be surprising since Monsieur Lincoln's name won't even be printed on the Louisiana ballot."

"Aimée!" Tante Dee Dee reprimanded, shocked at her lapse of good manners.

The men continued as if they had not heard her, but Jean Brisot's amused eyes found hers for a moment before he rejoined the animated discussion.

"Well, one thing is certain," the other man interjected. "If Lincoln is elected, the South will secede from the Union."

Prosper did not remain for long. He returned to Tante Dee Dee and Aimée, said his farewells, and left.

With Prosper gone, the heart went out of the conversation and the other two young men soon made their excuses and left.

"I hope you will not encourage that Jean Brisot, Papa," Tante Dee Dee said when he had gone. "He has 'a heart like an artichoke—a leaf for every girl.'"

Grand-père laughed. "He is an amiable young gentleman, Dee Dee, with fine ancestors. I knew his grandfather well. And do not be too hard on him just because he has not yet found a proper wife. It takes some men longer to look than others . . . and besides, he is giving Prosper competition in courting Aimée."

Chapter 2

$\mathcal{T}$he round of balls and *soirées* began, and Aimée, still strictly chaperoned, joined the gaiety. The Creoles, proud, aristocratic, saw nothing wrong in sampling life at its fullest; for one who was well in the morning could easily be dead by nightfall from the fever that struck so insidiously.

Fortunes were won and lost at the gambling tables; Creole gentlemen kept their quadroon or octoroon mistresses apart in little houses along the Ramparts; the land of sugarcane and cotton supported the habits of intense, fiery men, among whom the smallest slight, the merest hint of disapproval, brought a challenge with swords, and the fencing masters, housed along Exchange Alley, were the greatest gods of all, emulated and adored for their prowess with the sword.

Of course, Aimée, strictly brought up and educated by the Ursuline nuns, was supposed to know nothing of this underworld of society, but she had listened to the adolescent comments made by Etienne, and had seen for herself the beautiful young girls, dressed in fine clothes and jewels, out for drives in their own *calèches*. Many resembled their white half-sisters, and Aimée could not help wondering if one day she would see a girl with her same features, sitting in the upper tiers of the French Opera House . . . or whether when Etienne, Prosper, and Jean Brisot arrived late at one of the more formal balls they had not come from a Quadroon Ball, which was open only to aristocratic white men and chaste, young, well-educated girls of color, whose *mamans* made the necessary business arrangements for their daughters to become the mistresses of well-heeled young gentlemen, as they themselves had, years earlier.

Had Etienne yet chosen a mistress, or Prosper Gautier? How she would love to attend a Quadroon Ball herself, but *that*, Aimée knew, was out of the question . . . although she had heard the rumor that one daring married woman had masked herself and slipped into the Orleans Ballroom to see if her husband were present. And yes, she had found him. . . .

Although the Saint-Moreaus were no longer wealthy, their name was enough to open any door in New Orleans. Aimée, swept along in the frantic social rush, wore out one pair of satin dancing slippers after another.

Young gentlemen continued to call on her in the afternoons, and Prosper Gautier appeared often, always watching her across the room, always aware of her, yet saying practically nothing to her, under the watchful eyes of Tante Dee Dee. There were so many others that Aimée did not give much thought to him as a serious suitor. Jean Brisot, with his tall darkness and laughing eyes, appealed to her much more.

It was now a month since Aimée had been presented at the French Opera House and the gentlemen had begun calling on her in the afternoons. On this particular Friday afternoon Prosper came earlier than usual. He remained in the corner of the salon talking with Grand-père, but raised his voice, presumably for the benefit of Aimée, seated across the room.

"We are giving a ball next Thursday at Dresden— Maman, Papa, and I. They have asked me to extend an invitation for you all to come. You will, of course, spend the night, and I shall send the plantation boat for you that afternoon, if you accept." Again he stared at Aimée, while waiting for an answer.

"Dee Dee," Grand-père's voice inquired, "have we made prior plans for next Thursday night?"

"No, Papa, nothing definite," Tante Dee Dee replied.

"Then we shall be delighted to accept your invitation, Prosper," Grand-père acknowledged.

Time passed slowly until Thursday, with the array of afternoon callers the only diversion in the rainy, dreary week. Jean Brisot appeared again, but Prosper Gautier was not among the callers since he had returned to Dresden.

By Thursday the sun was shining and Aimée excitedly packed for the overnight jaunt to the Gautier plantation upriver from New Orleans, not because of Prosper, but because of the gaiety of the party.

Down by the levee Grand-père strolled leisurely up and down, his pointed goatee trimmed and neat and his high cravat stiff and white.

Ships in the harbor were being loaded and unloaded with the buzz of activity of a busy port—French and British ships, traders from New England, smaller vessels on their regular runs back and forth to the Indies, and steamboats, three deep, waiting for a place at the wharf.

River pilots sat at makeshift barreled tables, and played dice until it was time to lead the larger ships safely across the shallow places on their way to the Gulf and the open sea.

Michele and her *maman* and *papa* were also waiting for the boat to be taken up the Mississippi to the ball, and under Tante Dee Dee's watchful scrutiny, Aimée and Michele chatted until the boat arrived.

The two girls sat apart from the rest, holding their parasols to shade their faces from the sun. It was important to have a magnolia-white complexion; for the mere hint of a dark complexion was enough to start speculation as to whether a family had some small amount of *café noir* blood hidden away in the family line. But even then, the Creoles felt it was safer to marry among themselves, knowing the names and faces of every ancestor and relative.

"I hear that Prosper Gautier is going to make an official offer for you tonight, Aimée. That's why he's having this ball—so that your *grand-père* and his *papa* can get together to draw up the arrangements."

Aimée turned pale and faced Michele with a distressed look on her face. "But Michele, there must be some mistake. I . . . I am not ready to get married and settle down."

"Well, it seems that Prosper Gautier is ready, and that's all that matters. Would you dare turn him down and risk your *grand-père*'s displeasure?"

"I . . . I would not go against Grand-père's wishes, but he—that is, Monsieur Gautier—must give me time to get used to the idea. I . . . I don't even know him very well."

"Oh, Aimée, here you are, practically betrothed, and you are too shy to call him by his name. Will you still call him 'Monsieur Gautier' in the marriage bed?"

"Michele! You are embarrassing me. Do talk about something else. You can see how Tante Dee Dee is staring at us."

Michele laughed a high tinkling laugh. "I'm glad Maman does not watch me as carefully as your Tante Dee Dee watches you. But I do envy you—getting to be with Etienne every day." Michele glanced in Etienne's direction but he did not notice her.

The boat appeared and, surprisingly, Prosper was on board to greet them and ride with them upriver.

Aimée, dressed in a petal pink dress trimmed with white ruching, wore a fragile bonnet of the same color, with a saucy bunch of apple blossoms peeking from the underside. She lifted her dress daintily to walk across the plank and felt a hand at her elbow.

"You are enchanting," Prosper whispered as he helped her on board.

Michele laughed softly behind them. "You two had better be careful," she said in a low tone. "Everyone is listening."

"Let them listen if they wish," Prosper answered, suddenly defensive. "I am sure they would all agree with me."

"Agree with you about what, Prosper?" Etienne asked, making his way to the railing.

"That—that it is a beautiful day to ride upriver," Aimée hastily responded with an appeal to Prosper not to give her away.

The worst of the hot summer season was over, when

everything remained damp, either from rain or perspiration, and the insects constantly swarmed. There was a subtle change in the air as the travelers made their way upriver. Gone was the indolent drooping of plants along the riverbanks, the leaves attacked by flying pests and the baking sun. Instead, there was a new vigor and a pertness of flower heads and reeds. Aimée felt a common bond with the plants of having survived another season of mosquitoes, floods, and deadly fever.

Although the water was calm on the surface, there was still the threat underneath of whirling yellow eddies and constant erosion. Aimée would never feel comfortable again surrounded by water. She would always be reminded of that summer when she and Etienne had become orphans —when poor Maman and Papa . . .

"Your eyes are sad, Aimée," Prosper said. "Is anything the matter?"

Aimée was startled at his sudden appearance by her side. She immediately brightened and twisted her parasol back from her face.

"Sad, monsieur, when I am going to a ball? I feel quite gay and look forward to dancing till dawn."

"I also look forward to dancing tonight," Prosper said, looking down at her. "And I also hope that before the night is over, a certain *jeune fille* will not be too shy to call me by my name."

His hand moved toward the railing where Aimée's left hand rested.

"Aimée," Tante Dee Dee's voice interrupted, "will you please bring me my shawl? The mosquitoes are beginning to get annoying."

Aimée watched as the magnificent plantations dotting the river were pointed out to her, some visible from the bluffs, others screened from the river by the moss that hung from the large oak trees.

Just below Dresden lived a rich planter, a man of color, Monsieur Lavier, who had many slaves of his own. His daughters were convent trained, beautiful, and charming; his sons were educated in France. He was a proud man who was respected for his knowledge of music and literature, according to Grand-père.

"Monsieur Lavier," Grand-père said, "has not missed a performance at the St. Charles or the Opera House for the past twenty years. And when anyone wishes an expert opinion, he has only to listen to Toutant Lavier." Grand-père's eyes twinkled in amusement. "A pity that Monsieur Marin does not listen to him more often."

Two hours from the time it had first left New Orleans, the boat approached the landing at Dresden. Servants appeared quickly to take the baggage, and Aimée, walking between Tante Dee Dee and Grand-père, gazed in fascination at the beautiful white mansion before them. With the sun shining on its pillared columns, the house resembled a jeweled opal in a frame of moss-covered oak trees, magnolias, wax myrtles, and royal palms.

But there was no time to stop and admire the beauty. Aimée and Michele were whisked rapidly upstairs to rest, despite Michele's protests that she would rather see the terrapin pens and the *pigeonnier*. It was all because of Etienne, Aimée knew. If only she could feel about Monsieur Gautier as Michele felt about Etienne—wanting to be with him, to talk with him, to dance with him, to spend the rest of her life with him.

No, she would put that out of her mind. She would think only of the ball and the music. She would not think of more intimate things.

"Well, she certainly got you away from him in a hurry, didn't she?" Michele asked.

"Are you . . . speaking of Tante Dee Dee?" Aimée asked.

Michele nodded. "I find it very annoying not to be left alone with a man for a single minute."

The sound of laughter downstairs invaded the quietness of the room upstairs. "Just listen to the fun they're having, while we have been convented to hours of loneliness up here, away from them all. But tonight," Michele said with a mischievous smile, "tonight I shall make up for it."

"Oh, Michele, please do not get into any trouble. Tante Dee Dee might not allow me to see you again."

"I cannot understand why she is so strict with you,

25

Aimée. You would never guess that she had danced all night when she was a young girl, or that she was betrothed, much less married—"

"Tante Dee Dee is strict with me only where men and family honor are concerned, Michele. At home, she spoils me quite dreadfully. She is so kind and merry that I would not wish you to think she is an ogre," explained Aimée.

"If that is the case, then I am glad to hear it. Maman has told me that all the Saint-Moreaus were fun-loving, and that even your Tante Dee Dee was quite a belle when she was young. It's just hard, seeing her as she is now, to think that she was once sixteen, as we are."

Aimée giggled at that. "I cannot imagine Tante Dee Dee a slim debutante, can you? She has been so plump ever since I knew her. Michele," Aimée said with a horrified look on her face, "do you think we will turn to be the same way, years from now—plump and old, with a dozen children or more hanging on our skirts?"

Michele put up her hands in mock horror. She began to waddle across the room, calling in a nasal voice, "Come, Vincent and Bastile, leave your little sister, Felicité, alone. And Gabriel, stop your sniveling. I can't help it if Laurie bit you. Desirée, what are you doing trying to hide under Maman's crinolines?"

By this time Aimée was rolling on the bed and the tears of laughter gave a shimmering translucence to her turquoise eyes.

Suddenly the door opened and three other young female guests appeared with puzzled glances, sensing the abrupt cessation of laughter and movement.

Nadine, Julie, and Marie were sisters who lived upriver from Dresden. Their *maman* was a distant cousin of Prosper's *maman*. They were petite and pretty, and while Prosper was fair-haired, the girls were dark, with large brown eyes, resembling each other not only in looks but also in mannerisms. Soon they were conversing with Aimée and Michele as if they had known them for ages.

Although it seemed an eternity to the girls, they were barely ready when the gong sounded for dinner. Servants had run back and forth, bringing water for their baths and helping them into their crinolines and dresses—but what had taken up the most time was the surreptitious trying on of the rice powder and crushed rose petals that Michele had smuggled to Dresden with her.

"The petals will give our cheeks more color," Michele explained. "And it really isn't naughty. All the ladies in Paris use *paint* on their faces—so why can't we use a little color, too?"

They all walked downstairs together, bound by the conspiracy of rice powder and rose petals, and stifling their giggles with effort, the girls swept into the foyer that smelled of beeswax from the polishing of the elegant French furniture.

Aimée was hungry and the delicacies displayed on long tables presided over by smartly dressed servants caused in her an instant appreciation. Redfish and clam chowder soups, oysters on the half shell, pigeons *en compote*, and game—woodcock and brant and haunches of venison—filled two tables; while vegetables—peas, celery, baked mashed potatoes, turnips, and lettuce with brown gravy—filled another. But the dessert table caught her eye and Aimée could not choose among the *citron soufflage*, the *blanc manger*, and the plum pudding, so she decided to have a little of each.

"Don't forget Bastile, Vincent, and Desirée," Michele teased when she saw Aimée's plate piled high with food.

Aimée smiled at her, ignoring the insinuation. With a proud air, she walked gracefully toward her motioning aunt. A servant followed her, carrying her plate.

After the tables were cleared away, the older men, including Grand-père, retired to the game room to play bagatelle and brag, leaving the chaperonage of the young people to the eagle eyes of the women.

The dancers climbed the stairs to the ballroom where the musicians were tuning up their instruments for the long night ahead. When the music began, even the older women were swept up to dance with some of the young gallants.

"Look at Madame Gallier," Aimée whispered to Michele. "I thought she would be too weak to dance."

"Don't you know, Aimée, that every Creole woman, regardless of how delicate and frail she appears, can stay on her feet until the sun comes up if there's a partner for dancing?"

And it seemed true, for even Tante Dee Dee joined in the strenuous exercise without a hair stirring out of place.

Prosper had a proprietary air with Aimée, but the others refused to let that deter them from dancing with the petite, graceful Aimée for the first part of the evening.

"I do not like for you to dance with any other man, Aimée," Prosper said, claiming her again as his partner. "I did not have this ball for someone other than Prosper Gautier to hold you in his arms."

"But you are the host, monsieur," Aimée responded lightly, though inwardly shaking at his intimate words to her. "You have a duty to dance with the others. Would you wish me to be some drooping flower in a dark corner, waiting for you while you danced?"

"Yes," he whispered in a frustrated voice. "I would shut you away if I could so that no other eyes but mine could gaze on your beauty."

He tightened his fingers on her wrist and Aimée pulled back. "Monsieur," she said, and then with relief realized the music had stopped. He would have to let her go.

"Prosper," Grand-père's voice sounded near them, "may I claim my granddaughter for a few minutes?"

"Of course," he said, deferring to the old man's wishes.

Aimée, sensing why he had sought her out, reluctantly went with him, her feet dragging in uncertain step with her spirits, even though she would be relieved of Prosper's attentions for that period of time.

The door to the library closed, shutting out the music of the evening and Aimée, trembling, turned to her *grand-père* for the words she knew would seal her destiny.

"My child, I have good news for you." Grand-père smiled benevolently at Aimée, waiting for her to respond.

"Yes, Grand-père?" she asked in a shaky voice.

"Prosper Gautier wishes to make you his wife. His *papa* and I have been discussing the matter and we have reached an amicable settlement. Now, since you are both so young, we have decided it would be wise for you to wait at least six months before—"

"But Grand-père," Aimée broke into the explanation, "what if I do not wish to marry Prosper Gautier?"

Grand-père stood, looking at his granddaughter in uncomprehending astonishment. "You cannot be serious, Aimée," he replied. "It is an honor for you to have been accepted by the Gautier family as a suitable wife for Prosper."

"But I do not . . . love him, Grand-père," Aimée whispered timidly.

Grand-père dismissed her argument with an impatient wave of his hand. "You are too young to know of love, Aimée. That is what a husband teaches his wife—after she is married, not before. And just look around you, *ma chère*," his voice said coaxingly. "You will be the mistress of all this. Look at the fine books—do you think just anyone could afford such a library, such beautiful furniture—"

"But Grand-père," Aimée protested again, this time with tears in her eyes, "I wish to remain with you . . . and . . . and Dresden is so far away from New Orleans."

"Aimée, I would never wish you to do something completely against your will, but I am an old man. It has been my heart's desire to see you safely married before I die. Then I would not worry over what is to become of you."

"I . . . I am sorry, Grand-père. I did not know how you felt. If . . . if you wish me to, then I shall . . . marry Monsieur Gautier," Aimée said with a sinking heart.

Grand-père smiled at her. "Then let us call the impatient young man in and tell him of your decision."

The rest of the evening was spent in dancing, but now that Prosper Gautier had officially claimed Aimée, the other young men present did not dare risk his temper and Aimée received no other invitations to dance. Her betrothed now monopolized her time under the watchful beaming eye of Tante Dee Dee.

"We will spend our honeymoon here at Dresden, Aimée," Prosper informed her as they danced, "rather than New Orleans. I have a wish for a proper Creole honeymoon."

Aimée blushed and her heart fluttered rapidly. How

could she spend five days and nights in an upstairs bedroom, alone with Prosper, never seeing anyone else during that time but the servant assigned to care for them—when she found it difficult to spend *one* evening in his arms?

"You are adorable when you blush, *mon petit chouchou*," Prosper said, caressingly.

"Monsieur, people are looking at us," protested Aimée. "Please . . . do not say such things to me."

Prosper laughed and caught her up in his arms to glide across the room in rhythm to the music.

When dawn came, the dancers were given steaming bowls of gumbo and cups of thick black coffee. Soon the activity of the night folded and the dancers slipped to their bedrooms to sleep the morning away, leaving the scuffed ballroom floor as the only evidence of the energetic evening.

Several times a week Prosper Gautier paid court to Aimée, but they were never left alone. They walked in the French Market, stopping at the coffee stalls and buying hot pralines and honey cakes from the street venders; they went to Mass at the Cathedral and attended the opera and theater in the company of Grand-père, Tante Dee Dee, and occasionally Etienne. Rarely did Aimée's natural vivacity show through; more and more, her manner was restrained, her time taken up with the sober selection of trousseau and household linens.

But the tempo of life in the Crescent City quickened, and Aimée was swept into a fast-paced festivity of torchlight parades, fireworks and rocket displays, grand balls and barbeques and band music. Everywhere the golden promises of politicians rang out. It was the fall political campaign and each citizen, used to backing his favorite horse at the Metairie racetrack, now backed his favorite candidate instead for President of the United States. Clubs formed for Breckinridge, for Bell and Douglas, with each group intent on wooing the voters into their camps by the most eye-catching measures.

The people of New Orleans, who loved a parade even without a reason, delighted in the excitement of the vibrant diversion. Aimée, with Tante Dee Dee, watched the street parades from the balcony over Monsieur Tobin's shop on Canal Street, while Etienne and Grand-père mingled with their friends on the banquettes below.

Finally voting day came and the merrymaking and excitement of the campaign were shattered. The man whose name was not even on the Louisiana ballot was elected. To the stupefaction of the South, Abraham Lincoln was to be the next President of the United States.

The rumbling talk of secession became earnest. First, South Carolina and then other Southern states withdrew their allegiance from the republic of states and declared themselves free and independent powers. On a bleak, gray day in January, 1861, Louisiana, too, severed its ties with the United States.

The halls of the state house in Baton Rouge rang with the voices of the secession delegates. Translators rapidly turned English words into French ones for those delegates who spoke only French. When the final vote had been announced, the crowds waiting outside heard the cheering and applause of those who had overridden the opposition. They surged into the state house to add their voices to the cheering, and telegraph wires tapped the message of secession to other parts of the state.

In New Orleans, when the news came, bells rang; the pelican flag was raised and along the levee a deafening one-hundred-gun salute sounded. A holiday air pervaded the city as the Washington Artillery, dressed in full military regalia, marched down the streets.

On every corner, in every coffee and gambling house, the men discussed the probability of war.

"Cotton is king. The North needs our cotton and so does Europe. No one would dare invade the South."

"Gentlemen, I will wipe up with my handkerchief the amount of blood spilled because of secession."

"They cannot take away the rights of the states to decide for themselves on issues."

"I cannot imagine that Lincoln would actually send troops to try to hold the Union together."

"And has not the government caused this breach by raising such high tariffs on manufactured goods, designed to favor the North?"

"Not only that—they are trying to destroy our economy with their 'holier-than-thou' attitude that we must free our slaves, when their Northern ships were the ones to transport the slaves to our shores. They would not be crying so loud against slavery if the weather in the North had not forced their purchases South."

"There has been talk that some plan to arm their slaves, and will give them their freedom if they stand with them against the enemy."

"Gentlemen, I do not consider slavery the issue, despite the rabblerousers and abolitionists. It's a matter of the sovereignty of the states that divides us."

So on and on the conversations went about the inevitability of war. Young men were caught up in the fever of volunteering for an army even before a separate nation came into being. Both Etienne and Prosper joined the Avegno Zouaves, and they strutted proudly about New Orleans in the baggy trousers and tasseled fezzes of an elite company of volunteers.

Still, people talked about a compromise until that day at Fort Sumter when the favored Creole son of New Orleans, Pierre Gustave Toutant Beauregard, gave the order to fire on the military installation that threatened the Charleston harbor.

"Aimée, we are at war!" Etienne said excitedly as he dashed into the courtyard.

Aimée stood up, holding the sasanquas that she had cut to arrange for the Sèvres vase in the salon. She drew in a startled gasp of air and dropped the shears, making a clattering sound at her feet.

Aimée sat in the April dusk, remembering the nightmare quality of the day that had changed the direction of her destiny—crumbling the careful plans of Grand-père and Tante Dee Dee for her life. If it had not been for the excitement, the celebration, the unguarded flow of conversation about the war and the families they would leave behind, Prosper would not have been so quick to take offense and challenge Jean Brisot for brandishing Aimée's name in a public place for all to hear—and the dueling ground of St. Anthony's Close, behind the spire of St.

Louis Cathedral, would not have soaked up the life's blood from the body of Prosper Gautier.

So Prosper, the man to whom Aimée had been promised, had not gone to war with Etienne but instead was buried in the family mausoleum at the St. Louis Cemetery, with the words "Victime de son honneur" inscribed on the cold marble slab.

But death, clutching at Aimée's heart, grew and spawned additional tentacles until it had struck down Tante Dee Dee from the fever and Etienne at Shiloh. So now Aimée's world contained only a saddened, desolate *grand-père*, suddenly grown old. No one else . . . except the Yankee invaders.

Chapter 3

*E*ven before she opened her eyes, Aimée knew a heaviness of heart, a feeling that something was wrong. But she was not sufficiently awake to put a name to the heaviness pressing down upon her until her senses became bombarded by the acrid smoke and decaying odor in the street.

Now she remembered. The cotton at the warehouses had been set on fire the day before so that it would be of no use to the Yankees. Bales had been loaded on flatboats to float like funeral pyres toward the enemy, with the telltale billowing smoke leaving a trail of the journey downriver.

And the frenzied mob, not stopping there, had broken into the other storage places along the levee, pouring out molasses, destroying goods that might be of use to the enemy. There had been no one to stop them—for the army was in retreat—no one to stay the hand of the childish, destructive mob, reacting to the news that the Yankees were on their way.

Grand-père had sat in his enclosed world, seemingly oblivious to the carnage going on about him, disturbed only because Aimée had appeared on the street without a chaperon.

The rich Creole life had departed, bit by bit, and the few remaining pieces and patterns were patched and re-patched. The carriage house was now empty of both horses and carriage; the army had desperately needed every means of conveyance. A piece of furniture had been sold to buy the last tickets to the opera; an old dress had been retrimmed to wear to Mass and to stroll in the French Market; a shabby cravat, worn and thin from too many washings, had been turned to its better side; and the table, once loaded with delectable food, was now shabby with scant offerings because of the blockade of the once-busy harbor. And the silver tray that had held the rarest delicacies for guests contained only a small bunch of bananas, the cheapest food in all New Orleans.

Aimée looked at her thin wrists and her stomach rumbled with hunger. If she had only one tithe of the food she had piled high on her plate the night of the ball at the Gautier plantation, she would be happy.

But looking backward would not help. The problem was today—to get enough food for survival, to brave Grand-père's disapproval in walking alone to the market, now that she could not count on Lisette to help her with that chore.

Aimée struggled out of bed. After pouring cold water from the ewer into the basin, she washed her face, combed the tangles from her hair, and hurriedly dressed, anxious to do the marketing before the sun climbed too high and the streets became too crowded.

Grand-père, accustomed to sleeping late and having coffee and brioche in bed, was awake when Aimée took his tray into the room earlier than usual.

"Good morning, Grand-père," Aimée said, opening the door after knocking.

"Good morning, *ma chère*," he replied, his eyes showing his delight at seeing her.

She had gradually taken over the chore of fixing his breakfast, although Raoul still helped him get dressed for the day. But it was Aimée he watched for every morning, who, taking his breakfast to him, climbed up on the bed beside him to have her cup of chocolate and discuss the plans for their day.

"Grand-père," she started apologetically, "I . . . I will need more money for the marketing today."

"Do you think it wise to go out into the streets, Aimée?"

"The . . . the soldiers have not come yet, Grand-père. And since the Yankee sailors have gone back to their ships, it . . . it should be safe. And there is no food in the house . . ."

"Then Lisette must go with you."

"Grand-père," Aimée said, not wishing to burden him additionally, "I do not know how much longer we can . . . depend upon Lisette for anything."

"It is as bad as that?" he asked, not putting into words what was happening all around them.

"Yes, Grand-père," Aimée answered. "And besides, I went alone yesterday and nothing happened to me."

The pattern was already set—this was but further disintegration of the old life, and Grand-père, now ineffective in dealing with the new stubbornness in his granddaughter, let it pass.

There were few coins in Grand-père's purse. The remaining Confederate money was worth less than the dirty wrappers of the olive oil jars, and now that New Orleans was a possession of the enemy, Aimée knew that it would be impossible to buy anything with the paper money. The chimney tax was due soon—the city tax that was charged according to the number of chimneys on a house. That would leave almost nothing.

Hoping that there would be enough coins left over to buy Grand-père's *tabac*—his last small comfort—Aimée opened the iron gate, the market basket hanging from her arm. She walked to the end of the street and stepped over the open, dirty sewer ditch. It had not been cleaned in a long time, and with the addition of the garbage of the day before, it was clogged and malodorous. Aimée put her handkerchief over her nose to lessen the penetrating smell that made her ill.

Her beloved city was dirty and forlorn—no longer proud. It had an air of defeat and lethargy to match the faces of the few people who had ventured out upon its banquettes.

Aimée switched her basket from one arm to the other and, glancing back before crossing the street to the square, she saw Raoul following her at a discreet distance.

"Oh, Grand-père," Aimée said under her breath, "what a trial I am to your Old World conscience!"

Much later when she returned home, Aimée took the half-empty basket to the kitchen and set it down on the table where Lisette was finishing shaping the two small loaves of bread. Glancing at the meager contents, Lisette sniffed in disgust.

"Miss Aimée, how you 'spect me to fix a decent dinner for y'all tonight with no more'n this to work with?"

"Oh, Lisette, I did the best I could," Aimée replied, tired from wandering over the city. "There's hardly any food left in all of New Orleans. The French Market is nothing but a garbage heap of flies and mud—we're lucky that I found anything at all, with the Yankees still blockading the harbor."

"Well, the beans won't have no salt in 'em. I used the last pinch yesterday. And this tough old *coq*," Lisette added, pulling the fowl from the basket, "won't get tender, even if I cook 'im to doomsday."

"Just do the best you can, Lisette," coaxed Aimée and walked out of the kitchen, sighing, to find her *grand-père*.

"Aimée, did you remember my *tabac*?" the old man asked, seeing her in the hallway.

"I remembered it, Grand-père, but Monsieur Tobin's shop was closed. Someone said he left the city yesterday."

Grand-père became indignant. "Aimée, when a war disturbs a man's habits—habits he's had for over fifty years—I call that a mighty bad war. And I'm going to write Jefferson Davis and tell him so."

She put her hand on his arm. "Better to complain to

Monsieur Lincoln, Grand-père. His soldiers are the ones who'll be occupying the city soon."

"I have no intention of corresponding with that man," Grand-père said in a huff.

For the next several days New Orleans licked its wounds and shook from each rumor of its imminent destruction.

There was an order for all its citizens to evacuate—that the city was to be shelled because it refused a formal surrender. But there was no place for its inhabitants to go. Better to perish, they said, remaining where they were, than to die in an alien environment far from their familiar banquettes and walled courtyards.

So they remained where they were—Grand-père and Aimée, and the rest of the women, children, and old men —and waited for the navy to turn over the occupation of the city to the Union Army.

On the first of May they came, thousands of troops in the command of General Benjamin Butler, who marched at their head, anxious to keep in step and make a good appearance in the Crescent City. And the people, seeing their rotund, double-chinned conqueror, turned their backs on him and his soldiers. Stung by the cold reception given him, the commanding general immediately began the issuance of orders to bring the city under his thumb. The Yankees zealously identified those sympathetic to the Confederate cause, searching the houses for the smallest sign of loyalty—a sympathetic letter, a newspaper, a Confederate button or flag—and confiscated Confederate property. The more silver and beautiful possessions in a house, the harsher the punishment.

The city's police force and judges were relieved of their jobs and replaced with Union sympathizers who answered only to Butler's provost marshall for their actions. Profiteers, watching as a jackal watches a trapped gazelle growing weaker in its struggle, waited to feast upon the city's carcass.

Despite the official whirlwind about them, the Creoles ignored the order to indicate their allegiance, quietly retained their pride and empty stomachs, and sought to live in total insularity from the invaders.

Aimée ventured onto the streets only when it was necessary to go to market, to visit Monsieur O'Brie at the pharmacy to get something for Grand-père's cough, and to place flowers on the graves of Tante Dee Dee and her betrothed, Prosper Gautier. Once a week Aimée gathered flowers and took them to the cemetery, while Grand-père dozed in the chair that faced the flowered courtyard.

One afternoon, after the heat of the day had subsided a little, Aimée made her way to the cemetery. She knelt first by Tante Dee Dee's grave and a wave of loneliness flowed over her for the *tante* who, childless, had been a mother to her when her own *maman* had been swept away in the flood. And although she had never actually loved the man to whom she had been promised, Aimée felt a sadness that it was she who had been indirectly responsible for his death.

She stood before the Gautier mausoleum and replaced the dead flowers of the week before with the fresh ones from the garden. If things had been different, her wedding bouquet would have found its way to the cemetery to be placed on the grave of a beloved relative, or perhaps sent to the convent where she had been educated. But there was no wedding bouquet—only a handful of flowers to mark the grave of her intended husband.

Aimée knelt and her lips moved soundlessly for a moment before she rose, taking the dead flowers to dispose of them. Slowly she walked away from the cemetery and headed back toward the townhouse she shared with Grand-père—not fully aware of the soldiers opening the gate on Royal Street only a block away from her own house.

Troubling thoughts gnawed at her and she tried to convince herself that, for the moment, she and Grand-père were safe—she, because she had not reached her eighteenth birthday and therefore was not required to register with the marshall, and he, because he was old and no threat to the enemy.

Later, when she heard what had happened to Monsieur Corbeau, Aimée knew a trembling fear. The man was the same age as Grand-père and his years and white hair had not saved *him*. Would Grand-père also be in danger?

"I heard that the Corbeaus down the street left New Orleans yesterday," Aimée informed her *grand-père* at dinner several evenings later, "and that their house is now occupied by one of General Butler's officers."

Grand-père put down his knife and fork and looked up from his plate. "Did they try to make old Jean take the loyalty oath?" Grand-père questioned.

"Yes, and when he refused, they gave him only three days to dispose of his goods and leave New Orleans. It doesn't seem fair, Grand-père."

"These Yankees do not understand, Aimée, what we have always known . . . a gentleman does not give up his principles just because some upstart tells him to do so."

Aimée, with a sudden chill, had no need to ask Grand-père what he would do if the soldiers came to their house. Hadn't she heard him say time and again that when a man lost his honor, he had nothing left?

Aimée continued eating until the scanty meal was gone. All the time she was thinking how she could protect the old man. If the soldiers come here, Aimée decided, I will make sure they do not see Grand-père. I will find some excuse for him to be out of sight. And when I go to the market each morning, I will make Lisette promise to watch out for him and hide him if the soldiers come. Aimée felt much better after her decision.

The next afternoon the storm clouds gathered and Aimée, nervously watching in the direction of the levee, saw the gradual buildup of angry dark wisps, pushed by the wind's impatient hand to a swift journey across the yellow-tinged sky.

The smell of the storm was in the air, and like some long-forgotten ancestor standing on the battlements facing the sea, Aimée stood looking out her second-story bedroom window, her nostrils quivering, breathing in the danger of the impending clash between land and sea.

She paced restlessly in her room and then sat for a few minutes, only to jump up and return to her pacing. The gaslights no longer worked and Aimée, seeing the approaching false darkness, placed a treasured candle into the holder on her bedside table and prayed that she would not be coward enough to use it in the night ahead.

Supper was a short reprieve, lasting not nearly long enough to calm her completely, but at least she was with Grand-père and the storms did not seem nearly so terrifying when he was there to understand and share her terror. And although his eyes showed his sympathy, he never talked of it to her—this weakness of hers when the winds rose and the thunder and lightning began.

In surprise, the sun broke through the clouds for a while and Aimée visibly relaxed. Her knees found their strength again and she silently chided herself for being so afraid and weak.

She remained in the salon, content to sit and be near Grand-père, until time for bed. Only a slight wind scraping the limb of a crepe myrtle against the wall gave any hint that the storm was not entirely dead.

In the short time it took Aimée to undress, enshroud herself in the demure long-sleeved, high-necked gown, and climb into bed, the storm hit in a sudden eruption, bringing with it the old terror, so old that Aimée could barely remember anything but the feeling—stark and cold and dread.

Grand-père, reading by the flickering lamp at his bed, his nightcap askew, looked up at Aimée's silent approach. He smiled and motioned for her to climb up on the bed beside him.

It was a comforting, familiar old bed—high-posted with a carved head and foot. It had been made by the French cabinetmaker Lannuier as a wedding present for Grand-père, and many times Aimée had slipped into that haven, hiding from the storms that had raged outside.

"So, *ma petite* is still afraid as ever," he said, laying his book down on the bedside table to put his comforting arms around her.

"I . . . I cannot help it, Grand-père. The nightmare will always be in my mind."

"I had hoped, Aimée, that you would have gotten over being so terrified. It was my fault we did not speak of the tragedy for so long after it happened . . . but you seemed to have dismissed it from your mind, and the doctors suggested that I not speak of it until you were ready— until your grief was healed enough for you to remember and want to talk about it. But I see that was a mistake. Perhaps if we had brought it out into the open, you would not be so fearful when the wind rises and the thunder begins."

For a while he remained quiet, as if debating his next words. "How much do you remember of that night, Aimée?" he asked, seemingly intent on exorcising the ghost that came to life with every storm.

Aimée was silent at first, conjuring the past from her troubled mind, not thinking merely of that last eventful night, but of the days leading up to it.

"We were so happy that year at Thornfell—Maman, Papa, Etienne, and I—and when we went away for the summer to Grand Ile to escape the mosquitoes and the fever, we did not know that Papa had lost Thornfell and that we would never see the plantation again.

"He was so gay, so charming, and it was always fun when he was with us. On the island we built sand castles and played in the children's park, and sometimes Papa would take us for pony rides while Maman rested.

"And then one late afternoon, when Maman and Papa were in the hotel, Etienne and I stayed in the children's park and played on the whirligig—it was red and yellow, with bright blue bars and . . . and Etienne would push us round and round and then jump up on it, until it slowed again. The whirligig was on a little hill above the hotel and I remember . . . watching from it while all the pretty ladies strolled down by the beach with their parasols matching the color of their dresses. I could always pick Maman out from the rest. Even at that distance, you could tell she was the prettiest one. . . ."

The dredging of the dark fear from her mind continued and Aimée's words spilled from her lips in a rush.

"The ladies had disappeared back into the hotel when a sudden roar came from the sea, bringing waves and waves of water with it. We started to run back to the hotel, Etienne and I, but the waves knocked us down. And then Maman and Papa were beside us, lifting us back to the whirligig, since there was nothing else to hold onto. Then poor Maman was carried away by the rushing water and Papa went after her.

"We were so frightened, Etienne and I. The sun went down and Papa didn't come back. In the dark we were afraid we were going to fall off into the water . . ."

Aimée paused, still reaching back into her mind, bringing thoughts and feelings to the surface that she had buried through the years.

". . . I suppose what I remember most, besides the fear, was feeling sick while the wind pushed us round and round all night on the whirligig. And by morning we were all alone, with no sign of Maman or Papa . . . or the hotel. . . .

"Oh, Grand-père, why did we have to go to Grand Ile that summer and why did everyone have to drown?"

The tears from her eyes trembled on the long curved lashes.

"It was meant to be," the old man said sadly. "But I have often wondered why Providence should spare the two of you—you and Etienne—and no one else."

"And even Etienne is gone now . . . as well as Tante Dee Dee. I have no one left but you, Grand-père. And for you, I will try to be brave," Aimée said, attempting to smile, determined to conquer her fear of the storm. "*Bonne nuit*, Grand-père."

Aimée gave him a kiss on his cheek and slid from the bed.

"*Bonne nuit, ma chère.*"

Chapter 4

The storm had left the city bright and clear and Aimée, humming lightly under her breath now that the storm was over, gathered the food basket to make her usual morning trip to the market.

The old street vender sang out, advertising his seafood, and Aimée caught up with him to buy some prawns for dinner. Stopping to chat with the crippled man in the vegetable stall, Aimée felt a sudden happiness in the marketplace, the old arcade with its pillars and tiled roof. It was almost like the old days—but then a group of soldiers appeared, spoiling the picture, and Aimée hurriedly left the market to return home.

When she entered Royal Street, Aimée knew that something was wrong. The foreboding overwhelmed her and she began to run. But the weight of the market basket hampered her, and without thought of the food she had so carefully gathered, Aimée dropped the basket.

On past the row of townhouses she ran, until her own house came into view, giving no hint of what was happening inside because of the high wall surrounding the house.

Aimée, opening the iron gate, ran past the crepe myrtles lining the carriage drive to the door that opened from the worn brick courtyard.

"Grand-père, Grand-père," she shouted, but her cries were met only by Lisette's voice.

"They've taken him away, Miss Aimée."

"Who took him away—and where?" Aimée demanded.

"The soldiers. To Ship Island, I heard 'em say."

"Ship Island! But that's for prisoners," Aimée responded in an unbelieving voice. "Why have they taken him there instead of banishing him from the city?"

"They searched the house and found Mr. Etienne's Confederate flag. And then Mr. Jules wouldn't sign the loyalty oath either."

"Lisette, you promised me," Aimée cried, "that you would hide him if the soldiers came."

"Nuthin' I could do, Miss Aimée. The soldiers was here befo' I knowed it."

"But couldn't Raoul do something about it?"

"Raoul left, jes' after you went to the market. He's been promised a brand new uniform with gold buttons if he joins the Union Army."

Aimée, noticing for the first time that Lisette had on her hat, asked, "And are you leaving, too, Lisette, without permission?"

"Mister Lincum's gonna free us," Lisette replied in a sullen voice. "We don't need to ask nobody if it's all right."

Aimée stamped her foot in anger at Lisette's insolence. "Go then, and good riddance. But don't come begging to me to take you back when you're cold and hungry!"

It was almost dark but Aimée remained in the corner of the salon, with only an occasional sob to break the quiet. She had wept the entire afternoon, until there were no more tears to shed.

"Poor Grand-père," she said over and over. "Poor Grand-père."

Aimée gazed around at the shadowed room, her eyes touching the faded Chinese Ch'ien Lung rug on the floor, the upholstered chairs of apricot satin lampas, and the brown-wash drawings of Claude Lorrain on the walls— the landscapes that Grand-père had loved and treasured. His collection of enameled snuffboxes—the ones that had not been sold—lay on the table near the hearth. At the deadly stillness of the room, Aimée's tears threatened again.

Suddenly there was a short rap on the door. Aimée lifted her head and fresh terror swept over her. The knock sounded again and it was only then that Aimée remembered Lisette was no longer in the house and that she was alone. She went to the bolted door and opened it. In front of her stood an army sergeant, dressed in the blue of the enemy.

At the sight of the girl with her tear-stained face, the sergeant seemed temporarily startled. But he soon regained his composure and announced in short curt tones, "This house is hereby requisitioned by Major Garrard. You are to inform anyone living on the premises that they are to seek new quarters immediately."

"And does monsieur have any suggestions as to where I might seek shelter at this time of evening?" Aimée asked with a bitter tone to her voice.

A man, followed by two large white dogs, got out of the carriage and walked to the door with a frown on his face.

"What is it, Anderson? I was told the house was unoccupied."

Aimée stared at the immaculate well-tailored uniform, the polished boots, and the saber swinging at the officer's side. The tremendous height of the man blotted out the last rays of the afternoon sun. A saber cut, still jagged and rough across his cheek, made him even more malevolent looking. Perhaps he had been the one who murdered Etienne. Her brother would have had no chance at all with such a giant—a giant who also had ferocious dogs to do his bidding. Aimée shuddered but forced her voice to reply.

"The house will be unoccupied in a few short moments," she said haughtily before the sergeant could speak. "If monsieur will permit me to pack some personal things, I will give up my house to the chivalrous gentleman who makes war on women and children."

Major Garrard, with a snarl on his lips, stepped forward as if to silence her. Then his expression softened.

"Your name?" he asked.

"Aimée," she replied. "Aimée Saint-Moreau."

"And your family?"

"Grand-père was taken away this morning by the soldiers. He is my family," she answered defiantly.

"And you are now alone?"

She nodded.

"Even a soldier who 'makes war on women and children' would not push a child into the street," the major said. "I daresay there is enough room for both of us."

The anger showed in Aimée's voice. "I will move to the servants' quarters above the carriage house for tonight, monsieur. And by tomorrow you may have even the servants' quarters."

Aimée whirled from the door and fled up the stairs to her bedroom. It did not take her long to remove her things and seek shelter in Lisette's old room at the back of the courtyard. But by the time she was settled, she was tired.

Slowly Aimée put on the fresh, wispy nightgown made of fine lawn and brushed her long red-gold hair, counting automatically as she brushed. In the mirror she saw that the pink blotches on her face had cleared up, leaving her skin a smooth, delicate magnolia tint. She made a face at herself in the mirror, for she hated it that she turned so pink when she cried. Her friend Michele could cry so prettily with no hint of color to mar her cheeks and she could get anything she wanted just by shedding a few tears. But Aimée knew better than to try the same technique. Knowing she did not look her best, Aimée seldom cried.

The turquoise eyes stared back at her—that strange color that she had inherited from her great-great-*grandmère*. Every so often the exotic combination of red-gold hair and turquoise eyes as brilliant as some piece of Indian jewelry appeared in the family, and when it did, the daughter was always named Aimée for the first Saint-Moreau by that name.

Aimée never grew tired of hearing the legend that had been handed down to each generation of Saint-Moreaus as carefully as the family silver—how after the death of a Turkish sultan, the beautiful sultana named Aimée had been placed in a weighted sack to be drowned by the sultan's nephew. Instead of sinking to the bottom of the Bosporus, the sack floated to the surface and the sultana was rescued by a passing French ship. The Comte de Saint-Moreau, who was traveling on the ship, fell in love with her and later married her in France.

Aimée wondered if her namesake had also turned pink when she cried. Perhaps that was why all the women in her family had been so gay. They did not dare to be sad for fear of spoiling their looks. Even now, fresh tears threatened at the thought of Grand-père. But it did not matter because there was no one to see.

She tightened her hand on the hairbrush when she heard the boots coming up the outside steps. Aimée flew into the wrapper, hiding her thin gown, before the knock sounded.

"Yes?" she called timidly.

"The major's compliments, ma'am."

Relieved to recognize the sergeant's voice, she opened the door. He carried a tray of food.

"The major said you probably would not have eaten, so he has sent you a small repast."

He held out the tray for her, but Aimée shook her head angrily.

"Tell your major that I know he intends to be generous, but I do not accept charity from Yankees." And she slammed the door in his face.

She had been insulted twice that day by Major Garrard: called a child when she was almost eighteen, and now this—offering her scraps from his table.

Her breasts were heaving with anger and her breath came in short gasps. She threw off the hot wrapper, and climbing onto the small cot, she punched at the goose-feather pillow to rid herself of her anger.

Suddenly the door was flung open and the major stamped into the room, with the tray of food that she had spurned. Aimée watched in fright as he set the tray on the little table and strode toward the cot.

"It seems I have a spoiled child on my hands—who needs to be coaxed to eat."

She sat up and replied angrily, "I am no child, monsieur."

Major Garrard stared at her and his eyes narrowed, his gaze raking over her curved breasts barely hidden by the thin nightgown.

She blushed at his obvious interest and then turned pale.

"How old are you, Aimée?"

"I shall soon be eighteen, monsieur. But I did not give you permission to call me by my given name."

He laughed and the sound filled the room. "Such a little tiger you are, Aimée." He deliberately emphasized her name. "But your claws can always be trimmed. And now, you are to get off that miserable bed and eat your supper."

He walked a few steps and picked her up in his arms to carry her to the table.

"Monsieur," she protested and struggled to get out of his grasp. The chair almost turned over when he placed her in it.

"I expect you to eat it all, Aimée," he said, pointing to the tray.

With swaggering steps, the major walked to the door and the sound of his boots echoed down the steps to the courtyard.

In fury Aimée snatched up the tray, opened the door, and hurled the food into the courtyard. The breaking glass clattered on the bricks only a few feet from the major. Aimée noticed with satisfaction the bewildered stare on the man's face before she closed the door.

That night she slept fitfully, with recurring pangs of hunger, and she relived that rainy April day when the enemy had come, intent on destroying what was left of her small world.

Chapter 5

The barking of the dogs in the courtyard garden awoke her. How had they gotten in? Had she forgotten to lock the gate?

Then Aimée remembered . . . it was no longer *her* garden, *her* gate. The property had been confiscated by the enemy.

It was already warm and the day promised to be extremely hot. But the sun was shining and she hoped it would not rain until later in the day.

Aimée dressed carefully as she planned her morning. She would go to Michele's house and perhaps her *maman* and *papa* would take her in. If they could not, she was not sure where she would go. She certainly had no wish to return to the convent and be subjected to the strict ways of the nuns again—they even insisted that a girl take a bath with her gown on, for modesty's sake. She had had enough of that.

Aimée put on her camisole and tightened the laces to her corset, but she was so used to Lisette's doing it for her that she felt clumsy. Luckily her waist was so small that it did not matter if she was not laced as fashion dictated. Besides, she had never liked a tight corset. It was too uncomfortable. And she wasn't so vain as the girl she had read about in the Paris newspaper a few years before—the girl who had insisted on being laced so tightly that her liver had been punctured by three ribs! Grand-père had always agreed that it was not healthy for a young girl to be laced too tightly, and he had pointed to the story as proof.

Aimée pulled on her crinolines and the robin's-egg-blue dress that made her eyes even more vivid, and then the white fichu over her shoulders. In a spirit of defiance she fastened a little Confederate flag underneath the folds of the fichu.

The dogs watched her as she came down the steps into the garden. The animals, completely white, with no mark or blemish, stood silently, warily, as she came closer. To Aimée, they resembled wolves—wild, beautiful wolves, with their shiny white coats sleek and healthy, and their eyes as piercing as burning agates.

"Oh, you are so beautiful," she said impulsively and reached out her hand to them. But she became dizzy from hunger and quickly sat on the stone bench.

"I would not attempt to pet them if I were you," the voice cautioned.

Aimée saw the major and her exuberance vanished.

"Better to approach them gradually . . . wait until they become accustomed to you."

Aimée struggled with her weakness and attempted to remain calm in his presence. She noticed that the tray and broken glass had been removed. She was sorry that she had let her temper get the better of her. It was not the mark of a true lady. She would have to remember that.

But her attempts at being cool were lost in her interest in the animals. "What are their names, monsieur?"

"Fréki and Geri," he replied.

Aimée smiled fleetingly and said, "I thought only Odin had wolves by those names to protect him."

Major Garrard laughed. "So—a pretty face who knows her mythology. But they are not wolves, Aimée. They are white German Shepherds, an unusual breed." Then he added, "And they were in the garden to protect you—not me."

Aimée stood up and looked at him with a frigid glance. "Did I need protection, monsieur?"

He chuckled. "More than you realize, Aimée."

She left him in the garden and hurriedly walked out

of the courtyard and down the carriage drive to the street.

"Come back, Fréki, come back, Geri," she heard him call, as she closed the gate behind her.

Aimée walked down the street, avoiding the flags that General Butler had ordered placed up and down the streets and hanging over the banquettes. As she was crossing the street in a zigzag pattern, determined not to be caught under the enemy's flag, Aimée was looking down at the uneven ground and almost ran into the arms of a Union soldier.

She backed away as one of his companions teasingly said, "She'd be an armful for anybody, wouldn't she, Clyde?" And then he sniggered.

Furiously Aimée lifted her fichu to show the hidden Confederate flag and then swept swiftly past them.

"You wouldn't get by with that, miss, if General Butler saw you," he called after her. "He'd have you down to the provost marshall before you could wrinkle your nose."

The young girl walking a block away from Aimée did not fare so well. When she attempted to cross the street to avoid the flags, the guards who had been stationed on the banquette for that purpose by General Butler dragged her under the flags. Even then, the girl managed to put her shawl over her head, a small defiance to the enemy determined to remove every ounce of resistance to its occupation of the city.

Everywhere Aimée went there were soldiers. Each time, she crossed to the other side of the street to avoid them, and by the time she finally reached Michele's house on Chartres Street, she was hot, thirsty, and tired.

Aimée walked to the gate and tugged at the heavy knocker. The servant who came was one she did not recognize.

"Is . . . is Mam'selle Michele at home, please?"

The servant looked at her and replied, "Colonel Yates lives here now, missy. Don't know nuthin' about a Mam'selle Michele, unless she were in the fam'ly that was put over the lines yestiddy."

So they had felt the slap of the enemy as well. Aimée sighed in disappointment and turned to make her way home.

Where could she go? What was she to do? She was so hungry, she couldn't think clearly.

By the time she reached the house, Aimée had little energy to climb the steps to her quarters. Tears threatened to spill down her cheeks and she angrily brushed her hand across her face, determined not to give in.

When she opened the door, she saw the envelope on the floor. It must have been slipped under the door while she was away.

Aimée stooped down to pick the letter up, and when she opened it, the money fell out. Puzzled, she turned to the letter and its bold masculine writing.

"Aimée," the letter began, "Enclosed is the first month's rent. I trust you will not be so foolish as you were last night. And since you have no other place to go, I would consider it wise for you to remain where you are." It was signed "Major Bryan Garrard."

She had no pride left. She stuffed the money into her reticule and headed to one of the markets for food.

Aimée did not see Major Garrard for the next several days. But the dogs were in the garden each morning and soon they were friends. She scratched their ears and rubbed under their collars and they pressed closer and closer, enjoying her companionship and seeming content to remain in the garden with her. Aimée wished she could be as content as the dogs.

Occasionally Anderson came into the garden as he went about his duties. He walked with a noticeable limp, due, no doubt, to some injury in the war. It was not a pleasant reminder.

The sundial in the middle of the garden cast its shadows into her heart, warning Aimée that it was late—too late to find the peace that she had always felt while sitting in the shade of the oleander tree and breathing in the perfume of the flowers. It was too late because of the Yankees.

Yet the garden—that portion of the courtyard wedged between the main house and the carriage house—was the same as before the Yankees had come. The coral vines were in profuse bloom, spilling over the brick wall in their usual luxuriant growth, and the flower beds of geraniums, sasanquas, and ajuga running the length of the wall were covered in blossoms of pink and blue and white. Only Aimée was different.

The old fountain by the wall had long since ceased to pour its water through the mouth of the dolphin, to tumble into the little pond. Now the water was brackish and green algae grew along the tiled sides. Water jars sat nearby, holding the river water that was sweetened by charcoal and alum to make it suitable for drinking. The courtyard, deserted except for Aimée, resembled some ghostly replica of a garden where Ali Baba might have hidden among the huge jars.

Aimée stared at the statue of sea boy and dolphin, and the dappled movement of sunlight from sundial to fountain to jars and on to the iron railing of the stairs leading up to the carriage house made her eyes heavy. She rested her head in her arms, her flaming hair fanning out to give her the appearance of a water creature, akin to the sea boy and dolphin.

The fingers pushing her hair from her face made her smile at their caressing. But when her eyes opened, still in a dream state, she met the silver-gray inquiring eyes of Major Garrard. Aimée jumped in alarm and attempted to get up, but the man's hand stayed her.

"I did not mean to frighten you, little one," he said, "but the temptation was too much—to see if you were actually real, or merely a desire of the imagination."

"I . . . I do not know what you mean," said Aimée, still confused from sleep and the touch of the man's hand on her cheek.

She stumbled to her feet and Major Garrard reached out to steady her, but instead of letting her go, he held her gently against him and murmured, "Shall I carry you up the stairs, my little sleepy head?"

Angrily Aimée pushed against him, freeing herself from his embrace.

"Monsieur," she said in an assertive voice, "please do not touch me."

He laughed and replied, "You did not object to my touching you a moment before. In fact, you smiled when my hand caressed your cheek."

The fire flashed in her turquoise eyes, and hoping to disconcert him, she replied, "I . . . I thought you were someone else, monsieur."

"So now the truth comes out," he replied, still amused. "It was a man, of course."

"Yes," Aimée answered, adding, "I thought it was my . . . my fiancé."

Major Garrard's eyes darkened and his voice, suddenly grown cold, asked, "And this fiancé—did he leave you here alone, while he retreated to a safer place with your Confederate Army?"

"No, monsieur," Aimée replied. "He . . . he is still in the city."

"What is his name?" the man demanded, refusing to let her pass him until she answered.

"Prosper," Aimée announced proudly, "but for his own safety, I will tell you no more."

She hurried past him, her cheeks burning at the lies she had just told.

Aimée resolved never to go to sleep in the garden again. She could not risk another confrontation with that man. She must stay out of his way until she had decided what she would do. And even as she cut the flowers to take to the cemetery, she glanced over her shoulder to make certain that the man was not standing behind her.

Aimée had not gone far down the street when Fréki appeared at her side.

"Oh, Fréki, how did you get out?" The dog wagged his tail and continued beside her. If she took the time to walk him back down Royal Street and then retrace her steps to the cemetery, she would be so late in returning home that she was sure to bump into the major.

"Well, just this once, you naughty dog," Aimée said and walked rapidly down the street.

By the time she reached the cemetery Fréki was still beside her, and hesitating to take the dog inside, she took the ribbon from Tante Dee Dee's flowers and tied the dog's collar to the wrought-iron railing at the entrance.

"Wait here, Fréki, I won't be long," she said, giving him a pat before disappearing into the cemetery.

"I would appreciate it if you did not take my dog on your assignations with your lover," the man said icily, untying the dog from the fence.

Aimée held back the burning retort, knowing that any answer she gave him would be the wrong one. So she remained silent and turned from him, her contempt for him blazing in her eyes.

The tall dark-haired man stood watching her go, and with Fréki by his side, he walked casually into the cemetery.

That evening the weather was muggy and the carriage house was uncomfortably hot. Aimée slipped out into the darkness to sit on the steps half hidden by the oleander tree growing up beside them. There was a movement in the garden and a short ecstatic bark. Fréki and Geri had found her hiding place.

Aimée whispered to them, "Go back, Fréki, go back, Geri." And she gave them both a slight push when they bounded up the steps to her.

"I'm afraid it's too late," the hated voice commented with an insolent arrogance. "Your hiding place has been found."

"I . . . I am not hiding, monsieur," Aimée said, biting her lip. "It . . . it is hot and I . . . could not sleep."

"Neither could I. But it was not the heat that made me restless." His voice had suddenly become more human, without the tinge of arrogance she had noticed at first.

"I am afraid I should apologize for my accusation this afternoon."

"Why should you, monsieur?"

"Come now, Aimée. I know your secret—I found his grave this afternoon."

"What . . . what are you talking about, monsieur?"

"Do not pretend, Aimée. Your flowers gave you away. That, and the name you mentioned—Prosper . . . Gautier, was it not? The man you loved—"

"Prosper is a common name in New Orleans. And . . . and I took no flowers this afternoon."

"Oh, Aimée, you are no good at lying. Even the ribbon

you used to tie Fréki to the fence matched the one on the flowers in the cemetery."

Aimée stood up, her tiny figure dwarfed by the height of the man standing before her. "I . . . I have no wish to continue this conversation. You may believe what you wish. Good *night*, monsieur!"

Aimée walked the rest of the way up the steps and went into the hot little room. She wished she had never had the misfortune to meet the man who could cause her such dismay.

The atmosphere in New Orleans was still tense and Aimée wished she could leave the city. But as long as her *grand-père* was a prisoner on Ship Island, she would stay.

For days she had felt uneasy about him, but it was the disturbing dream on that airless, humid Tuesday night that caused her to seek news of him. Aimée had dreamed that her *grand-père* had fallen while filling bags of sand in the prisoners' yard on Ship Island, and had been kicked by one of the guards. In her dream he had lain in the hot sun all day, and when he had asked for water, there was no one to hear.

She woke with such a sense of dread that she was determined to get news of him. Boarding the trolley, she started out on her destination to the offices of the provost marshall.

The provost marshall had given orders for imprisoning more and more of the citizens of New Orleans and he had not finished. General Butler seemed to be at war with the entire populace of the city, resolved to remove the stiffnecked pride of the people still loyal to the Confederacy. He had punished the young man responsible for lowering the flag by hanging him, had sent the man cheering for Jefferson Davis to prison, and had sent an elderly schoolteacher to prison because she happened to have a newspaper favorable to the Confederate cause in her possession. Where would it end? What other offenses would be punished by imprisonment or the taking of a life?

The voices of the two women sitting in front of her floated back to Aimée, interrupting her thoughts.

"My dear, did you know that 'Beast' Butler has sent three of the Protestant ministers to prison for refusing to pray for the President of the United States?"

"General Butler may be commander of the enemy forces, but even *he* doesn't have the authority to tell a man of the cloth how to pray," Aimée heard the other woman reply.

"And not only that," the first woman continued, "I heard the editor of the *Crescent* has been fined and imprisoned for printing the names of the Confederate soldiers who had died or were wounded."

"One poor woman has been trying to get a pass to leave New Orleans to visit her wounded son, but the Beast won't give her one. He seems to have absolutely no regard for the feelings of a mother."

"The man is clearly no gentleman, as evidenced by his treatment of women. And I fear things will get much worse. He has already sent one poor lady to Ship Island —Ship Island! Can you imagine the degradation for a lady of being a prisoner, guarded over by former slaves— just because she laughed when a Union funeral cortege passed her house? And the general would not even listen when she explained that a child's birthday party was taking place at the time."

"Well, I for one will fight him with my dying breath!"

The trolley stopped and a Union officer got on. The two women glanced at each other and promptly left the trolley, even though, Aimée was sure, they were not at their destination.

At the next stop Aimée stepped down from the trolley and crossed the street, for she had reached the military offices of the provost marshall.

It was a gloomy place, with little furniture in the waiting room. Benches with no backs lined the walls and at one end, over the desk by the door to the inner office, hung a picture of Abraham Lincoln.

Aimée was surprised to see the room so crowded. She would have a long wait if the provost marshall had to deal with each one personally. Still, the wait would not matter if she could hear news of her *grand-père*.

Hesitantly Aimée walked toward the desk, and when

the man seated there did not acknowledge her presence, she cleared her throat and said, "Monsieur . . ."

He looked up from his papers and Aimée continued, "Monsieur, I have come to seek news of my *grand-père*, who was taken to Ship Island last week. I must know if he is . . . well."

"The name of your grandfather?" the clerk asked in a businesslike tone.

"Jules Saint-Moreau," she replied. "He is an old man and not accustomed to . . . manual labor."

"I doubt that we will have news on the welfare of any of the prisoners . . . unless they're dead. And anyway, the marshall will not be in until later."

"I will wait, monsieur," Aimée said with a determined voice and sat back down again, prepared to stay all day if necessary.

She had waited for nearly two hours, hearing one name called after the other. An occasional sound of weeping disturbed the waiting room.

A beautiful dark-haired woman supported by another woman walked dazedly back into the waiting room on her way out.

"You must be brave and strong, *ma chérie*. Pierre would not wish you to break down in front of these Yankees," the companion said to the distressed woman.

"But he has given me only three days to sell my property," she replied weeping, "before being put out of the city."

So she had refused to take the loyalty oath, thought Aimée. She could easily envision the woman's life right now with her husband fighting for the Confederacy.

Profiteers had been able to acquire, at the auctions held regularly, fine old furniture and family heirlooms for a fraction of their value. Former slaves paraded on the streets wearing velvets, silks, and satins. The woman who had just left was faced with the same dilemma so many others were—of trying to get what money she could before being forced to seek shelter over the lines.

She would burn everything, Aimée vowed, before letting someone buy her *grand-père*'s beautiful things. Even as it was, an enemy was using them. . . .

The door opened from the street and the room was filled with the man's presence. Major Garrard surveyed the room for an instant. Seeing Aimée on a bench, he quickly walked toward her.

"Are you in trouble, Aimée?" he asked sternly.

"No, monsieur. I am here because I fear for my *grand-père*. But no one will give me news of him."

"I will see what I can find out," he said, leaving her side to walk through to the inner office.

After being gone a short time, Major Garrard was again at her side.

"Come, Aimée. I will take you home."

"But Grand-père—I must stay until I get news of him," she protested.

"I . . . I have news of him, Aimée."

"Then tell me, monsieur, tell me what you have learned," she requested with urgency.

"In the carriage, Aimée. Wait until we are in the carriage."

He took her by the arm and led her through the crowd to the carriage on the street. Her only concern was for her *grand-père*, so she did not protest further.

As the horses started down the street, she looked up at Major Garrard. She was alarmed by the look on his face, but she waited for him to speak.

He stopped the carriage when they were out of the congested traffic. The major looked into her eyes and with a sad, pained voice, he said, "Aimée, your grandfather is dead."

Her face turned white and a buzzing noise filled her ears. Had she heard him correctly?

"Dead? Grand-père is . . . dead?"

"His . . . heart was evidently not strong. He died two days ago."

The tears slipped silently down her cheeks before she became aware that she was crying. And then an audible sob reached her throat.

"Go ahead and cry, Aimée." He put his arms about her and drew her to his chest and Aimée cried as if she were flooding the levee. She was unaware of her surroundings, unaware of whose shoulder her tears soaked. Only her grief was reality. Nothing else touched her.

His soothing words finally reached her brain and she jerked away from him, now conscious of the one who comforted her. She quickly gathered up her skirts, and before he could stop her, Aimée jumped from the carriage and ran down the street.

"Aimée, where are you going?" Major Garrard shouted. But she continued running and did not stop until she had reached the Cathedral of St. Louis.

With her tears blinding her, she stumbled across the marbled entrance and groped for the door. But the door would not open—the church was barred—locked, upon orders of Beast Butler. With no strength left, Aimée sank to her knees, her hands pressing upward toward the closed doors. And there, upon the weathered stone step, she prayed for the soul of a proud old man.

Chapter 6

There was now nothing to keep her in New Orleans. She had no wish to remain, surrounded by the enemy that had taken away everything she had ever loved. For Aimée, the city was only a reminder of what she had lost.

The strains of the "Bonnie Blue Flag" wafted from the harbor and Aimée brightened at the message of sympathy from the British ship waiting to sail. No doubt, General Butler would issue another order forbidding any foreign ship to play that song while anchored in the harbor. But with the playing of that particular melody, strangers had given her fresh courage.

Yes, she would leave New Orleans as soon as possible —as soon as she could send word to her *papa's* distant cousin that she was now alone and needed shelter.

What a strange twist of fate that she might once again see Thornfell, the home where she had been born. When Papa had lost it in the gambling house—the lovely old home and the rich sugarcane fields that went with it—it had been discreetly purchased by a distant member of the family who had decided to move back to Louisiana.

Cousin Clotilde and her brother Jorge now occupied it —that is, if it was still standing. There had been many forays into outlying areas, with Union forces carrying off the slaves they were supposed to be freeing to force them to work on the canals and ditches. Any resistance on the part of the owner was met with the firing of their plantations. Perhaps the house had already been burned to the ground. If not, how could she be sure that Cousin Clotilde was still alive, or that she had not sought safety elsewhere?

Aimée did not dare leave New Orleans until she was certain that she had a place to go. But how could she find out? Could she get a letter to Cousin Clotilde when there was little traffic going in and out of New Orleans— and that by strict regulations?

Perhaps Monsieur O'Brie at the pharmacy would know a way. He had sent medicine to the Confederate troops before the city had fallen, and she had heard that somehow, small portions of quinine and morphine were still getting through. Could her letter be sent the same way?

The next day Aimée went to the pharmacy near the square.

"Monsieur O'Brie, do you know if there is any way that I could get a letter through enemy lines?" Aimée asked the stoop-shouldered man behind the counter.

He looked up to make sure she had not been overheard. He then closed the door to the street.

"Where is it to go, Aimée?" he asked cautiously, adjusting his spectacles on the bridge of his thin nose.

"To Cousin Clotilde at Plantation Thornfell. It is across Lake Pontchartrain, toward Bayou St. Moreau."

"If you care to leave the letter with me, I will see what I can do."

Aimée did not ask how he could get it past the sentries. And he probably would not have told her if she had asked.

While she waited for an answer to her letter, Aimée joined in to show contempt for the enemy, for she was bitter about the death of her *grand-père*, who would not have harmed *un petit pou*, and she blamed every Yankee for the shabby treatment that had led to his death. She, too, left the trolley when a Union officer boarded. She held her nose each time she could not avoid passing an enemy soldier. (Since many of them had not taken a bath for months, their odor really was offensive.) And when the soldiers made vulgar remarks, she sang snatches of "Bonnie Blue Flag" to show her loyalty to the Confederacy. She had sewn Confederate buttons on some of her dresses and she displayed the little Confederate flag whenever she could.

Aimée had heard that General Butler was livid over the behavior of the ladies of New Orleans, who banned his officers from their drawing rooms and contemptuously swept their skirts out of the way of his soldiers at every turn. And Aimée was glad that he was upset. It was the only weapon they had to wound the enemy—and they would continue to use it until New Orleans was free of the invading army. The Beast would soon learn that he could not defeat the women merely by rules and regulations. Their hearts were more loyal than that.

But even Aimée was not prepared for General Butler's next move in his personal vendetta. She gasped in dismay as she read the order in the *Daily Delta*—the order designed to disgrace every loyal woman and force her into submission to the whims of any soldier.

Order Number 28

As the officers and soldiers of the United States have been subjected to repeated insults from the women (calling themselves ladies) of New Orleans . . . it is ordered that hereafter when any female shall by word, gesture,

or movement insult or show contempt for any officer . . .
she shall be regarded as a woman of the town plying
her avocation.

By orders of: General Benjamin Butler

Aimée was furious. This was the final straw. The pot-
bellied, double-chinned Beast had shown his true colors
and had declared war, not on the Confederate soldiers,
but on the defenseless mothers, wives, and sweethearts
of men who could not defend their honor.

Aimée was still seething in indignation when she approached the pharmacy. No letter awaited her, and in a
state of disappointment she walked home in the vast heat
of the late afternoon.

Daily Aimée sought out Monsieur O'Brie, but still no
letter appeared from Thornfell. I must get away, Aimée
thought. I cannot stay in New Orleans a moment longer
than necessary. She felt stifled and trapped.

Aimée was too absorbed in her troubles to see the
drunken soldier weaving his way into her path.

"How 'bout a l'il kiss?" the soldier said, taking her
by the arm.

Aimée recoiled from his touch and the odor of his
breath. "Remove your filthy hand from my arm at once,
monsieur," she ordered in a frigid voice.

"Not till you give me a l'il kiss,' 'the soldier replied
stubbornly, leaning closer to her.

"Leave the lady alone, Corporal," a voice called out.

The drunken soldier looked up to see the officer de-
scending upon him. He attempted a salute.

"Sir, thish woman insulted me—I'm taking her to the
marshall's offiish—off-ice." He tried to stand with dignity
but his equilibrium was too far gone.

"That's not necessary. Just leave her with me," the
major ordered.

The man's inebriated eyes brightened. "You want 'er
for yourself, Major?"

"No. I just want you to leave her alone."

"Ish all right . . . you can have her . . . shish too l'il for me, anyway. I like 'em bigger." He turned and staggered in the opposite direction.

Aimée, her anger flashing as brightly as her red-gold hair, started to go past her rescuer, when he stopped her.

"May I escort you home, Aimée?" Major Garrard asked.

She looked at the arrogant, swaggering invader who had taken away her freedom, her house, and had tried to regulate even her thoughts by orders upon orders. She saw the blue uniform with gold buttons glinting in the afternoon sun, the saber clinking against his side, and silver-gray eyes staring down at her—amused and teasing. It was more than she could bear. Aimée retaliated and showed her hatred the only way she could. The strains of the "Bonnie Blue Flag" came from her lips and she lifted the small flag from her bosom to wave in front of him.

"Are you crazy? Do you want to be put in prison?" Major Garrard reached for the flag to crush it in his hands, but Aimée eluded him and darted down the street.

He took up the chase, his face black with rage. His long soldier's legs were a decided advantage, but Aimée knew the city better than he and she managed to escape through the alleys.

Panting, and with her long silky hair loosened from its coiffure, she reached the gate of the townhouse and hurried into the courtyard to seek shelter in the servants' quarters before his return.

A sudden breeze lifted her hair and the low-hanging limb of the crepe myrtle entwined with coral vines clutched at her hair as if the tree had become a druid spirit reaching out to harm her. The more she pulled the strands, the more helplessly entangled she became.

The gate opened and the major walked into the courtyard, stopping short when he saw her predicament. He laughed in unexpected enjoyment and stood watching her ineffective efforts to free herself.

"I wonder what the feminine of 'Absalom' is?" he said, as if he were thinking aloud. "I'm sure he could have given you advice on the dangers of catching your hair in a tree. His neck was broken, Aimée, as a punishment for his disobedience. And you, my dear, have come close to having your pretty little neck broken—by my own hands."

He continued staring at her.

"I wonder which name would suit you. The pagan goddesses had names ending in 'roth' or 'loth' . . . Absaroth? Absaloth?"

He stood over her, making her feel impotent against such a giant. When he reached out to pull the strands loose, she protested, "I do not need your help, monsieur," and in an insulting, unladylike gesture, she spat on the ground before him.

Again the dark rage spread over his face, the gray eyes became slivers of steel, and his brow furrowed in deep wrinkles. The scar was even more vivid against the dark flush of his face.

"You have gone too far, Aimée, with your damned insolent pride, taunting me. I told you once your claws should be trimmed, and by God, this night I shall do it! I have put up long enough with your insults!"

He freed the last remaining strand caught on the vines and lifted her, carrying her toward the house. "General Butler is right," Major Garrard muttered, looking down at her, while she kicked and scratched to get out of his grasp. "You *should* be treated as a woman of the street."

Anderson quickly smothered the look of surprise on his face when the major walked into the house carrying the struggling Aimée.

"Anderson," Major Garrard said, "I want you to go out and buy the most vulgar red dress you can find, with suitable undergarments—and a feather for the hair . . . something that any woman plying her vocation would be proud to wear."

He tossed his money clip toward Anderson. With a poker face, the man caught it and left the house to do the major's bidding.

By this time Aimée was alarmed. She had started something that refused to be stopped. Major Garrard carried her up the stairs, pushed her into his bedroom, and locked the door from the outside.

"Please, monsieur, let me out." She could just as easily have saved her breath.

Three quarters of an hour later the door opened and Aimée could tell that the man was still angry. In his arms Major Garrard held the gaudiest red silk dress she had ever seen—with layers of white petticoats.

"Put these on," he ordered, throwing the clothes on the bed.

She lifted her chin; her eyes flashed and seemed to burn. "Never, monsieur! You cannot make me!"

"Oh, can't I?" He accepted the challenge and with one swift jerk he tore her dress down the back. She was taken by total surprise and she grabbed the dress to keep it from sliding off her shoulders.

"Do not be so modest, my pretty," he said, seeing her embarrassment. "Before this night is over, we shall know each other very well."

With another jerk, he removed the dress and crinolines from her, and she stood trembling in her camisole and pantaloons.

"What, no corset?" he jeered. "Have you perhaps—what is the phrase you Creoles use when a spinster gives up hoping for marriage—have you 'tossed your corset on the armoire,' my dear? Well, tonight no woman of the street would be seen without one."

"Have you no regard for a lady, monsieur? Must you insult me this way?"

"You did not mind insulting me, Aimée. Why should I mind helping you to dress for the part you are to play tonight?"

He picked up the white corset, put it around her waist, and turned her away from him. She struggled to remove the stiff garment from her body, to free herself from his grasp.

"Be still," he ordered, as he began lacing the corset tighter and tighter.

"Monsieur," Aimée protested, "I cannot breathe. Please, monsieur, not so tight!"

"Call me Bryan and I'll think about it."

She remained silent and he pulled the laces even tighter.

"Please, monsieur," she gasped, and he tugged again on the corset strings. "Monsieur . . . Bryan," she said feebly.

"What did you say, Aimée?"

"Bryan," she cried out in a louder voice.

The corset strings eased and she was able to breathe again.

The red dress that he had placed over her head, nearly smothering her, gave her a cheap look, with her red-gold hair and vivid eyes. Like a room furnished with too much opulence, Aimée also looked too opulent for propriety. The corset had pushed her breasts upward and they looked as if they might spill out of the dress at any moment.

Bryan turned her around and viewed her with satisfaction. "I think you look sufficiently vulgar to play the part. I won't be long, Aimée. Just make yourself comfortable in the chair."

"Are you . . . going to . . . dress in this room?" she asked, aghast.

"You may turn around and close your eyes, if your modesty becomes too enraged."

"I would hate to be your wife, monsieur—Bryan—if this is how you treat her."

"I have no wife, Aimée. I have been far too busy defending my country from hotheads," he replied.

Bryan began removing his shirt and Aimée turned her back and closed her eyes.

She was still trembling when she felt his hands on her shoulders. She opened her eyes and his devil's face was handsome and alarming looking down at her.

"How could I ever have mistaken you for a child?" he asked in a hoarse voice as he surveyed her once again.

Suddenly his lips were on hers and the soft butterfly touch hardened into something more passionate and demanding. Her heart fluttered in alarm. Then he released her, with a surprised look on his face.

"I would not have thought you were that experienced, Aimée, to arouse a man so quickly by your kisses. Perhaps your fiancé taught you more than young girls are usually taught before marriage."

She furiously rubbed her lips with her handkerchief. Scornfully she retorted, "No man has dared to kiss me before . . . Bryan. Not even my fiancé. And if this is what kisses are like, I can well live without them!"

He laughed. "Do not judge by a short sample. There will be enough time for you to decide just what you like and don't like," he threatened. "Before this night is over, you will be begging for more than my kisses."

"You are arrogant, monsieur, to think that I would beg you for anything!" she said haughtily, as her eyes flashed in anger.

"All women are the same, Aimée . . . pretending to dislike a man's touch, yet inviting him by their flashing eyes and seductive beauty. Even you, my little Rebel, know how to play the game, while insulting me with your outrageous behavior."

Aimée gave an unladylike snort.

"Oh yes," Bryan assured her. "And you may protest wanting to be my wife—it's a challenge to the strongest of men—but I have eluded the marriage knot for all of my thirty-two years and I shall continue to do so. I have no intention of being caught by the challenge you have flung in my face."

Aimée was furious. "You do not have to worry, Bryan. Rather than become your wife, I would cut my throat."

Bryan laughed in delight and touched her cheek. "Such a little spitfire . . . we will get along well, indeed, this night."

By the tone of his voice it was more a threat than anything else. Aimée bit her lip to keep from retorting, for now she was afraid of this giant who stood beside her, overwhelming her with his sheer physical presence.

Chapter 7

$\mathcal{T}$he hired carriage, turning down the cobbled street on its way from the Vieux Carré to the French Opera House, took the same route as another night in Aimée's life.

Aimée remembered the virginal white demure dress she had worn less than two years before, the imported lace fan she had carried, and the debutante's bouquet of flowers tied with long satin streamers.

Now she was again on her way, but this time she was dressed in a harlot's dress—red, vulgar, gaudy, its scantiness barely covering the top portion of her body.

In her embarrassment Aimée shrank farther back into the carriage, out of sight of any curious passerby.

The man beside her, aware of her sudden movement, leaned over and taunted, "Are you trembling in anticipation of the night ahead, my love?"

Aimée met his amused glance and with a stiff mien, she replied, "The only thing I could look forward to in anticipation is *your* falling under the wheels of this carriage!"

"Watch your tongue, Aimée," Bryan cautioned sternly.

The rest of the journey was made in silence.

Crowds of people milled around the Opera House and Aimée felt speculative eyes on her as Bryan handed her down from the carriage. There was a murmur when she came into the light, but Aimée, determined not to show Bryan what it was costing her to appear in this total disgrace, held her head even higher on her slender neck, and sweeping the long, curved golden lashes downward, kept her eyes open only wide enough to see the space immediately in front of her.

Up the red carpeted stairs they climbed, she and Bryan, his hand under her elbow to guide her. The brilliant chandeliers broadcast a silvery luminescence, offering no shadowed escape to Aimée.

Voices wove in and out, a tapestried polyphony made up of earlier voices combined with the veiled whispered ones surrounding her.

"At least he had the sense to hide her in the *loges grilles*."

"Do not speak of her, Aimée. For you, such creatures do not exist."

"My son, your timing is off. You should not have been seen conversing with Madame Calti under the watchful eye of the *jeunes filles*' mothers."

Madame Calti—Aimée had dismissed the woman from her mind. But now as she sat in the horseshoe-shaped open box, visible to everyone, Madame Calti assumed an overwhelming importance—an educating, elucidating force. For now Aimée had entered the same shabby world. She had been made to appear another Madame Calti, being whispered about, referred to, glanced at greedily by men and disapprovingly by women. It did not matter that she was still an innocent girl. Her reputation was tarnished, as much as if she had actually become a woman of the streets. And it was all due to the devil who sat beside her, pretending to be her lover and all the while amused at her discomfort.

When the music finally began, Aimée knew that her face was almost as red as the feather in her hair. She could have been mistaken for one of the dancers on the stage or any of the dozen trollops lolling outside, waiting for business after the performance.

Aimée tried to ignore her bruised feelings and to shut out the interested glances on all sides by concentrating on what was happening on stage. But the production was amateurish, far below the standard before the Yankees and their hangers-on had ruined the city. And so even the action on the stage was no help to her in forgetting. The most ironic part of all—that the Opera House was closing at the end of the week's performance—made Aimée bitter. A few days more and it would not have been the scene of her disgrace.

Bryan's hand stole to the nape of her neck and caressed a curl that had fallen at the back. Aimée stiffened at the attention. Chuckling softly, Bryan removed his hand, seemingly acquiescing to her frigid manner, until he could think of new mischief.

Just when she began to succeed in gaining some interest in the music, Bryan's teasing began all over again, ending in a lingering kiss on her shoulder when he knew he was being watched.

When the performance was over, Aimée breathed easier, not aware that the worst moment of all—a final humiliation—was yet to come.

They stood upon the banquette, waiting for their carriage. At its arrival, Bryan lifted her into the vehicle in the same manner that he would have helped an actual woman of the street, giving Aimée a playful smack across her *derrière*, to the accompanying titters of the crowd around her.

Furiously Aimée scrambled away from him as he seated himself beside her. When the carriage drew away from the Opera House, she could no longer contain her anger.

"You . . . you are no gentleman, sir," she sputtered with dagger-honed glints in her eyes. She reached out to pummel his chest but he laughed and caught her hands, replying, "And you, my little hellcat, are no lady."

Her hands were caught fast and her attempt to free them was not successful. Aimée remained still, caught, pulled beside his strong, muscular body—ineffective with her hands trapped in his. Her lips moved and the vague whisper reached his ears.

"Are you praying for my forgiveness, my pet, for that last display of temper?'

"I . . . I am praying to Our Lady of Prompt Succour that she will send a lightning bolt and strike down a certain miserable specimen of a man."

"Aimée, Aimée," he replied in mock hurt, "do you mean that all my efforts tonight to rid you of your excessive pride have been for naught?"

"Yes," she hissed venomously at him. "There are some things you will never take from me, even if I *am* trapped like some sparrow in the clutches of a hawk!"

"You do yourself an injustice, Aimée, to liken yourself to a little brown sparrow. You are far more like some exotic jungle bird, with flaming plumage, that could never be hidden from its predator. But come," he said, releasing her hands, "we are at our destination."

Aimée looked out to see the restaurant before her. So, she was still being punished—not allowed to go home and hide from her evening of disgrace. The humiliation was to continue, Her head was not quite so high, nor her step so lively as before.

The atmosphere was gay and Aimée shrank from the boisterous laughter emanating from the supper cubicles on either side of them. She sat still, aloof, not aware that the meal had been ordered and was now before them.

Lost and defeated in her shame, she did not at first hear his question spoken across the table.

"You are not eating, Aimée. Is the food not to your taste?"

"I . . . I am not hungry, Bryan," she answered in a subdued voice.

"The prawns are unusually good . . . I think you would enjoy them, if you tasted them."

He ate heartily but she could force nothing down her throat. She waited and watched in agitation as he ate leisurely, in no hurry to cut short the evening. Again the loud laughter from another cubicle penetrated the air.

"Oh, Bryan," Aimée pleaded, her eyes threatening to fill with tears, "please take me home. I . . . I can stand no more."

He rang for the waiter and it seemed Bryan's eyes softened toward her.

On the way home they were both silent. Perhaps it had been a mistake to suggest leaving to go home. Had he not intimated that there was more to come? But she could not abide being in the red dress a moment longer than necessary . . . could not abide the knowing looks and Bryan's enjoyment of the entire episode. Did he not realize what he had done to her?

"I will walk you to your room, Aimée," he said quietly when they entered the court. So he had become tired of the charade, too, thought Aimée. But she was too heartsick and exhausted to feel relief that her shame-filled night had come to an end.

Bryan walked up the steps with her and lit a candle on the table. "Good night, Aimée."

"Good night, Bryan," she answered, barely forming the words.

She closed the door and stood mute with shame. But at that moment her hunger overrode her shame and she walked to the little cupboard to find one of the peaches that she had hidden there that afternoon.

The sharp fruit knife lay on the table and its handle gleamed in the candlelight. Aimée picked it up to peel the peach, but suddenly her foot slipped on candle tallow that had spilled on the floor. As she fell, Aimée hit her head on the corner of the table and the peach rolled out of sight under the cot.

She was barely conscious when the knock sounded. "Aimée, let me in—I wish to talk with you."

She could not answer and the voice called again. "Aimée, I have come to apologize."

When there was still no answer, Bryan pushed open the door. The candle flickered, giving the room a shadowed, lonely feeling.

She lay in a crumpled heap on the floor, the knife protruding from her body, with the red blood darkening the red of the gaudy dress.

"Aimée!" Bryan cried as he rushed to her side. He picked her up in his arms and shouted for Anderson.

"Get a doctor at once, Anderson—there's been an accident. Hurry! In God's name, hurry!"

She felt his arms around her and his face against her hair. "I didn't mean to hurt you . . . please don't die . . ."

Voices thundered and receded around her. Snatches of conversation impressed themselves for a while on her brain—the soft voice of Anderson, the harsh, deep voice of Bryan, and others that she could not recognize.

"I have done all I can," an unfamiliar voice intoned. "A priest seems to be what you need."

She drifted and slept, waking, yet still unable to speak. Last rites—extreme unction—words for the dead—and the hands upon her, gentle, priestly hands.

"There is only one reason why the child would attempt this, Major," she heard in the distance. "Creoles are a proud people—they cannot live with shame and dishonor. Are you guilty, my son, of dishonoring her?"

No one answered. And then Bryan's voice admitted, "I . . . I was not kind to her, Father . . . and I realize now the shame she felt . . . but it is too late to make amends . . . the damage is done, however much I regret it."

"There *is* one way you can help to set things right, if you would . . ."

The priest was speaking to her gently. "Aimée, this man seeks to make amends and return some measure of honor to you. He has agreed to marry you, my child. Do you understand?"

Aimée's eyes fluttered open and she became aware not only of her pain but also of the dark, all-seeing eyes of the priest who was seated before her.

"No," she said, "he is my enemy . . ." Her voice was weak and the priest leaned closer to hear her whispered protest.

"You must, my child," the priest admonished. "It is the only way you can regain what you have lost."

She had no strength left to argue or to try to explain what had happened. "The peach" was all she could manage to whisper, but no one heard her.

The priest's words droned on and she felt the heavy ring pressed onto her finger by strong hands, imprisoning hers. "Till death do you part. . . ." And death stood at the door, beckoning her.

Down, down into a kaleidoscope of whirling colors she went—bits and pieces of colored glass that changed before she could find their meaning. She tried to fit the pieces together, but they changed too rapidly for her to grasp them and put them in place.

"Do not try to talk," a strange voice commanded her. And then a cloth was pressed across her brow.

"Hot—so hot!" she whispered, and she struggled to remove the covers smothering her.

The heavy ring encircled her finger, squeezing the life blood from her, draining her strength as some evil leech. With a giant effort, she pushed the ring from her finger and heard it drop on the floor.

Free—free at last from the enemy's grasp. Now, she could sleep.

It was the wind that woke her, teasing at the loose shutter, banging it noisily to signal the approaching storm.

She opened her eyes and watched the flickering lamp. A thin wraithlike figure moved across the room to stare at her. A smile filled the small freckled face, and without a word, the figure tripped out of the room and left the door to the bedroom open.

"Major Garrard," the childish voice called, "I think she's awake."

There were steps along the hall and the clicking of dogs' paws, closer and closer. The giant now stood at the door with a dog on either side of him. Odin, the god, with his wolves. But no, that was not his name. What had the girl called him?

She tried to sit up but the pain prevented her. What had happened? Why was she in bed? And why was the man staring at her so strangely?

"Aimée," he said from the doorway, with vast relief in his voice. He quickly came to her and bent over her, his eyes searching her face, as if to assure himself that she was all right.

"Who . . . who are you?" the girl asked, puzzled.

He tried to suppress the startled look on his face but was unsuccessful.

"Do you . . . not know who I am, Aimée?"

"Am I supposed to know you, monsieur?" she asked.

"I am your husband," he replied. "Do you not remember?"

She stared at him in disbelief. "I don't even know your name, monsieur," she answered. "How can you be my husband when I have never . . . seen you before?"

He gave a barely audible groan before sitting down beside the bed. He gently took her hand in his and stared at her finger that was now bare of the heavy gold ring.

"There was an accident and you are still in shock. But it's not very flattering, you know," he said with a wry smile, "to be forgotten by one's wife. My name is Bryan."

"I . . . I am sorry, monsieur," she replied with a tired whimper. "But it is disconcerting to have someone I don't know announce that he is my husband. . . ."

Her voice drifted away and she closed her eyes in exhaustion.

"Sleep, my little one," he said, and he brushed his lips across her forehead before leaving the room.

The storm gathered force from the south. Soon the trees were bowing low before the sodden earth and the lightning became a bullwhip across the sky, stinging Aimée awake with its deafening crack.

She trembled at the noise of the thunder and the rain striking against the windowpanes. "Odin," she cried aloud. "Odin."

The child asleep in the chair beside the bed stirred at her voice.

"It's a bad storm, Mrs. Garrard—but it won't hurt you none. I been through worse storms than this 'un and come out all right. But I'll get the major, if you want 'im."

"No, no—it's all right," Aimée said, and once more felt exhaustion pressing heavily upon her.

"What is it, Tink?" Bryan's voice demanded from the doorway.

"Your wife was calling for you, Major. She was afraid of the storm, but she's quieted down now."

"You may go to bed . . . I'll stay with her the rest of the night."

Another flash of lightning filled the room and Aimée shuddered. "The storm—I'm so afraid of storms."

His arms encircled her. "You're safe, Aimée. Don't be frightened."

She rested her head against his shoulder, content and safe in Odin's protection.

Aimée awoke with arms still around her. She pushed herself out of his reach and gazed at the man lying quietly beside her. She memorized every feature—the shiny black hair with highlights of blue, the jagged scar cutting across his cheek, and the square, angular jaw shadowed by the night's growth of beard blending into trimmed sideburns below his ears. She had confused him with Odin, but he was not a god, after all. He was the man who had claimed to be her husband.

Oh, why can I not remember? she asked herself. Everything was strange. She had no idea where she was or how long she had been ill. She vaguely remembered seeing the man in uniform the evening before, and the girl had called him "Major." And the girl? Who was she? The child had an odd manner of speaking and she looked as if she had never had more than a mouthful to eat at any time in her life. She looked to be about twelve years old, but of course, with little to eat, she could be small for her age and much older.

There was a knock at the door. The man beside her stirred.

"Major, you will be late this morning, sir, if you do not hurry. I have prepared a bath for you in the other bedroom."

The man stretched and opened his eyes. He met Aimée's turquoise eyes staring at him and she blushed at the knowing, sardonic look he returned.

"Just a moment, Anderson," he answered.

She did not feel married, although there was something familiar, yet disturbing, about this man. He had called her Aimée the night before and she had responded automatically to the name. But there was something puzzling about their relationship . . . something unnatural. She had noticed the watchful look in his eyes the previous night and it was there again in the morning light . . . almost as if he were waiting for her to discover something unpleasant. What could it be?

He left the room and she did not see him again until evening.

Aimée lay on the chaise, with a light shawl thrown over her feet. Tink had brushed her hair to a burnished red-gold, but had not attempted to dress it in a coiffure. It lay long and shining against the soft blue of the chaise, and the white dogs were on the floor beside her, keeping her company.

She looked up to see him standing in the shadows of the hall. He watched her with a frown on his face.

"Good evening, Bryan," she greeted her husband uncertainly.

"Good evening, Aimée," he answered as he stepped into the room.

Again there was silence and an air of tenseness surrounding them.

"Is it . . . all right for the dogs to be inside, Bryan?" she asked, trying to find some reason for the stern look on his face.

"If you wish it, Aimée," the man replied.

She remained quiet, trying not to show her anxiety, even though she was uncomfortable in his presence. What was bothering him? Had she done something to disturb him?

Did he think her forward for her behavior the evening before, clinging to him in fright over the storm? To Aimée, it seemed only natural for a wife to reach out to her husband for protection. But she knew that only the greater fear of the storm had made her forget her wariness of the handsome giant.

Aimée watched as he unbuckled the saber at his waist and unbuttoned his coat.

"I have become acquainted with Tink today, Bryan," she offered, to fill the silence. "She told me you found her wandering the streets and you were so kind to her. She said she has no kin, and she appeared grateful to you for giving her a place to sleep and food to eat."

He turned with an embarrassed grimace. "She will earn her keep," he said roughly, "so it wasn't all charity, Aimée. She will be quite helpful in caring for you."

Aimée attempted to leave the chaise but Bryan's voice stopped her.

"Just what do you think you are doing?"

"I am getting up to look out the window at the garden, monsieur. Do I need permission?"

"Yes, Aimée. I will not allow you to walk about so soon . . . it is not good for you to be up."

"But I am not an invalid," Aimée protested. "Just because I cannot remember the past does not make me totally incapable of moving."

"You have lost a lot of blood, my dear, and I will not allow you to do anything to lengthen your convalescence," he said, overriding her protest.

The stubborn jut of her chin gave warning to her feelings.

"Surely, you do not intend to force me to remain inactive, monsieur?"

Bryan laugher at her display of temper, "I see that your spirit is still intact. That's a good sign," he teased. Then his face darkened and he threatened, "But do not think I would hesitate to keep you a prisoner if it meant that you would get well sooner. Do you understand, Aimée?"

"Yes, monsieur," she said with a trembling, frightened voice. He was so fierce when he was crossed.

"Do not call me 'monsieur.' We have been through this before. My name is Bryan."

"Yes, Bryan."

She would have to be sensitive to his moods and not make him angry. But it was all so confusing, not knowing.

He leaned over and said lightly, "Does your husband get a kiss when he returns home, Aimée? I believe that is the custom."

She obediently lifted her head to kiss his cheek, but before she could accomplish the deed, his lips found hers. Her heart beat rapidly as his ardor grew. He pressed her to him and a tingling sensation enveloped her. She was visibly shaken when he stood again, his back to her.

"I think . . . your kisses are far more . . . exhausting for me than walking to the window."

Again he laughed, as he faced her. "You have mentioned my kisses before, Aimée, but your response each time belies your protest. But do not worry. I shall give you time to recuperate before demanding anything more from you."

Chapter 8

For the next week Aimée rested during the day, asking questions of both Tink and Anderson, since her husband evaded so many of the questions and her memory had not returned. But Anderson was noncommittal and Tink did not know anything since Aimée had been ill when she first came to the house. Aimée was aware that both Anderson and Tink watched the major with loyal, adoring eyes.

Each day her husband bombarded her with acts of care and kindness, as if he had only a limited time in which to capture her love. And this was what was so baffling to her.

Aimée could not believe that she had married a stranger willingly. Had he swept her off her feet by his gentle and tender wooing? Or rather, had he forced her into marriage with the same whirlwind force that caused her to tremble the few times he had shown his anger in her presence?

She was no match for his physical strength. In his arms Aimée felt much like a ripe dandelion that could be blown away to nothingness by one strong puff of his tremendous chest. There was a fierceness about him, barely hidden by his civilized words, and perhaps it was for this reason that she was so frightened, looking for some small assurance that he would not unleash this awful power to destroy her.

If she could only remember. . . .

"But evidently you do not wish to remember," the doctor admonished.

Aimée looked at him in bewilderment. "But you told me I fell and hit my head," the girl protested.

"Only a minor concussion—not severe enough to cause this amnesia. No, Mrs. Garrard, something so painful to you must have happened that you wished to erase all memory of it from your mind. I have seen it happen in young girls before, usually when they have experienced some event that was shocking to them . . . a form of hysteria."

"And my . . . husband? Has he talked with you about it?" Aimée questioned.

The tall heavy-jowled man hesitated. "Your husband refuses to discuss anything at all with me. And I have been unable to talk with the doctor who attended you on the night of your accident."

Aimée fidgeted in her chair, clasping her fingers and then releasing them, while the doctor studied her.

He began to speak again. "*Physically,* Mrs. Garrard, you are well—at least I can say that," he added, smiling with pride. "But I will not consider you completely well," he said, a sober tone replacing the lighter one, "until your memory returns—until you have come to terms with whatever is troubling you."

The doctor got up from his chair and Aimée also stood. "I am dismissing you as a patient, since I can do no more for you. But I pray that it will not be long before you have gained a complete recovery."

"Thank you, Doctor Floud, for . . . for your kindness," Aimée responded, seeing him to the door.

Soon after the doctor had left, Bryan returned to the townhouse. As he opened the door, he called for Aimée.

"I am in the salon, Bryan," Aimée answered.

Her husband took up the entire opening of the door, making the room and indeed the entire proportions of the townhouse seem too small. He stood for a moment before coming toward her and he gently took her in his arms and gazed at her, searching her face before demanding the kiss that had become an unnerving daily ritual.

"Did Doctor Floud pronounce you well today?" he asked.

"Yes, Bryan. He said physically I am as good as new."

The news seemed to change Bryan's gentle behavior toward her. He refused to release her, but instead let his hand trail down her back, causing her to shiver. And then she was lifted against him, her body molded to his, and Aimée's heart began pounding as he took a second kiss, his body straining against hers.

Aimée became frightened at the sudden change in his behavior—at the intensity that her news had brought. The gold buttons and the metal buckle on his uniform dug into her soft flesh, and she pushed away from him. "Bryan, your uniform—it is hurting me."

Instantly he released her and stood with a contrite expression. "And I have frightened you, haven't I, little one?"

She nodded, feeling a miserable consternation. "I . . . am sorry, Bryan, but somehow, I . . . don't feel like a wife yet." She stared down at her ringless left hand, and although she said nothing further, he seemed to understand what she was thinking.

He smiled, coaxing her to return his smile, and in relief that he was not angry with her, her turquoise eyes lit up in a dazzling display, as her lips quivered and then turned up at the corners, until her tiny white teeth showed in perfect rows.

"For now, you are safe, Aimée," he teased. "I have waited a long time to claim you. I can wait a while longer."

Bryan put his arm about her and together they went upstairs in time to prepare for dinner.

"I have waited a long time to claim you . . ." Bryan's words taunted her that night, and still no memory returned to give full meaning to his words.

Had she not actually become his wife in the marriage bed? Was that why she still felt so virginal with him, with no memory of being loved by him? Yet they had shared a bed—that high, carved ornate bed that for some reason gave Aimée a sense of security. She had lain beside the man who called himself her husband. Only he had never touched her, except to take her in his arms the night of the storm. She had thought he was being kind to her, patiently waiting for her body to recover from the wound. But what if they were not married at all? How could she be sure that what he had told her was the truth, with no sign of ring or marriage paper?

"Bryan," she whispered in the dark.

"Yes, my love," he replied sleepily.

"Are you really my husband, or . . . or are you merely playacting in some . . . some comedy? How am I to know that all this is . . . is real?"

She felt his stirring and then heard his gruff reply. "Do not tempt me to prove it this night, Aimée. I informed you earlier that I am ready to convince you at any time. Your illness at first, and then your fright, have stayed me so far from taking what is mine by law."

"I only wish . . . I could remember," Aimée said sadly in a little girl's voice, unaware of the fires that she had stirred in Bryan's loins.

Aimée sat in the garden and watched the lengthening shadows take form and spread their blue tints to every part of the walled courtyard.

It was the time of day that Aimée loved best, the time she called "the edge of yesterday," with the breeze whispering words of forgotten love songs—remembering, remembering. But there was no song or memory of the past for her. Aimée's life was contained in the shadow of the weeks that Major Garrard had announced that she was his wife.

She was like the coral vines that had finished blooming and now, stripped of their beautiful flowers, lamented their lost perfume and lay dormant under the summer sun, waiting for another time, another season.

Sighing, Aimée stared down at the bare finger of her left hand. When she had questioned Bryan about a wedding ring, he had a ready explanation. The heavy gold signet ring that he had placed on her finger at the time of their wedding was far too large and it had dropped from her finger when she was ill, or so he had said.

It must have been a hurried ceremony not to have a ring. And the accident had sounded strange also . . . almost as if she had deliberately fallen on the knife, even though Bryan had called it an accident.

Another thing bothered Aimée. Bryan had refused to answer when she questioned him about the scar across his cheek. Perhaps he had just gotten tired of all her questions.

While she sat, thinking of him, wondering what it would be like to be loved by this frightening giant, the gate opened and Bryan came into the courtyard. The moment she saw him, Aimée knew there was a difference about him this day. He was a stalking tiger and she had the uneasy feeling that she was his prey. The look in his eyes told her that he was willing to wait no longer. He had given her a week—a week to ponder what it would be like to be his wife—and now he stood with the bearing of a man ready to take what was his.

"Aimée, come here," he commanded, with a strange light in his silver-gray eyes.

She obeyed him as a slave would obey her master. Her feet moved woodenly along the walkway until she was beside him. Aimée watched while he took the gold circlet from his pocket and solemnly placed it upon her finger.

"If you had doubts of our marriage, this should reassure you," he said gruffly.

The shadows in the garden had grown deeper and there was a stillness, as if the very leaves were listening and waiting.

"You are mine . . . always remember that, Aimée." Bryan's voice was threatening and he leaned closer and closer until she was in his arms, her body pressed against his hard, muscular thighs.

Aimée attempted to draw back but his hands caressed her cheeks and moved down her throat, sending shivers through her body. And then his hands became more insistent, stroking the flesh that overflowed from the bodice of her dress. The sudden warmth made her weak and helpless before Bryan's sensual assault on her body.

He unloosened the buttons to her dress, his hands

fondling her body through the thin material of her camisole. And acting immediately impatient of the obstruction that hid her breast from sight, he slipped the camisole from one shoulder, exposing her bare breast to his view.

"So beautiful," he murmured, bending his head to kiss the silky, soft globe.

"Bryan, someone will see," Aimée protested, attempting to push herself from him.

But Bryan, ignoring her protest, impatiently lifted her in his arms, making no effort to right the devastation to her camisole. His arms cradled her, already possessing her with their intent, as they carried her past the sundial, past the oleander tree, up the curving stairs to the second-story quarters of the carriage house at the back of the garden.

Her mind refused to function. Aimée was aware only of his strength, his power over her, and a vague, discomforting, alien thing that frightened her even more—this awakening of her body. And so she struggled against him until his voice commanded, "Let me love you, Aimée. I have waited so long to make you mine. . . ."

She stopped struggling. The softness of the pillow under her head and the movement of the cot were forgotten as she felt his strong, muscular body straining against her own. Like an entrapped, fluttering bird, her heart beating rapidly, in frightened fascination she watched the two shadows on the wall merge into one.

Suddenly the fear and the pain were swept away by a new sensation and her eyes widened in surprise.

"Aimée, I'll never let you go," the emotion-filled voice of the man cried out. "You are mine and you can never escape. . . ."

The emotion was now spent. Aimée lay quietly in her husband's arms and timidly traced the angle of his jaw with her finger. He gazed down at her and she saw fierce love and complete possession written in his eyes. She would never be free of him. She was his—his alone, grafted to him by the ancient mystical rite of becoming one flesh with him. Apart from him, she would be half-whole, incomplete—she was destined to blossom and flower only in his presence. And because of this, she shuddered.

"I did not know love was so . . . consuming," she whispered.

The giant laughed and gathered her to him again. "Your heart is fluttering, Aimée. Are you still so frightened of me?"

"No, Bryan," she said, refuting the small twinge of remaining fear. "But you must give me time . . . to become used to being . . . your wife."

Each day Bryan left early and returned in the late afternoon to the house where Aimée waited for him.

He was gentle with her, initiating her into the subtleties of love, until she was no longer embarrassed, no longer afraid of him. As her trust grew, she began to fulfill her duties as a wife with a naturalness of spirit unknowingly drawn from the first Aimée, who had possessed all the secrets of love from the seraglio of a lusty sultan.

Each night she gave herself in good measure to her husband, inflaming his desire with her smooth, tempting young body and her silken Lorelei hair.

"Your hair broadcasts your passionate nature, my love," he teased. "I knew the moment I saw you that you would be a feast for any man."

"I come by it naturally, monsieur. My great-great-*grand-mère* was the sultan's favorite." Aimée stopped speaking, wondering how that bit of information had come to mind, but she shrugged it away and turned to other things.

When her husband was away, Aimée was careful not to impinge on Anderson's territory. He kept the house clean and tended to the major's clothes. All the other things, Tink and Aimée did together, going to the market each day, finding good things to put on the table at mealtimes. And when the marketing and cooking were done, they cared for the garden, cultivating the strawberries and scuppernongs. When that was finished, the two pulled the weeds from the flower beds along the wall.

The bees flitted from blossom to blossom and were chased by Fréki and Geri until each had been stung on his tender nose. Then they kept their distance from the insects, content to find a cool spot in the dirt to hide from the burning rays of the summer sun.

And when the strawberries were ripe and plump, Aimée gathered them to save for her husband's dinner.

"Are you sure you are not feeding me lotus blossoms, Aimée?" Bryan asked teasingly as he took a bite of the strawberry dessert. "I find it increasingly hard to leave you each morning and I can't keep my mind on my work, for thinking about returning to you."

Aimée smiled with a coquettish glint in her turquoise eyes. "Make no mistake, Bryan. With your appetite, if I had lotus blossoms in my garden, I would certainly feed them to you."

He pushed back his chair and stood up, drawing her to him.

"Your garden is already filled with untold delights, my love," he said, caressing her.

Aimée laughed and retorted, "I was speaking of my garden in the courtyard, monsieur."

Bryan pulled her closer, sliding his hands down her waist, and making a path on each side of her dress to her hips. "You tantalize me, Aimée. My desire grows stronger for you each day. Even now, I can wait no longer."

He pushed her out the door and toward the stairs and she went willingly with him.

He unloosened her dress, and driven by passion, jerked it impatiently from her shoulders. At this action she shuddered and her body froze.

"What is it, my darling? Did I hurt you in my impatience?" Bryan asked.

"No," Aimée reassured him, "but for a moment, there was . . ." She stopped, puzzled at the fleeting feeling of terror, but then dismissed it from her mind, and helped him to unfasten the crinolines that separated her body from his.

A few days later Aimée and Tink were in the kitchen preparing dinner. As usual, Tink took down the china to set the table in the dining room for Bryan and Aimée.

"Tink," Aimée spoke, "there is no need for you and Anderson to eat in the kitchen each day. Please put four settings on the dining table. From now on, we will all eat together."

"I'm not sure Anderson would . . ." Tink replied uncertainly, unable to express her feelings in appropriate words.

"You think Anderson would object to our eating together?"

"Yes ma'am—with the major, that is."

"Then I will speak to him about it."

On the way to find Anderson Aimée heard the door open and she went into the hallway, where Anderson was helping Bryan remove his coat.

"And what has my flaming-haired wife been doing today?" Bryan asked teasingly, holding her in his arms for the greeting he demanded each evening.

"I have been rearranging the . . . mess, as you would say, Bryan. I thought it would be much easier for everyone concerned if Anderson and Tink had their meals with us in the dining room . . . but Tink thinks Anderson might object to my change."

Bryan laughed, and turning to Anderson, said, "What about it, old fellow? Do you have any objections?"

"Sir, you know I do—I do not think it . . . appropriate."

"We shared many a tree stump before as our dining table—and sometimes ate from the same tin plate. No, Anderson, you are overruled. Mrs. Garrard shall have her way."

"Is that . . . an order, sir?"

"Yes, Anderson, it's an order," Bryan snapped.

Aimée could see that Anderson was not happy with the change. And though he had quickly disguised it, she had seen the slight flicker of annoyance on Bryan's face when she had first mentioned it. But Aimée felt relieved that she would not be the only object of the brooding, penetrating looks of her husband.

The days passed and the incessant heat of New Orleans baked every living thing in its path. With the heat came additional problems for the Union forces. By August Bryan could hardly hide his irritation each day when he came home. But one day he met Aimée with a fury that she had never seen before.

"That damned martinet!" he exclaimed. "One of our own colonels is killing more of our soldiers than the Rebels ever did by making them dress out with full packs to march in this damned heat. It was a hundred and ten degrees out there today, but do you think the colonel would forego the marching? No! Not even when the poor fools were dropping like flies."

Aimée listened to her husband and then another voice was speaking to her. "New Orleans can almost defend itself against the Yankee soldiers. What with the heat and the fever, the poor fools will drop like flies."

"Etienne," she said under her breath. The face of her brother became clear and she could hear him as he repeated the words. And then she realized the awful sadness —Etienne was dead.

"What is it, Aimée? What is wrong?" Bryan asked.

Aimée turned her ashen face toward him and faltered, "I . . . I just remembered . . ."

"What did you remember, Aimée?" Bryan was shaking her and she saw the fierce look in his eyes.

"You are hurting me, Bryan," she whispered, suddenly afraid of her husband.

"I'm sorry, Aimée," he said, loosening his hold on her, "but I insist that you tell me what you remembered."

"My brother—I had a brother, Etienne. But he is dead."

The fierce look disappeared and in its place came one of relief.

She did not understand him, this husband of hers, but hiding the despair and sadness she felt in her heart, she looked up at Bryan and said, "Come into the house. I want to show you what Tink and I did today."

Aimée, having experienced Bryan's reaction to her memory's returning, did not mention to him the little things that popped into her mind. Sometimes while holding a certain vase or looking at a porcelain figurine, she had a fleeting glimpse into the past. But so far she had been unable to remember anything about their courtship —or their wedding day.

Chapter 9

$\mathcal{N}$ews of increased fighting farther north came, and Bryan was away more of the time, inspecting the forts and fortifications along the river.

When he returned home, Bryan always brought something designed to please Aimée. He secured bolts of cloth from one of the foreign ships in the harbor, now that President Lincoln had lifted the blockade, and he hired an old Negress to sew clothes for both Aimée and Tink.

One afternoon when Bryan had been away for a few days Aimée heard a commotion outside the gate. She looked out the upstairs window to see what was happening. There stood Bryan with a handsome *calèche*, pulled by a beautiful black pony. Aimée rushed down the stairs to greet the grinning Bryan.

"A little love offering, my sweet, designed just for you."

"Oh, Bryan, it's beautiful and *he's* beautiful, too!" she exclaimed enthusiastically, rushing to stroke the head of the placid, sleek pony.

"You and Tink will be able to enjoy cool drives along Lake Pontchartrain when I am away," explained Bryan. "And it seems I shall have to be away more often than I would wish."

Aimée's eyes that had showed her delight with the gift now turned dark with sudden worry. "Will you be in the fighting, Bryan?"

He shook his head. "I will be far too busy seeing to the levee and the flooded waters and supervising the building of bridges for the river crossings. You do not have to worry on my account, Aimée," he assured her.

Then a new worry assailed her as she looked again at the expensive gift. "Can we . . . afford all this, Bryan?" she asked, not knowing what a major received in pay. "After all, there are Tink and Anderson and you and me to provide for."

He laughed at her. "Not on a major's pay," he teased, "but you need not worry about the picayunes."

"Bryan, you are not . . . trading across the lines, are you?" she asked, suddenly fearful. The news was all over New Orleans that General Butler had allowed his brother, Andrew Butler, to trade back and forth with the Confederates and it was rumored that if anyone else wanted to trade, he would have to get a permit from Andrew Butler. Already the man was supposed to have made millions of dollars selling goods at exorbitant prices, charging as much as twenty-five dollars for a two-dollar sack of salt.

"Aimée, you cannot think that I am part of that carrion, making profits from war!" he scolded.

"Then how *do* we manage?" she inquired.

"You do not have to worry about money, Aimée—the Garrards have always had more than enough. But it has not always been a blessing. So many mamas were so determined that I would share my portion with their thin-nosed, haughty daughters that at times I felt inclined to give it all away, just so I could be rid of the matchmaking mamas."

Bryan looked down at his wife, touching her hair and caressing her cheek with his fingers." But no one could accuse *you*, little Rebel, of marrying me for my money."

Even though Aimée knew that money was not an issue, she was frugal with the amount Bryan gave her to do the shopping, attempting to find the best bargains. But she was always silent and sad when she returned from the market, for it was a heartache to see aristocratic old ladies haggling over the price of a rancid piece of bacon or a cast-off pair of shoes that Aimée knew they would not have been caught dead in a few months before.

"You are so silent, my love," Bryan said to Aimée at

the dinner table that night. "Has something happened to distress you?"

Bryan and Aimée were alone, since Tink and Anderson had eaten earlier.

"I went to the market today, Bryan, and it always . . . distresses me when I see children and old people looking hungrily at food they cannot afford to buy. Why is it, Bryan, that war hurts the ones least responsible for it?" Her troubled turquoise eyes looked to him for some answer or understanding.

"It has always been that way, Aimée. But I fear the hard times are just beginning."

"But the city has surrendered, Bryan," Aimée protested. "Must the people be deluged with new indignities, fresh hurts each day, until nothing is left? Their homes have been taken away, their livelihood is gone, many have been forced to take the oath against their principles just to stay alive. And yet, General Butler seems determined to strip them even of their pride, the last thing they possess. I cannot understand it."

"You forget, Aimée, that this war is not one between enemy nations, with honorable conventions of surrender and settlement handled with dignity. It's a *blood feud* within the same family, with hate measured out on the same scale that once measured love. And when the fighting is over between brothers, there is never forgiveness—only a nursing of grudges, with the victor determined to strip the last vestiges of pride from the vanquished.

"No, Aimée, there *is* no dignity of surrender between brothers," Bryan said bitterly. "And your brother Etienne is far better off dead than rotting away in some prison camp."

Aimée looked at her husband's unhappy face and she knew that he must have inspected one of the prisons that day. His words chilled her and Aimée shivered.

The intense humidity remained with them, but the fever, usually rampant at that time of year, had not appeared. To his credit, General Butler had cleaned up the city and had strictly observed quarantine on the boats that came from the West Indies, more often than not with yellow jack as their principal cargo.

To celebrate that good fortune, a lavish ball had been planned by the general's staff for the third Friday evening in September.

Aimée dressed for the ball with mixed feelings. She did not look forward to an evening surrounded by Union officers, even though her husband was one of them, but she could not resist wearing the beautiful ball gown that Bryan had brought home to her.

The dress itself was made of pale yellow watered silk—yards and yards of it, its skirt supported by a large metal hoop and six crinolines. The front of the skirt was inlaid with turquoise embroidery in a diamond-shaped pattern, sheltering the bouquet of flowers in the center. Each flower fluttered its silken sheen, catching the light as Aimée turned. And the same turquoise embroidery decorated the low décolleté of the bodice, enhancing the magnolia tint of her bare arms and shoulders.

It was as if magician and designer had collaborated to create and clothe a masterpiece—exotic red-gilt hair and strangely glowing eyes of turquoise above the pale yellow silk . . . no earthly creature, but a gossamer desire conjured in Merlin's cauldron to dazzle mortals' eyes before disappearing at the caprice of the wizard's wand.

Tink had helped Aimée with the hoop skirt and the crinolines, and stood in awe when Aimée slipped the ball gown on.

"Jus' like a fairy queen, Mrs. Garrard," Tink said, with her mouth agape. "I never seen—saw—anybody so beautiful." In her excitement Tink had lapsed into her more rustic speech.

Tink was not the only one who seemed overwhelmed. Bryan, attired in full-dress uniform, stood in the hallway, and when Aimée descended the stairs and walked toward him, his eyes met hers in silent tribute.

When he spoke, his voice was tinged with emotion. "Aimée," he whispered, "if I so much as touch you, I'm afraid you'll disappear. And without you, I should be lost forever."

Aimée laughed delightedly. "Come, *mon chevalier*, and

give me your arm. I wish to dance with my husband this night."

There was a brightness, a frivolity in the air, as the carriage, carrying Bryan and Aimée, approached the hall. The musicians were already at work, the violins' tones floating out to greet them.

The gown itself was enough to attract attention when Aimée walked into the hall on Bryan's arm, but her beauty was a magnet, drawing all eyes to her face, her hair, and the marble smoothness of her white shoulders. The other officers surrounded Bryan, demanding an introduction to the vision beside him.

Bryan had kept the two parts of his life separated until tonight, but now it was no longer possible, and with a petulance that Aimée could not fail to notice, he grudgingly introduced her to his fellow officers.

"Garrard, you always did have the most uncanny luck! No wonder we have not seen you lately at our poker games—Lady Luck dealt you a far better hand than we could ever hope to match!" The colonel slapped him on the back and headed for the punch bowl.

Others murmured their compliments as well, but Bryan impatiently removed Aimée from their stares and flowery words and led her onto the dance floor. For a man so large, he danced well and Aimée enjoyed the waltz with him. But she had to pay close attention to her hoop, making sure not to get too close to him, for if she were not careful, the back of the hoop could easily flip up, leaving her in an embarrassed position with exposed undergarments showing.

Soon Aimée was claimed by other officers and Bryan was dragged away to perform the duty dances with wives of his superior officers. The colonel she had met earlier, Colonel Tilson, led her once again into a waltz and it seemed his only intent was to draw her as close to him as the skirt would allow. The very thing that Aimée had feared happened. The hoop flipped up from the back. Quickly Aimée stepped back, freeing her hand from the colonel's grasp, and the hoop fell once more in full circle about the floor.

The man was amused at her embarrassment. "Would you care for a cup of punch, Mrs. Garrard?" he asked, now that they were no longer in step to the music.

"Yes, please," Aimée responded, anxious to leave the dance floor.

"There's a little nook over here where you can make yourself comfortable," he said, guiding her by the arm, "while I get the refreshments."

Aimée sat down, half hidden by the potted plants, her eyes searching the room for Bryan.

A woman's voice penetrated from the other side of the high-backed couch. "Did you see the little baggage on the dance floor just now?"

"Yes," another woman answered, laughing. "I think she did it deliberately—turning up her hoop like that. Or maybe she's just out of her element, dressed in such a fine dress. Wonder how she trapped Bryan into marrying her?"

"All men are fools when it comes to a pretty face," her companion replied. "But I must say, he has tamed her down since I last saw her. My dear, you could not imagine how vulgar she looked at the theater not long ago—dressed in a bright red dress, and a red feather in that brassy hair, advertising her wares to every man in the theater. Even Charles noticed her, and you know that in itself is an indictment of how gaudily she displayed herself. But I *am* surprised that Bryan had no more sense than to marry a woman of the street!"

A woman of the street—the red dress—the red feather. Aimée suddenly remembered it all—Bryan's voice taunting her, Bryan forcing her to wear the dress, his enjoyment of her dismay—and with the remembrance, her hate for the enemy returned, surging over her. She gazed wildly about her and saw that she was surrounded by them. What was she doing here, dancing with them, laughing with them, when her Etienne and her *grand-père* had been murdered by them?

Aimée fled from the ballroom, gasping for breath and fighting back the angry tears. She passed by the surprised guard at the door and did not reply when he asked if he could be of help.

Down the street she sped, staining the beautiful yellow

ball gown with mud from the wet street in her hurry to escape. By the time she reached the house, Aimée did not care that the ball gown was ruined. She climbed the steps to the bedroom and snatched up the nightgown that Tink had laid on the bed for her—the bed that she shared each night with her husband Bryan—and sought refuge once again in the servants' quarters at the back of the garden.

It was not long before she heard Bryan's voice calling her. She did not answer. Yet she knew she could not hope to remain hidden from him.

Aimée listened to the noise on the steps and then the door was jerked open and her husband was standing in the doorway.

"Aimée," he said in a stern, thundering voice, "why did you run away tonight, embarrassing me in front of my fellow officers—and why are you hiding here in the servants' quarters?"

She looked at him and said in a surprisingly calm voice, "Why did you disgrace me, Bryan, by treating me as a woman of the street?"

Bryan gave a groan, and closing the door, walked toward the light.

"So you remembered," he said.

"Yes."

There was complete silence in the room. Finally Bryan said in a subdued tone, "I can only apologize, Aimée. Your haughtiness to me was a constant goad, driving me to vengeance. I had no idea at the time that it would affect you so—that you would feel so dishonored."

"Dishonored!" Aimée pounced upon the word. "Yes, I felt dishonored that night. But it was nothing in comparison to the dishonor I feel this moment at being your *wife*! I would far rather be paraded in front of my enemies as a woman of the street than to be paraded in front of them as your wife!"

"But that night you felt shamed enough to try to take your own life," he accused.

"Take my own life? What are you talking about, monsieur?"

"The knife, Aimée . . . do you not remember that you stabbed yourself with the paring knife?"

Aimée began to laugh and then could not stop. She kept on and on until Bryan shook her and slapped her across the cheek. "Stop it, Aimée. You are hysterical. Get hold of yourself."

The slap checked her laughter.

"I was only hungry," she replied, the tears welling up in her eyes at his violence to her. "I started to peel a peach and my foot slipped. I must have hit my head on the table when I fell. . . ." And then, Aimée began to laugh again. "You were trapped into marriage, monsieur, by your own arrogance—not by any shame of mine," she taunted.

The color drained from his face and Bryan stared at her incredulously before finally walking out of the room and slamming the door hard behind him. When he was gone, the tears began to spill down Aimée's cheeks in earnest.

"Oh, Bryan . . . Bryan," she cried. "Why did I have to fall in love with you?"

The next day Aimée awoke, remembering that she had spent the night alone in the servants' quarters. And she also remembered that it was her birthday. She was now eighteen years old—old enough to register as an enemy of the Union before leaving New Orleans for good.

Chapter 10

Aimée walked to the pharmacy, intent on seeing if she had a letter from Cousin Clotilde, a reply to her request, forgotten until now.

"I wondered what had happened to you, Aimée," Monsieur O'Brie greeted her. "It has been several weeks since the letter arrived."

"I . . . I have been ill, Monsieur O'Brie—a slight accident. But now I am strong enough to travel, if Cousin Clotilde will have me."

Aimée stood near the counter and hurriedly glanced at Cousin Clotilde's message.

"You are planning to . . . leave New Orleans?" Monsieur O'Brie asked cautiously.

"Yes. As soon as I can pack a few things and get a pass to leave the city."

Aimée should have felt glad to leave New Orleans and the arrogant Bryan Garrard who had married her out of guilt. But her heart was heavy as she packed the few necessary items and clothes that she would be able to carry in the small valise.

She touched the stained yellow ballgown that she had worn the evening before, and then pushed it out of sight in the farther part of the armoire. She had been so excited when Bryan had brought it home to her. But now the dress was a symbol of pain—the instrument of her rude awakening to Bryan's harsh treatment and degradation of her. He could never have truly loved her if he had annihilated her honor so completely. Yet even now her body trembled, remembering the ecstasy that his lovemaking had created. And her sadness mixed with the anger she felt toward herself that her body betrayed her by still wanting him. He had made it evident that the only reason he had married her was because after losing her honor, she had attempted to take her own life . . . or so he had thought. And instead of dying, she had lived, binding him to an agreement he had not meant to last a lifetime.

"Oh, Bryan, how could you split me apart like this? Why didn't you let me die that night instead of saving me, making me well—to experience what life could be like with you, only to have my heart wounded anew with your indifference?"

Aimée finished packing and left the townhouse, leaving no note, no indication that she was gone forever. She had sent both Anderson and Tink away on errands, and while they were gone, she slipped away. Bryan had left while she was still asleep in the carriage house. Only the dogs, Fréki and Geri, protested her leaving, whining at the gate, eager to follow her, as her steps disappeared down the banquette.

Aimée waited her turn, quietly but firmly signing the register as an enemy, giving up all claim to any possessions she had left behind. Armed with the pass out of the city and the valise under her arm, she walked to the Pontchartrain rail junction in the heart of the Vieux Carré to make the five-mile trip to Lake Pontchartrain, before switching to the ferry that would take her across the lake to Confederate territory and the protection of Plantation Thornfell.

It had been three years since Aimée had ridden the train to the resort on the lake—to the fine old hotel where she had spent a weekend with Tante Dee Dee, Grand-père, and Etienne. She wondered if the empty freight car that was used as a jail for weekend drunks and pickpockets was still attached to the Saturday morning train. It had been sad knowing that the last train to New Orleans on Sunday evening had that extra car attached, filled with lawbreakers who would be turned over to the police as soon as it reached the junction in the Vieux Carré.

The wheels made a clacking sound and the farther away from New Orleans she went, the louder the message of the wheels. "Don't look back! Don't look back!" they seemed to say to her. She must forget the heartache and the pain. She must wipe away all memory of her life with Bryan Garrard.

Aimée felt the slowing of the train on the rails. She had finished the first short stretch of her journey. Taking her valise, she moved from the train that had come to a squalling, screeching halt, amid bellows of soot and smoke, and made her way to the ferry. Aimée stood in line while the guards checked each pass before allowing the passengers to board. Her red-gold hair was covered by a subdued bonnet and her turquoise eyes dulled by sadness. The guards gave her only a passing glance.

There was a steady stream of people leaving the city, with few possessions except the bit of money they had managed to get from the sale of their goods—the Federal money that was necessary to buy food now that the Confederate dollar was only a curious, worthless piece of paper.

Aimée joined the line of refugees from a changed, alien world. She carried the contraband morphine sewn between her petticoats. From the sounds of the guns in the distance, the Confederate doctors would have need of this gift from the pharmacist, Monsieur O'Brie. The letter from Cousin Clotilde was packed in a more accessible space—her valise.

"My dear child," it read, "Of course you may come to us. We have grown in number with the war. Besides my brother Jorge and me, there are now Cousin Vickie, a recent widow, and her three children, and Cousin Juba, who is recuperating from wounds suffered in the battle of Shiloh. We are all managing well, despite the noise of war around us. . . .

"We are looking forward to having you with us. Come soon, Aimée. Our hearts grieve with you in your sadness."

"Our hearts grieve with you in your sadness." The phrase turned over and over in Aimée's brain. Little did

Cousin Clotilde know the anguish she felt at that moment, caught between opposing sides—her brother and *grand-père* dead by the enemy's hand, and her heart dead by the hand of her husband, Major Bryan Garrard, U.S. Army. But she was determined not to look back, only ahead.

All day long the procession of refugees continued, many telling of Yankee raids and burning of towns along the levee. What the Yankees did not ruin was shelled by the Confederates to try to force the enemy to withdraw, so the people had almost nothing left but a few pieces of bedding and furniture not demolished in the crossfire.

"Here, little lady, there's just room for one more," an old man said, as Aimée walked by the side of the road, carrying her valise.

Aimée gratefully climbed up on the wagon and found a seat on a trunk shared by two white girls and a little black servant girl. They all seemed to be dressed the same, the white girl's clothes no better than the other's.

Aimée was relieved that no one thought it peculiar that she was traveling alone. The people in the wagon accepted her as one of them, no different from any of the others on the road. With the hidden packages sewn into her petticoats, Aimée was afraid that something would give her away—that the words "spy" or "carrier of contraband goods" might be engraved on her forehead for all to see.

Gradually she relaxed and entered into the childish chatter around her, content to travel the few miles in the rough conveyance until she drew near the assigned rendezvous.

It had not mattered to her that Monsieur O'Brie had asked her to travel miles out of her way, beyond Mandeville and above, to reach the appointed destination with her important contraband. She had a lifetime to retrace her steps and head back to Bayou St. Moreau and Plantation Thornfell, hidden but a few miles beyond the eastern neck of Lake Pontchartrain, where only twelve miles of water would separate her from New Orleans.

The little shack to which Monsieur O'Brie had given

her directions was standing in a patch of briars in a deserted field just off the main road. It was an apt place for a rendezvous; no one would have chosen to stay there, since the roof looked as if it would cave in at any moment.

Aimée waited, the loneliness giving her a strange feeling. What if a Union soldier should happen upon it and find her there? How would she explain being there? To meet her lover? To rest before traveling farther?

Aimée felt the pistol in the pocket of her dress—her *papa*'s pistol that she had hidden and then forgotten about when Etienne left for the war. But before leaving New Orleans, she had found it again . . . and now she might have to use it to defend herself.

She had been inside the shack for at least an hour and she was getting drowsy, her eyelids closing and her head nodding. The soft whistle in the woods aroused her and Aimée became alert again.

She returned the whistle and waited with her hand in the pocket of her dress. The door opened slowly and Aimée watched from the dark corner.

He was not in uniform, this man who stood in the doorway. Aimée had the advantage over him. She could see him easily, but he, used to the glare of the hot sun, was virtually blinded for a few seconds upon entering.

His hand was on his pistol, still undrawn at his side, when Aimée called out, "I would not attempt that, monsieur. There is a gun pointed at you."

The man gave a low chuckling laugh. "So—a very cautious little Rebel. And if I give you the password, will you promise not to shoot me?"

"Yes," answered Aimée.

"Beauty and the Beast," he responded and Aimée lowered her pistol.

The man chuckled again as he gazed at her. "An appropriate password, don't you think? I had no idea anything would be delivered by such a beauty."

"But surely you knew it was coming from the city of the Beast," Aimée joked, continuing in the same vein.

There was a whinny from the woods and the man grew cautious. "Quickly . . . hand over what you have. My horse is getting nervous. There are too many raiders lurking, much as I would like to stay."

"Do you have a knife, monsieur?" Aimée questioned.

He handed it to her in silence and she turned her back to rip the petticoats apart for the hidden packages containing the morphine and the accompanying letter. Handing both the knife and the packages to the man, Aimée watched as he walked hurriedly out of sight into the woods.

After a few minutes Aimée also left the shack, to find her way back to the main road.

It was toward evening when she reached the road to Plantation Thornfell. Only once after she had delivered the letter and the morphine had Aimée been taken up in a well-sprung carriage for a few miles. After that she had walked. She was exhausted, covered with dust, her nose tender from the sun, for even her bonnet had been unable to protect her face entirely.

Her journey had almost come to an end. Aimée's heart quickened as she recognized the terrain, the approach to the plantation where she had drawn first life. And now Aimée hoped that Thornfell's healing balm would make her feel life was still worth living.

The plantation, when Aimée saw it, was a serene picture—a haven from the flight taking place only a few miles away. The moss-hung oaks, framing the old familiar white-columned mansion with its winding steps, swayed in the slight evening breeze.

The *pigeonnier*, a few yards from the house, emitted soft coos as an occasional pigeon, tinted a strange purplish glow from the twilight, flew toward its safety to roost for the night. The kitchen orchard on the other side appeared as the last recognizable part of the landscape, pointing the way to the deep, dark stretches of cane fields beyond the house.

The cane fields came alive and Aimée, a child again, watched from the gallery of the plantation house and listened to the sounds of her distant childhood. She looked again at the cane fields, the deep, haunting shadows, and the mirage of memories disappeared before her eyes.

Except for the pigeons, there was no evidence of life

around her. Then a light came on and Aimée saw someone coming across the front meadow toward the road to meet her.

"Welcome home, my dear," the woman said.

Cousin Clotilde and Aimée both stood in the road and cried. Then with arms about each other, they began to walk once more toward the house. An old servant came to take Aimée's valise.

She did not see the rest of the family that evening. She was left in a small room at the end of the upstairs hallway, too exhausted to be companionable, too tired to do anything but remove her dusty clothes, eat the food from the tray brought to her, and crawl into bed to sleep—with any luck, no haunting dreams would disturb her.

But she was not lucky. Dreams formed, one upon the other, becoming a jumbled collage, layered by the red dress, the laughter of the women at the ball, and the furious face of her husband when he learned he had been tricked into marriage. A strange wedding scene took place in the garden, with the dogs Fréki and Geri the only attendants, being chased by bees, while she carried a bouquet of ripe red strawberries to match the red feather in her hair.

Gratefully Aimée awoke the next morning to the noise of children playing outside.

"Hush yo' mouth, chil'ren. You'll wake Miss Aimée up with yo' loud talkin'. She's had a *hard* time and needs her rest," a servant's voice scolded.

The children immediately quieted and Aimée smiled. She had heard that tone of voice many a time. She remembered as a child how subdued she had managed to be for a few minutes, before forgetting and building the whispers to a noisy roar again. Confirming her remembrance of children's ways, the voices outside rose in pitch, as excited as before.

Aimée stretched and climbed out of bed to wash her face in the basin of water left near the bed. Remembering her jumbled dreams, she fingered the gold ring that she had removed from her finger to hide on a chain about her neck. She would not tell Cousin Clotilde about her marriage. It would be easier not having to explain.

Aimée dressed, feeling pangs of hunger, for her supper had been light and she had eaten little before leaving New Orleans. Following the sound of voices, she walked down the stairs and into the dining room to face the strangers seated at the table. The conversation stopped in midair, but Cousin Clotilde held out her arms in a welcoming gesture to Aimée, while the two men stood up, waiting to be introduced. Cousin Clotilde began the introductions with her brother Jorge.

He was rotund, with faded blue myopic eyes that lit up when he saw her. "Ah, yes . . . I remember your father well, Aimée. When he was a boy, we used to—"

"Now, Jorge," cut in Cousin Clotilde, "don't start on one of your long reminiscences . . . plenty of time for that later."

Cousin Jorge smiled apologetically at Aimée and, kissing her cheek, proceeded to pass her down the line.

"This is Cousin Vickie," Clotilde continued. "Actually, she's not related to you—only to Jorge and me through Tante Julie, on our mother's side of the family. Tante Julie is the one who married the American, you know."

It would always be so, thought Aimée—one was still considered an outsider after many years in Creole society. Vickie murmured a not too cordial welcome and Cousin Clotilde turned to the last one at the table.

"Cousin Juba is your blood cousin through the Saint-Moreaus, Aimée. He's lucky to be alive after that dreadful battle at Shiloh."

Juba Barnard impetuously took Aimée's hands to bring her forward to his frank gaze, and when Aimée would pull away, he resisted her efforts and said, "No, little Aimée . . . if Jorge is a kissing cousin, so am I." And he leaned down and kissed her cheek before she could demur.

"Cousin Juba always *did* take advantage of a situation," Vickie commented with a drop of acid in her voice.

"Would you like the same treatment, too, Widow Brittain?" Juba asked with dancing, teasing eyes. "Do you feel neglected already, with another pretty girl at the table?"

"Not at all," Vickie responded in a cold voice. "You would do well to limit your advances to where they will be appreciated. At least, *she* seems to enjoy them. Perhaps you will get further with her than you did with me."

"Vickie!" Cousin Clotilde's voice sounded in alarm.

With her lips compressed tightly into a prim line, Vickie shrugged and returned to the business of eating.

"My dear, you will have to excuse Vickie. This war has not been kind to her and I fear she does not always weigh what she says," explained Cousin Clotilde.

Aimée looked at the tall thin woman, her gray hair falling in little wisps about her neck, her face showing such anxiety that Aimée, in an effort to reassure her that she would not be a party to a family tiff, nodded and said, "Of course, Cousin Clotilde. I'm sure she did not mean any harm."

The older woman relaxed once more and the air at the table did not seem so frigid even with Vickie's petulant silence. Soon the others were chatting and Aimée joined in the conversation.

"I must show you my garden, Aimée, after breakfast. It's my pride and joy. I have some of the most marvelous flowers, envied for miles around." Cousin Clotilde took a sip of tea and wiped her mouth daintily with the embroidered napkin.

Juba grinned and elaborated. "You're in for a shock, pretty cousin. Clotilde did not tell you that it's a musical garden—that everything in it has some name like 'trumpet vine' or 'coral bells'—pity the poor sunflower or the cowslip. Even the wisteria would be treated as a weed and pulled up if it ever forced its way into her garden."

"Now, Juba, stop your teasing. You know very well I allow the wisteria to grow on the south side of the house," Cousin Clotilde explained with a serious demeanor.

"Well, she couldn't help that," joined in Jorge. "There's a good reason for it. Papa planted the wisteria. I remember when he brought the plants home. It was the spring of 1852 . . . or was it 1853? Anyway, I remember we had a rainy winter and the ground was so soggy that . . ."

Clotilde lifted her eyebrows in consternation and Aimée was amused at the woman's reaction as she sat back, resigned to hearing the long familiar discourse from her brother.

Juba winked at Aimée in conspiracy, then gave his polite attention to the rotund man, who was reveling in relating his mundane recollections to a new listener.

Chapter 11

*C*ousin Clotilde's garden was a mass of blooms. The yellow Spring Song petunias vied with the pink-colored Sonata shrub rose. As Clotilde showed Aimée through the garden that she had created not far from the house, she used the time to confide in her.

"I feel I must explain about Vickie, Aimée, since her dislike of you is so pointed." Cousin Clotilde was embarrassed but she continued. "Juba had a sister and her name was Aimée also—she had the same red-gold hair and the same turquoise eyes. You see, you are not the only one to have inherited that combination.

"Juba's sister was here at Thornfell when Vickie and her new husband, Geoffrey, came to visit us. Geoffrey could not keep his eyes off Aimée—he was smitten with her beauty and he showed it. And I must confess, Aimée did nothing to discourage him. Poor Vickie was so jealous. She was madly in love with Geoffrey, but he was poor and I suspect he had married her more for money than for love. And so you see, my dear, you are a painful reminder to Vickie of that unhappy episode in her life. It would be unfair to you to let you think it might be something that *you* had done that has set Vickie against you. When she looks at you, she is really seeing the other Aimée, who nearly destroyed her marriage."

"Thank you, Cousin Clotilde, for telling me. I . . . will try to be kind."

"And now, let me show you the rest of the garden," Cousin Clotilde said, dismissing the subject of Vickie.

"This variety," explained Clotilde, pointing to one of her tea roses, "is called 'Daughter of the Regiment,' named for Donizetti's opera by that name."

Walking over to the small althea tree at the edge of the garden, Clotilde snipped one of the blossoms to hand to Aimée. "This is also one of my favorites—'Midsummer Night's Dream.' Don't you think that's a good name for such a lovely white blossom?"

Aimée looked at the flower in her hand and politely agreed.

"Of course, it was originally the play by Mr. Shakespeare," admitted Clotilde, "but Felix Mendelssohn composed such beautiful music by that name."

Clotilde's voice trailed as she walked to another part of the garden, lost in her thoughts. "When I was growing up, many people said I was talented enough to become a concert pianist. But of course Maman would never have allowed such a thing. It would have been a *scandale* for one of her daughters to perform on a public stage. So now I play for my family and take care of my musical garden."

Then, as if she just remembered the girl beside her, she began speaking directly to her. "Do you enjoy music, Aimée?"

Aimée nodded her head. "Very much, and I shall enjoy hearing you play, Cousin Clotilde."

The woman seemed pleased. "And do you play the piano, too?"

"No—I used to play the lute quite a lot and sing. Tante Dee Dee taught me before she died."

Cousin Clotilde could not hide her excitement at the mention of the lute.

"Don't tell me the lute is the one that belonged to your great-great-*grand-mère*! If it is, I hope it's in a safe place. It must be quite valuable by now."

"It . . . it is in the attic of the townhouse. I do not know if it is . . . safe," replied Aimée.

"What a pity that you could not bring the instrument

with you! There is so little social life here, with the war and all. We pass the time in the evenings with music and a little reading and sewing. It would have been so delightful . . . but we can still have an enjoyable performance tonight after supper. You can sing and I shall accompany you."

Clotilde impulsively put her arm around Aimée. "I am glad that you are here, Aimée. You will add so much to our little family—and Vickie will soon soften her attitude toward you."

That afternoon Aimée's mind was restless, dwelling too much on the life she had resolved to forget. The children, Faith, Hope, and Charity, were playing near the edge of the orchard behind the house, watched over by Lizzie, the black servant, and neither Vickie nor Cousin Clotilde had come downstairs from their afternoon rest. Even Juba was resting; for it had not been long since he had gotten the ball in his lung, and one had only to notice his pallor and hear his muffled coughing to know that he was a sick man.

Aimée read for a few minutes, her eyes remaining on the same paragraph, and then she got up from her chair to stand at the window and look out. Again she seated herself, not really seeing or noticing anything because of her unhappy thoughts. Bryan's memory refused to be put to rest.

"Aimée, my dear, do you ride?" Cousin Jorge's voice startled her and she jumped.

"It . . . it has been a while, Cousin Jorge, but yes, I do ride."

"Then wouldn't you like to have Sagefly saddled for a bit of exercise?"

"Oh, could I?" Aimée asked eagerly.

Jorge nodded. "If you like, I will walk to the stables with you, as soon as you have changed. And perhaps you will ride away some of that restlessness," he added with a smile.

"I do not have a riding habit with me, Cousin Jorge, but the skirt and blouse that I have on are old . . . they will do to ride in."

"Well, if you are ready, shall we make our way to the stables?"

Once Aimée had the reins in her hands, the old dexterity returned. She hoped the ride *would* dissolve the knotted tension within her, as Cousin Jorge had suggested it would.

Once on horseback, Aimée heard his words following her in a cautioning reminder. "Remember, Aimée, to turn around at the twin forks. It would not be safe for you to go any farther alone."

The sun had gone behind thick clouds, although the air was still hot and humid. The exercise was good for her troubled mind and Aimée did not object to the heat sifting down through the trees, though her skirt and blouse were dampened with perspiration. The ride had begun its curative powers.

Within a short time she was at the forks in the road. She slowed the horse and felt the peace and deserted air around her. She had reached the forks too soon . . . far too soon to turn around and go back home. Surely there would be no harm in galloping a little farther. She and Etienne had gone much farther on their ponies when they were small.

Aimée brought Sagefly to a stop in the road, at war with herself as to whether she would heed Cousin Jorge's warning or not. Making up her mind, she urged the horse into a gallop, turning down the left fork, with the steady hoofbeats on the road the only sound around her.

Farther and farther she rode, and a new joy rose up within her. She was alive. Contemplating this new surge of feeling, Aimée did not at first notice the darkening sky. But at the sound of thunder she lifted her head to survey her shadowy surroundings and the old feeling of uneasiness enveloped her.

One drop of rain splashed Aimée in the face, and then another mammoth drop bounced on the dirt, leaving an indentation in the sandy road. Soon other drops joined together and Aimée pulled Sagefly into a clump of trees in an effort to find shelter from her fear and the drenching rain.

Someone else was now on the road, the sound of the horse barely penetrating the noise of the storm. The sudden flash and crack caused Aimée to jump. Had it been thunder or a pistol shot?

The pounding of hooves was louder, and Aimée peered out from her shelter in time to see the bleeding man fall from his horse a few yards from her feet.

The riderless horse continued galloping down the road and Aimée, jumping from the saddle, rushed to the man lying on the ground. She bent down beside him and the same brown eyes that had gazed at her in the abandoned shack beyond Mandeville now gazed unbelievingly into the turquoise eyes of an astonished Aimée.

"Well, my little red-haired Rebel, you do turn up at the oddest of times."

"You are hurt, monsieur," she said, ignoring his attempt at humor and staring at the stain on his right thigh. "I must get help for you."

"There's no need. I am already a dead man. If I do not die today, they will get me tomorrow."

"You mean . . ."

"I am a marked man—of no further use." Suddenly he reached into the inside of his shirt and pulled out a letter. "Will you do me a favor, little Rebel—take this back to Monsieur O'Brie in New Orleans as soon as possible?" He pushed the letter into her hands and continued, "Hurry! Take the communiqué before the man returns to make certain that I am dead."

"But I cannot leave you here, monsieur," Aimée protested.

"There isn't much choice—and the letter is more important than I am at the moment."

"I did not know a man could give up so easily," Aimée angrily retorted. "I suppose it would be simpler for you to lie here and die than struggle to stay alive."

"It would be far simpler for you. If you are caught helping a spy, it will not go well with you."

"Monsieur, if you do not attempt to get up and climb on my horse, then I shall stay here as well . . . Either you come with me, or I stay."

Aimée, without another word, removed the sidesaddle

111

and dropped it into the bushes. The two would have to ride bareback, with Aimée sitting astride, behind the man.

The man grinned at her action, and in spite of the obvious pain, he pushed himself up, and holding onto Aimée, dragged himself to Sagefly.

Cousin Jorge, with an anxious expression on his face, stood on the gallery and watched as the horse approached the house and galloped right up to the steps. The wounded man slid from the horse and fell into a faint before the surprised little man.

The next few moments were full of action and commands, with the entire household looking on. And when the man had been taken into the house to be attended to, all Aimée could see were the hostile eyes of Vickie staring at her, and the tight-lipped line of her disapproving mouth.

"How is he?" Aimée asked Clotilde when the older woman appeared in the hallway, carrying the basin of stained water.

"The bullet is now out of his leg and he will live," answered Clotilde. "But I fear his leg is broken and it will be some time before he can walk again."

Vickie opened her bedroom door that had been partially cracked and faced Aimée with no effort to conceal her ill will.

"You have put us all in danger, Aimée, by bringing that man here. You might as well destroy my three sweet little angels with your own hands. For if the Yankees find out we are harboring a fugitive, we will all be killed, and you, Aimée, will be guilty of murder."

"I would also be guilty of murder if I had left the wounded man by the side of the road to die, Vickie," Aimée answered, suddenly weary.

"There will be no further discussion of this," Cousin Clotilde said with fury in her voice. "You are being overly dramatic, Vickie, but if, at any time, you feel the danger in this house is too great for you, you are free to leave."

Vickie stared at Clotilde in amazement at the display of anger from the mild-mannered woman, and then twirling from her, sought safety behind her closed bedroom door.

That night there was neither merriment nor music in the house. Instead of singing to Cousin Clotilde's accompaniment, Aimée, with her hooded cape about her, galloped toward the shore of Lake Pontchartrain on her mission to deliver the letter to New Orleans. She was glad the storm had stopped.

Juba rode silently beside her, each horse keeping pace with the other, until they came to the hidden boat that the wounded man, John Runefelt, had assured them would be waiting.

"I will be here with the horses tomorrow night, Aimée. You must be careful to get across the lake tonight in time to take the last train to the city. The guards are lax that time of the evening, I'm told. And it will be easier for you if they don't check passes. . . . And don't start back tomorrow until well after dark," he added.

"I will be careful, Juba," Aimée assured him.

"I wish I could go instead," Juba said, before a fit of coughing stopped his speech.

"But you do not know the city well, Juba," Aimée whispered. "It's better this way . . . and I feel safe, knowing you will be here waiting when I return."

Juba gave the little rowboat a shove and soon there was only the softly lapping sound of dipping oars in the darkness as Aimée started her watery journey toward the city to which she had said good-bye only a little over thirty-six hours before.

The small copse of willows growing out into the water was a good hiding place for the boat on the southern shore of the lake. Somewhere near here the voodoo queen was supposed to hold court. Deserted little cabins built on stilts dotted the swampy land and Aimée was glad that few people ventured into this place, convinced that it was haunted by spirits that would destroy them if they trespassed on Marie Laveau's land.

The moon gave a silvery glow to the landscape, making it unnecessary for Aimée to light the lantern she had brought with her. Gingerly she stepped out of the boat, not sure that the soggy earth would hold her weight. Her slippers sank only a little way, and holding her dress high so that the hem would not become stained, Aimée proceeded to walk out of the swampy area toward the rail station.

She did not dare go to the ticket window where the guards were more observant and would be sure to see the effects of the watery trip across the lake. Aimée had cleaned the mud from her slippers, but her dress had gotten damp around the hem, after all. Instead of purchasing her ticket at the window, she would pretend to the conductor who came to collect her ticket after the train had started that she had gotten to the station too late, and she would give her fare directly to him.

The surge of people trying to go through the stile to get on the last train of the evening to New Orleans presented a problem to the guards checking passes. Waving their passes high as they passed through, the people became a rolling mass of movement. Aimée hid behind an extremely large man loaded with an armful of packages and was carried along with the crowd, unobserved.

There were few seats left in the passenger car by the time Aimée got in. Seeing a vacant seat by a fat woman holding a chicken coop containing two scrawny white roosters, Aimée, realizing why the seat was still vacant, wedged herself into the uncomfortably small space and immediately pretended to go to sleep, her head drooping to her chest with her bonnet shadowing her face from anyone who happened to walk down the dimly-lit aisle.

"Miss! Miss!" the conductor's voice sounded in her ear. "Your ticket, please."

Silently, she handed the fifteen cents to the man and hoped he would not protest.

"Another one," the conductor said disparagingly to the fat woman, above the noise of the roosters. "Always hopin' to get a free ride. And if I didn't check so well, the train line would go bankrupt."

He took a ticket from his pocket, canceled it, and returned the stub to Aimée, who had not spoken throughout the procedure.

When the train stopped at Pontchartrain Junction near

114

Elysian Fields, Aimée followed closely behind the fat woman with the chicken coop, pretending to be part of her entourage. Once she was safely out of the train, she dashed hurriedly away from the station, her hand reaching briefly up to her camisole. The crackle of the letter assured her that she had not lost the message hidden there.

Now she walked in a westerly direction toward Jackson Square. From lake to train to the Vieux Carré, the trip had taken a little over four hours, but the time going back would be shorter, for now she had the knack of steady rowing. Probably her arms would be sore the next day from the unaccustomed rowing, but if that were her only casualty, she would not mind.

Aimée realized that she had been lucky. She could have been stopped by the guards, or the conductor, if he had wanted to, could have caused a scene. But now she was safely at her destination—the pharmacy belonging to Monsieur O'Brie. Only then, seeing the pharmacy in sight, did Aimée realize how tense she had been throughout the night.

For the first time that evening she ran into difficulty. The living quarters attached to the back of the pharmacy seemed to be deserted and no one came to the door to answer her persistent knock. Aimée knew she could not remain outside for long. Someone was sure to see her.

Hearing footsteps, she darted away from the door, into the darkness, and crouched low behind the bougainvillea on the fence. She watched as the man took a key from his pocket and inserted it into the lock.

"Monsieur," she whispered, coming from her hiding place.

The man turned, and seeing Aimée before him, he hurriedly pushed her into the building without uttering a word.

Once inside, he relaxed and in a surprised voice asked, "What are you doing here, Aimée? I thought you had left the city for good."

"I . . . I am a . . . substitute messenger, Monsieur O'Brie. I have a letter for you, since Monsieur Runefelt has been wounded." Aimée reached into the bosom of her dress and retrieved the letter to hand to the pharmacist.

"A poor war, when one has to use a young girl," Monsieur O'Brie muttered, as if speaking to himself. "But tell me, Aimée, will the man be all right, and is he safe?"

"He is at Plantation Thornfell with Cousin Clotilde. His leg is broken and he will not be able to walk for some time. As to whether he is safe," Aimée continued, "I do not know. The Yankees now know about him."

Monsieur O'Brie groaned. "That makes our job twice as hard then," he said with an expression of regret. "But come, Aimée, I'm sure you are tired and hungry. I will fix you something to eat and then you can rest. Do you plan to stay in New Orleans?"

"No, monsieur. I will leave again tomorrow evening, if I may hide here until then."

His concerned eyes rested on Aimée's red-gold hair. "You must be very careful. Your appearance will easily give you away. And you run a double risk, since this place is often under surveillance. General Butler has bragged that he has a spy behind every man and family in New Orleans, to report anything that even *looks* suspicious."

"I am not afraid, monsieur," Aimée answered with a proud tilt to her head. "And if you care to send a message, I shall be glad to take it back with me."

The next evening Aimée left the pharmacy, with her hooded cape hiding her hair from the luminous streaks of moonglow. She walked down the street and, on impulse, turned away from her route to the train station. She knew it was dangerous to be wandering the streets. She should hurry back to the station, for each additional moment she stayed in New Orleans heightened her chances of being caught. But she had an overwhelming desire to see her house on Royal Street.

Deep down, Aimée knew it was not the house she wanted to see. It was Bryan her heart ached to see—one glimpse, and then she would return to Thornfell.

Aimée carefully avoided the lights on Royal Street. The sound of a carriage coming up the street made her dart into a darkened doorway, and as the carriage passed by, she recognized the open *calèche* that Bryan had given her and the sleek black pony pulling it.

He was not alone. Seated beside him was a woman in a blue velvet cape, and the two—Bryan and the woman—were laughing together.

Tears stung Aimée's eyes. Bryan had wasted no time in finding companionship after she had left. At that moment Aimée was sorry that she had given in to her impetuous urge. And for Vickie's jealousy, she had only understanding.

She walked quickly, hoping to make up the lost minutes. One train had already left, and another, its engine noisily puffing out its built-up steam, was announcing its immediate departure. When the guard left his position, convinced there were no more passengers to check, Aimée ducked under the stile as the train was set into motion. The conductor, standing in the open doorway, had already taken up the steps, but he held out his hand to help her.

"*Merci*, monsieur, I thought I had missed the train."

He followed her to her seat, and again she took out the money for her fare. Luckily it was a different conductor from the evening before, but this one—middle-aged, with a slight bulge to his stomach—seemed much more curious than the first.

Feeling his eyes upon her, Aimée became uncomfortable. Was he wondering what a young girl was doing traveling alone in an almost deserted passenger car? And then it dawned upon Aimée—the only type of woman about at night alone was a woman of the streets. Was that why he was peering at her so strangely?

Aimée could not show her fear, could not give away that it was not the most natural thing in the world for her to be traveling in this manner. Sighing, she made up her mind to play the part he had assigned her. She had been made to play the part before, so perhaps she would be convincing.

The conductor made periodic trips up and down the aisle past her, and by the fourth time Aimée was prepared. She had adjusted her bonnet to a more seductive angle and had assumed a less prim position on the seat.

The conductor's pace slowed as he drew nearer Aimée. Clasping her hands nervously in her lap, she forced herself to meet his gaze with bold eyes and to smile dazzlingly at him.

At first the man appeared surprised. Then with a wolfish glint in his eyes, he returned her smile, straightened his shoulders, and walked the rest of the length of the passenger car with a jauntier air.

"My Lady, I am in trouble," Aimée prayed to her patron saint. "Help me out of this predicament, *s'il vous plaît.*"

Her source of trouble approached again, this time stopping to address her.

"You are going to Milneburg?" he asked.

"Yes, monsieur. I am going to visit a . . . friend."

The conductor smiled. "Will you be returning to New Orleans tonight?" There was a hopeful note in the man's voice.

"No, monsieur, I plan to stay a little longer."

The disappointment showed in the man's face, but he pursued the conversation in a determined manner. "If you . . . come back on the last train on Sunday night, we could have a meal together when we get to New Orleans. I am free from duty once that last train gets into Pontchartrain Station."

Aimée pretended to be offended at his offer (which, in actuality, she was). Her eyes widened as she looked up at him. "But monsieur, I . . . that is, we have not even been introduced. I could not . . . accept an invitation from a stranger. I am not that kind of girl."

The man, recognizing the stock reply, said, "Then let me introduce myself. I am Gaston Ferbes. And your name?"

"Cécile," Aimée replied, letting the syllables roll out in lazy enunciation.

"Well now, Cécile, is it a bargain?"

"You are a most charming man, Gaston. It would be difficult for me to refuse. But I am not sure . . . that I shall be returning this Sunday. Shall we say *some* evening soon instead?"

Again he grinned. "I'll have to be satisfied with that, although I'd rather . . ."

The train slowed and the conductor did not finish his

sentence. He left to attend to his duties and Aimée felt relief that he had not become suspicious.

The boat was even harder to get into the water than Aimée had imagined. She pushed, straining her arms and legs, but the boat did not budge. Again she pushed, and all at once the thick wet grass gave way and Aimée fell as the boat shot into the water, the sudden lurch causing an oar to rattle against the side of the boat. Quickly she glided out of the safety of the willow trees, into a more vulnerable section of open lake.

"Halt! Who goes there?" the voice of the guard called out of the darkness.

Aimée did not answer. Neither did she stop, but rowed as hard and fast as she could to escape the sentry.

"In the name of General Butler, I order you to halt!"

Still, Aimée continued, heaving at the effort to put as much distance between her and the guard as quickly as possible. The shots rang into the air, landing in the water beside the boat. They were shooting at her!

Now she did not dare move. If she made any noise with the oars, they would be able to trace the sound on the water and reach her easily, so she stayed still, crouching in the boat, feeling not only paralyzed panic but also a throbbing pain in the ankle she had wrenched getting the boat into the water.

"What is happening, Private?" another voice questioned.

"I . . . I thought I heard someone just now, sir," the soldier replied.

A frog leaped into the water with a noisy plop, making a hoarse croak as he leaped, and the inquisitor laughed.

"It's getting to you, Private, this night duty. You will be jumping at your own shadow next. Can't you tell the difference between a friendly bullfrog and a Rebel?"

The voices grew dim in the distance as the men walked away. Relieved, Aimée took up the oars again, and forgetting the muscles that ached from the exertion, she rowed her way across the lake.

Juba was not at the assigned place when Aimée dragged herself from the boat. She had almost gone to sleep on the water, but knowing Juba would be waiting for her, she had continued rowing. Once she finally reached the point of numbness, she was able to keep on, no longer feeling tired, no longer needing to sleep . . . her only thought to reach safety where Juba waited for her.

Had something happened to him? Had the Yankees come to burn the house, killing all within, because they had given shelter to a wounded man? Had Vickie been right in her accusation?

A horse whinnied, and in relief Aimée sat up from her hiding place and limped toward the sound.

"Cousin Jorge," Aimée said in disbelief, seeing the rotund little man standing in the woods, holding onto the two nervous horses.

"Aimée, am I glad to see you!" he whispered. "I did not know the exact spot where you would come ashore. I was so afraid I would miss you, even though Juba gave me careful instructions."

"Juba," Aimée repeated, suddenly afraid. "Has something happened to him?"

"No. He is hiding in the attic. Yankees came to Thornfell this morning, searching for Runefelt. Before we could get him out of bed and into a hiding place, the Yankees had forced their way inside and found him. But before they could take him away, Clotilde convinced them he was Cousin Juba, and showed his discharge papers to prove it. Now Juba does not dare show his face outside until the man is well again."

"Oh, Cousin Jorge, I have given you nothing but trouble," lamented Aimée.

"Nonsense, child . . . I felt so old and helpless before, but now I can hold up my head with pride, knowing we are doing something for the cause."

Chapter 12

*H*ow John Runefelt could carry on a war of espionage while in bed, Aimée would never know, but in the morning a man appeared at the colonnaded summerhouse to take the letter she had brought back with her.

Throughout the morning there was a tenseness in the air and Aimée found it hard to relax. She sat in the drawing room in the latter part of the afternoon, keeping the uneasy silence that had settled upon Thornfell, with Cousin Clotilde, Jorge, Vickie, and Juba. The only ones missing were John Runefelt, who could not come down the stairs because of his leg, and Vickie's three little girls, who were playing on the gallery.

"Is your . . . attic room comfortable, Juba?" Clotilde asked.

Juba coughed as he breathed in air to respond. Everyone politely looked away, pretending not to notice, until the spasm was over and he could put an answer to the question directed to him.

"Yes, quite comfortable, Clotilde. It's very . . . cosy under the eaves. I just have to be careful not to stand too suddenly," he said, attempting a light touch. "My head has come in contact with the sloped ceiling more than once, when I have gotten out of bed."

"That is your penalty for being so tall, Juba," Cousin Jorge maintained. "It is too bad that you and I could not exchange places. I would have no such trouble with the ceiling."

Aimée smiled, envisioning the endearing little rotund

man hiding away in the secret room in the attic.

Juba laughed. "But that would defeat the purpose, wouldn't it? The man upstairs could not take your identity. You are too well known. But I—I know no one around here. So I can easily fade into the attic at will—especially to save someone important."

"But *you* are important, as well," Cousin Clotilde protested.

"I fear that my days of contributing something worthwhile to the Confederacy are over," Juba lamented. "Except for my discharge papers. At least they have served their purpose."

"You have given more than your share, Juba—even at the risk of your health. We are proud that you are a part of this family. You fought honorably, and now you must get well. That is the important thing." Cousin Clotilde spoke fervently, showing her pride in Juba, and there was a murmur of agreement in the room.

"And your room is . . . warm enough? It's too bad there is no opening in the chimney wall for a fire," the woman continued.

"Do not worry so about me," Juba said, smiling. "The warmth from the bricks is quite adequate."

Vickie continued her needlework, while Aimée glanced out the window, seeing nothing. Silence enveloped the room again. It was as if they were all listening, waiting for something outside.

The uneasiness was suddenly broken by the eruption of a squabble taking place on the gallery. The childish voices were raised high in argument, and Vickie put down her needlework and hurried to the gallery to arbitrate the dispute.

Aimée suddenly felt that she could stay no longer in the drawing room, could no longer be a prisoner of her memories. "If you will excuse me, I think I'll take a walk."

"Take someone with you, Aimée," Cousin Jorge suggested. "You cannot be too careful. And I hope you will not go far."

"Only beyond the orchard toward the cane fields, Cousin Jorge. But I promise I will not go out of sight of the house."

Vickie returned to the drawing room as Aimée was leaving. "Those children—they are so exasperating," mused Vickie, with a frown on her face. "Hope should know better than to try to get her way with the other two."

When Aimée walked out onto the gallery, Faith and Charity, the baby, were playing happily together, but the middle child, Hope, still blinking away her tears, sat alone on the winding steps. The forlorn little face touched Aimée's heart and gently she said, "Would you like to go for a walk with me, Hope?"

The child looked up gratefully at a kind voice, and immediately her face brightened. She stood up, placing her hand in Aimée's, and together they completed the winding steps and walked across the yard toward the orchard.

"You are so . . . pretty," the little girl confided to Aimée. "I wish I had your red hair."

"Thank you, Hope. But your hair is lovely," Aimée replied. "So silky and fine. And when the sun shines on those blond locks, you might be the Princess Rapunzel, leaning her head out of her tower."

"You . . . really think so?" the child asked. "Sometimes Papa teased me—calling me 'princess.'" The little voice trailed away, weaving a wreath of tragedy with the small sad wisps of longing for the father who had been killed in the war.

If I were her mother, Aimée thought, I'd love her so much that she would not feel so alone. To be a mother—how would it feel? Aimée's lips curved in a bittersweet smile. If she and Bryan could have had a child. . . . Instantly she dismissed the thought from her mind and turned her attention to the little girl who needed love and understanding and an opportunity to share her grief.

"You know, *ma petite*, when I was a little girl, I lived here at Thornfell—together with my brother Etienne and my *maman* and *papa*. And then, when I was about your age, I had to leave my home here, just as you had to leave your home. And . . . and I lost my *papa* too, as well as my *maman*. And I had to go to live with other people."

"You did?" Hope asked in a surprised voice.

"Yes. It was hard at first—it's always hard to lose the ones who loved you best—but time has a way of helping. You don't ever forget the ones you loved . . . but somehow, as you grow up, the pain becomes a little easier. And I always thought I was lucky to have had them to love for even a little while."

"I . . . I had not thought about it that way. It hurts so much to think of Papa. But—but it would have been worse if I had never had him to love me, wouldn't it?" Hope said, as if making an important discovery.

"Yes, Hope. It would have been much worse."

The dull ache throbbed in Aimée's veins. Never to have had Bryan to love her—yes, that would have been worse, much worse. Her efforts to console Vickie's daughter gave Aimée a new insight into herself.

"And you are lucky to have your mother, who loves you," Aimée continued.

"Yes," Hope said uncertainly; her eyes showed that she was not at all convinced this was true.

The two of them, Hope and Aimée, gathered apples from the orchard, and giggling together, returned in a much brighter mood, taking the apples to the kitchen to be baked for supper.

That evening the tenseness of the day had eased and after supper Aimée joined the others in the drawing room and settled down to listening to Cousin Clotilde's expert music drawn from the beautiful square rosewood piano that was placed near the window.

"Come, Aimée, and sing for us," Clotilde coaxed.

"No—I would much rather sit here and listen, Cousin Clotilde. Your music . . . helps us all."

"Now, Aimée, its your turn to entertain us. We need some new excitement in this tired old room, and you're the one to give it to us," Cousin Jorge persuaded.

"Yes, Aimée, do as your elders tell you," Juba said in a teasing mood. He sat in the chair, relaxed and relatively free from the cough that plagued him many hours of the day.

Aimée got up from her chair to sit reluctantly beside

Clotilde on the soft-cushioned bench that was long enough to accommodate them both.

"Do you know this one, Aimée?" Clotilde asked, turning the pages to "Bonnie Blue Flag," the song that had gotten Aimée into so much trouble.

"Dare we . . . sing it, Cousin Clotilde? What if someone hears us?"

"*Pauvre* Aimée! Your mind is still in New Orleans," teased Juba. "Here, we are in Confederate territory with no one to say us nay, and no one but maybe some old Choctaw, creeping back from his refuge in the cypress swamps, to hear us. We will all sing it together and hope the noise carries all the way across the lake to the headquarters of the Beast himself!"

Juba stood up to join them, walking to the piano with Cousin Jorge.

"Vickie, won't you come and join us, too?" Clotilde asked.

A faint smile crossed Vickie's lips. "I will leave the singing to you—and be your audience," she added, with no trace of the antagonism that had colored her speech previously.

Clotilde played a few measures as an introduction, and soon the music rose in a rousing noise. The sound of John Runefelt's deep bass voice from above the stairs joined with the voices downstairs and for a little while they all found joy in the song that echoed their beliefs—that served as a rallying song for those determined to defend their country from the invader.

> We are a band of brothers, and natives to the soil,
> Fighting for the property we gained by honest toil;
> And when our rights were threatened, the cry rose near and far,
> Hurrah for the bonnie Blue Flag that bears the single star.
> . . . But now, when Northern treachery attempts our rights to mar,
> We hoist on high the bonnie Blue Flag that bears the single star.
> . . . Then here's to our Confederacy; strong we are and brave;
> Like patriots of old we'll fight, our heritage to save,

And rather than submit to shame, to die we will prefer;
So cheer for the bonnie Blue Flag that bears a single star.

It was too much to hope for—that they would be left alone. The next day a raucous noise in the yard sent Juba to his hiding place in the attic.

Faith, the oldest of the little girls, barely eight, came running into the house, her face a pallid white and her large brown eyes wide with fear.

"There's . . . there's an *Indian* in the yard," she gasped, clinging to Vickie.

Aimée ran with Vickie to snatch the other two children from the gallery and take them inside—Vickie picking up the baby, Charity, and Aimée clasping Hope's hand.

"Oh, lordy, they'll kill us all!" Lizzie's hysterical voice cried out.

"Hush, Lizzie. Stop carrying on and hide the silver," Clotilde ordered.

There was a frantic scramble in the house while the noise outside filled the air—whoops and yells and the snorting of horses. War paint on the faces of the men gave them a vague resemblance to an Indian raiding party, but the saddles were Union issue and the features of the men were not Choctaw features.

Cousin Jorge stood at the door in a protective stance, but he was pushed aside in an abrupt manner and the ruffians, boldly walking into the house, eyed the valuables on the mantel and the genteel furnishings.

Aimée did not wait to see what would next catch the eyes of the scavengers. She slipped out the back door and ran to the stable to let the horses loose before they could be taken. She gave Sagefly and Dark Lightning a slap and they bolted into the woods.

Looking around, she spied the hen's nest in the straw and, acting nonchalant, she strolled back into the yard. As if her only purpose had been to gather the eggs, she calmly carried them in her handkerchief.

"I'll take those eggs, little lady," a voice ordered beside her. The man's face was covered with white stripes, with a touch of blue on each side of his nose.

"But monsieur, they are for the children's breakfast.

You would not wish to starve three little children, would you?"

"Better for them to starve than one hungry Indian brave," he answered, taking the eggs forcibly from her hands.

"The Indian braves are in the cypress swamps," Aimée said indignantly. "Are Union soldiers such cowards that they have to hide behind Indian war paint?"

"Hold your sharp tongue, little Rebel, or I'll take more than the chicken eggs from you," the man answered with a threatening tone.

Aimée took flight and ran back into the house, while the coarse laughter of the soldier sounded behind her.

The men left a trail of destruction behind them. Pieces of furniture, old paintings, and the mantel clock were taken from the house, and outside, the cries of the pigeons and the squealing of the pigs told their own story. Hams were taken from the smokehouse, and all the flour, sugar, and potatoes were confiscated from the pantry behind the kitchen—the food that Clotilde had carefully guarded so they would have enough to eat for the next several months. Now all of that was being carried away. And the animals that the raiders could not carry away alive were shot and left in the yard. Like bullies with no one to stop them, they rode their horses over the yard, tearing down fences, wrecking the outbuildings, and, worst of all, trampling Clotilde's flower garden until there was no sign of blossom or shrub left.

"My beautiful little box," Clotilde exclaimed with sadness, while Vickie attempted to quiet the children, who were crying from fright.

Cousin Jorge stooped down beside his sister, helping her to retrieve the little mementoes on the floor that the crushed box had once held. "Do not cry, Sister. We must all be brave this day."

"Why should they destroy what was valuable only to me? The baby curls from Sister Jeannette . . . and Mama's and Papa's wedding picture." Clotilde picked up the pieces that remained of the picture.

"Well, look at this, Clotilde," Cousin Jorge commented, with the paper in his hands. "Your baptismal certificate—

why, I remember that day so well . . . you had a touch of colic. . . ." And once again, Cousin Jorge was deep in his memories, forgetting, for the time being, the raiders' devastation of his home.

Clotilde's grief over the teakwood box was nothing in comparison with her reaction when she saw her musical garden in ruins. The althea tree had been stripped of its leaves and flowers, and the slender trunk had been hacked to the ground. The petunias and roses were no more—only an essence crushed into the ground by unloving hands. Taking one disbelieving look at the garden that she had loved and cared for as tenderly as for a child, and seeing it in complete shambles, Clotilde seemed to lose the will to live. She took to her bed and refused all comfort—refused to come to the table for the little bit of food they could scrape together for a meal, refused to play the piano, refused any consolation offered her in her grief. She closed out the world, wanting no more of a life that could be so cruel.

It was the rapid deterioration of Juba's health that brought an end to Clotilde's self-imposed exile. She arose from her bed to tend the sick man, whose agonized coughing could not be disguised.

Even the children were affected by the dismal air in the house. Faith, Hope, and Charity did not quarrel anymore, but kept up their Sunday manners, sensing the grief that hung over Plantation Thornfell like a cloud of doom, ready to spill its tears at any moment.

Vickie took on a measure of worth, doing her share in nursing Juba and seeing to the needs of the other man, John Runefelt, who now hobbled around his room with the aid of a stick, still berating himself that he had been of no help when the raiders had come .

Aimée also took turns nursing the sick Juba. Now too weak to come downstairs, he remained in bed most of the day, his strength ebbing away by the incessant coughing.

"Read to me, Aimée," Juba requested one rainy afternoon when she was sitting with him.

"What would you like to hear, Juba?" Aimée asked.

"Your voice, Aimée. It doesn't matter what you read —just so I can lie here and listen to your voice." He finished the sentence with a fit of coughing and Aimée went to him to lift him up, to make it easier for him to breathe.

"I am going to die, Aimée," Juba confided.

"No . . . no, Juba! You must not say that. You are going to get well," Aimée insisted.

"We need not pretend, little Aimée. We both know the truth . . . I do not have the strength to live. . . ."

His voice was low and Aimée leaned close to hear the last words.

"Juba . . ." Her heart was distressed at his resignation.

"Sit in the light, so I can see your golden-red hair, Aimée . . . so I can remember the happy times when we were children."

At that moment Aimée knew that Juba was not seeing her, but his sister who had died two years before.

She found her place near the window, and despite the lump in her throat, she took up the book lying on the table and read in soothing low tones until Juba's eyes closed in sleep.

Aimée tiptoed down the attic stairs to her little room at the end of the hallway, and there she cried for Juba and for herself—for her utter loneliness . . . destined never to be with her husband Bryan again . . . never to feel his arms about her . . . never again to be loved by the strong giant who could be so gentle. . . .

The funeral for Juba was a quiet one. He was buried in the family plot, with the minister sworn to secrecy. Even the headstone conspired in the secret—the name John Runefelt was chiseled in crude letters on it. For the man upstairs—the man with the broken leg—was now Juba Barnard to the outside world, with the discharge papers to prove it.

Two days after Juba's funeral the new Juba Barnard waylaid Aimée in the hallway when she was returning to her room.

"May I . . . speak with you for a moment, Aimée?" he

asked in a serious voice. He looked up and down the hall as if to make sure that no one could overhear them.

"Of course, John. What is it? Or would you rather I called you Juba?" Aimée felt the pain at speaking Juba's name, but was not aware that it showed in her eyes.

"No. When we are alone, I'd rather you called me . . . John."

"You know, I have a feeling that even *John* is not your right name," Aimée said in confidence.

The man smiled at her but made no comment.

"What is it that you wish to speak to me about?" Aimée prompted.

"Are you . . . willing to make another trip into New Orleans?"

Aimée did not answer at first. She realized how lucky she had been not to get caught the first time. And now that the conductor knew her as Cécile, it would be dangerous to bump into him again on the train—especially on a Sunday evening. And she could not continue to slip through the guards without a pass.

"If . . . if I could find some means other than the train of getting into New Orleans, I would not mind, John. But it was dangerous without a pass, and I would not wish to try *that* again."

"If I could arrange to . . . have a horse waiting behind one of the deserted cabins on the south shore, could you ride down the Bayou Road into the city?"

"Yes, I could do that. But what about the horse? Is there somewhere that I might leave it before I got to the pharmacy? Monsieur O'Brie said that the pharmacy is being watched, and a horse in front would certainly cause comment."

"The horse could easily be left at Talbot's Livery Stables, Aimée. And you could claim it again on your way back. Just make sure you ask for Henry . . . no one else."

"How . . . how soon do you want me to go?"

"I can make arrangements for the horse by tomorrow," John said, wrinkling his brow in deep thought.

"It's too bad you couldn't get some extra passes from General Butler's office. That would solve the problem, wouldn't it? And then I could go in and out of New Orleans at will, without being stopped," she tossed in flippantly.

"That's an idea, Aimée. We'll see what we can do about that." John suddenly grinned at Aimée's astonished expression.

"You mean . . . it might be possible?"

"Who knows?" John replied, shrugging his shoulders.

The next evening, as soon as the sun had set, Aimée, with the help of Cousin Jorge, launched the boat into the water. John's last words still rang in her ears.

"Basalt is a free man of color. You need not be afraid of him, although he is an outlaw. He will be at the back of the cabin set on the tallest stilts, a hundred yards from the willow copse."

Chapter 13

*F*rom that time on, Aimée settled into a weekly routine of carrying messages back and forth into New Orleans.

Once a week Basalt had the horse waiting for her and Aimée skirted the swamp, galloping down the Bayou Road, until she reached the livery stables.

On one particular Wednesday night Aimée traveled into New Orleans as usual, reaching the stables with no mishap to mar the trip. But her eyes and ears were finely tuned to the sights and sounds around her.

It was the stillness of the figure across the alley from the stables that first made Aimée uneasy. She looked quickly at the inert figure, a light-skinned woman of color, a woman who looked as if she was waiting for something or someone.

The lantern hanging at the side of the stables flickered and in its soft glow Aimée felt peculiarly vulnerable to the watching eyes as she alit from Gaspard, the bay horse.

Hurriedly she left the horse in the stables, covering his sweating flanks with the blanket that had been draped over the sides of the stall. Then, standing at the edge of the open door, she looked up and down the street.

The woman had disappeared and Aimée relaxed. She must not become so tense at every glance in her direction, she thought, as she darted out onto the banquette.

The street was dark and Aimée, aware of the seamier side of New Orleans that appeared at the first stroke of darkness, walked more rapidly down the banquette to remove herself quickly from the dubious life around the livery stable.

"Pretend you do not know that I am walking by your side."

The voice came from the woman of color who had reappeared to walk in an easy gait, moving her mouth but little with the words.

Aimée, startled, did not turn her head, but listened and kept her eyes on the street ahead, catching only a glimpse of the plump woman in the periphery of her vision.

"Soldiers are watching Monsieur O'Brie's pharmacy tonight. I will take you to safety where they cannot find you."

How could Aimée be sure that this was not a trap? Or that this woman was not working for General Butler and taking her into the arms of the enemy?

"How do I know that you are telling me the truth?" Aimée asked in a low tone.

"Angeline does not lie. But Monsieur O'Brie told me to mention the name 'Cousin Clotilde' if you did not trust me," the woman said matter-of-factly.

Immediately Aimée knew that the woman was actually a messenger from Monsieur O'Brie. There was no more doubts. Only *he* had heard that name from Aimée's lips.

"I will walk ahead of you, so that we will not be seen together," the woman of color remarked, beginning a faster pace until she was a half-block away from Aimée. Aimée strained her eyes and quickened her own steps, afraid that she would lose sight of the woman.

Music flew across one section of the city, blaring and loud, and raucous laughter jarred her taut nerves. A small group of revelers, with no certain destination in mind, stopped at the street corner before turning around and staggering in the same direction from which they had come. A drunk, lying on the banquette, barred the way but Aimée walked around him, stepping back on the broken tile of the banquette once past the barrier.

Union soldiers appeared suddenly at the far end of the street. The woman Angeline had vanished near the alleyway at St. Anthony's Close, and Aimée, her spirits plummeting, reacted without thinking and began to run.

The soldiers broke rank and ran after her. In a moment she would be trapped into one corner of the alleyway, where she could not escape the fence looming up before her.

The hand reached out just as she ran by, and Aimée was snatched quickly from sight. Aimée stiffled her sudden sound of alarm when she recognized the woman of color beside her.

"*Mon Dieu*, they are everywhere tonight," the woman managed to say to the trembling Aimée, pushing her ahead with a determined hand.

The sound of running footsteps behind her gave her new impetus to move, but her hungry lungs ached for the air denied her by the lacing of her corset. Still, she had no choice except to keep running. If she slowed down, the soldiers would close in.

A block away, Aimée and the woman stumbled into a lighted courtyard where tropical trees and shrubs hid small tables that were set for two. Aimée looked up toward the balcony that oversaw the courtyard and heard the music coming from the room above. She headed toward a chair behind one of the shrubs but she was stopped before she could sit down.

"Not yet, *ma petite*."

Gasping for breath, she followed the woman up a back staircase to the rear of the ballroom. One last glance toward the courtyard told Aimée that it was well she had not remained outside. Her pursuers were still following her trail like hounds hot on the scent. How could she escape them? How could she hide from them, dressed as she was?

She was hardly aware of the elongated high-ceilinged room or the sound of laughter rippling over the lilting music of the fiddlers. She saw only blurs of moving color on the dance floor, as the hand behind her pushed her until she was in one of the small gaming rooms back of the ballroom.

"Wait here. I will be back soon," the woman whispered and Aimée was left alone.

The blurs of color Aimée had seen, now that she had time to think about it, became clear and focused in her mind. She was in the Orleans Ballroom, at a Quadroon Ball, and the bits of moving color she had seen were the beautiful young quadroons, octoroons, and *griffes* dressed in rich satins, jewels, and plumes, and dancing with the white men intent on forming an alliance with them that night.

Despite the danger, Aimée felt a trembling of excitement as well. She would never have the opportunity to see this again. While she was at such close range, she would make the most of it. She opened the door quietly and peered out on this strange phenomenon—a unique situation that could only occur in the Crescent City.

"Close the door, *ma petite*. You do not wish to be seen," Angeline said, slipping into the small game room, carrying a load of clothes in her arms.

"The . . . soldiers—are they . . . ?"

"Yes. Some have stationed themselves at the doors and others are searching the rooms. We haven't much time. The only way I can get you out safely is to dress you like the others."

"The others? Do you mean that I will have to . . ."

Aimée swallowed, not able to finish the thought aloud. To watch was one thing, but to become a part. . . .

"*Oui, ma petite*. You will have to become one of . . . them tonight, and I pray *le bon Dieu* that you will not be noticed overmuch. There is a black wig in the case from

Justine, the hairdresser. And the mask, I hope, will hide those giveaway turquoise eyes."

The woman spread out the white satin gown and the other paraphernalia and began removing the cape and modest traveling dress from Aimée's body. "We must hurry and hide your street clothes."

"Whose . . . dress is this?" Aimée asked, looking at the elegant ball gown.

For a moment the woman did not answer. Then she replied, "A pretty young octoroon who will have to wait until the next ball to form an alliance."

"But didn't she mind—having her dress taken from her?"

"Naturally she was disappointed. But her *maman* understood the need."

There was a knock on the door, and a basin of water was pushed inside to Angeline's waiting hands. And Aimée submitted to the hurried but effective ministrations of the woman. A slight bit of color had been rubbed on Aimée's cheeks and the black wig almost secured in place when the door burst open.

A rattle of abusive French greeted the ears of the Union soldier, who backed away in apology, closing the door behind him, and Angeline's hands shook as she completed the toilette. "Monsieur O'Brie would skin me and stuff my hide if something happened to you. That was a *narrow* escape, *mon enfant!*" Angeline croaked.

The woman now turned to her own needs, placing the red satin dress over her head. She twisted uncomfortably in the borrowed corset. Taking one last glance at Aimée, Angeline opened the door. The same soldier stood outside, as if waiting for a closer inspection of the girl he had surprised.

"Uh oh! Trouble is at the door and does not plan to leave."

"Then what can we do, Angeline? The soldier will begin to suspect that something is wrong if I do not go past him to the ballroom," Aimée whispered.

"You will have to dance with some of the gentlemen, but do not worry. I will pretend to be your *maman* and will watch over you carefully. If some man approaches you to form an . . . alliance, tell him that he will have to see me to make the . . . necessary arrangements."

Angeline's voice became loud enough for the soldier to hear. "Come, Delphine, it is time we go into the ballroom."

Aimée, feeling timid and strange, followed Angeline in much the same way that a young girl, unused to being with men, would enter a room filled with them. She must remember her name—Delphine—if anyone should ask.

The white satin dress rustled and Aimée, wishing to be ignored, could not have chosen a worse time to enter. The music had ceased and all male eyes turned to the blushing girl as she stopped uncertainly beyond the threshold.

Angeline vanished into the crowd and Aimée was left completely alone. Near panic, she watched as one of the guards stared and headed in her direction. Rapidly she turned her back and took several steps toward the door from which she had entered, but a hand at her elbow stayed her.

"Most enchanting," the man said in a connoisseur's voice, while he eyed her up and down. "May I have this dance, my dear?"

The guard hesitated and Aimée glanced from the soldier to the man and then frantically searched the room for Angeline. The woman sat in a gilt chair at the edge of the ballroom. Focusing her attention upon Aimée, she inclined her head, as if giving permission for the girl to dance with the man at her side. There was no way that Aimée could tell her that this man presented an added danger.

"And what are you called, my dear?" the man asked, taking her hand and placing it in his own.

"D-Delphine, monsieur," she stammered, feeling the pulse leap in her throat.

"And I am Colonel Tilson," the man said.

She was not apt to forget it. He was the same man who had been much too forward with her at the Officers' Ball, who had caused her disgrace on the dance floor, and here she was dancing with him at a Quadroon Ball. Would the mask and the black wig be sufficient to prevent him from recognizing her? If he discovered her identity, he would know she had no business at all being present in such a questionable place. And he would not hesitate to call the soldiers who had stationed themselves at all the exits.

The colonel took her in his arms and his eyes did not move from her face. "You remind me of someone I have seen before," he said, "and yet, you are also different."

It would not take long before he placed her, Aimée knew, and then her disguise would be to no avail, unless she thought of something quickly.

"Ah, ha," he said, with a sign of recognition. "Those eycs—those remarkable turquoise eycs." And then he began laughing. "And what Creole gentleman claims you as his daughter, little Delphine?" he asked, with the evidence of the joke still in his eyes.

Aimée frowned. Was he planning to toy with her, teasing her until he eventually turned her over to the soldiers?

"It is true my *papa* was a . . . Creole gentleman, monsieur, but I do not choose to give you his name," Aimée answered indignantly.

"You do not have to—I have guessed your secret!"

"You . . . you have?" Aimée asked uncertainly.

"Of course. I have danced with your white half-sister, Aimée—whom you resemble a great deal. You cannot deny what is written in your face. Your father was a Saint-Moreau."

"Your white half-sister, Aimée." Then he had not discerned her secret after all. In relief she smiled at him and said coquettishly, "I see, monsieur, that you are much too smart to be fooled. There seems to be no secret a girl can keep from you."

He swept her into a gay, abandoned waltz, holding her much too closely, but she was not at liberty to protest. For a while at least, she was safe. The soldier had gone back to his post at the door and Colonel Tilson had not discovered her identity.

The music continued and the man kept her in his arms. Occasionally Aimée looked over her shoulder. The guards had not moved from their fixed positions. But they watched her, followed her movements with their eyes, and waited while she continued to dance. And Angeline sat serenely in the gilt chair and also watched Aimée.

It was a nightmare, dancing to the music, being mistaken for a half-caste, and being forced to keep up the farce. Aimée's initial curiosity had been satisfied and in its place was a degraded feeling and a wish to leave the ballroom, to escape before her disguise was stripped from her.

"I am already mad about you," Colonel Tilson said caressingly in her ear. "And I want to be your protector. What do you say to such a proposal, little Delphine?"

She blocked out the unpleasant feeling of his paunchy stomach pressing between them.

"Please, monsieur, you must not speak to me of things I do not understand. My . . . *maman* is the one you must address."

"Ah, yes, I understand. But your mama should have no objections whatever. I am already prepared to settle a large sum on you—and buy you a little love nest in the Ramparts. Shall we seek her out now, my love?"

What could she say? Would Angeline be able to handle him without offending him? Undecided, Aimée answered, "Let us . . . finish the dance, monsieur. For this is my first and last ball in the Orleans."

He acceded to her wish. Still searching her face as they danced, Colonel Tilson remarked, "A pity that you did not inherit the red hair as well—but I suppose that would have been too much to hope for."

Colonel Tilson seemed to be enjoying himself, and in a burst of exuberance he crowed, "I wonder what Bryan Garrard would say if he knew his aristocratic and proud little beauty of a wife and my quadroon mistress were related? That would put him down a peg, I expect."

Aimée winced inwardly, hearing Bryan's name spoken. "I . . . am an . . . octoroon, monsieur," she said, wishing to correct him about something, however minute.

"My apologies," he said. "One more step up to being white—I see."

The waltz was over and Aimée reluctantly led Colonel Tilson to the place where Angeline was sitting.

"Maman," Aimée began, "this gentleman, Colonel Tilson, wishes to . . . discuss an . . . arrangement with you." Aimée blushed and her head bent low in embarrassment.

"But certainly, *ma petite*. The gentleman is . . . enchanted with my Delphine, *n'est-ce pas?*"

"Yes, madam. And I am an impatient man," he added. "I should like to make the arrangements tonight."

"Tonight, monsieur?" Angeline asked in a surprised voice. "*Oui*, you *are* an impatient man, monsieur," she said, grinning at him.

Aimée frowned at Angeline, but the woman continued, "And does monsieur have his carriage outside?"

"Yes," Colonel Tilson answered.

"Then perhaps monsieur will not object to taking us home where the . . . necessary details can be discussed much more pleasantly and agreeably over a glass of wine."

"I will call for the carriage at once," Colonel Tilson said, leaving a flustered Aimée with Angeline.

"What . . . what are you doing to me, Angeline? He will betray me easily when he is crossed."

"Wait here and trust me, *ma petite*. The man is offering us safe escort past the Union soldiers. We cannot refuse." The woman left quickly to speak in another woman's ear. She in turn nodded and disappeared. Aimée watched the activity. Would Angeline's friends be able to help them?

By the time Colonel Tilson reappeared, Angeline was again at Aimée's side. The man took Aimée's arm and guided her out the door, past the Union guards. He helped her into the waiting carriage and Angeline clambered up under her own steam.

The woman gave the black driver directions to a house on Rampart Street, but robbers and cutthroats stopped the carriage a few blocks from the Orleans ballroom. Amid the screams of the two women, Colonel Tilson and his driver were thrown from the carriage and the vehicle, with the two women inside, was confiscated by the cutthroats and driven away into the darkness of the night. . . .

"Thank you, Angeline," Aimée said later, "for taking care of me."

"It is nothing," Angeline assured her, seeing her into the unguarded pharmacy shortly before dawn. "And I trust the colonel will not look too long for his little Delphine," she said, still chuckling over the events of the evening.

Chapter 14

Aimée was aware that John Runefelt had begun to watch her, his eyes lingering much too long on her hair and on her mouth. And sometimes Aimée would remember the times Bryan Garrard had gazed at her in that tender way, and she would feel the pain anew—a phantom pain, now that her life with him had been severed.

The war was not going well. Even though she had not started out to be a spy, Aimée saw how necessary it was to bring news of troop movements or carry the packets of quinine or morphine that the Confederate surgeons so desperately needed. Any strike against the enemy was worthwhile—anything to cut down on the killing, the bleeding, the slow starvation that was insidiously enveloping the entire South.

Day after day Union troops passed in and out of New Orleans and were replaced a few days later by the casualties of war—not only Federal soldiers, but an increasing number of wounded and captured Confederates, their uniforms in tatters, their feet encased in rags or ill-fitting boots taken from some less fortunate friend who needed them no longer.

While Aimée sat, thinking of the war and of her husband, John also sat, watching Aimée in silence, until he put his thoughts into words.

"Are you certain that you want to continue these trips

back and forth to New Orleans, Aimée?"

Startled at his voice, Aimée did not answer his question for a while. Then she said, "Yes, John. Someone has to go while you are still unable to do so. And I have been lucky so far."

But the brown-eyed man was dubious, and to Aimée, this gradual change, this possessive urge to protect her, was not in character with the hard core of the man she had first met. Was not a spy supposed to be completely heartless, putting principles and ideals above human relationships? He had done so before—but now he was being swayed by his personal feelings. He was changing.

"But luck will last only so long," John countered. "There is a danger in being *too* successful. You are fast becoming a legend, and I do not want you to become too well known. Butler is bound to hear of you sooner or later and put a price on your head."

"Let him hear," Aimée retorted. "Just so he doesn't catch me," she said in a softer voice.

When Aimée made her next trip into New Orleans—for despite John's reservations, she had continued—the city's banquettes were alight from the flares of torches and people swarmed in and out of the busy streets in a holiday mood.

Crosses of dried immortelles and wreaths of paper roses hung on the walls by the banquettes; stands lining the banquettes contained images of plaster and curled paper of black and purple and white for sale; everywhere there were fresh-flower venders with vast supplies of chrysanthemums and roses.

Even the war could not prevent the people from following their time-honored custom of observing the festival of the dead—*le jour des morts*—that important holy day when the graves of their ancestors would come alive with flowers and wreaths and tokens of loving memory, when the poorest of the poor spent their last pennies to honor their dead.

Aimée slipped past the stands with her face hidden from the unwelcome brightness of the torchlight, and weaving in and out between the street venders calling out their wares of pralines and *pain-patate*, she escaped the crowds to find her way to the pharmacy.

Just beyond the fence at the back of the pharmacy, she gave the signal to let Monsieur O'Brie know she was there. She counted to herself the proper number of times, to wait for Monsieur O'Brie to unlock the back door and leave by the front, strolling down the street as he usually did, to draw away any of General Butler's spies who might be lurking in the darkness.

The time was up and Aimée hastened to take the few remaining steps to reach the safety of the pharmacy, and once inside, to lock the door.

A few minutes later Aimée heard the front door open. Monsieur O'Brie had returned.

"Aimée," he whispered, groping his way into the room.

"I am here," she replied.

Monsieur O'Brie lit the lamp and his eyes glowed with joy at seeing her.

He's like my *papa*, Aimée thought, seeing the expression on his face. There was a comfortable closeness between them from the sharing of a common danger. A pity that a war had brought them together in this close relationship.

He still wore his pharmacist's apron and he looked old and tired. The strain was beginning to tell on him, Aimée thought, but she could sense an added strain that had not been present before—as if he were almost torn apart.

"What is wrong, monsieur?" Aimée asked, feeling the agitation that he could not keep hidden.

"The general's spies are hard at work, Aimée, and it's paying off, much to our hurt. Two of our best men were caught this week—a terrible blow for us."

He removed his spectacles, cleaning them on his pharmacist's apron as he continued.

"So now I am wrestling with my conscience, not knowing which way to turn. I have a . . . dangerous cargo that needs to be taken across Lake Pontchartrain within twenty-four hours, and there is only one person left who can take it. I have even thought of taking it myself, but I would be stopped before getting to the end of the street. . . ."

"That's my problem, Aimée—I cannot ask that person to take such a risk, even knowing that it might save the Confederacy."

"You are speaking of me, are you not, Monsieur O'Brie, as the one who could carry your . . . dangerous cargo?" Aimée asked matter-of-factly.

"Yes, Aimée, I am speaking of you," he replied unhappily.

"Will you explain to me the danger and . . . what I must do?"

Monsieur O'Brie sighed and for an interval remained silent. Then he began to speak.

"I will give you the facts and then you must decide for yourself. . . . But I will not hold it against you if you decide the risk is too great."

Aimée sat across the table from the stoop-shouldered man and listened.

"You have already heard that General Grant is determined to take Vicksburg and split the South in two?"

Aimée nodded.

"Twice he has tried it, and twice the Yazoo Delta has defeated him. Each time his heavy cannons have gotten bogged down in the delta mud before they were close enough to the city to do any damage. . . .

"But now, we have received word that a new offensive is to be launched. This time it will come from two sides at the same time—one from the land side, and the other from the Mississippi.

"Aimée," he said, with rising fervor, "we have *got* to stop them from reaching Vicksburg by the river!"

"But how can we do that, monsieur, when our guns could not stop the boats coming from the Gulf of New Orleans? How could we stop them this time?" Aimée inquired.

"We will be using something better than guns. We will be using underwater explosives—mines—in the river to blow up the boats as they pass a certain point."

"Mines?" Aimée was incredulous.

"Yes. It has proven effective in the James River, and I am told that it has made the whole Union Navy tremble."

"But what is small enough that I could carry?" a

puzzled Aimée asked. "What is this dangerous cargo?"

"Fulminate of mercury," Monsieur O'Brie replied. "It's used for the fuses."

"And it will . . . explode?" Aimée questioned.

"Yes. But if one is careful in carrying it, it will be all right. The danger lies in its being dropped or knocked against something."

Aimée started to speak but Monsieur O'Brie stopped her.

"No, Aimée . . . we will discuss it no further tonight. You are tired and hungry. There will be enough time tomorrow, before you leave."

Off and on during the night Aimée kept waking, troubled by the decision facing her. Never before had she been in such a dangerous difficulty. If she decided to take this fulminate of mercury, there was a chance that she would not live beyond the day.

And if she did not take it? Hadn't Monsieur O'Brie said this cargo might be the means of saving the Confederacy?

Etienne had given his life for what he had believed in . . . and so had her *grand-père*. Was she any less loyal?

Bryan's face loomed in her mind, haunting her with his silver-gray eyes. If there were even a remote possibility that Bryan would be on one of the boats traveling upriver, Aimée knew she would never be able to agree to the venture. But Bryan had told her himself that he saw only to the fortifications along the river. He did not go upstream beyond the portion of river that the Yankees had taken. And he did not defend those fortifications.

Oh, why had he come into her life, making her loyalties so complicated? Before he became her husband, she was able to hate each Yankee equally. Now that was no longer possible.

Aimée knew that, for her, life would always be bittersweet. She could only look back to memories and regrets; she had nothing to look forward to after the war. If she did not survive, there was no one to care. Everyone who had ever truly loved her was now dead, except for Monsieur O'Brie . . . and he loved the Confederacy even more.

Remembering his troubled face, Aimée made her decision. Turning over on her side, she closed her eyes and slept peacefully in the storage room, just off the main room of the pharmacy.

Aimée awoke to the noise of the thunder and the rain —combined with the wind, these always sent a shudder of fear through her. It was a bad omen for the night ahead.

All during the day the rain continued. And by dark, when it was time for Aimée to leave, Monsieur O'Brie refused to give her the satchel and begged her to stay another day because of the stormy waters of the lake—as the sea backed into it, freshets of salty waves disturbed its usual placidity.

"You cannot go, Aimée. It is too dangerous," Monsieur O'Brie said for the tenth time.

Despite her fear of the storm, Aimée tied her cape around her and said, "The satchel, monsieur . . . I am ready. I do not wish to remain here any longer."

The man slowly walked into the pharmacy and returned with the satchel. "May heaven forgive me, Aimée—and the Lord be with you this night."

With that final benediction, Aimée began her journey home.

Throughout that day she had been conscious of the ritual taking place at the cemetery, and she had no comfort knowing that Tante Dee Dee's tomb remained bare of ornament—no flower, no wreath. Prosper's family would see to his tomb, but there was no one to honor Tante Dee Dee on this most important day.

From the shelter of the pharmacy Aimée had listened to the people walking by in the rain on their way to join the All Souls' Day procession, in which the priest carried the silver crucifix before them. But it should not have rained. The sun should have been shining for the procession, for the fragile, gnarled little ladies who sat on iron chairs to receive their guests at the family mausoleums, for the orphans standing at the gate with the Sisters to remind the people of their destitution.

Aimée pulled her cape closer to her, feeling the wetness on her face. The streets were deserted except for one lonely vender, who was folding up his table to take inside. Aimée saw the wreath of paper roses hanging on the wall beside the stand, and on impulse she rushed up. "Please, monsieur—I should like to buy the wreath," and she dug into the pockets of her cape for the money. It was madness to do it, but the cemetery was not far out of her way.

The gates had been left open and Aimée, with the satchel over her shoulder and the paper roses in her hand, walked in past the tombs stacked tier upon tier, the soggy earth partially hiding the ones underneath that had sunk from the weight of those added on top. And everywhere were roses and chrysanthemums, crosses and draped paper, all soaked from the rain.

"Forgive me, Tante Dee Dee, for being so late," Aimée said, her voice echoing the loneliness of the place, as she hung the wreath on the hook embedded in the wall.

"Miss Aimée, Miss Aimée," the voice called out.

Aimée's mind returned from her sadness with a jerk, and recognizing Lisette, she broke into a run to elude her former servant.

"A spy behind every Rebel family in New Orleans!" Was that not what Monsieur O'Brie had said? Who better than Lisette to spy on her and give her up to the enemy? And what better place to find her than at the St. Louis Cemetery on All Souls' Day, near Tante Dee Dee's grave? Lisette must have been paid well to remain so long. Most would have been frightened away before dark.

Aimée hid behind an ancient mausoleum and listened to the woman's steps pacing back and forth and her soft tones whispering Aimée's name, alternately close and then farther away.

The whispering voice returned, closer and closer, and Lisette's foot was now visible at the edge of the mausoleum.

"Miss Aimèe, I know you' hidin' in here somewhere. Why don't you answer?"

Any closer and Lisette would be able to hear her rapid breathing. Aimée glanced at the satchel she was carrying. While she was worrying, Lisette stood still, listening.

A flash of lightning crossed the sky and fresh rains

descended. Then Lisette's foot moved away from sight and her footsteps disappeared into the stormy night.

Shaking with the realization that she had almost been caught, Aimée kept her mind on her escape. And then her heart was chilled by another thought. . . . Had she pulled the boat sufficiently far enough from shore to be safe from the encroaching water? At times the water rose several feet when it rained, and the rain had not ceased all day. It would be the ultimate disaster to find that her means of escape had floated away, forcing her to return to the pharmacy. More trouble—not only for herself, but also for Monsieur O'Brie.

With eyes and ears alert to the slightest movement and sound, Aimée hurried from the cemetery to the stables where her horse would be waiting. Lisette had evidently given up.

Traveling toward the lake, Aimée stayed just off the main road—straining to see in the rain and the terrible darkness, not daring to put the horse to a gallop because of the cargo she was carrying. She prayed that the horse would not stumble and fall, for that would be the end of them both.

Miraculously Aimée reached the cabin and left the horse in its makeshift corral.

If the rain had caused danger for Aimée, it had also helped her in one respect. The guards were more relaxed and less attentive to their duties at the edge of the lake.

"This weather ain't fit for fowl or peahen," Aimée heard a guard's voice comment.

"Not even a Rebel with wings could get across this water tonight," another voice agreed.

"Then let's go get some coffee, Henry. Ain't no use soakin' our backsides sittin' here in all this rain."

When the voices receded, Aimée crossed the open area that was always the most dangerous spot, and proceeded to grope her way in the rain toward the willow copse. The area was covered in water and there was no sign of the boat. It had disappeared.

If she wanted to get across that night, it was evident to Aimée that she had to find another boat to use. Disheartened, she walked along the shore, searching for a skiff, for anything seaworthy that would float her across.

Why had so many obstacles been placed in her way tonight, of all the nights since she had started going back and forth to New Orleans? Was she destined to be caught —to be thwarted in the most important undertaking she had ever tried?

Angry with herself and angry with the rain that had done this treason to her, Aimée retraced her steps until she was almost in sight of the guards' hut. Their voices returned to her ears, laughter and conversation over the cups of coffee. It was by their light that she saw the boat tied to the pier jutting into the water—her boat, which the guards must have found and retrieved.

For the first time in several hours Aimée felt a sense of relief. Carrying the satchel close to her body, she boldly walked down the pier, placed the satchel in the boat, untied the craft under the noses of the guards, and escaped out onto the lake.

Her fear of the storm and the water returned to plague her, and each moment on the lake became an eternity. At times Aimée thought she might be swamped by the water in the bottom of the boat and the waves lapping against the sides, but she and her cargo finally got across.

Exhausted, she sank upon the dirt, the wet dirt that was soaked with so much rain. She clutched the satchel in her hands.

The clouds began passing overhead, revealing clumps of stars in the heavens, and Monsieur O'Brie's words came back to her: "The Lord be with you this night."

The stars went out, one by one, and then Aimée was clinging to the horse—frantically trying to stay upright in her seat. Jorge's words were compelling, coaxing her to stay awake. He was beside her, leading her horse with his own.

"The satchel," Aimée whispered, shuddering from the cold. "You must be careful."

"It's safe. I have it here, Aimée. Just hold on—we'll soon be home."

When Jorge and Aimée reached Plantation Thornfell, Clotilde appeared out of the darkness, the pale darkness edging toward the dawn. When the front door was closed, she lit the lamp and held it high to guide the two bedraggled people up the stairs.

At the sound of steps, John Runefelt, making a thumping noise with the wooden splint tied to his leg, stood in the doorway of his bedroom and watched the mute procession.

Aimée, her turquoise eyes much too large for her face, looked up into the fierce, angry brown eyes of the limping man before passing on to her room.

"You know, you should stay in bed all day," Clotilde told Aimée when bringing the tray of food to her room the next day toward noon.

"I am not an invalid, Cousin Clotilde. And you have far too much to do to be waiting on me. I should be helping you instead."

"My dear, you were soaked to the skin last night. If you are truly serious about giving me less work, then you will stay the rest of the day in bed. So I won't have to nurse you back to health," Clotilde added, with a smile.

Aimée sank back onto the pillows. She *was* tired and her throat did feel a little sore. Fall had almost gone and winter was approaching. No wonder she had felt chilled in the rain the night before.

"All right, you win, Cousin Clotilde," Aimée acquiesced.

"Good! I'm glad you are agreeable," responded Clotilde. The woman glanced at the fireplace and the darkened ashes. Immediately she called for Lizzie to build up the fire to make the room warm.

After Lizzie had gone and the fire was blazing warmly on the hearth, Aimée heard a thumping walk down the hall and then a knock on her door.

"Come in," she called and the door opened to reveal John Runefelt.

"How are you feeling, Aimée, after that rainy excursion last night?" he asked.

"Thankful to be home," she replied.

He shifted his position, and seeing how uncomfortable he was standing, Aimée asked, "Wouldn't you like to sit down, John?"

He left the door open, and finding his way to the chair by the bed, stretched his splinted leg in relief.

"This blasted leg! What a terrible time to be laid up. But I wanted to tell you, little red-headed spy, how furious I am with you for putting yourself in such danger." Then he smiled and said, "But the satchel is already on its way, and if all goes well, you, my dear, may turn out to be the heroine of this war."

"Please, John," said Aimée, suddenly embarrassed. "I . . . I do not feel like a heroine."

Just then a draft slammed the door to her room.

"Shall I . . . open the door again, Aimée? I would not wish to damage your reputation."

Aimée laughed, and thinking of his leg, she said, "Don't bother, John. After what has happened in the past two days, a closed door is not very important."

"You are very brave, you know, besides being very beautiful." He stared at her for a moment before continuing. "I was half out of my mind last night when you didn't come for such a long time. And when I found out what you had brought with you—" Impulsively he reached over and took one of her golden-red strands of hair in his hands, stroking it as he talked. "Not many girls would be brave enough to do what you did last night."

Suddenly the door burst open and Vickie stood triumphantly inside the room.

"Just as I suspected," she said. "First it was Juba—and now it's this . . . this spy. And heaven knows who else in New Orleans that you spend your nights with."

Aimée was aghast at Vickie's accusations, but the anger belonged to John Runefelt.

"You will apologize to Aimée immediately," John ordered, "for even thinking such a thing about her. She has risked her neck for you, Mrs. Brittain—risked her life to save the Confederacy from being trampled underfoot and ruined. And if I thought I could save Aimée from any more of your vicious attacks on her character, I would be honored to make her my wife. But I love her too much to put her life in any more danger than it is already."

John stood up awkwardly and walked menacingly toward Vickie. Vickie shrank back and said deprecatingly, "Well, the door *was* closed. What else was I to think? But . . . if I'm wrong, I'll apologize—"

John ignored Vickie and turned back to Aimée. "Rest well, Aimée. We will finish our conversation later."

Chapter 15

*W*hen the news came, Aimée and John were jubilant. The mines had prevented the Yankees from reaching Vicksburg by the river and General Grant's cannons had gotten stuck in the delta mud. Vicksburg was still free.

But amidst their jubilation, both knew it was only temporary. Grant was not used to defeat. He would keep on trying. If only they could keep the river blocked. . . .

Again Aimée crossed the lake. The November sky was dark, but Aimée was by now so used to the trip on the water that she could have crossed the lake with her eyes shut. But it was not her usual Wednesday night. This time it was Sunday, and Aimée hoped that Basalt had gotten the message to have the horse, Gaspard, waiting for her.

When Aimée reached the copse, she hid her boat and fled through the vulnerable open space of reeds and marsh grass. She stumbled on a burned-out pine knot before coming to the assigned cabin. At first it did not disturb her that the horse was not there, for she was early and the bit of time waiting for Basalt would give her an opportunity to rest before going the remainder of the way.

There was an eeriness to the atmosphere that night—a

feeling that the place was not quite deserted, as if it had been recently occupied.

Ever since All Hallow's Eve, fires had been sprinkled along the lakeshore, lighting up the sky so that the glow was apparent all the way across the lake to the northern shore. Aimée knew that Marie Laveau had a cabin hidden somewhere near—Maison Blanche, it was called—but no one had ever found it. There had been rumors of secret rites and sacrificial ceremonies, and Aimée shivered just thinking about it.

She waited, becoming more uneasy as the time passed. If Basalt did not come soon, she would have to decide whether to cross the lake back to Thornfell or to take her chances on the train.

Aimée deliberated back and forth, deciding one way and then the other. When it seemed definite Basalt would not come, she reached a final decision. She would take the train, keeping her fingers crossed that Gaston Ferbes, if he were still the conductor, would not remember her, or else not hold her to the promise made to him much earlier.

Aimée, walking toward the station, kept her cape close to her, wondering if she was doing the right thing in continuing the trip.

"There she is," a voice called out. "We'll get her this time."

Aimée looked back and saw the guards running toward her. She, too, began running—running toward the train, the last train of the evening. Her path toward the lake was cut off and her one desire was to elude the guards.

People swarmed to get on the train and for a second or two Aimée was lost in the crowd. But the hood of her cape fell, revealing the flaming red hair, and the shouting began anew. Wildly, Aimée looked around, seeking escape from the approaching guards.

"Cécile, what a surprise!" The man reached out to steady her and Aimée looked up into the face of Gaston Ferbes, seeing the delight in his eyes at her sudden appearance.

"Oh, Gaston," Aimée whispered frantically. "Help me—I am being followed."

Seeing the guards bearing down upon them, the conductor hesitated only an instant.

"Come quickly. I will hide you."

He led her through the passenger car to the ground at the other side and pushed her to the back of the train.

"Don't be afraid, Cécile. There's only one person in the freight car, and he's too drunk to harm you. I'll let you out when we reach New Orleans . . . no one will think of looking for you here."

The freight car! The last car attached to the Sunday evening train, for drunks, pickpockets, and lawbreakers being delivered to the police back in the city.

"You promise me you will let me out when we reach New Orleans?"

"Of course. Do we not have a date for a late supper?"

He slid open the door and lifted her up into the dark opening. "Here, take my lantern—but make sure you cover it with something until we get underway. There must be no signs of light coming from this car."

The sound of the bolts sliding back into place gave an awful finality to what she had done. Even if she decided now that she did not want to go to New Orleans, it was too late. She was locked away—completely in the hands of a middle-aged man who was helping her because of his own desire for adventure after his dull routine on the Pontchartrain line.

The train remained in the station. Why did it not start up? Aimée, sitting in the darkness of the freight car with her cape over the lantern, heard only the loud drunken snore from a corner of the freight car, and voices outside, nearer and nearer, until they sounded beside the freight car.

"And what is in here?" the voice questioned, while a hand thumped the sides of the car.

"The drunk you handed over to me to be taken back to jail," the conductor replied.

"Oh yes, the pokey car—I can hear his snore now. Well, the girl couldn't be hiding in there, that's for sure."

"Are you certain you saw her coming toward the train?" the conductor asked.

"She came this way, all right. But she's eluded us before. Guess she's done it again," the man said in a disappointed voice.

"Would you like to go over the train again?" Gaston's voice inquired.

"No, that's not necessary. Well, guess you can be on your way. I won't hold you up any longer."

The voices evaporated and within a short time Aimée heard the building up of steam and the release of the brakes, setting the wheels into a slow, jerking motion until the wheel parts, forced to travel in the same direction, began to work smoothly together. The whistle sounded, and only then did Aimée feel she had escaped.

But one dilemma was swapped in Aimée's mind for another. How could she avoid spending the rest of the evening with Gaston Ferbes, her rescuer?

A sudden wave of nausea swept over her. It was not surprising because of the constant rolling motion of the freight car, coupled with the stench of the straw that she was forced to sit upon. But the lantern was a comfort, chasing away the dread and utter darkness. Aimée glanced uneasily in the corner, but the man had not stirred. Soon the trip would be over. The terminus was not far away.

The toot of the train announced their arrival into the station. Quickly Aimée blew out the lantern and traveled in darkness the last remaining yards. There was a busy, swarming hum of noise—the passengers leaving the train. And then Aimée could hear only the belching of steam, the cooling of fire from the tired old iron dragon, home at last.

Aimée waited in the darkness. Surely the conductor had not forgotten her. Why did he not come? Suddenly the sound of voices reverberated along the tracks.

"I will bring him out for you," the conductor offered. "There's only one tonight."

Aimée fled farther into the dark corner when the bolts scraped against the wood. The conductor, not even glancing toward her, dragged the drunken man out of the freight car as he talked to the policeman nearby.

The doors were bolted again, and in her fright Aimée almost called out to Gaston. Her fingers gripped the bar

154

on the inside of the door, and she clenched her teeth hard to keep from crying out.

He was coming back for her—of course, he was coming back . . . after he had gotten rid of the policeman. He would not forget her in this foul-smelling freight car. He could not!

When the bolts finally sounded again, Aimée was almost hysterical with relief.

"You may come out, *L'Ange flambé*. The coast is clear," the voice said with an element of awe.

"Why . . . why do you call me that?" Aimée whispered.

"All of New Orleans calls you that—the Flaming Angel. You have become famous, my dear—a thorn in the flesh of General Butler—coming in and out of New Orleans at will, and disappearing in the very faces of the men he has hired to track you down. But do not stand here—I know you must hurry."

"You mean . . . you are not holding me to the . . . promise?"

"It is too dangerous for you—much as I would like an evening with you," he replied in a disappointed voice. "But if you ever need help again, you know where to find me."

"Thank you, Gaston," Aimée said humbly, and rapidly disappeared, her cloak wrapped around her to hide her flaming hair—*L'Ange flambé*.

It was now the third week of November and the South was crying with hurt. Vicksburg was once more laid to siege, this time faced with the most powerful army Grant could gather. The town had become another Jericho, with Grant's Army of the Tennessee surrounding it, blowing its ram's horn to tumble down the walls. And the whole South shook at the devastating noise.

This time Basalt had received the message and was waiting with the horse in the usual place. Aimée, leaving John in steaming agitation at Thornfell, slipped into New Orleans. She had not told John of her near capture, but he had guessed.

"At all costs" the communiqué read. And this time Aimée pursued her mission knowing that if she failed to return with the precious chemical, the cost would indeed be great. "At all costs" meant that the chemical used for the fuses was more important than her own life. Aimée would guard it with just that—her life.

She slept hard in the little storage room that night at the pharmacy. And she was content to rest throughout the next day until it was time to leave.

Monsieur O'Brie looked far older to Aimée than he had the last time she had seen him. This time he did not even attempt to hide from her his increasing illness .

"Time is running out for many of us, Aimée. But if we succeed in this effort, I shall die happy, knowing that we have done our part. This is the last of the chemical, Aimée. I can get no more, so—"

Monsieur O'Brie did not finish his sentence. The noise at the front of the pharmacy interrupted him. The crash of the door sent Aimée out the back in a scurry, with the satchel in her hands. She had no time to gather up her cape or say good-bye—or think of anything but escaping from the soldiers with the fulminate of mercury.

Out of the darkness Lisette appeared and the shocked Aimée realized that once again Lisette had trailed her. Running down the street away from Lisette as fast as she could sprint, her red-gold hair flying behind her, Aimée dared not look back, although she knew they were following her—the soldiers and Lisette—spreading the net to snare her.

The moon was bright, too bright for a clandestine mission, too bright to hide the golden-red hair.

The catch in her side was painful and Aimée knew she could not keep up the tortured pace for long. Her lungs screamed for air, gasping and gulping hungrily. Yet she continued running, knowing that the horse, hidden in the stall at the livery stables, was lost to her as a means of escape.

She was the fox chased by the hunter, the red fox flushed from her den by the hounds, her only hope of escape to reach the lake and the waiting boat.

On through the night she fled, with her pursuers behind her. The enforced rests, snatched now and again, were not nearly long enough.

Heading in the general direction of the lake, almost five tortured miles in the distance, Aimée lost her way. She reached the shoreline by a new route and now she was nowhere near the place where the boat lay hidden.

Exhausted from carrying the burden, the satchel hanging heavily from her shoulders, Aimée felt it impossible to go farther without rest. Collapse was inevitable if she could not find a place to rest for an adequate time before running again.

The hunted deer sometimes ran itself to death before the steady pursuit of the hunter. Could humans succumb to the same fate? Aimée's heartbeats now had a swishing sound—the rushing of her life's blood pumping from her heart and lungs in answer to the demands she made on her body. She could go no farther. She must hide from the moonlight that lit up the old shell road and the scrubby pines—the voluptuous light of the full moon that made a mockery of the darkness.

An eerie whitewashed cabin loomed before her—a place to hide and rest. But somehow its menacing air made Aimée hesitate to use it. She went instead to one of the cruder, smaller cabins dotting the shore nearby. The cabin she chose had a look of total desertion, with its boarded-up windows and sagging steps. Weeds grew through the rotting treads in a tangled mass and threatened to trip her as her feet moved toward the porch. The small weight of Aimée's body made the little porch groan.

Pushing against the closed door, she expected it to come open easily, but the wood remained firmly latched. She tried again until the voices of her pursuers and the fanning lights made her abandon her effort and seek another shelter.

On to the whitewashed cabin she went, forgetting her earlier foreboding. The door opened easily and she stumbled into the unlighted hallway and waited, listening for the voices outside.

Footsteps sounded on the porch of the other cabin. The porch protested by its creaks and groans, and Aimée, still breathing hard, listened as her pursuers, attempting to get inside the abandoned cabin, discussed her.

"She's around here somewhere," a voice stated positively.

"Maybe she's hiding in one of the other cabins closer to the water."

"Well, we'll just have to spread out and search every cabin."

The voices grew fainter, indicating that the men were concentrating their search closer to the lake. Aimée's hands trembled and she wiped the nervous perspiration from her forehead.

It was hard to wait, knowing that they were searching for her. But having eluded them so far, she must not do anything foolish to draw their attention to her or her hiding place.

Aimée's gasps for air were now quieting, and her breathing, although much too fast, showed signs of returning to near normal. Her senses, previously aware only of the danger of being caught and of the voices outside, now took in her surroundings.

She wrinkled her nose at the odor of smoke and the aroma of food. Had someone else recently used the cabin as a hiding place? Or worse—was someone still inside, not declaring himself by light or motion? At the thought, her scalp prickled and she moved toward the door. Aimée's hand groped for the knob, her mind undecided where the greater danger lay—inside or out.

At the sight of the veiled light, she quickly jerked her hand back and turned toward the intruder coming down the hall.

"Thought I heard the door open. It took him long enough to send it. Do you have it with you?" the woman asked.

"What . . . what do you mean?" Aimée croaked.

"The whiskey, girl, the whiskey," the impatient woman replied.

Aimée clung to the satchel and replied in a frightened voice, "I . . . no . . ."

Chapter 16

The black woman took the satchel from Aimée's hands even as she protested.

"We may have enough without it, but I wouldn't want to run out. Not good for the business, you know." She took a deep look at Aimée, noticing her rapid breathing.

"What's the matter, child? Are you afraid?"

"No—that is . . ."

The woman laughed. "I know what it is. This is your first time and you're not sure you want to meet the spirits that Mama Rousseau is going to conjure tonight."

"Yes, that's it," Aimée quickly admitted.

"Well, come. The others are waiting. Just put your money in the plate at the door."

Reluctantly she walked with the woman, but upon entering the room, Aimée realized that she had no money with her. It was in the cape that she had left behind.

"I . . . I do not have any money with me," she whispered to the woman.

"Then take your place in the circle. You can pay later," the woman said in a hurried voice.

Noticing little but that the woman was placing her satchel on the hutch, Aimée sat down on the floor in the space that had been made for her. Assured that the satchel would remain safe for a while, she looked around the circle at the people. Black and white together they sat, their attention completely on what was happening in the center of the room.

No wonder Aimée had felt reluctant to seek shelter

here. The room cried with the silent, protesting voices of spirits that did not wish to be awakened. But the priestess had willed it, and even now was preparing the road to reach the spirits of the dead.

In the center of the room was a table with a black candle, knife, and bowl. Seated at the table was a gigantic black woman, Mama Rousseau, dressed completely in white. The white tignon on her head magnified the glistening black satin of her skin and the black eyes appeared strange and compelling in the candlelight.

Caught up in the drama, the circle of people sat forward, as if afraid to miss one movement of the ritual. The priestess's helper brought a white rooster to the table and offered it to Mama Rousseau. With an expert twist of the knife, the woman in white cut the rooster's neck and allowed the blood to drip into the bowl. There was a murmur of approval at the deed and the crowd settled back while the helper restrained the rooster's dying spasms.

Aimée turned her head, sick at the sight, but she dared not leave. The soldiers were still outside.

While Mama Rousseau began her incantations over the bowl of blood, the helper went to the large kettle hanging on the hook over the hearth. As she stirred the mixture—gumbo by the odor—Aimée watched her. The woman lifted something from the pot and laid it on the hearth. It was a large snake that had been cooked with the gumbo.

Aimée gasped in stunned disbelief. But of course—the snake worshippers. She should have remembered. But who would have the stomach to eat the gumbo prepared in the voodoo way?

Even as she shuddered at the thought, the woman filled individual bowls with the gumbo and began passing them around the circle of people who sat in semidarkness.

Aimée hurriedly passed each bowl that came to her until the woman next to her stated, "No, that one is for you." And she was left with the unwanted bowl in her hands.

She stared at it, unable to force herself to partake.

"Drink it!" the woman urged. "Or Mama Rousseau will be offended."

Aimée shut her eyes, and gripping the bowl with a determined hand, placed her lips on its rim as the others were doing and pretended to drink. The mutterings in the center of the room mercifully took the attention from Aimée, who quickly rid herself of the offensive bowl.

The woman in the white tignon stared at the light of the candle. Her lips moved in a more agitated manner and she began to shake and roll her eyes.

"The spirit's comin' on 'er," a man uttered.

"Hush!"

"I see . . . flaming hair and danger."

Aimée jumped at the woman's sudden pronouncement.

"Etienne—Etienne is coming to warn you . . ."

The strangeness of the room did things to Aimée's eyes. As if hypnotized by the ritual, she could almost see Etienne standing by Mama Rousseau's chair. She rubbed her eyes to clear them and the outline disappeared. But Mama Rousseau was walking toward Aimée and taking her by the hand.

"No," Aimée whispered in fright, but Mama Rousseau could not hear her.

"Go with her, child," the helper urged.

Aimée was now in the center of the room. The shredded moss, hanging near the fireplace, was draped over her head, hiding the red-gold hair, and the dingy white, foul-smelling cloak was wrapped around her body. Mama Rousseau, dipping her hands into the bowl on the table, smeared Aimée's face with the rooster's blood just as the door burst open and the soldiers strode into the room.

Mama Rousseau cried out another incantation, paying no attention to the soldiers.

"What do you know—a voodoo ritual. Heard about 'em, but never seen one."

The helper glared at the soldier as if to silence him.

The two soldiers stared at each person in the half-lighted room. Then, satisfied that their prey was not among them, they closed the door and left.

In no hurry to finish the ritual, Mama Rousseau continued with her incantations, and just when Aimée felt she could stand it no longer—this participation in such a bizarre ceremony—the moss was removed from her head, the blood wiped from her face, and she was allowed to find her place again near the door.

By this time the people in the circle were drinking the whiskey that had been passed around. Mama Rousseau began to shake again as another spirit seemed to grip her. While everyone drank and watched the large black woman, Aimée looked to make sure that the satchel was still in its place on the hutch. Stealthily she got up from the circle and fled from the room, taking the satchel with her as she left.

"Wait! The spell is not set yet! You don't have the *gris-gris* to throw in the enemy's path!"

The helper ran toward her but Aimée was already down the hall and out the door.

The boat—if I can make it to the boat, Aimée thought. Carefully she headed down the swampy path. The willow copse had to be somewhere near.

Her legs had to be urged to move on, for she was still weak from her strange experience. Rubbing her cheek, Aimée still felt the rooster's blood and she shuddered, remembering the moment when Mama Rousseau had used the knife.

But at least the room had provided a temporary haven. It was almost like the Passover long ago in Egypt, thought Aimée, when the lintels of the houses had been smeared with blood to keep all within safe when the Angel of Death had passed over. She herself had been smeared with blood, and the soldiers had passed her by. She would have to think of this more fully when she had the time. Now she was concerned only with reaching the boat.

The night had become quiet—unusually quiet—and Aimée pushed herself until the willow copse was finally in sight. A few yards more and then—the boat. Was it possible, after all, that she had escaped?

The water had a welcoming look and Aimée sighed in relief. But her relief was premature. The guards suddenly emerged from the darkness and blocked her path. Lights appeared everywhere, pinning her against the darkness, and hands reached out to grab her.

Aimée quickly flung her satchel into the water and fell to the ground. . . .

"She's the one, all right. A regular little red-headed hurricane, this one."

The voice floated through the air and Aimée's body ached from the jolting of the wagon on the road.

"Wonder what they'll do to her?"

"Couldn't even guess. If she was a man, she'd be hanged more'n likely, but bein' a mere slip of a girl, it don't seem right somehow. Maybe they'll jus' keep her a prisoner in the Castle till the war's over."

"And maybe the colonel will let her warm his bed durin' the waitin'. Gets mighty lonely in a prison, I'm told."

The two men chuckled. In anger at their words, Aimée tried to sit up. But her hands and feet were bound tightly, restricting her movements. She fell back against the side of the wagon.

At the sound, one of the men turned and stared at her. "Well, little Miss Rebel, ya finally came to, did ya?"

"Where . . . where are you taking me?" Aimée demanded.

"To the Castle," the heavy man in the blue uniform answered. "But if ya think you're goin' to be the fairy princess there, you'll be sadly disappointed."

Both men laughed at the joke.

Aimée ignored the laugh. "The Castle?" she questioned.

"Used to be a castle," the same heavy man explained. "Now, it's a prison. And once inside, ya never get out. It's on the canal, with a moat surroundin' it. Even the rats can't escape. Some fancy gent built it for his fine lady, with turrets and a dungeon and everything. I think you'll find it an interestin' place."

The sentry's voice calling through the darkness cut the explanation short.

"Who goes there?"

"Corporal Johnson, with a new prisoner for Colonel Hubel," the soldier on the wagon shouted. "Let down the drawbridge."

In a few minutes the wagon rumbled across the bridge and into the yard of the old castle. Soon the wagon came to a creaking stop and Corporal Johnson stooped beside

Aimée, untying the ropes that bound her hands and ankles.

"Up you go," he said, helping Aimée to her feet. But Aimée could not stand alone. Her feet crumpled under her. He reached out and caught her before she fell.

"Reckon you're still pretty stunned," the corporal said.

The man carried her into the Castle where he laid her on a cot and again stooped beside her, this time to rub vigorously her hands and wrists that were swollen from the ropes. "Got to get a little circulation back into ya, girl."

"Private," he yelled over his shoulder to the soldier on duty, "get some hot coffee in here in a hurry."

"Thank you," Aimée whispered. "You're very kind."

"Got a daughter 'bout your age. Reckon you've gotten under my skin a little, even if ya are a Rebel," he commented gruffly.

Before long the private was at the door with the coffee. Aimée looked up and standing before her was Raoul, her *grand-père*'s servant, now in Union uniform. He gave no hint that he had ever seen her before, but handed the tin cup of coffee to the corporal and left.

Offering the cup to Aimée, the corporal stalked out of the room without another word. The door closed and the key turning in the old lock made a squeaking sound.

Aimée sat trembling, drinking the black coffee, and then, exhausted, she lay down on the cot not knowing what the day would bring.

At the sound of the key turning in the lock, Aimée sat up and brushed her tangled hair out of her eyes. Her head ached and she was cold. There had been no blanket on the cot and her body was stiff, as if she had curled into a knot in an effort to keep warm.

The soldier with a sergeant's stripes on his sleeve stood looking at her for some time from the doorway before removing the key from the lock and coming inside, holding the key in his hand.

"So you're the new prisoner," the soldier said with a grinning leer.

Aimée remained silent, still sitting on the cot, the only piece of furniture in the room.

"I can see the colonel is going to have his fun questioning you—but lucky for me, he won't be back until later in the day."

The sergeant closed the door and locked it from the inside, dropping the key into his coat pocket. He walked slowly toward Aimée. At his action, she stood up, her heart quivering in fear.

"I think, little Rebel, that the colonel owes me a little fun, too."

Aimée clenched her fists in anger and said in a cold voice, "Do not touch me, monsieur."

He laughed as Aimée backed farther away from him. He reached out for her, drawing her to him. Like a spitting cat cornered by an enemy, she reached up and clawed his face.

"Why, you little—" He felt his face with one hand while holding her with the other.

Then using both hands, he picked her up and threw her on the cot, tearing at her dress immediately. Her protests were drowned by his hot, moist lips covering her mouth. The violent creaks of the cot told of her struggle, but she was no match for his strength, which had fanned to a flaming anger at her repulsion of him. He pinned her down and she was now helpless against him. When Aimée thought all was lost, a knock sounded at the door.

"Damn!" he muttered, raising himself from her. "What is it?" the sergeant demanded in a disgusted voice.

"I see the major comin' for inspection, Sergeant Lugby. You tol' me to tell you when I saw him." It was Raoul's voice coming through the slit in the door.

The sergeant took the key from his pocket and unlocked the door. Raoul peered inside and Aimée turned red with shame at being so degraded before her former servant.

"Out!" the sergeant's voice yelled. "Out, little Rebel. You don't think I'm going to let the major spoil my fun, do you?"

He turned to Raoul. "Delay him, Private, until I've

returned from hiding this tasty piece from his prying eyes."

Sergeant Lugby twisted her arm and forced Aimée through the doorway, down the hall to the winding stairs. She had no strength to fight him as he half dragged her down the steps.

"Where . . . where are you taking me?" For the second time in a matter of hours Aimée had need to ask the question.

"Every castle has a dungeon," he answered. "It's dark and filled with rats, but maybe that's just what you need to take a little spirit out of you. But don't worry—I won't let you stay there long."

"Please," she begged, swallowing her pride. "Please don't leave me in a dark dungeon."

He twisted her arm even more, forcing her on ahead of him. Then a door opened and Aimée was thrust inside, with no hope of being found by anyone.

She sank to the floor amid a scurrying sound, and the tears that she had vowed she would never shed again spilled down her cheeks in an agony of terror.

This was far worse than any fear that she had ever experienced—worse than the terror she had lived with from childhood. She was locked away . . . and if the sergeant forgot her, she would be left to die in the dark, alone. Her only hope of being rescued lay with the sergeant, who had already promised her another kind of death.

The gnawing sound of the rats reminded her that she was not alone, after all. Suddenly Aimée stood, kicking at the furry creature that had brushed across her foot, but the strangled scream of terror was stuck in her throat.

Finally she sank down onto the cold dark floor, her knees unable to support her body. Paralyzed with fear, Aimée lost all feeling of time. It could have been hours, it could have been only minutes, when she heard the whining and clicking of dogs' paws on the stone floor.

"What is it, Fréki? Geri, what's the matter, boy?"

Bryan! It was Bryan's voice!

The sergeant replied, "They're probably smelling out rats in the dungeon. That's all that's down there, Major.

Wouldn't you rather go on upstairs? There's a nice lunch waiting for you, and some good wine, too."

"My job is to inspect the entire facilities, Sergeant. And that means every inch." Bryan's voice was firm.

"Well then, wouldn't you rather leave your dogs with the private on duty? He'll take good care of them."

"The dogs go with me," the major answered.

Aimée reached toward the door and her mouth opened to call to Bryan. But no sound came . . . her voice was gone.

It had happened in her nightmares—the sudden loss of voice when she was unable to scream for help, unable to do anything but wait for some menace to envelop her. But it had never happened in real life. Desolate and lost, Aimée realized she was caught up in a nightmare, and all cries for help were denied her.

The whining grew louder and then Aimée could hear the frenzied scratching at the cell door.

"Open it, Sergeant," Bryan ordered.

"But I don't have a key," the sergeant resisted.

"Find one, Sergeant, or I'll shoot it off."

"Yes, sir."

The door creaked open and the light of the lantern blinded Aimée's turquoise eyes, wide with terror, as hands reached out to take her.

"Aimée—Aimée," the voice said, over and over. She was lifted into strong arms, up, away from the darkness and into the light.

His hands bathed her face and attempted to adjust her torn dress. His low, threatening voice, cold as ice, far more dangerous than his shouts, talked to the sergeant—but still, Aimée was unable to speak. She sat where Bryan had put her, not moving, while the whirlwind went on around her.

"If you had harmed one hair of her head, Sergeant, you would now be floating in the moat, face down."

"But, Major, you can hardly blame me," the sergeant protested. "She's a tasty little dish, even if she *is* a Rebel spy. You can't blame me for wanting to have some fun with her before turning her over to the colonel. The colonel will have his fun with her, you can bet your bottom dollar."

"You will not be turning my wife over to the colonel," Bryan replied.

The sergeant choked when he realized what Bryan had said.

"Your . . . your wife?"

"Yes, my wife," Bryan repeated. "And I am taking my wife with me. Get the papers for me to sign, Sergeant. And when your colonel returns, you can tell him that she will be under my parole. I will take full responsibility for her."

"Yes, sir!"

Chapter 17

Bryan carried Aimée to the waiting carriage and tucked the army supply blanket and lap robe around her. The horse he had ridden to the Castle was tied to the back of the carriage and the two army mules, harnessed to the borrowed carriage, trotted across the drawbridge and onto the road leading into New Orleans.

Bryan kept his anger under the surface and talked quietly and soothingly, aware that the fragility of Aimée's emotions could be shattered by a harsh or unkind word.

Aimée sat, mute and tense, with an occasional shiver as the only outward sign that her body was responding to anything. Bryan, pulling the lap robe about her, kept up an inconsequential monologue whose low, unhurried monotony lulled Aimée into a more relaxing posture, although the meaning of his conversation was beyond her consciousness.

Still, no words came from Aimée. It was as if by remaining mute she could suppress the feeling from the dungeon—suppress the wild scream of agony that lay trapped in her throat, waiting to erupt.

The shining benign turrets of the Castle, their peaks caught in the glistening sunlight, gave no hint of the dark regions beneath. There was no outward sign of the malignant terror that she had experienced in the dungeon.

Aimée finally turned her head from the Castle to stare with hurt, bewildered eyes at the man beside her.

Bryan's features had grown more sharply distinctive in the months that had separated them. He had lost weight and the mark on his cheek had toned down from an angry red welt to a white raised scar, not quite so noticeable or malevolent-looking as before.

Aimée listened in stillness to Bryan's voice as his words began to make sense. He talked about the weather, the stormy, snowy winters spent in Massachusetts, his childhood home with his parents and his brother Clay. Then Bryan's voice stopped the strange, soothing monologue to speak to the mules, giving them encouragement as they plodded through the muddy ruts on their way home. . . .

Home? Where was her home? Aimée had refused to think of the house in the Vieux Carré as home these past months. Thornfell was now her home. As she thought of Thornfell, she wondered if the Yankees had already destroyed it. But if the Yankees had connected her just with Monsieur O'Brie, perhaps Thornfell was safe. Only the raiders had seen her at Thornfell, and they would not connect the girl gathering eggs on a remote plantation with the notorious spy who crossed the lake to New Orleans. And Lisette did not know of Thornfell, so she could not inform the authorities.

John Runefelt and the others would wonder what had happened to her. She must send word to them that she was safe, even if she had failed in her mission. But how to send word? And was she sure that she was actually safe from reprisal by the enemy?

It was all so exhausting, just thinking about it. Aimée

was tired—tired of the war, tired of a life that took the best of a person and used it to feed the animosity that divided human beings. If the Yankees would just leave them alone, let them have the freedom to be a separate nation—as the colonies had separated themselves from England—instead of forcing them to their knees and then trampling them to the ground.

Aimée closed her eyes in exhaustion and then a hand was touching her gently, a voice saying, "Aimée, wake up. We're home."

Her eyes fluttered open to see Bryan leaning over her and she drew back in sudden fright as the horse, tied to the carriage, whinnied at the same time, causing the mules to move forward with a lurch.

"Whoa," Bryan yelled, grasping the reins to stop them.

The noise drew Anderson out of the house, onto the street. The taciturn man's eyes met Aimée's and the expression was one of relief. He took charge of the horse, mules, and carriage once Bryan explained it was borrowed equipment, and acting as if he were charged with overseeing army mules each day, disappeared with them while Bryan carried Aimée into the house.

Aimée slept a long, troubled sleep, crying out in fear, her voice freed at last.

"It's all right, Aimée. You're safe." The man's voice was kind and reassuring and, with a little dry sob similar to an infant's that has stopped crying but is still sad, Aimée settled down to sleep once more.

The crackling of the fire was a pleasant sound. As Aimée awoke, her eyes gradually grew accustomed to the light and the sparks shooting from the hearth. The logs shifted, sending a jutting of surprised embers against the fire screen. Lizzie must have come in while she was asleep to light the fire.

But the room was not the safe haven under the stairway to the attic at Thornfell. This was the room in the Vieux Carré—hers and Bryan's room. And as this knowledge sank in, Aimée's eyes found the still, silent figure of her husband, slumped in the easy chair, his face partially hidden by the shadows of the room. In quietness Aimée watched Bryan, his troubled face taut, even in sleep.

Her heart went out to this man as she realized what her actions must have cost him. Of course he was angry with her. And why shouldn't he be? But she had not asked him to marry her. And he had been aware of her feelings toward the Union Army. It was the age-old story of a divided heart—her love for one of the enemy struggling against her fierce loyalty to her people. And at that moment Aimée knew only torment.

If Bryan could feel some measure of understanding for what she had done . . . but he was a man who saw only one way—*his* way, which he believed was the right way. Aimée knew his character was much like Grand-père's—he, too, would never back down from his beliefs—and she knew he would never forgive her for her role as a spy. He would never be able to love her as she loved him.

The terror of the dungeon slipped away and her heart became manacled to a new terror—that by some word or action she would inadvertently show that she loved him. She must not allow this to happen. She could risk Bryan's hate and his contempt for her, but never his pity. Better for her to play the recalcitrant spy who hated the enemy. She must never let him guess what she felt for him, how much she loved him.

Bryan stirred. Watching with wary eyes, Aimée sat up in bed, throwing back the long strands of hair that had half-covered her face in sleep.

The movement caught Bryan's attention and he stretched his long frame before getting up to stand beside the bed.

"So, you are awake now," he said, smiling that strange, taunting smile. "I trust you are feeling better, Aimée, after your traumatic ordeal."

Aimée looked at him, sensing his challenge for her to speak. Her voice was low but clear .

"At least with the rats, monsieur, I knew my fate. Now, with you as my jailor, I am uncertain."

The anger sparked from his eyes into the clipped, harsh words with which he responded to her gibe.

"You are lucky, Aimée, not to be sharing that cell still with the rats. If it had not been for Raoul—"

"Raoul told you I was in the Castle?" Aimée cut in.

"Yes, but he had no idea where the sergeant had hidden you. Perhaps you would have preferred the sergeant as your jailor . . . to me?" Bryan questioned with a biting tone.

Aimée quickly shook her head.

Bryan continued, forcing his voice to remain quiet, and the coldness alarmed Aimée far more than the words.

"Since I have no alternative except to be your jailor, I want you to understand how you will be treated. I will not pretend to ask for your promise not to escape. Knowing you, you will attempt it as soon as my back is turned. So when I am away there will be a guard at your door. You will remain here with Tink and Anderson and you will not be allowed outside this house. There will be no more carrying of dangerous goods across the lake to your precious Rebels."

Aimée swept the covers from her, and turning her back to him, walked toward the fire.

He followed her and grabbed her by the arm. "Do not turn your back on me while I am speaking, Aimée."

His touch electrified her and she tried to escape from his grasp but it was futile. He tightened his grip and with a fury seldom seen by Aimée, Bryan said, "You little fool! Did you not realize the danger you were constantly in? You could have been shot, Aimée, for your foolishness."

"I *was* shot at, monsieur, but Yankee bullets so often miss their mark!"

Bryan's face turned white. "So you were in even more danger than I had imagined. When did that happen?"

"When . . . when I crossed the lake that first night, with the letters and the medicine."

"Aimée," he groaned, pulling her closer to him, "would you want your face marred as mine is? To have people turn their eyes away in disgust? Were you willing to be blown to pieces or be maimed for a losing cause? Your Rebels cannot win . . . you know that. Why do you persist in such foolishness?"

"Is it foolishness to fight for what one believes in, monsieur?" Aimée retorted. "If that is so, then you are foolish as well. And if someone told you today that you

172

could not win the war, would you lay down your arms and refuse to fight?"

Again the anguished moan came from Bryan's throat. "Would that a tiny particle of such loyalty had been transferred to your husband. You have no idea, Aimée, what I have suffered because of you."

"I . . . I am sorry, Bryan, that I have been such an embarrassment to you. Do you think you could explain to your friends that I was your mistress and not your wife? Then your chances for promotion would not be hindered. After all, I did not ask to be your wi—"

His cruel kiss cut off her words and she struggled in his arms. Then he held her at arm's length and muttered in a menacing tone, "But you *are* my wife, and you shall be treated as such, even though you despise your husband. And as your husband, I will see to it that you do not get into any more trouble while this war lasts—even if I have to tie you to the bed!"

"Is that the only way you Yankees know how to fight women? To tie them to a bed and force your attentions on them?"

He pushed her from him and stumbled from the room. Her taunting words hung in the still air.

Chapter 18

Aimée heard the click of the key. Once again, she was a prisoner in the bedroom. She could not forget the humiliation of that first night that Bryan had locked her in the bedroom, only to return with the outrageous clothes that he had forced her to wear. And now Aimée knew another kind of humiliation that she could not brush away. She was a prisoner, paroled to her own husband, and if he lived up to his threats, he would see that she had no opportunity to escape either his shackles or his attentions.

Aimée paced restlessly up and down the room the rest of the afternoon, stopping now and then to peer out the window into the garden that lay bare in the November mist. The place where the strawberries had grown was now a barren spot of earth, and the coral vines lay dormant, waiting for spring.

The gate into the courtyard squeaked and Aimée, standing and watching for Bryan to return, saw a soldier with rifle in hand take his place before the door that opened from the house into the court.

The guard that Bryan had promised—and he was in place so soon. It had taken Bryan little time to make sure that she was watched. If she attempted to leave, would the guard shoot her? If he had his orders, it would not matter that she was a girl, for she was a spy—a dangerous enemy to the Union.

Aimée heard the noise of someone unlocking the door to the bedroom. The tray of food appeared first, followed by the young girl, Tink. But her appearance was vastly different from that of a few months before.

"Tink, is it really you?" Aimée asked, delighted to see the girl.

Tink reacted with an embarrassed air and a coolness that Aimée had not thought possible.

"This is your supper, Mrs. Garrard. The major won't be comin' home for supper, and he . . . he asked that I bring a tray up to your room." The girl looked around and set the tray on the table before the fireplace. "Would you like some tea, or would you rather have coffee?"

"I'll have coffee later—but come, let me look at you, Tink," Aimée said with a lilt to her voice. "You have grown so much since I saw you. And you are so pretty."

Tink flushed and reluctantly stood still before Aimée. "The major says I'm getting to be a . . . regular beauty," she volunteered, forgetting the initial coolness.

"How old are you, Tink?" Aimée asked.

"Almost sixteen, Mrs. Garrard." Then Tink stiffened and said, "I must be getting back. Just ring if you want anything else."

"Thank you, Tink," Aimée said gravely as the girl turned and opened the door to leave. Aimée heard the key turn in the lock.

She stood gazing into the fire, thinking of Tink and realizing that the girl must be in love with Bryan from the way she acted. She had dismissed the idea previously, thinking that Tink was just a child, but actually, Tink was only two years younger than Aimée herself, and capable of a woman's feelings for a man.

Oh, Tink, not you, too. Did Bryan have the power to make every girl he met fall in love with him? He had been so arrogant, talking about the matchmaking mamas, so sure of himself.

And why shouldn't he be? Had he not made her fall in love with him? And was she not trembling, longing for his kisses even now—waiting for him to return to claim her as his wife? She ached for his touch, ached for his caresses, and she was ashamed that she wanted him so much.

Aimée heard the wheels of the *calèche* as it came into the courtyard. She ran to the window to watch for Bryan and her heart fluttered with a quickening beat.

Bryan did not come into the house. Tink had evidently been waiting for him in the doorway and he stepped down only long enough to help Tink into the carriage before turning the *calèche* and leaving the courtyard.

The fire that had blazed through the evening had been reduced to a few glowing coals, silently dying on the hearth. Aimée rose from the fireside and climbed into bed. Bryan was not coming to her room. She would share nothing with him that night. He had preferred Tink's company to hers. Again, in utter loneliness and desolation, Aimée sought the forgetfulness of sleep.

The next morning there was a knock on the bedroom door.

"Aimée," Bryan called through the door. "You are to appear before the board of inquiry at two o'clock today.

175

I will be back for you about one. Do you understand, Aimée?"

"Yes, Bryan," she answered, still feeling drugged from sleep.

It was after he had gone that the full impact of his words hit her. What would they do to her? Was this an official investigation, and would she be asked to betray her friends? And if she refused, would Bryan have the power to save her? But if she were shot as a spy, it would be much simpler for him, for Bryan would then be free of the marriage he had been tricked into.

Aimée was despondent all morning and she was no better when Bryan came home.

"Are you not ready, Aimée?" he asked after unlocking the door.

"Someone will have to help me with the dress. I . . . I cannot manage alone," Aimée said in a quivering voice. She averted her eyes to avoid letting him see her in such an emotional state.

"Here, let me help you," he said, and while helping her remove her wrapper, he spoke to her in the same soothing tone he had used in the carriage on the way home from the Castle. "You do not have to be worried, Aimée, about the inquiry. Just answer the questions truthfully. It is not something anyone would look forward to, but it should not last long."

The carriage and a uniformed driver waited outside. Bryan, taking Aimée by the arm, led her out the door. She shivered and Bryan glanced down at her, asking, "Where is your cape, Aimée?"

"I . . . I lost it," she replied. "But it doesn't matter. I am not that cold."

He still frowned as he helped her into the carriage. There was an awkward silence between them and neither made an attempt to speak as the horses clopped upon the cobblestones monotonously.

They were seated at a long table—four official-looking officers with grave faces. Aimée was led to a chair before them and asked to take her place. She was not certain that Bryan had even remained in the room.

"Mrs. Garrard, you realize the seriousness of the charges that have been brought against you." The officer speaking looked at her, waiting for an answer.

"Yes," she replied, looking him straight in the eye with her unwavering turquoise gaze.

The man cleared his throat and then looked over her head, as if embarrassed.

"You have been accused of carrying goods across Lake Pontchartrain to the enemy, and were caught while carrying a Confederate satchel, which you saw reason to dispose of in the lake. What was in the satchel, Mrs. Garrard?"

Why was he asking such a question? Did they not have the satchel, then? Or was he trying to get her to admit her guilt?

"The satchel speaks for itself, monsieur. Did you not look inside?"

Again the man cleared his throat. "Mrs. Garrard, the board of inquiry asks the questions, not the prisoner," he said in a severe tone. "Now, will you please inform the board what you were carrying?"

"I . . . I am not sure, monsieur."

"Come now, Mrs. Garrard. You are making it difficult for yourself." The man appeared angry, as the officer next to him whispered, "Maybe she did not know what it contained."

"Why were you in the city to begin with, without a pass?" the man continued, ignoring the response of his fellow officer.

"I . . . I was visiting a friend," Aimée replied.

"And that friend's name?"

"I cannot tell you."

"Mrs. Garrard, this is getting us nowhere. You say you are not sure what the satchel contained. You also refuse to give the name of the person you were with. We already have the answers to both questions. We merely wish you to admit to them. This reluctance on your part will not dispose the board to leniency in your case. So for your own safety, I suggest you answer the questions."

Aimée remained silent.

"Who were your contacts in the enemy's territory?" one of the other officers asked.

"Contacts? Do you mean where did I seek shelter after having my home here confiscated?" Aimée asked.

"That will do, Mrs. Garrard," the interrogator ordered. "You do admit then that you are opposed to the Union, even though your husband is a Union officer," he added sarcastically.

"I registered as your enemy before I left New Orleans, monsieur. I am listed as such in the official records."

Again the prosecutor appeared angry. Without saying anything else immediately, he glanced at the pocket watch he had placed on the table earlier.

"I think the board will adjourn to the square for a certain period of time. After the . . . er, spectacle, Mrs. Garrard, I believe you will be more kindly disposed to answering my questions. This board will recess until after the . . . er, event in the square."

The four men stood and Aimée also stood, not certain what was to come.

"Colonel, do you feel that this is . . . necessary?" Bryan was at Aimée's side, questioning the prosecutor.

"Yes," he said with a cool voice. "Your wife is proving a difficult prisoner. Perhaps seeing what happens to spies will loosen her tongue."

A look of anger crossed Bryan's face. "Colonel," Bryan said, lowering his voice in an anxious tone, "my wife is but a young girl . . ."

"If you are concerned for your wife's welfare, Major Garrard, I give you permission to accompany us."

Aimée was puzzled at the reluctance of the other officers to adjourn to the square. But at the insistence of the colonel, they left the inquiry room, acting as if they wanted no part of what was to follow.

By the time the official group reached the square, a crowd had gathered. Aimée looked up at the wooden scaffold placed in the square and then she noticed the hanging rope.

Was she to be witness to a hanging? Who could it be and what was to be gained by forcing her to watch? Aimée felt sick and she held onto her husband's arm. "Bryan," she whispered in a distressed voice.

"It's all right, Aimée. I'm beside you. Try not to look. Just close your eyes."

But Aimée did not close her eyes. She watched to see who the unfortunate person was—the one to be hanged publicly for his misdeeds.

The stoop-shouldered man walked slowly and proudly toward the scaffold. He turned his head and looked at Aimée, and for a split second there was recognition; then he passed on, walking up the steps.

Monsieur O'Brie! He was the one to be hanged! And the colonel was forcing her to watch.

Monsieur O'Brie took off his spectacles and handed them to the man beside him. The crowd was quiet. There were no derisive hoots for the condemned man—only silent homage for one willing to die for what he believed in, and for his part in trying to defeat the enemy.

Only the raucous sound of a crow flying overhead and the mild squeaking of the scaffold in the late November wind disturbed the silence.

The noose was put around the old man's neck, and then the block was knocked from under his feet, leaving him dangling in the air, his hands outstretched toward the rope around his neck. . . .

Aimée cried out, and in that moment a merciful darkness descended to blot out the view.

Chapter 19

Aimée was in the swaying carriage and Bryan held her in his arms. To go on forever feeling his strength was all she wished . . . never to wake up again . . . never to face the horror that she had just lived through . . . but the scene was indelibly stamped on her memory.

As the carriage rocked back and forth, Aimée saw the swinging of the rope, the surprised face of Monsieur O'Brie, and she uttered a cry.

"My darling," Bryan said, tightening his hold on her, "we will soon be home . . ."

Aimée would not be consoled. She sat by the hearth, huddled in her misery, and she shivered as if she would never be warm again. The supper tray lay untouched on the table and Bryan sat silently, broodingly, in the easy chair near her, making no attempt at conversation, but watching her, Aimée could feel, with his stern silver-gray eyes.

Bryan had stayed in the room with her, having his supper brought up on a tray also, as if he did not dare leave her alone even for the brief time it would take to eat downstairs.

The bleak day had fast turned into an early darkness and Bryan picked up a book to read by the lamplight. Finally Aimée leaned her head against the hearth stool, her eyes closed in emotional exhaustion, but the haunting terror would not leave her.

"Aimée, I think you would be more comfortable in bed," Bryan's voice gently admonished. "You cannot sleep the night on the hearth." He got up to walk toward the bell pull. "I will call Tink to help you get undressed."

"No!" Aimée's voice dissented. "I do not want Tink . . ."

Bryan stopped and looked at her questioningly, surprised at the vehemence in her voice. He walked to her, and taking both hands, pulled her to her feet. She turned her head from him, not wanting him to witness her tear-stained face.

"Aimée, Aimée," he whispered, holding her in his arms and stroking her hair. "I did not know that Colonel Lewe would be so heartless today. If I could only take away your distress . . ."

At his comforting words, she could no longer contain her grief. "Oh, Bryan," she said with a sob, "it was terrible." And she laid her head against his chest.

"Hush, my darling. Don't think about it. Erase it from your mind."

"I can't," she replied. "I will always remember his face, his handing his spectacles to the man, before—"

"Aimée!" Bryan's voice was stern. "You are not to think of it," he commanded. Then his voice softened and he said, "Where is your gown? It's time for you to be in bed."

"In the lower drawer," she responded. "But I am afraid to go to sleep."

"That doesn't sound like my fierce little Rebel," Bryan said in a cajoling manner.

He walked to the bureau and took out the nightgown that she had not taken with her to Thornfell. Then his gentle hands were helping her out of her dress and holding the gown to slip over her head, as he had done many times. Aimée did not protest his help. Numbed with grief, she was beyond the desire to resist and she clung to the strength that was Bryan.

It was bound to happen . . . in her need to be comforted. His lips brushed past her cheek and found her mouth and Aimée, forgetting her vow to be cool to him, responded.

She felt the tightening of his muscles and the sudden expiration of breath. His hand, caressing the small of her back, moved in a sensuous pattern along her spine and his lips found the vulnerable spot on her neck.

The quickening of heart and flesh made her alive as she had not been for the past two months, and Aimée did not protest when Bryan carried her to the high-post bed where, as a child, she had sought comfort of another kind from the terrors of the night.

It did not take long for Bryan to shed his clothes and Aimée, soft and compliant, nestled against his chest, seeking his warmth, his strength. For the first time that day she felt a pervading warmth through her body. The fires, long banked by their separation, took spark and blazed with an intensity that could not be ended.

His endearing words drowned out the harshness of the courtroom, the cruelty in the square, and Aimée responded to his needs with a matching need of her own—to be comforted, to be desired, to be loved.

Later in the night her troubled mind cried out, her sleep interrupted by unsettled dreams, but each time she awoke, she felt Bryan's sturdy frame beside her and, reassured by his nearness, she went back to sleep—if not entirely content, at least a little more resigned to her sadness of the day past.

Aimée awoke to the light streaming through the window. Bryan was not beside her. The remembrance of the night slowly flared over her. The empty place beside her slowly mocked her for her shameful behavior. At Bryan's touch, she had become weak, clinging to him, responding to him, until, out of pity, he had made love to her.

How could she face him when he came home that evening, knowing that she had reacted to his comfort as a beggar starving for a few cast-off crumbs? Now there would be no doubt as to how she felt. Bryan was probably pitying her at that very moment—the poor, lovesick girl so eager for his kisses that, in the heat of her desire, she had forgotten what the enemy had done to her friend, Monsieur O'Brie.

Idiot! Aimée reprimanded herself. Can you not keep anything from him? In her anger she became determined to show Bryan that the night had been a mistake. She would never again reveal her vulnerability to him.

Aimée heard the key in the lock and Tink opened the door to bring her breakfast tray to her. The girl was still distant, not lingering to chat, and Aimée willingly let her go.

Drinking the hot chocolate and eating the brioche, Aimée sat in bed and fumed and fussed, knowing she would never dare to say the things that came to mind to Bryan's face. A well-brought-up Creole girl was not supposed to have any desires of her own—she was only supposed to suffer the desires of her husband. Yet there was now no doubt of her fiery, passionate nature. And Bryan had been a witness to it.

The water in the ewer was cold and Aimée longed for a warm bath in the old brass tub. Instead she settled for a cold makeshift bath before dressing for the day.

She did not have many clothes and she missed the few that were at Thornfell, the clothes hanging in the bedroom under the stairway. And her cape . . . had the soldiers found it in Monsieur O'Brie's pharmacy? Were they holding it as evidence against her, to surprise her at the next inquisition?

It was the coldest part of the year, and if she ever needed the cape, it was now. But if she was to be kept a prisoner in one room, never allowed to go outside, then the cape was not such a loss after all.

The morning passed with the rapidity of a snail taking his daily walk. By the rattle of the tray outside her door, Aimée knew it was finally midday. Anderson, following behind Tink with the tray, also came into the room, carrying a box.

"This just came, Mrs. Garrard," the sergeant explained.

"Thank you, Anderson," Aimée said. "Just set it down anywhere."

She deliberately showed a disinterest in the box and waited for Tink and Anderson to leave. Despite the disappointment in their faces, Aimée did not dare open the box until they had left the room. What if it contained a message from John Runefelt or Cousin Jorge or Clotilde?

Finally her curiosity getting the upper hand, Aimée tore open the wrappings and a blue velvet cloak came into view. As she pulled it out of the box, the card drifted to the floor, but Aimée, not taking the time to retrieve it, tried on the cloak, looking at herself in it in the cheval glass. It was elegant and warm and suited her eyes. Bryan must have gotten it for her since he had asked her about her cape the day before. She hugged the cloak to her body, feeling its softness, and her thoughts about her husband softened.

And then she stooped to pick up the card, wondering what it would say. It was in the same bold masculine handwriting as the note slipped under her door that day in May—"In partial payment for a night of love . . ."

In payment! She gazed at the words, suddenly feeling like one of the girls at Madame Josephina's who sold her love to the highest bidder night after night, and was rewarded with some fancy trinket if she had been especially accommodating.

The cloak had a familiar look to it. Aimée had seen one like it before . . . that night, when she had watched Bryan with the woman in the *calèche*. The woman had worn one very similar. Was hers also in payment for a night of love?

Aimée felt sullied, degraded. Was this the way Bryan thought of her, no better than someone who sold her love for a trinket? Was this his revenge for her behavior the previous night? Or did it go back further, to the night he had been tricked into marriage?

Folding the cloak, Aimée returned it to the box and hid it in the armoire. She would never wear it, never acknowledge it. She would act as if that night had never happened.

Pacing restlessly up and down the length of the bedroom, Aimée picked up the whorled walnut box and wound the music mechanism. When it ran down, she studied each face in the daguerrotypes along the wall, and then picked up Grand-père's pipe that still lay on the mantel. She ran her fingers over the smooth wood and silver inlay before putting it back in its place.

What could she do to keep from going raving mad, locked away for the rest of the war in one small room filled with relics of another age? If she remained in the room much longer with nothing to do, she would get as crazy as Madame Blanc down the street.

The lute . . . the lute stored in the attic. Aimée remembered singing the old songs and playing the lute for Grand-père until Etienne teased her so much that she had put the instrument away, despite Grand-père's protests. She had not thought of it again until Cousin Clotilde had questioned her about her music. Were the strings still good? And would Anderson let her go up to the attic to find the instrument? She had to do something to wipe out the hurt of Bryan's note.

Aimée tugged impatiently at the bell pull, and when Tink came to the door, she called out, "Tink, please ask Anderson to come to the door . . . I need him."

She listened for the limping walk, and in a few minutes

Anderson was at the door asking, "Did you want to see me, Mrs. Garrard?"

"Yes, Anderson," she answered. "I . . . I would like to go up to the attic to get something. Will you take me, if I promise not to run away?"

There was an embarrassed silence, as if Anderson were uncertain as to what to do with her request.

"The guard is outside, is he not? You can give orders to him to shoot me if I attempt to leave."

The sound of the key in the lock gave her Anderson's answer. "That will not be necessary, Mrs. Garrard," he said with a red face. "Your word will be sufficient."

"Thank you, Anderson."

Aimée walked quickly toward the stairs, the strange attic stairs that had no railing to hold onto. As a child, Etienne had dared her to run up and down them, until Grand-père had stopped the game, saying it was too dangerous. Now Aimée gathered up her skirts, and while Anderson waited on the landing, she dashed up the steep steps to the attic.

Everything in the attic was covered with a layer of dust, despite the covers over the larger pieces of furniture. Aimée poked and searched, lifting covers until the sudden dispersal of dust made her sneeze. She found her sketch-book and the colored pencils, and Etienne's toy soldiers in a box, but the lute remained hidden from her.

She did not know what prompted her to open the little window in the attic dormer. Perhaps it was the dust, or it could have been the musty smell. But as she stood for a moment, breathing in the fresh air, a figure moved across the street.

It was John Runefelt! And he was watching her house. How long had he been there and what was he planning to do? Now was the time to get a message to Cousin Clotilde, while Anderson waited unsuspectingly on the landing.

Quickly Aimée tore one of the sheets from the sketch-book and with a dark pencil hurriedly wrote a note telling him that she had been released from the Castle and was safe for the moment, although under house arrest, and

185

asking him to give the news to Clotilde, who would be worried about her.

After folding the sheet into smaller squares, Aimée pushed it out the dormer window and, with crossed fingers, watched the paper glide slowly downward. A breeze lifted it and for a moment Aimée thought it might sail back into the walled courtyard. But it changed directions and landed on the banquette.

The man made no move to cross the street to retrieve it. Had he not seen it? Just when she had given up hope, he limped from his hiding place, picked it up, and quickly put it in his pocket.

Another limping walk echoed up the stairs and Aimée closed the window. Anderson appeared in the doorway and Aimée hastily lifted another dust cover.

"I know it's here," she said, speaking casually, "but I can't seem to find it."

"What is it, Mrs. Garrard? Perhaps I can help you find it."

"It's a lute, Anderson, stored in a case somewhere in one of the corners. I remember bringing it up myself, with the music."

His foot touched a leather case hidden under one of the dust covers. "Could this be it?" Anderson asked, pushing aside the cover.

"Oh, Anderson, how marvelous! You found it . . . thank you." Aimée impulsively kissed him on the cheek and then, recalling where she had stored the music, opened the drawer to the lowboy nearby.

Anderson stood up, holding the lute case in his hands, his uniform covered by fine dust and his face an apoplectic red.

"I think we had better be going, Mrs. Garrard. The major said he was coming home early today and I wouldn't like for you to be out of your room when he returns."

Sighing, Aimée said, "I wish you were my jailor, Anderson. You have been so kind to me."

Carrying the sheets of music, she left the attic. Anderson, with the lute case, followed behind.

Back in the room, she determined not to think of John Runefelt or the note she had surreptitiously gotten to him.

She became engrossed in tuning the lute and practicing the fingering. Without looking at the notes, she picked out a *maqam* that her great-great-*grand-mère* had played for the Comte, weaving an exotic spell about him with the Arabian music.

The old familiar feeling returned, and Aimée began to think of the lute as "al 'ud," the name the first Aimée had called it, and again she felt the atmosphere of the seraglio, with the melodies and rhythmic patterns of a long-ago age. This was why Etienne had teased her; for when she touched the strings, it was almost as if she were the beautiful sultana herself. Now Aimée realized that her ancestor had been a prisoner also, with a fat eunuch guarding the door. Somehow her story did not seem so romantic as it once had.

Aimée put the instrument aside, and looking out the window, saw the Union soldier guarding the courtyard. Over a hundred years apart, both Aimées had jailors. Ironic. At that moment Aimée felt closer than ever to her great-great-*grand-mère*.

Her anger flared again. How could Bryan treat her this way, locking her away and acting as if she were a mere bit of fluff, lightly giving her favors to him? The soothing power of the music disappeared as she heard the whistling in the hallway. Aimée did not turn her head when the door opened, but continued looking out the window.

"What? No kiss to greet your husband, Aimée?" he teased.

He was taken by surprise at the angry glint in the turquoise eyes. "And what price kiss, Bryan?" she said, confronting him. "What will you pay for a kiss?"

Bryan seemed confused at this attack.

"No amount could induce me to kiss a Yankee. I have been degraded enough by your actions of last night." In anger she had forgotten her resolve to dismiss the night from her memory.

The silver-gray eyes staring at her grew cold. "I was not aware that you were . . . averse to my actions last night, Aimée."

"How could you tell my true feelings, monsieur, when

187

you took advantage of my grief and then offered me payment, as if I were one of Madame Josephina's *filles de l'amour*?"

"Payment?" Bryan's puzzled look cleared and he laughed a hearty laugh that filled the room. "So that's what you're bristling about—my note with the cloak. Perhaps that was an unfortunate choice of words. How would you prefer that your husband show his gratefulness to a warm, loving wife? Or are your sensibilities so horrified that your Yankee husband could be so crude as to mention anything that happened under the covers? You did not seem to mind before."

"I do not wish to discuss it," Aimée said, staring out the window.

Her neck jerked at his sudden grasp, whirling her around to face him.

"We *will* talk about it, Aimée," Bryan argued.

In exasperation Aimée blurted, "Why didn't you let me stay at the Castle, Bryan, instead of bringing me back with you?"

"You may be back at the Castle sooner than you think," Bryan scolded, "if the marshall's office has its way."

Aimée lost the color in her cheeks. "What . . . what do you mean?"

"Just that I have maneuvered all day to counteract the colonel's orders that you be returned to the Castle. Your appearance before the board did nothing to endear you to them, or cause them to look favorably on your case."

Aimée noticed for the first time the strained look on her husband's face.

"I . . . I am sorry, Bryan. I did not mean to be such a shrew."

His cool indifference took command again. "I realize it is not pleasant for you to be locked up, Aimée, but I promise you that during your period of parole to me, you will not again be subject to my unwanted advances."

Then, opening the drawers of the bureau, he removed his shirts and all personal belongings, and as he did so, Aimée sat at the window, reduced to despair. She could never win against him.

Chapter 20

The forced inactivity of remaining alone with nothing to do was telling, and Aimée, so used to walking and riding, felt drained, not only emotionally, but physically as well. She had no appetite for food. She had no will to do anything, and on the third day she remained in bed, too weak to fight the slight nausea and the lethargy that pervaded her spirit. The lute lay, untouched, on the window seat.

She did not even look up when the door was unlocked.

"Are you ill, Aimée?" her husband asked, standing beside the bed. "Tink tells me that your meals have been untouched."

It must be the middle of the afternoon, she thought. What was Bryan doing home so soon? Aimée made no attempt to lift her head. And when she answered him, her voice was weak.

"I . . . I have not been hungry."

Bryan leaned over and put his hand across her brow. "You do not seem to have any fever, yet there must be something wrong. You are far too pale."

Aimée did not respond, and Bryan again stood, as if he were deep in thought.

"It could be the lack of fresh air," he suggested. "I think we will have to allow you an hour each day in the courtyard. I will tell Anderson before I leave New Orleans and he will see to it."

"You are . . . leaving?" Aimée asked.

"Yes. And I am not certain how long I will be away."

"When . . . will you be going?" she asked.

"Tomorrow morning," Bryan replied.

Again there was silence and Bryan, seeming uncertain, hesitated before finally walking toward the door and locking it behind him, leaving Aimée alone.

In the early hours of the next morning Aimée heard Bryan leave. He had not even come to tell her good-bye. But what could she expect from an estranged husband?

Later Anderson knocked on the door and waited until Aimée was dressed to help her down the stairs and into the garden.

It was a beautiful, pale sunny day, with little breeze, one of the soft delta days that occasionally crept unobtrusively into the winter calendar, a prelude to the early spring. Anderson fussed over Aimée, carrying her to the chair and covering her with a lap rug, as if she were some fragile creature who might disappear with the first gust of wind.

The young guard eyed the girl with interest, but Aimée ignored him and closed her eyes against the sun to drink in the fresh air and the peace of the still, quiet garden.

All too soon the hour ended and Aimée was taken upstairs to her prison. But she felt better and now had something to look forward to each day—one hour of relative freedom. Soon she spent the time walking instead of sitting and her appetite increased.

Sometimes she took her lute into the garden and quietly sang some of the old French *virelais* that could be traced to early Arabian music. She had no desire to sing "Bonnie Blue Flag." She had gotten into enough trouble for that to last a lifetime. And even the time at Thornfell, when it had been permissible, it brought too much sadness to her.

There was a new dimension to Aimée, a certain peace and tranquil blooming that had come upon her, and sometimes, as she sat in the garden, she smiled, hugging her secret to herself. For the past two months she had missed her time, and Aimée knew that she was with child. Even during the trips when she had slipped in and out of New Orleans, her destiny had been decided—to bear the son of Bryan Garrard.

What would it be like to have Bryan's child? Would he have the same dark hair, the same silver-gray eyes? And how would he feel, cuddled in her arms?

Her arms ached to hold her baby. She would never possess Bryan, but at least she would have a part of him in the child—a part that he could never take away from her. "*Merci*, Madame," she prayed in the garden to the Virgin Mother, who had given her a blessing amid all the sadness and uncertainty of the past months.

Now Aimée was no longer jealous of Tink, of the times that Bryan had spent with the girl. More and more she turned to Anderson who, remaining silent, watched over her, seeing to her comfort, to her diet, and making sure that she was well wrapped when in the garden. If she had not known better, she would have thought by his actions that he had been ordered to take care of her as some precious possession.

The dogs, Fréki and Geri, lay at Aimée's feet and warily watched the soldiers taking turns marching up and down the banquette by the gate. Sometimes Aimée looked up to catch their curious glances, but the soldiers soon disappeared from sight to continue their marching back and forth.

It had now been three weeks since Bryan's departure and Aimée wondered if he would ever return. In the garden she sat, enjoying another day of balmy weather as the sun shone down its healing rays. But she sang a plaintive song, filled with loneliness and exotic beauty.

Lost in the mysticism of the poetry that Zazal, the lutenist of Baghdad, had made famous, she did not at first notice the two men standing inside the gate and listening. But some unknown force caused her to lift her head, and she saw Bryan, standing and then walking toward her, with a tall, gaunt stranger at his side.

Aimée laid down the lute, and forgetting in her excitement at seeing her husband that they had not been on the best of terms when he left, she rose to meet him with a smile on her lips.

"Aimée," Bryan said, lifting her chin to see her face. "The fresh air seems to have been of benefit." He searched her face, as if hungry for the sight of her, and then remembering the man beside him, he said, "Aimée, this is my brother, Clay Garrard. Clay, my wife."

Aimée stared at Bryan in surprise, and then back to the young man who had a black patch over his eye. His height was almost the same as Bryan's, but he was far thinner.

"Well, dear sister," Clay greeted her, "I see this prison is not so mean as the one at Point Lookout, and the company is much improved. Perhaps it will not be too bad here, after all."

Point Lookout? Aimée did not understand. That was a Yankee prison camp.

"Were you a . . . guard at Point Lookout, monsieur?" Aimée asked, still puzzled.

Clay laughed. "No, little sister, I was on the other side of the bars. I was a prisoner until recently."

"But I do not understand—"

Bryan interrupted impatiently. "Clay was in the Confederate Army, Aimée, and captured during the riot at Baltimore. But he has been exchanged and has taken the eagle oath to return his loyalty to the Union. There'll be no more fighting for him during this war."

Again Clay laughed. "Bryan, your wife seems surprised. Evidently you have never told her we were fighting on opposite sides, or that you and your man, Anderson, were the ones responsible for my capture."

Aimée could see that Bryan did not like the turn of the conversation. "Come, let's go into the house," he said, taking Aimée by the arm. "There will be enough time for conversation later. I am tired and hungry."

"But my hour is not up, Bryan," Aimée protested.

Bryan tightened his hold. "You can make up for it tomorrow."

There was nothing for Aimée to do but go along with him.

That evening was a special occasion for Aimée. She did not have the usual supper tray in her room. Instead the three sat down at the dinner table—she, Clay, and her husband Bryan. Tink had eaten earlier with Anderson.

It was a strange feeling seeing the two brothers facing each other, both with the signatures of war on their faces —one with a jagged scar across his cheek, the other with an eye patch. Aimée could feel the undercurrent and she wondered how it came to be that they had fought on opposite sides. But then, many families were divided by the war. Now she understood Bryan's words concerning Etienne—"He is far better off dead than rotting away in some prison camp." Bryan had been thinking of his younger brother.

The sudden thunder made Aimée remember. She jumped to her feet, murmuring an excuse, left the table, and dashed for the door into the courtyard. She had not gone far when an arm encircled her from behind with such force that the breath was knocked from her.

"Just where do you think you are going?" Bryan's angry voice sounded.

"My lute," she whimpered, struggling for her breath. "I . . . I left it in the garden and it . . . it is going to storm."

Bryan relaxed his hold on her. "So you were not trying to run away."

Aimée became angry at his insinuation, angry that the peace of the garden had been destroyed.

"What chance have I of running away, monsieur, when I am watched from every side . . . when I am not permitted to leave the house, except to be questioned or watch a friend hang . . . when a guard stands at the gate all day long, ready to shoot if I so much as venture onto the banquette?"

Her eyes were dry but her lips quivered with emotion.

"Aimée, Aimée, do not be so vehement. This is not of my own choosing. You brought it on yourself and there is nothing I can do but obey orders to keep you locked up, especially while your case is being considered."

"Some women spies have been banished to the Confederate lines and told never to cross into Federal territory again. Why can I not be allowed to leave also?"

"General Butler would never permit it . . . and neither would I."

"You are both cruel then, Bryan—so wrapped up in your self-righteousness."

He responded to her accusation in a low resigned voice. "Not half so cruel, Aimée, as you have been to me."

"I? Cruel?" Aimée asked in surprise.

"Yes. Do you not realize how you have taunted me from the moment I set eyes on you—with that little face blotched with tears? I wanted to take you in my arms to comfort you, but you were a little tiger, spitting out your hatred. And then, when you lost your memory, I dared to hope things would change between us. Now I see that it is impossible. I pray to God that I can forget those days when you behaved like a loving wife!"

"Bryan . . ." Aimée, disconcerted by his odd manner, said his name in a soft voice and reached out to lay her hand on his arm.

But Bryan shook it off as if he had been touched by a leper. "But regardless of how you feel, there is one thing I insist on, Aimée." She felt the harshness in his voice. "While my brother is here, you are to appear outwardly as my loving wife. I ask nothing else of you."

At his hostile and intimidating words, Aimée lost the fleeting feeling of pity and gathered fresh invectives to hurl at him, but another rumble of thunder and the beginning rain dispatched the two hurriedly toward the house, Aimée carrying the lute that she had left in the garden.

"Have you always been afraid of storms?"

Aimée, holding her arms tightly around her body, looked up to see Bryan watching her as she paced up and down the bedroom.

"How . . . how do you know that I am afraid?" she asked, suddenly vulnerable to his question.

The lightning flashed, sending its quick spurt of light into the room, and as the thunder sounded seconds afterward, indicating that the hit was near, Aimée jumped and fled to the high-post bed.

Bryan's laughter trailed her, following her mercilessly. "Your actions speak for themselves, Aimée. And I remember when you were recovering from your . . . accident, you were afraid."

194

Standing over the bed, he towered in his superiority, and Aimée felt a desire to lash out at him for his smugness. "And by what right have you to feel so superior, monsieur? You, who have never known fear, gloat because each time it storms, I relive that time in my life when my *maman* and *papa* were swept away by the flood, and when Etienne and I were left at the mercy of the storm, with trees and bodies floating past us all night. And then, the next morning when we were rescued, there was no one left on the island."

Bryan, with a chagrined look, attempted to stop her, but Aimée's words continued spewing out the horror of her nightmare. "I ran to the bodies washed up on shore—those horrible, bloated bodies that no longer resembled people —searching for Maman and Papa, until the rescue workers dragged me away. And I never found them."

"Don't," Bryan whispered. "Don't torture yourself, Aimée. I did not know. I would never have teased you if I had had an inkling . . ."

". . . And that is why I am afraid."

Aimée, jerking away from him, refused the comfort of his arms, and he got up from her side, muttering an oath under his breath, as if castigating himself for mentioning the storm.

While Aimée sat, cradled in fright, Bryan left the room and locked the door behind him.

It was impossible for her to remain calm when he was around. There was something about him that caused her to lash out at him, and now she had spoiled his homecoming and had not honored the request he had made of her in the garden—to act outwardly as his loving wife.

The cold, chilling rain lashed against the windowpanes and the shutters creaked and banged. The rainstorm surrounded the townhouse and filled the low-lying areas of the garden with pools of water.

Voices sounded outside the bedroom door and then the door opened. "Anderson is bringing in more firewood, Aimée," Bryan said. Casually holding a glass of milk in his hand, her husband came into the room with Anderson following.

Aimée brought up the covers so that only her long

flaming gold hair showed against the pillows. After laying the logs on the hearth, Anderson placed some of them upon the fire and turned to go out as silently as he had come in.

"Here, drink this. It will make you feel better and will relax you."

Bryan held the glass of milk to her lips and willed her to drink it. The warmth at first disguised the taste, but Aimée coughed when the unusual strength of the liquid added to the milk reached her throat.

"What . . . what is it?" Aimée inquired.

"A little sugar, a little brandy, and lots of warm milk," he said, grinning at her wrinkling nose. "And I will not let you turn up your dainty nose at it. You must drink it all."

Aimée obeyed him, finishing the glass. He leaned over, kissed her on the forehead as one would kiss a child, and said, "Now go to sleep. There's no more need to be afraid of the storm. I will keep it from our doors." His eyes twinkled and Aimée said sleepily, "Yes, Odin," while her lips curved softly and her eyes shut out the flickering light from the hearth.

The sunlight coming into the window penetrated the room and Aimée, when the filtered light reached her half-closed eyes, felt a warm sensuousness spreading over her body. Still half-asleep, she smiled, thinking she was still in her dream, with the soft kiss part of it.

She felt Bryan's mouth moving down her body, sending waves of desire throughout her. Her love-starved soul responded to the feast offered her. Never once did she open her eyes or gaze at him. Suspended in a semidream state, Aimée lay against her husband and breathed easily and slowly, her red-gold hair caught by his arm. Later, when she opened her eyes, he was still beside her. Had she merely dreamed that they had made love? Had she desired him so much that her body, unable to possess his, had created the dream?

The wave of early morning nausea nagged at her as it had while Bryan was away, but the nausea reminded her of her secret, and fresh joy swept over her.

"You are smiling in your sleep, my love," Bryan whispered in her ear.

Aimée's eyes flew open with a startled expression. "What . . . what time is it?" she inquired.

"It's late—but I do not have to report for duty until tomorrow. We have the entire day, Aimée. What would you like to do?"

"You mean you will take me somewhere?" Aimée asked incredulously.

"I think it can be arranged," Bryan said, laughing at her amazement at this unexpected change. "Of course, the guard will have to ride post, but we can ignore him."

Aimée giggled. "Am I so formidable, monsieur, that you would require help in subduing me if I should attempt to escape?"

"You make a man weak, Aimée. I had resolved not to touch you, and yet, the first night I am back, I break that resolve. How do I know what wiles you would use on me to let you escape."

He took her long hair in his hands and she laughed, pulling her hair away from his grasp and standing up, suddenly feeling happy and impatient for the day to begin.

Chapter 21

"*I* think we will take a trip down the bayou," Bryan said at breakfast. "Clay, I'm sure you can find something to occupy you today. Since I've been away for three weeks, I wish to spend the day with my wife."

Clay looked at Bryan and laughed. "How did you ever unbend enough to court a Secesh?" he asked mockingly. "I thought you cared for nothing but duty and honor."

Bryan frowned and his tenseness made the scar on his cheek stand out.

Clay turned to Aimée. "Did you know, Aimée, that Bryan and I have never agreed on a single thing until yesterday?"

"Oh? And what was that, Clay?" Aimée asked, more interested in breaking up the angry feelings between the brothers than curious.

"That your beauty could enslave any man. I can see how cold, dark Bryan would respond to your flaming hair, like a moth to the fire. But come now, confess. Don't you ever get a little cold from his hard, flinty manner?"

His words were teasing, but underneath them there was an antagonism, as if Clay were trying to let her know that he thought she had made a mistake in marrying his brother.

Aimée blushed, aware of the morning spent in Bryan's arms, and the two men, noticing the blush, were both affected—Clay amused, and Bryan tender and protective.

"Clay, you need not embarrass my wife so soon after you have come."

"My apologies, Brother. Evidently your wife has seen a side of you that you have kept hidden these many years."

Again the sardonic tinge to his voice was apparent. Clay watched Aimée and she had the feeling that, as he watched her, he was mentally placing a subtle barrier between them. Was it something she had done that had caused this reaction? Or was it that merely by being Bryan's wife she was automatically relegated to this position? No wonder Bryan had insisted that she behave like a loving wife while Clay was present.

The knock at the door gained their attention and soon Anderson stood at Bryan's side with the official-looking order in his hands.

"This has just come by special courier," Anderson said, handing the paper to Bryan.

The exclamation filled the room as Bryan read the order. His dark brow wrinkled in a massive frown and he pushed himself from the table.

"What is it, Bryan?" Aimée asked. "Will you have to report for duty today, after all?"

His words were slow and lethal. "The *Cairo* has been blown up by a mine in the Yazoo River, and in retaliation you are to go back to the Castle immediately. The board has turned down my request, Aimée."

Stunned, Aimée stared at her husband speechlessly. The quiet desperation flowed over her as she remembered her terrifying experience at the Castle, And now she looked at her husband's unfathomable face.

Aimée said, "I will go and pack," and with dignity, she left the room. The angry voices of the two brothers raised in argument trailed her.

"Even the Customs House is a better prison than the Castle," Clay's voice pointed out. "Surely your commanding general will listen to the request of one of his officers. Why not go to him?"

"He would not listen, Clay. There is a . . . breach between us because I have questioned some of his actions. And Aimée was known to be carrying fulminate of mercury for the mines."

Aimée heard no more. She shut the door to the bedroom and closed out all sound except the erratic beating of her heart.

Did being an obedient wife mean she should make no protest at being taken back to prison? But Aimée knew she would gain nothing by protesting.

With slow, dazed movements, she changed her dress for the purple velvet outfit that Bryan had bought her for wintertime. It had been too warm to wear when she left New Orleans for Thornfell in September and she had left it hanging in the armoire. There had been no occasion special enough to warrant its use since—her only venture outside had been to the board of inquiry, and to her, that had not been an important enough event.

Now, glancing at the dress with its nipped-in waist and short jacket similar to a Spanish dancer's, Aimée, with a rising bit of pride, was determined to look her best when she was taken to the Union prison. She would neither look nor act like a nonentity. She was a Saint-Moreau and she would appear with her best foot forward, even if that foot was never to step toward freedom again.

Aimée was not sorry that she had helped her people. She was proud of it and would do it again. She had no regrets on that part. Her one regret was that her baby would have to suffer with her. She had heard of the hardships of expectant mothers in prison and that their babies seldom lived. But she had too much pride to beg the enemy for either her life or that of her unborn child.

The valise was packed, and while Aimée waited for Bryan to come for her, she surveyed the room that had meant so much to her. She walked to the mantel and, fingering Grand-père's pipe, thought of the happy times that she had seen in this house and had shared with her brother, her *grand-père*, and Tante Dee Dee. At least no one could take the memories away, regardless of what else was taken. She would always remember, whatever the months ahead brought.

Bryan walked into the bedroom, but Aimée, recognizing his walk, felt such emotion that she kept her back to him.

"I swear to you, Aimée, that I will not rest until I can have you removed from that place."

Aimée made no reply and Bryan continued. "It is not official, but I have heard that General Butler is being relieved of his command here any day. The French government has protested to President Lincoln because of his harsh treatment of the Creoles. . . ."

"Trust me, Aimée." Bryan's voice was closer, whispering in her ear. "I will petition the new commander, as soon as he arrives, that you be released in my custody. And I will see that Sergeant Lugby is transferred immediately. You need have no worry on that score."

Aimée handed her valise to Bryan and walked toward the door.

"Where is your new cloak?" Bryan asked, appraising her with his sober gray eyes.

"In the armoire."

"Get it and put it on," he commanded. "The air is cold. I do not wish you to become chilled."

It was useless to argue with him. She walked back to the armoire and removed the cloak from the box. She made no effort to put it on but laid it across her arm.

Downstairs, Bryan stopped her, took the cloak in his hands, and held it for her to slip into. He covered her hair with the hood, and appearing satisfied that she was well wrapped, held open the door for her to walk into the courtyard to the waiting carriage.

There were no blossoms from the garden to perfume the December air, but for a fleeting moment Aimée smelled the scent of the oleander tree and the tea roses that had once bloomed along the wall. She lifted her head to see the bare coral vines, their tangled brown tendrils looking somehow pathetic and naked against the old brick of the courtyard.

The sound of the wind scraping the creaking gate back and forth matched the dull roll of the wheels of the *calèche*, as Bryan started the carriage down the drive and pulled out into the street.

Aimée turned her head to take one last look at the house. Anderson and Tink stood in the courtyard and watched them leave. Clay was nowhere in sight. The three-storied pink house with its black shuttered windows appeared the same as it had before the Yankee invaders came . . . as it would doubtless appear long after she had gone.

"I have taken the liberty of putting your lute in the carriage, Aimée," Bryan informed her. "You seem to derive a great deal of pleasure from your music. Perhaps it will be a comfort to you for the next few days."

Still, Aimée did not dare speak, but sat rigid and tense, with her hands clasped together under the blue velvet cloak. She was determined to show no emotion.

For some time they traveled, past the city streets, out into the countryside, until they were on the rutted, muddy road toward the Castle. Because of the constant motion of the carriage, the nausea swept over Aimée until she could ignore it no longer.

"Please, Bryan, you will have to stop for a moment."

"Are you ill, Aimée?"

Barely in time Aimée jumped from the carriage, and turning her back to Bryan, who waited and watched by the shrubs at the edge of the road, she lost her breakfast. It was degrading that she had no privacy. But she might as well get used to it for at the Castle she would be in full view of the guards at all times.

Aimée, with what dignity she could muster, came back to the carriage, ready to resume the trip. But Bryan, with an inquiring look, stopped her and asked, "Aimée, is it possible that you are with child?"

"Would it matter to you if I am?" she asked quietly.

Bryan, furiously angry, grasped her by the shoulders as if he wanted to shake her. Then he released his hold and stared at her pale, wan face.

"I insist that you answer me, Aimée. Are you carrying my son, even now?"

"Either your son or your daughter, Bryan," she admitted.

In a display of fury, he clenched his fist and hit it against his open palm.

"Of course," he said, speaking to himself. "How could I have been so blind? Even before I left for Point Lookout, I should have known . . ."

Then his anger turned on Aimée. "How far along are you?"

"Almost three months."

"But why didn't you tell me, Aimée, instead of letting me find it out for myself? If you had not become ill just now, I would have taken you to the Castle, not knowing."

"It would have been best, Bryan, for you never to have suspected. I am told that babies do not often survive being born in a prison," she answered.

Her words, with no trace of pity for herself, seemed to provide the final decision for him. "Aimée, get back into the carriage," he ordered. "We are turning around . . . I cannot take you back to that cold, unhealthy place."

"But the orders," Aimée argued. "You cannot disobey orders."

"The devil take the orders. No army can expect me to send my wife and unborn child to prison, even for a day. I will gladly fight for my country—I will bleed and die for it—but this is asking too much. You will go back to the townhouse and I will—"

Men on horseback galloped from the wooded area, and Bryan, consumed with the problem concerning Aimée, did not notice them until it was too late. The shots rang out and Bryan fell to the ground, the rest of his sentence unuttered.

Aimée screamed and ran toward her fallen husband, but a man from the marauding group wheeled his horse in front of her, cutting off her path. He leaned down to sweep her into the saddle with him, but she ran from him toward the *calèche*.

The man swung himself to the ground and Aimée, seeing that he intended taking her with him, held to one of the wheels of the *calèche* and repulsed him with a kick to his shins.

"Damn you!" he muttered. "We're trying to rescue you. Why are you fighting me, you little bitch?"

"Bryan," Aimée screamed, but he lay on the ground, unable to defend either Aimée or himself.

The man grew impatient with her, and as he forcibly jerked her hands from the wheel, the fingernail was ripped from her little finger and the blood rapidly spread over the blue velvet cloak.

The ties to the cloak had come loose, and as she fought a losing duel with her abductor, Aimée's cloak fell into the muddied road. Still, she struggled against him, but he lifted her into the saddle, and urging his horse into a gallop, sped off with the other horsemen, leaving the *calèche*, the Union officer, and the bloodied cloak by the desolate roadside.

Chapter 22

$\mathcal{F}$or some time they galloped—Aimée and her abductor —while the man occasionally looked back to make sure they were not being followed. His hold finally lessened, but even then, it would have been impossible for Aimée to escape because of the speed at which the horse traveled.

With each jolt of the horse, Aimée's finger throbbed from the pain, although the bleeding had subsided. But a deeper pain that pervaded her, filling her with an unceasing sorrow, taking her mind off her physical pain.

For the first time Aimée's stunned turquoise eyes took in the appearance of the other men traveling with them. They were a motley, dirty group—unshaven—outlaws. Was her fate to be far worse than returning to the Castle? Why had they kidnapped her and where were they taking her?

At one point they stopped, but Aimée, hoping that the jolting journey was over, was disappointed. Fresh horses were waiting for them, and soon, without a word, they were on their way again, skirting the swamps and crisscrossing the bayous that made little islands of the land.

The shabby shacks built on stilts began to become more numerous, and oddly-dressed men, wearing coolie hats, stared as the group slowed down and headed toward the center of the village.

The Chinese shrimp workers. Aimée had never seen them before, but she had heard Etienne speak of them— the shrimpers of St. Malo who, with their nets, supplied New Orleans and the surrounding countryside with the seafood from the Gulf. Silent and morose, the villagers watched, giving no welcome by either word or gesture to the group coming in on horseback.

Finally the horsemen stopped in front of one of the shacks, no better and no worse than any of the others. But at least someone welcomed them instead of looking at them as if it would take no effort to slit their throats, and Aimée, grateful that they had stopped the jarring ride, was lifted off the horse and firmly guided inside.

"Go with her. She will see to your needs," her abductor said curtly, indicating the yellow-skinned woman waiting in the shadows of the darkened room.

To protest would be futile, Aimée thought, going with the woman to the little room adjoining the hut.

"Please," Aimée whispered to the woman, "help me." But the closed door made no difference. Again Aimée repeated it, this time in French, but the woman gazed uncomprehendingly and led her to the small mat on the floor. She pointed to the mat and indicated by gesture that she was to lie down and rest. Either the woman chose not to understand her, or she had little comprehension of any language other than her own. But she had seemed to understand Aimée's abductor. Why could she not understand Aimée?

Aimée gave a defeated sigh. Lying down, she closed her eyes, but the jumbled scenes and the horror of the day invaded her thoughts.

"Bryan, Bryan," she whispered with restless anguish in her voice, until the sound dwindled and she lay sleeping upon the mat, exhausted and heart-torn, her face pink and stained with tears.

"Missee! Missee!" The voice of the woman was soft but urgent.

Aimée sat up, rubbing her eyes, disoriented because the room was in near darkness. The aroma of the food was tantalizing as the woman thrust the bowl into Aimée's hands. Taking a bite of the curried rice with shrimp, she felt an emptiness, and in spite of her despondency, she ate.

A knock sounded on the door—merely a signal that someone was opening the door to come in. Aimée's abductor stood before her, staring down at her, as she continued eating the rice.

"We will need to be on our way. Come." He reached out, taking the bowl from her and lifting her to her feet, with no regard for her and her unfinished meal.

"Where are we going?" Aimée asked in a voice stronger than before.

"You will find that out soon enough," he muttered, still holding her by the arm and leading her to the door.

Aimée shivered and the man looked at her, as if realizing for the first time that she had no outer wrap and might be cold. In a strange sing-song voice he issued a command and the petite, shriveled old woman quickly brought the blanket from the mat where Aimée had rested and handed it to the man before her.

Again Aimée found herself upon the horse, with the man astride the saddle behind her. The blanket was thrust around her, binding her closer to the man and restricting her arms. It was a position she might as well get used to, Aimée conceded and reconciled herself to another leg of the journey before them. At least the blanket would shield her from the wind that had begun its icy whistle through the drab landscape of scrubby pines and gnarled oaks.

The ride on horseback finally ended and Aimée was carried to the large pirogue that lay hidden in the bayou. Her abductor handed her over to the two men in the pirogue. Then, going back to his horse, he wheeled around and in an instant vanished from sight. She was now seated between the two men—once again a prisoner. Her skirts, so heavy when wet, would assure that she drowned if she made any attempt to escape. And she was disoriented, not knowing which way to flee if she were fortunate enough to escape.

The men must have known the waters well, for they went steadfastly on their way, slipping in and out of the treacherous network of byways like ones born to the water. Aimée knew that they were traveling in a southeasterly pattern. That was her only certainty.

Slowly sinking into the earth, the sun, now at her back, unwound its shape and diffused its strength in all directions until its last thread spun into darkness. Dark branches loomed overhead as the pirogue wove in and out through the black waters. Blackness surrounded them, and Aimée, exhausted in heart and spirit, let the darkness lull her to sleep, along with the movement of the unceasing lapping waters. . . .

The movement became rougher and the softness was exchanged for a roaring rush of waves waxing and receding against the constant swinging of the waters.

Aimée, opening her eyes, expected to see the same darkness overhead, the same satin shadows of menacing black branches and vines that had traveled with them. Instead there was a flickering small light swinging back and forth above her. She was no longer in the pirogue, but in a cabin and from the sound of voices and creaking chains, Aimée knew she must have been put on board a ship while she slept. But the ship was lifting anchor, getting ready to sail. Where was she being taken? And why?

She did not have to wonder for long. The door to the cabin opened and Aimée stared unbelievingly at the man beside her—John Runefelt.

"John," she whispered, "what is happening?"

He walked back to close the door behind him while shaking his head. In a low tone he said, "We must be quiet until we are safely out of the Gulf. We could still be caught."

Out of the Gulf? They were leaving Louisiana?

Aimée struggled to her feet in alarm. She had to get back. Bryan had been hurt—perhaps even killed.

John Runefelt put his hand over her mouth to keep her from speaking further. Then his hand was replaced by his lips seeking hers. She struggled against him, feeling nothing. "Oh, my darling, I've wanted you so much," John whispered in her ear. His lips brushed lightly across her hair.

"John, I must go back," Aimée resisted. "Bryan needs me."

"It's too late, Aimée. We are already sailing. There is no turning back." And he barred her escape through the door.

At his words, Aimée lost all hope that she would be

allowed to return to Bryan. Wearily she laid her head against his chest, while he comforted her.

After leading her to the cabin bunk, he sat quietly with his arms about her. Then, after a long silence, he asked, "This Bryan . . . what was he to you, Aimée, besides your jailor?"

"He is my husband," she confessed with a sob.

The news cast a brooding silence over him and his shoulders looked as if they had been newly burdened. "I am sorry, Aimée. I did not guess. I only knew that you were being returned to the Castle and it would have been impossible to free you from that place." He lifted her head and looked into her troubled, tear-filled eyes. "But why would your husband return you to the prison, Aimée? He must not have loved you very much if he did not attempt to hide you or help you escape."

"It was to be just for a few days . . . Bryan was going to petition the new commander when he arrived . . ."

"A strange way for a husband to act," John said, almost to himself.

Aimée bristled and felt a need to defend her husband. "He was an officer and had to obey orders, regardless of how he felt about them."

"Yankees must not have the same regard for their women as Southerners do. No one in the Confederate Army would ever have issued an order to put a woman in the Castle or on Ship Island!"

"Where are we going, John?" Aimée asked, deliberately changing the subject.

"To England, if all goes well."

"England?" She was incredulous. "But why?"

"I have a special mission to get help from the British. Things have not been going well. England is now hesitant to recognize us as a separate nation, because of the slave issue. A brilliant strategy by President Lincoln," he complained bitterly.

"As long as the issue was kept to whether we had the right to secede from the Union, and the Yankees were the invader, we had the moral war won. But now that Lincoln has thrown in freeing the slaves to muddy the diplomatic waters, Britain is hesitant to recognize us. And without their official recognition, we are lost!"

Aimée's tears fell silently down her cheeks. John was speaking of an abstraction while Bryan, her husband, who was flesh and blood, lay mortally wounded, far from her.

Aimée winced when John touched her hand. He immediately held it up to the light and saw the caked blood.

"Aimée, you're hurt," John said in surprise.

"It . . . it is nothing," she responded, moving her hand to escape his view. But she was not successful. It remained in his grasp while he stared at the finger where the nail had been ripped from the nailbed.

"Did you . . . resist being rescued?" he asked.

"Y-yes," Aimée stammered.

John continued holding her hand in silence, his eyes hooded from view. Then he said, "The finger will have to be taken care of before it becomes infected. I'll get the things from the ship's surgery."

"Is it safe for you to move about?" Aimée asked, remembering his caution a few minutes before.

"We have not been challenged so far. And it is almost dawn," he replied. "We will be safe once we are out on the open seas." Despite his answer, Aimée knew from his manner that he was uneasy.

John stood looking down at Aimée, his eyes narrowing when he saw her dress was still damp from her trip through the bayous. Her shudder was almost imperceptible, but even that did not escape his notice.

"We must find you some dry clothes. It seems there are several things that I did not think of in my hasty plans to free you," the man said ruefully before leaving the cabin.

"No such luck as the captain's wife leaving some clothes on board. Looks as if you will have to be content with sailors' garb if you want some dry clothes."

Aimée stared at the trousers, shirt, and heavy sweater that John held in his hands.

"I cannot wear *trousers*, monsieur!" Aimée protested indignantly.

John's hearty laugh cut through her protest. "Only until we reach England. I promise to buy you the most fashionable dresses in all of England, when we get there."

Aimée did not tell him that she would have no need of fashionable dresses by the time they reached England. It was not the time to inform him that she was with child.

"Now hurry and get these on, and I will be back to attend to your finger. And by the way, I am known as Juba Barnard, so you might as well start calling me 'Juba.' "

Aimée, when alone, removed the velvet dress and jacket that she had put on—was it the day before? And with distaste and a wrinkling of her nose, she slid her legs into the sailor's trousers and pulled on the rough shirt and the heavy navy-blue sweater. She smoothed out the velvet skirt of the dress, dropping it over the end of the berth— hoping that it had not been completely ruined by the dampness. She did not relish dressing like a sailor the entire trip.

"I . . . I am dressed now . . . Juba," Aimée called out.

He came back in, carrying the basin of water, the brandy, and the bandages from the ship's surgery, and without comment on her unusual attire, proceeded to work efficiently, gently cleaning the finger with the brandy and bandaging it. When it was done, the man said, "Now try to get some sleep. I'm in the next cabin, so you need not be afraid."

"Thank you, Juba."

He turned at the door and Aimée saw the amused look in his brown eyes. "If you don't want a mutiny on the ship I think you had better remain in your cabin while you're dressed like that. You're far too fetching for the sailors to keep their minds on the ship."

At his frank appraisal Aimée blushed and gladly saw him leave. Lying down on the bunk she hoped to get a little respite from the fragmented thoughts bombarding her brain, but the constant rolling pitch of the ship would not let her forget that she was with child—Bryan's child.

Aimée stayed below hidden from view during the day, and emerged at night to be taken up on deck by John for fresh air. She now had a change of clothes—another suit of trousers and shirt—a gift from the smallest sailor aboard ship.

The second day out Aimée walked along the deck with John. She sensed a nervousness in him that had not been present before. He finally stopped her from continuing the walk and led her to the railing.

"Aimée, all day long I have rehearsed what I was going to say to you tonight and now I find that I can't remember any of the words."

Sensing that the words were ones she did not wish to hear, Aimée drew back, but there was no denying them. They were destined to be said at some time. Slowly she exhaled, trying to relax the tense feeling of her body, waiting for him to continue.

"You must have guessed how I felt about you at Thornfell, Aimée—especially after the scene with Vickie. And when you did not return from your trip into New Orleans, I was in agony, wondering what had happened to you. I was ready to start looking for you when word came to me that both you and Monsieur O'Brie had been captured. But then I found that you were back in your own home— a prisoner, true, but at least in better surroundings than Monsieur O'Brie. We tried to save him, but he was too well guarded.

"And then this trip to England was being arranged and I started watching the townhouse where you were kept, to see if you were ever permitted outside.

"I had to move fast when I found you were being taken back to the Castle. The . . . arrangements were not the best, Aimée, but I had to use what was immediately available. I understand that your . . . husband was shot and left for dead."

At the pain in her face, the man posing as Juba Barnard said softly, "I am sorry, Aimée . . . that it had to happen this way."

Silence hung between them like a shadowed curtain. Then he continued. "We are on a British ship, heading for England, and the captain thinks that you are my wife."

Aimée gave a start, but John laid his hand on her arm. "Please let me finish before saying anything. We may be in England as long as two years. Your husband is almost certain to be dead. But if, by some chance, he is still alive, I will see that your marriage is annulled. I want to take care of you, and the only right I would have in doing that is by marrying you. It would be awkward for you to marry again in Louisiana, when we are not certain about your husband, but in England, it will not matter."

"And would it matter," Aimée asked, enunciating each word slowly, "that I am already carrying his child?"

John stared at her, belatedly comprehending what she was telling him.

"You are going to have . . . his baby?" he asked, as if he had been given a mortal blow.

Aimée nodded. The ship rolled and Aimée, struggling for her balance, found herself enclosed in his arms.

"Oh, my darling, of course it doesn't matter. I will claim him as my own because he will be a part of you."

"But I cannot marry you," Aimée said, pulling herself from his embrace. "If there is one remote chance that Bryan is alive, I must return to find him. I . . . do not wish to live without him."

The tears flowed steadily and John, his voice dead, said, "Hush, little one. I can't bear to hear you cry. If you love this husband of yours, and there's a chance that he's still alive, we will work something out, somehow."

Chapter 23

She began screaming, fighting the hands reaching out for her, but they pinned her down and the voice whispered in her ear, "Aimée, Aimée, wake up! The entire ship will think you're being murdered."

"They're keeping me from him," she cried, still in her nightmare. "I must get to him—I must! No, I don't want to go with you—I must stay with Bryan. Bryan! Bryan!" she called in anguish, and then her eyes were open, seeing John—no, Juba—leaning over her, trying to shake her awake. Her sobs quieted but, still caught up in the horror, her body trembled and her wide candescent eyes still saw the man she loved struck down while she was being forced from him.

The older man, standing in the doorway, held the lantern high. The light reached the bunk and the flaming red hair massed in a luxurious cascade on the pillow.

"Is there something I can do for her?" the man asked John in a decidedly British accent.

"Thank you, no, Captain," he replied. "I am sorry we disturbed you. My . . . wife has had another nightmare, that is all."

The captain walked farther into the small cabin and he brought the light closer to survey the girl in the bunk. In the lantern light her eyes shone like jeweled tears reflected in an azure Grecian sea.

"Who is this Bryan that has caused your . . . wife so much anguish?" the captain suddenly asked John.

"Bryan?" John repeated, caught off guard. "I did not hear her speak of anyone by that name."

The captain, continuing to hold the lantern high, looked back and forth from John to Aimée, with a pondering expression on his uncompromising face.

"Tomorrow," the captain said, as if suddenly making up his mind, "I will give orders for her things to be brought up to the first mate's cabin. He will not mind being dispossessed for a short time."

"That is not necessary, Captain," John began, but his speech was interrupted.

"When I suggested she be given this cabin, I did not know how fragile your . . . wife was. She needs fresh air and a chance to stretch her legs during the day. The trip is hard enough on her without this added discomfort. No, I have made up my mind, Mr. Barnard."

The captain bent his head as he went out the door, and

Aimée, still groggy from her interrupted sleep, did not guess the sudden blazing of antagonism between the two men.

The next day Aimée did not understand why she had been moved from the cabin next to John's. She only knew it had something to do with her nightmare, and she felt guilty, as if in some way she had betrayed him.

"My dear, if you wish to walk out upon the deck, you may do so. And from now on, you are to take your evening meal with me."

Aimée looked at the captain in surprise, for he had begun to assume a guardianship over her—transferring her from John's care to his own. And he had not invited John to dine with them.

Tight-lipped and morose, John did not like the captain's attitude and told Aimée several times in one afternoon.

"But he is very kind. And I . . . feel much better above. The rolling of the ship does not affect me so much in the cabin that I am in. I think the captain is only trying to be nice to me. But I am sorry he has taken a dislike to you."

"Forgive me for being selfish, Aimée. I know you are more comfortable on the upper deck. But I resent the captain's removing you from my care. He does not seem to trust me. Oh, God, why couldn't I have remained impersonal, content to do the job I was assigned to do, rather than falling in love with you?"

John turned around and stamped angrily away, his limping walk more noticeable as he strove to put as much distance as quickly between himself and the source of his fretfulness.

"I believe the man does not appreciate my overbearing ways," the quiet voice sounded behind her.

"He . . . he is most unhappy, Captain, but the trouble does not lie with you."

The captain met her glance and she saw his approval of her appearance, for Aimée, tired of the trousers and shirt, had dressed in the velvet dress and jacket, even though the hem showed the visible signs of her journey by horseback and pirogue.

"Is Juba Barnard actually your husband?" the captain

asked with a disconcerting directness.

Aimée saw no need to continue the lie. "No, Captain," she answered.

There was a growl in the captain's throat that was quieted with effort. "The sailor on duty told me you were carried aboard by two men, but I assumed at first that it was because of your exhaustion from the trip. Were you brought here by force?"

Aimée chose her words with care. "Captain, the man, Juba Barnard, is my friend, and I would not wish you to think ill of him. I was being taken to the Castle . . . to prison, because I am . . . was a spy. That is all he knew. He thought he was rescuing me."

"And this Bryan that you cried out for in your sleep, who is he?"

"Major Bryan Garrard, under General Butler's command. *He* is my husband. He had been ordered to take me back to the Castle, even though he had tried to keep me under his parole—but it was to be only for a few days. General Butler is being replaced and Bryan . . . felt the new commander would be more lenient."

The captain was incredulous at the complicated situation.

"Your husband is a Union officer—yet you were helping the Confederacy. And this man, Juba Barnard, your fellow conspirator, was not . . . aware that you are married?"

"No, Captain, he did not know until I told him aboard your ship. Or that I am . . ." Aimée blushed and stopped, biting her lip at the secret she had almost divulged.

"Or that you are what, my dear?" he prompted in a gentle but demanding tone.

Sighing, Aimée answered, "That . . . that I am expecting a child."

She was suddenly tired and did not wish to answer any more questions, but the next one she could not avoid.

"And this Major Garrard, who is your husband, where is he now?"

"He . . . he was shot when I was . . . rescued. And I do not know whether he is alive or dead."

At the sound of the torment in her voice, the captain

said, "I beg your pardon for being so inquisitive. I only wished to understand the situation, not to stir up your sorrow."

The captain walked with Aimée back to her cabin, and in a comforting voice said, "I am told that even the officers under his command have become sick of the general's tyranny toward the people of New Orleans. We are aware of the hardships you and your people have suffered, Mrs. Garrard. The general has already been condemned in the House of Lords for his actions, and the British people will rejoice with you on the day he is removed from command."

A small comfort, Aimée thought bitterly. But perhaps it was an indication that John's mission might be a success, after all.

They were headed for the Bahamas, to take on fresh water and cargo before braving the colder waters of the Atlantic toward Liverpool.

Captain Denby, accompanying Aimée on her afternoon walk on deck, turned to the girl beside him and confided, "We will soon be in Nassau, Mrs. Garrard. And I am sure that you will enjoy selecting some suitable clothes to add to your wardrobe." He glanced at the velvet dress, no longer fresh, and Aimée was disconcerted.

"That is not necessary, Captain," Aimée replied. "I can make do with what I have until we reach England."

"If it is money, my dear," he said, "do not be so hesitant. I shall consider it an honor if you will allow me to purchase them for you."

"Thank you, but no, Captain. I cannot accept—"

The voice of the sailor stopped the conversation.

"Ship approaching on the port stern."

The captain's attention was immediately riveted to the horizon. Aimée, with a sudden stab of fear, strained her eyes at the ship approaching.

"Can you see the flag?" Aimée asked, praying that it would not be a Union ship.

"From this distance it looks like an American flag, Mrs. Garrard," Captain Denby responded, but at the expression on her face he hastened to assure her. "You need

216

not be worried, ma'am. We are in international waters."

"Will that make a difference?"

"They do not dare stop and search a British ship. It would be an act of aggression, a breach of maritime law." His voice was calm, giving no hint of alarm.

Still, Aimée watched, not completely convinced by the captain's assurance.

For the next day and a half the U.S. man-o'-war trailed them. The ship occupied Aimée's mind, and she watched in increasing tenseness as it grew larger and larger on the horizon.

The meal that evening was eaten in an uneasy atmosphere. The U.S. ship was now so near that it could not be ignored, and a cold premonition swept over Aimée. John stood no chance if the U.S. Navy insisted on removing him from the British ship to take him back to New Orleans. He would be hanged as surely as Monsieur O'Brie.

"What will happen, Captain, if the Federal ship asks you to hand over . . . Juba?" Aimée asked, showing her concern for John Runefelt.

"I do not believe they would make such a request," he answered, "and if they did, of course the request would be denied."

"And if . . . they boarded without permission?"

"That would be extremely foolish. You must remember that we are quite close to a British port—less than a day away, actually."

"Still, they have been trailing us consistently," Aimée argued, not content with his answer. "And if we are only a day's time from Nassau, would it not be to their advantage to try to remove Juba before we reach port?"

"That is true, Mrs. Garrard, if they planned such an act of aggression. But I really think you are worrying unduly."

The meal was over and the captain rose from the table. "Shall we take an evening stroll on deck, Mrs. Garrard? The air is quite balmy tonight."

Aimée stepped out on deck with the man, and although she knew Captain Denby was growing impatient at the discussion (though he was too much of a gentleman to tell her so outright), she could not change the subject.

"Is there any way that Juba could escape to port tonight, without the other ship's knowing?"

Her turquoise eyes, wide and concerned, peered directly at the captain, and he flushed under the unwavering scrutiny. He tugged at his closely-cropped beard and said reluctantly, "I suppose we could lower a lifeboat if we felt that such a danger were imminent. He could slip through the darkness to meet us again in port. But what about you, Mrs. Garrard? Are you not in the same danger?"

Aimée's smile was alloyed with pain, "The enemy has not yet *hanged* a woman, Captain. But far too many men have lost their lives at the end of a Federal rope. No, Captain, I am not in the same danger as Juba Barnard."

"U.S. man-o'-war *Corinthian* requests permission for commander to board ship, sir!"

The captain bristled upon hearing the request and fired back to the young man, "Permission denied. Flag them back, Higsby, to that effect."

"Aye, aye, sir!"

Aimée stood and watched while the flags, barely discernible in the twilight, waved their message to the other ship.

"Mrs. Garrard, I think you had better go to my cabin, just to be safe. I would prefer that you be out of sight in case something unpleasant occurs. Lock the door, and do not open it again until I tell you."

Aimée, fleeing from the deck, left the captain, who became busy at once, issuing instructions to his sailors on duty. But instead of obeying him immediately, she climbed down the ladder to the lower deck.

I must warn John, Aimée thought. He will have to be prepared to leave the ship if the Federal Navy insists on stopping and searching the ship. Aimée knew the British ship was not equipped to do battle against such strong guns.

"John, where are you?" Aimée shouted, running down the passageway and forgetting to call him by his alias.

He opened the door to his cabin and smiled when he

saw Aimée, but her agitated manner wiped the smile from his face.

"John, you must be prepared to leave the ship right away. The man-o'-war has requested permission for its commander to come aboard. That can mean only one thing—he must know that you're on this ship." Aimée was breathless from running, but she continued to choke out the words. "Captain Denby said he will lower a lifeboat for you to get to port if they insist on boarding."

John did not appear surprised at the news for he, too, had been watching the progress of the *Corinthian*.

"And if I go, are you planning to come with me, Aimée?" he asked.

"No, John—I would only be a detriment and slow you down."

John looked out the porthole to the island visible in the distance. "But I could never leave you, Aimée. I would never forgive myself if I were such a coward."

"Do not be so stubborn, John," she said in a rising tone of anger. "I am in no danger of being hanged, but you are. And I could not bear to see you . . . like Monsieur O'Brie. You must try to escape if they force themselves on board. Please, John."

"Aimée. Aimée." He reached toward her, taking her in his arms. "Must you always spur me on to place you in greater danger while seeking to save myself?"

"You have a mission," she argued. "It's important that you reach England. Promise me, John, that you will try to escape."

"What can I say?" John asked in a defeated voice. "It will be hell either way."

"Then promise me," she said, the fire alight in her eyes. "Promise me, John!"

"Only . . . if there is no other way," he said sadly.

The burly sailor loomed in the doorway. "Hurry, Mr. Barnard, The captain has ordered a lifeboat lowered. The U.S. commander and his sailors are forcing themselves on board. We do not have much time to get away."

"John, you must go," Aimée urged. "Hurry!"

There was no other way now. Planting a quick kiss on Aimée's forehead, John picked up the small valise and followed the sailor leading the way down the passageway.

Aimée, her mission accomplished, hurried back to the upper deck, to the captain's cabin, to lock herself in as she had been directed. With relief, she saw that the lingering twilight had given way to darkness.

The long silence penetrated the corners of the cabin and Aimée, denouncing the lack of sound, listened for some slowing down of the ship, some clue as to what was happening.

How could she stand it, not knowing whether the ship had been boarded or not? Or whether John had actually kept his promise and was now rowing through the darkness to safety?

"Sir, this is monstrous. My government will make an official protest to Washington." The captain's voice broke through the silence, loud and angry. "To board my ship forcibly is a breach of maritime law!"

"You have on board one spy, for sure—possibly two, Captain Denby. We wish you to turn them over to us, and you may go on your way. My government does not wish to molest your ship in any way—only to claim two of your passengers."

"I must warn you, sir, that the lady aboard ship is the wife of one of your American officers. She is expecting his child, and if any harm comes to her, or she is ill treated in any way, you will have more than one man to answer to!"

"We will treat her with the utmost respect, I assure you, Captain," the American voice promised. "And now, if you will kindly open the door to your cabin . . ."

The British captain was silent, and the American voice, a trifle more impatient, repeated the request.

"I do not wish to damage the door, Captain, but if you force me—"

"That is not necessary, monsieur," Aimée said softly, opening the door.

"You understand, sir, that Mrs. Garrard had no part in this. She was kidnapped at gunpoint, and I hope you will inform your superiors of this," Captain Denby pointed out with ire in his voice.

"My husband," Aimée said timidly. "He was shot when

I was taken. Do you have news of him?" She addressed the commander, who stood staring at her in an impersonal way.

"I was not informed of the circumstances, ma'am. I'm sorry I know nothing of your husband."

Aimée's shoulders sagged. How long before she would be told what had happened to Bryan—whether he had been found in time to be helped, or whether he was already dead.

"There is no American aboard ship, sir," the boy in navy uniform informed the commander of the *Corinthian*. "A lifeboat is missing. That is all we found."

Aimée and Captain Denby silently exchanged glances of relief. At least John Runefelt had gotten away.

"Good-bye, my dear," Captain Denby said a few minutes later, as Aimée departed with the commander. "Perhaps it is for the best. I do not know. I pray that you will find your husband alive when you reach New Orleans."

"Thank you, Captain, for being so kind to me," Aimée responded, saying with her eyes what her lips could not— that she was grateful the British captain had allowed John Runefelt to escape.

Chapter 24

The waters were rough on the return trip to New Orleans, and the man-o'-war rolled with the swells and the waves. Rain lashed the decks and Aimée, a victim of *mal de mer*, remained the majority of the time in the cabin assigned to her.

Seasickness was not the only toll of the rough seas. Nagging back pain had bothered Aimée the entire day, and she was alarmed at further visible signs that all was not well with her unborn child. She might be in danger of losing this child of Bryan's—the baby she wanted so much.

"Oh, Tante Dee Dee, if only you could be with me now," she lamented aloud, feeling the anxiety of having no one to give her advice. She remembered the whispered conversations of older women discussing some pending birth or the difficulties of being *enceinte,* but whenever she had come within hearing, the whisperings had ceased and the conversations had turned to something more suitable for a young girl to hear.

She did the only thing she knew to protect her baby: Aimée rested in bed. Had not her own *maman* rested in bed for some time before she herself had been born? Had her *maman* experienced the same difficulties that she was now having, the spotting and the nagging back pain?

The swing of the sea denied Aimée physical comfort even in bed. She longed for the waters to become a placid-looking glass, reflecting the calm cerulean blue of the sky. Instead they were an angry, churning somber green and black, clashing and roaring their vibrating dissonances against the hulk of the ship.

The next day Aimée was relieved to find that the storm that had swept in from the Indies in stealth had gone away in stealth sometime during the night, and the nagging ache in her back and the spotting had disappeared.

The *Corinthian* now lay anchored in the Gulf, close to the mouth of the Mississippi. Nearby was the gunboat. They were waiting for the waves to quiet enough for Aimée to be transferred to the smaller vessel to complete the journey to New Orleans.

The man-o'-war did not dare cross the sandbar and the waters that had to be dredged continually of the silt that clogged the mouth of the delta. Ships had been marooned before in shallow waters when the tide was out. The Federal Navy had learned of the Mississippi's treachery in sand and tide the hard way.

When waiting for the storm to subside, a curious thing had happened to Aimée. She had lost her fear of the storm—the old terror that had plagued her from childhood. There was a quietness of strength that shone from the turquoise eyes—she was a new being, tempered by adversity. As she was handed over to the care of the other vessel, the men, seeming to sense a special destiny in the young woman, accorded her more respect than they had originally intended.

Aimée rode past the forts, upriver toward port. An occasional brown pelican moved from its perch to lumber into the air and hurl itself, with pouched mouth open, into the water to scoop up menhaden for its dinner. Only the young in the rookeries dotting the lagoons had the power to cry out for food, for the pelican lost its voice in maturity. Aimée watched the silent old pelican swoop and ride the waters patiently. His survival and that of his family depended upon no one else but himself.

Aimée did not enter New Orleans in the most triumphal manner. She had been given little fresh water with which to bathe, and the velvet dress that she had been so proud of was now limp, dirty and unappealing. There were no pins to bind her hair, no comb but her fingers to brush out the tangles, and the forlorn and tired look in her turquoise eyes, smudged by shadows underneath, broadcast to anyone with a sensitive eye the price that the past week and a half had exacted from her.

Aimée saw the Union soldier standing by the carriage near the levee. He was waiting for the gunboat to dock so that she might be delivered like some piece of goods—no different from the other cargo being loaded and unloaded on the busy levee.

With all its intense activity, the port showed no visible signs that a war was going on. Goods overflowed, traded back and forth, loaded and unloaded from the vast warehouses. The port of inanimate structures of wood and metal and water was not capable of sensing, as Aimée was, the subtle change of feeling—the transfer of ownership from the native shipper to the enterprising outsider who had taken the river and its harbor as the spoils of war. What did the river know of the heartache and near starvation of the people who lived along its banks? It flowed and moved toward the sea, carrying the cargo as it had always done.

The gunboat berthed between two larger ships and Aimée, under escort, walked across the planks laid down until she reached the built-up banks, the levee holding back the water that could so easily inundate the entire city.

"Mrs. Garrard," the young officer waiting on the wharf said to her in a kind voice, "you are to come with me."

Nervously Aimée wet her lips. "My . . . my husband—he was found?" she asked, dreading to hear the answer, yet not able to stand the suspense any longer.

"Yes, Mrs. Garrard. He is in an army hospital but . . ." He hesitated and Aimée willed him to continue.

"But what, monsieur? He is . . . gravely ill. Is that what you are trying to tell me?"

"He has a debilitating fever and . . . has not regained consciousness."

"I must go to him, monsieur," Aimée begged, her voice unable to control the quaver.

"Ma'am, I am afraid it will be impossible, until you have talked with General Banks."

"General Banks!" Then, that meant—

"General Butler has been . . . replaced?" she asked.

"Yes, ma'am. About a week ago."

The relief was overwhelming. Surely any commander would be kinder—would not keep her from her husband. Perhaps he would even let her stay with Bryan to nurse him back to health.

As Aimée rode in the carriage beside the young officer, she closed her eyes in exhaustion, grateful that at least Bryan was alive.

It was now the coldest part of the year, when the dampness swept in from the water to freeze the bones with its icy broom. Aimée shivered, feeling the cold dampness that blotted out the memory of warmth and balmy breezes from the tropical waters as the carriage sped through the streets to General Bank's office.

The general was not there. Instead Aimée was hand-delivered to his aide, who sat across his desk and took down all pertinent information as she was questioned. And the file, with Bryan's petition, lay before him on the desk. But Bryan had not had an opportunity to apply to General Banks—he could not have done so before he was hurt—it must be the old petition he had made.

"Mrs. Garrard," the man said to her, "I see here that you have been under your husband's parole, but that an order was issued for you to be removed to the Castle as a prisoner on the day you . . . disappeared."

"Yes, *monsieur*, that is correct."

"Will you tell me about that day, what happened? There are only rumors. Your husband was shot and there was a question as to whether you had been hurt also, since your cloak, found beside your husband, was covered with blood. But the man who found Major Garrard insisted it was the major's blood, and not yours."

Aimée began calmly enough, but when she reached the moment when Bryan got hurt, she became so visibly distressed that the aide got up from his desk and walked to the window to give her time to recover.

Aimée struggled with her emotions, and by the time the man sat down again, she had regained some control.

"Mrs. Garrard, was there any reason for stopping at that particular spot?" he continued questioning.

"I . . . I became ill, *monsieur*. That was the only reason."

The man nodded as if corroborating her story. "Your husband was too delirious to be questioned the day I visited him, but he kept speaking of his son—that he would not have his son born in a prison."

"If I had been able to keep the truth from him—if I had not become ill—Bryan would not have been caught off guard." The tears fell onto the velvet skirt. "He would have seen the men and been able to defend himself."

"Against so many, Mrs. Garrard?" His look was doubtful. "You love your husband very much." It was not a question but a statement.

Aimée nodded and then looked away. The aide continued to stare down at the file before him.

"Mrs. Garrard, I have discussed your . . . case with

General Banks, and if you are prepared to sign a statment that you had no foreknowledge of your rescue and that you will engage in no more activities against the Union, you will be allowed to remain in New Orleans with your husband."

At first Aimée did not understand. "Do you mean . . ."

". . . that you are free to go so long as you can fulfill the requirements of this document," he finished for her, handing her the pen with which to sign.

"And now I think you would wish to . . . become more presentable before visiting your husband. I will have Lieutenant Johnson drive you to your house."

Never before had she been told that she looked like a veritable hag, but Aimée was not insulted. She smiled, grateful for the kindness that had been shown her.

"One word of warning, Mrs. Garrard—"

The man's voice stopped her at the door and she turned toward him, waiting for him to continue.

"You realize, of course, that you will be watched. If there is ever any indication that you are again giving aid to the Rebels, then . . ." He moved his hands in an expressive gesture.

Understanding the threat, Aimée nodded her head and left.

Across the city she went, once again, until the familiar pink stucco and brick townhouse told her she had come home.

"My God, Aimée, I thought you were a ghost!" Clay stood in the open door and stared at her unbelievingly.

"I assure you, Clay, I am real," Aimée said wearily. "And now, if I may come in . . ."

He immediately stepped back to allow her to pass through the opening.

"But where have you been? We all thought you were dead. With Bryan raving mad, unable to do anything but hold that damned bloody cloak next to him—"

"I was kidnapped, Clay. But I do not have time to tell you the whole story. I must hurry and freshen up, so that I can go to Bryan."

"You mean, you're no longer a prisoner?" he asked.

'I am . . . as free as you are," she replied. And then

looking around, she asked, "Where are Tink and Anderson?"

"They're at the St. Charles Hotel—taking care of Bryan."

"Hotel?" Aimée was not sure she had heard him correctly.

"Yes. The town is overflowing with the wounded. Every available space is being used for a hospital—even the hotel ballroom. And they've hardly left me with a bowl of soup these past ten days," he complained. "Always at the hotel . . ."

Moving past Clay, Aimée climbed the stairs to the room she had shared with Bryan. It was just as she had left it that day when she had packed her valise to take to the Castle.

Less than an hour later Aimée was on her way to the St. Charles, the hotel that General Butler had taken over when he was refused the choice suite. Since Anderson was using the *calèche*, Aimée was forced to ride the trolley. It was late in the afternoon when she arrived, and the man standing guard before the door stopped her. "I am sorry, but you cannot go in without a pass."

"Oh, please," Aimée begged. "My . . . my husband is in there. I must go to him."

"Orders are orders, ma'am," he said, shaking his head. "If you wish to visit, you will have to have a pass."

"Where do I see about this pass?" Aimée asked, wilting from the extra obstacles thrown in her way.

"At headquarters in the Customs House. But the offices are now closed for the day. You will have to wait until tomorrow."

The aide must have forgotten to give her a pass, Aimée thought dejectedly. She turned to walk down the steps when a voice stopped her.

"Mrs. Garrard! Mrs. Garrard!"

It was Anderson, limping toward her, and she rushed to meet him.

The questions tumbled out quickly, one after the other, while she clung to Anderson. "How is he? Is he conscious? The guard said I would have to obtain a pass to see him. Is Bryan going to be all right?"

"Now that you are here, there is a . . . chance," he said, taking her by the arm. With an intimidating expression, he displayed his own pass to the guard and dared the man to stop them.

The cavernous ballroom was crowded with men on pallets side by side, which left almost no space for walking. The glistening chandeliers were an incongruous sight, shining down, not on some gay *soirée* or *bal du salut,* but upon the horror of suffering—crowded bodies that had been mutilated by war. Everywhere were men in pain and the steady groans rose up to greet Aimée in a macabre chant.

"Why . . . why are there so many, Anderson?" Aimée asked, touched at the sight, as she followed the path he made through the room.

"The battles are increasing upriver," Anderson replied, "and there are many casualties on both sides."

Aimée's eyes searched for Bryan at each pallet as she walked, her concern for him becoming more alarming with each step. Then she spied Tink, kneeling in the far corner of the room and wiping a man's fevered brow.

Aimée hurried the rest of the way, dropping down beside Tink, the anxiety showing in her pale face. Tink, seeing her, reluctantly gave up her place beside Bryan and stood back in the shadows of a pillared column.

The man thrashed restlessly on the pallet, his lips moving in a low, agonized voice. His chest was wrapped in bandages and beside him lay Aimée's blue velvet cloak, stained with blood and mud.

"Bryan, Bryan," she whispered. "Can you hear me, my darling?"

The giant of a man clutched at the cloak beside him and his voice, weak and low, cried out, "Aimée—I cannot take you back—they cannot force me. My son—Aimée, are you carrying my son?"

Aimée placed her hand on his hot brow. "I am here with you, Bryan. And your son is . . . safe."

Bryan opened his eyes and Aimée smiled, but there was no recognition. He continued in his tortured delirium, not seeing her at his side.

"She is . . . dead. Aimée is dead." His head moved

back and forth and fresh beads of sweat appeared on his forehead.

Aimée took the cloth, and gently touching his brow, she wiped away the dampness.

"I am here, Bryan—Aimée is here with you," she repeated, but the man kept up his agitated movements until finally, in exhaustion, he loosened his hold on the cloak and his breathing became less labored.

"He will sleep now, Mrs. Garrard," Anderson informed her. "The . . . delirium always exhausts him."

"And . . . he has been like this, ever since they brought him in?"

Anderson looked at her with sympathy in his eyes. "He was evidently on the ground for a long time before being found. The dampness could not help but hurt him."

"And it was all your fault," Tink's voice accused, speaking quietly to Aimée from the shadow of the nearby column.

"Child, I think you would do well not to place blame where it is not warranted," Anderson said severely. "Mrs. Garrard had nothing to do with the major's being shot."

Ignoring Tink's accusation, Aimée addressed the man. "Anderson, will they allow me to stay the night here?"

"One of us has been staying each night with him," he replied, "because they don't have enough help. I don't believe there would be any objection, since we already have permission for someone to be with him."

"Then I should like to be the one to stay with him tonight," Aimée affirmed.

Anderson and Tink left, and Aimée, sitting on the hard floor beside the pallet, kept vigil, surrounded by the pained voices in the night. She did what she could for the ones nearby, giving them water when they asked for it and replacing the blankets that had slipped to the floor, but it was Bryan who claimed her heart. In his restlessness he cried out off and on but Aimée was beside him to soothe him with her loving hands.

The first light of morning, coming through the windows, spread its filtered shafts of gold into the dark places of the ballroom. Aimée had dozed, but now the light teased her into waking. Her hair, having become unpinned during the night, tumbled down in a frivolous display, and Aimée sat up to repair the ravages of the night to her appearance. But Bryan moved his arm, entrapping the silky strands. The movement pulled at her scalp and Aimée turned to lift Bryan's arm, but as she turned, his hands began to stroke the red-gold mass, slowly at first, then with stronger movements, caressing it between his fingers, and Aimée did not dare move.

Bryan's eyelids opened and a strange expression shone from the silver-gray haunted eyes. "Aimée?" The voice was faint, and then his eyelids closed.

"Bryan?" Aimée waited but there was no further sound except her husband's breathing.

Had he recognized her, or was he still lost in the dream that had haunted him for days?

The limping sound across the floor told her that Anderson had come early.

"Clay is waiting outside in the *calèche* to take you home, Mrs. Garrard. And don't worry about coming back so soon. I have brought enough food to last the day."

Aimée looked around at the activity, now that the others were waking up. "Anderson, how can they all possibly be looked after well, with so few to do it?"

"They're sent to the convalescent camps as soon as they can walk—the Union ones, that is. And I guess the others are . . . taken to the Customs House."

"To the Customs House." As prisoners of war. Aimée glanced sadly around her. She had promised to give no comfort, no aid to the enemy—her own people—in exchange for being with her husband. It was a difficult promise to keep.

Again she glanced at her husband. "If Bryan—Major Garrard—could be moved back to the townhouse, he would stand a better chance of getting well. The floor is so cold here for him to be lying on. He would be much better off in a clean bed, with a fire warming the room. Do you think it would . . . injure him further to be moved?"

"It was too risky even a few days ago, Mrs. Garrard, but I'll have a talk with the doctor while I'm here and see if he's changed his mind. He might welcome one less patient."

"Thank you, Anderson." Aimée hurried out of the ballroom so that Clay would not be kept waiting too long in the cold.

They rode down the street, the black pony trotting gingerly along the rough cobblestones. Aimée and Clay made no effort to converse until she remembered the lute that Bryan had placed in the back of the *calèche* that day they left for the Castle.

"Clay, when Bryan was found, was my lute still in the *calèche*?"

"I think so, Aimée. It seems to me that Anderson said something about it."

"Do you know where it is now?"

"I believe Anderson put it in the attic, Aimée."

Aimée nodded and rode the rest of the way home in silence.

By the time Aimée returned in the late afternoon Anderson had good news for her. Since the wound was healing, the doctor had given his consent for Bryan to be moved, if she could find a safe means of getting him home.

"The fever, Mrs. Garrard," the doctor explained, "is the thing to watch and worry about. I have seen it make a man as weak as a baby. But your main problem is lifting such a big man without injuring him further—and then moving him. The army ambulance is rough enough to jolt a man's teeth loose . . . so I wouldn't advise that."

"I once saw the sugarcane workers on my *papa's* plantation lift an injured man into a cane wagon to take him out of the fields. They used a gate covered with soft leaves stripped from the stalks," Aimée said, searching back in her memory. "If I could hire a dray and some workers on the levee, they could line the wagon deep with cotton to prevent any harsh jolting and . . . and if we could find a door to lift him . . ."

The doctor was smiling when Aimée looked up at him. "I see you have solved the problem, Mrs. Garrard. If you are this determined, then I expect you will have your husband well in no time."

231

It was too late that day to accomplish the move, so Aimée remained overnight by Bryan's side. There was no change in the fever, no recognition, and Bryan, still agitated, cried out in his delirium, breaking Aimée's heart with each haunted cry.

In the middle of the night Aimée became aware of the rain—the driving, slashing rain—and she feared that it would continue during the next day so that they could not get Bryan home. She listened to its sounds, hopeful when there was a slackening. Then her hope plunged when the torrents sounded afresh on the roof.

The morning was gray and chilled, with a slight mist rising from the river. An unpromising day. Would she put Bryan's life in even more danger if she took him home in such weather? Aimée had already been blamed by Tink for being responsible for his injury . . . and no doubt she would be blamed for any setback, any mishap, because of moving him. But she had to take the chance. Wasn't it better to take him to warm quarters than to leave him where he was, when the weather was getting colder and his fever was making him weaker each day?

Bryan was her responsibility now and Aimée would have to make the decisions, and pray that they were the right ones. There was no other way.

Tink stayed with Bryan while Aimée went directly to the levee with Anderson to arrange the transportation of the sick man.

An hour later a strange procession moved through the streets of New Orleans—a strong, low wagon without sides pulled by a set of mules with Anderson as the driver; muscular dock workers, protecting their passenger while sitting along the sides of the dray with feet dangling; and the *calèche*, with Aimée and Tink, moving slowly behind the dray.

Chapter 25

The fire crackled on the hearth and the bed where Bryan lay was far different from the uncomfortable, bare, makeshift pallet that had been his bed for over ten days.

The room in the townhouse had assumed an air of peace and Aimée, grateful that her husband was resting quietly, also rested in the chair beside the hearth, her mind wandering here and there over events of the past days. The sound of the church bells wafted in from the street. Aimée sat up with a jolt—it must be Christmas Eve. It had completely slipped her mind.

She must get to the cathedral and light candles for Bryan's recovery—for all her loved ones—and also have a priest hear her confession.

Aimée took one last glance at Bryan, who had not stirred, and remembering the warmth of Tante Dee Dee's old black cape, probably still hanging near the kitchen pantry, she walked quickly to the kitchen area. She bumped into Tink, who was walking in the hallway toward her.

"Oh, Tink, I am going out for a few minutes. Will you please sit with Major Garrard while I am out?"

Tink, looking at Aimée with the same accusing expression that she had given her earlier, nodded and climbed the stairs toward the bedroom where Bryan lay asleep.

When Aimée reached the kitchen, Fréki and Geri lifted their heads from the beds to which Aimée had relegated them earlier that day so that Bryan would not be disturbed by their barks or whining.

Seeing Aimée putting on the cloak, they stood up, ready to follow her. "Stay!" Aimée ordered, and the dogs settled again, succumbing to the warmth radiating from the iron range, as Aimée closed the door behind her.

The candles before the altar twinkled in sputters and spurts. Aimée, after purchasing her candles, joined her entreaties with those of the others, her prayers forming with the lighting of each candle from the main one in the center. She knelt in the cathedral, her head bowed and her lips moving soundlessly to form the word "Bryan" over and over. Bryan—the man who had stolen her heart; Bryan—the father of her unborn child. And it was then that she made her vow.

Tired from the long day, she left the cathedral to trudge home in the cold wind that whipped the somber black cloak from her petite, fragile frame.

The small crêche—the manger scene made of French porcelain—had been carefully wrapped and stored in the attic. Aimé brought it downstairs to a place of honor in the salon that night—the one reminder in the house of that holy day. And as she placed Mary and Joseph and the Wise Men with their gifts about the manger, she continued praying for the most precious gift she could receive —Bryan, her husband, restored to health.

He slept fitfully, exhausting himself with his delirious outbursts, until a cool hand, a cold cloth, gave him peace again. And so it continued, each person in the house taking turns sitting with him. But each night it was Aimée who insisted on being in the room with Bryan, so she could get up from the chaise at his slightest movement or murmur.

Staring down at Bryan in his fevered delirium, Aimée had the same stricken feeling she had had that year the epidemic had hit the city full force . . . the year Tante Dee Dee had died. She had cared for her, had sat up with her at night to sponge her hot, fevered body with vinegar water, had tended to her during the day as well, never leaving the sick room except for a few minutes at a time. Yet Tante Dee Dee had grown gradually weaker each day, and Aimée had not been able to prevent her from dying.

A heavy cloud of stagnant air had hung over the city those terrible weeks, a dark shroud, smothering and hovering with a blackness that drove even the birds away. And the undertakers and grave diggers had staggered under a never-ending job until finally, after thousands had died, the storm had cleared and purified the malignant air—something the cannons, ordered by the authorities to be shot along the streets each evening, had never been able to do.

Now Bryan, his body already weakened by the gunshot wound, lay drenched in perspiration as he struggled to throw off the enervating fever. And Aimée, remembering Tante Dee Dee, redoubled her efforts to give him relief.

On the fourth day his brow seemed a little cooler and he did not appear so restless. His outbursts were now less frequent and Aimée's hopes soared that the fever was beginning to break.

That night Aimée lay on the chaise with the downy soft quilt wrapped around her shoulders. The wind whistled down the chimney, and toward morning the rainstorm hit the city with a violent anger from the sea. The fire, giving out little warmth from its banked embers, was in danger of dying completely and Aimée, shivering, got up from her bed to lay fresh logs on it.

She knelt by the hearth and hugged the warmth to her body, covered by the white long-sleeved gown, her face framed by the glowing tongues of fire licking at the rough, jagged bits of bark. A low, haunted voice suddenly cried out, startling her.

"No! Leave me alone! Go away!"

Aimée stood, straining her eyes in the darkness.

"Bryan?" she questioned.

She took a step closer to the bed, but the voice halted her. "Can't you leave me in peace? God! Do I have to be tormented the rest of my life, seeing your face before me?"

Aimée was stunned by the outburst. The first words that Bryan had spoken to her—the ones she had waited so long to hear—were heartless, cruel words, chilling her

235

far worse than the grip of the storm.

The pressures that had built up over the past days closed in on her and Aimée could no longer control her aching heart. He hated her—he did not want to look at her!

She sank to the hearth in despair and her body shook with deep, racking sobs that matched the deluge outside. Her grief was no longer disguised, her tears no longer held back. Aimée laid her head in her arms and gave full vent to the desolation that was in her heart.

"Aimée? Aimée?" the voice called out. There was a question in the voice now, and Aimée raised her head, staring in Bryan's direction, not able to see him, not certain what was to happen next.

There was a movement in the high-carved bed, as if the man in it were attempting to sit up.

"Am I . . . home?" he asked in a puzzled, weak voice.

"Yes, Bryan, you're home," she answered quietly.

"And you're really . . . with me? You're not a . . . ghost?"

"I'm with you, Bryan. No, I'm not a ghost."

"Why . . . why are you so far away . . . from me?" he asked. "Will you . . . come closer?"

Aimée obeyed him, her bare feet making no sound as she approached the bed and stood before him, the sadness still revealed in her face.

Bryan reached out to touch her, and like a blind man he let his fingers trace upward until his hands were cradling her face. A finger brushed across her wet cheeks and he asked, "Are you crying? Aimée, why are you crying?"

"You . . . you told be to . . . go away—to leave you alone." Her voice cracked on the last word.

His trembling arms drew her to him and he buried his face in her hair. "Oh, my darling, I thought I was being . . . haunted again. I have been in a nightmare—I dreamed you were . . . dead."

"Then, you are . . . happy to see me?" Aimée asked, with a glimmer of hope.

"Happy . . . I . . ." His voice dwindled away and his arms relaxed his hold on her. The deep, slumbered breathing was all she heard, and grateful that he had regained consciousness even for a short time, she drew the covers over him and slipped back to her bed.

The sound of the hungry leaping flames woke Aimée. She opened her eyes slowly, taking in the fresh fire on the hearth, her body feeling warm and snug in the quilt. Not wanting to move or disturb the comfortable peace of the room, she remained where she was until a disturbing feeling gradually crept over her—a feeling that she was being watched.

Sitting up quickly, Aimée let her eyes wander to the bed where Bryan lay. But he was not lying down. He was sitting up, watching her, and she was embarrassed under his careful scrutiny.

"Bryan, you're awake," Aimée said, forgetting the episode of the past night in her joy at seeing him propped up on the pillows. The quilt fell from her in her haste to stand.

Bryan smiled at her and said, "I've been awake for some time."

"Why . . . why didn't you call me then? I have been such a sleepyhead," Aimée fretted.

"I was in no hurry. I was content just to sit here and watch you."

"Watch me?"

"Yes—to make sure that you were real, and that you wouldn't disappear again."

Aimée pushed back her long golden-red hair. "But you must be hungry. I'll get you some breakfast."

"Anderson has already been in. He's bringing breakfast soon."

Aimée hurriedly put on her robe and turned toward the door, but Bryan protested, "Don't leave me, Aimée. I . . . can't bear to let you out of my sight."

There was a weakness in his voice, an absence of strength that touched her as nothing else did. There was no trace of his former insolence or arrogance—only a tiredness, a terrible exacting of the fever that had left his face gaunt, his eyes with an unnatural brilliance.

"I . . . thought I had . . . lost you."

"Don't try to talk, Bryan. You'll waste your strength."

He reached out for her and Aimée came to sit on the bed, to take his hand, while he fought the weakness that caused him to close his eyes, his body exhausted from the few words he had uttered.

"He has gone back to sleep, Anderson," Aimée apologized when he brought in the breakfast tray. "I'm afraid he's not going to want breakfast for a while."

Bryan drifted through the next several days—emerging off and on from the sleep that was renewing his tired and weak body, but only long enough to be fed and to make sure that Aimée was at his side.

In the afternoons, when he was apt to sleep longest, Aimée put on the old dark cloak and went to the cathedral. She never stayed long for fear that Bryan would wake and miss her.

It was during one of the trips out of the house that Aimée decided to stop at the French Market before returning home from the cathedral.

As she walked in and out of the stalls in the arcade, looking for something to tempt Bryan's appetite, she overheard the news of the latest Confederate victory that the Union-controlled newspapers would not dare print.

Excited whispers told her that Van Dorn had raided Grant's headquarters, capturing the city of Holly Springs, Mississippi, and fifteen hundred Union soldiers. He had destroyed Grant's winter's supplies, disrupting the general's advance southward.

All along the stalls unconcealed smiles greeted Aimée, and the whispers continued, until a Union uniform in their midst would force mouths to close. At the uniform's disappearance, the whispers would start again.

"Grant's mules won't have such a fine accommodation after all. Guess the first thing Van Dorn will do will be to remove the animals from the churches."

"Couldn't say I like the idea of the Yankees using a church for a stable."

"Maybe the general thought they'd get a little religion," chuckled one old fellow, picking up a banana to purchase. "Mules can be mighty ornery at times."

When Bryan had been home for a week, Aimée hurried back to the townhouse from her usual afternoon trip. As she turned to open the iron gate, she saw the wagon rumbling down the street. She squinted against the late afternoon sun, trying to see the figures in the wagon as it approached.

The wagon slowed and came to a stop several houses away, and a child jumped down onto the banquette. She walked to the faded wooden door, looked at the name plate, shook her head, and then climbed up again on the wagon.

The child resembled Faith, Vickie's oldest daughter, with her long brown hair tumbling over her shoulders, but of course it could not be the child. She was safe at Thornfell with Cousin Clotilde and Jorge. She would not be on a wagon with household goods and people.

Aimée watched while the wagon rolled closer. Alarm came with the sudden recognition. It *was* Faith, and Hope as well, with Vickie, Cousin Clotilde, and Jorge, and seated in the rear of the wagon, Lizzie holding the baby, Charity.

What had happened? Had Thornfell been burned? Had Yankee raiders not left them alone after all?

Aimée rushed toward them. "Cousin Clotilde," Aimée called, "what has happened?"

The tall gray-haired woman shivered in the cold, but her eyes, upon seeing Aimée, lit up with joy, even as she apologized. "We are seeking shelter, Aimée. There is nothing left at Thornfell."

"Nothing left? Do you mean . . .?"

"The Yankees have burned everything—the sugar house, the slave cabins, and Thornfell. The house is just a shell," Cousin Jorge said ruefully.

"But . . . why?" Aimée asked, still unable to understand the reason for such destruction.

"Oh, we were not the only ones," Cousin Jorge hastily explained. "Other plantations nearby were burned as well. It seems that an army supply wagon was ambushed and the driver wounded. So the Yankee soldiers retaliated by burning everyone out for miles around."

"And it wasn't even their own supplies," Faith piped up. "They had stolen the food to begin with."

"Faith, don't interrupt," Vickie admonished.

"And this is all you were able to save?" Aimée asked, looking at the contents of the wagon.

"We were luckier than some of the others," Cousin Clotilde quietly answered with a weary droop to her head.

"At least you are all safe," Aimée said in relief alongside the wagon, while directing them down the courtyard drive. "We can put the wagon in the carriage house for tonight. All of you come in—I know you're cold and tired from the trip. I'll get someone to help you unhitch the horses, Cousin Jorge."

Aimée looked with pity at the two fine saddle horses forced to do a mule's work in pulling the wagon such a distance.

She led the women and children into the house and Anderson and Clay, who had heard the sound of the wagon in the carriage drive, came to Cousin Jorge's aid, unhitching Sagefly and Dark Lightning, to put them in the stall of the carriage house, beside the black pony.

"My dear, we have been so worried about you. We did not dare think what had happened when you did not return to Thornfell . . . and then John brought your note to us. We were so thankful that you had not been . . . harmed."

Aimée saw the inquiring look in Cousin Clotilde's face but there was no time for explaining anything, with Bryan upstairs ready to wake at any moment. As soon as she had gotten them into the salon by the warm fire, Aimée dashed upstairs to see if Bryan had awakened from the noise, but his eyes were still closed and his breathing was steady and even. So she returned to the salon where Clay and Cousin Jorge had joined Cousin Clotilde and Vickie. The children vanished with Lizzie into the kitchen at the mention of honey cakes.

To explain Clay as her brother-in-law, when they did not know she was married, created an awkwardness for Aimée. Vickie's sharp eyes had not missed the slight thickening of Aimée's waist, visible after she removed the black cloak. Aimée was wearing a loose-fitting garment, with no corset, and she saw that look appear in the deep brown eyes watching her—the speculative look only one who has borne a child can give another.

"I am afraid we have created quite a problem for you, with so many of us . . . especially with a sick man in the house," Cousin Clotilde said in a concerned voice. "Clay has told us that your husband has been wounded. Perhaps it would be better if we tried to find another place—"

"Nonsense. You gave me shelter when I needed it. And the least I can do is return the hospitality. There will have to be some reshuffling to find enough bed space, but other than that . . ." Aimée was thoughtful, mentally planning where she could put everyone.

"I can help solve that problem right away, Aimée," Clay said. "Why not have the men move to the carriage house? Anderson and Cousin Jorge and I would get along very well in bachelor quarters."

Cousin Jorge smiled at Clay. "A good idea—our very own *garçonière*. I remember when we boys reached the age of sixteen, we were moved from the main house to a wing set apart from the rest. It will be just like the old days."

So that left Cousin Clotilde to share Tink's room, Vickie in the larger bedroom with the two older girls, Faith and Hope, and Lizzie with two-year-old Charity in the smaller adjoining bedroom-nursery.

By this time, with bedroom space settled and steaming cups of black coffee with honey cakes served, Aimée was anxious to see to Bryan.

"If you will excuse me, I must see to my . . . husband," Aimée said, leaving the salon to walk to the stairs.

Bryan was awake, and seeing her, he asked in a puzzled voice, "Aimée, what is all the activity downstairs? What is happening?"

Aimée closed the door, walked to the bed, and leaned over to feel his forehead. Bryan took her hand, and kissing the palm, held onto her when she straightened, intending to sit down in the chair.

"Bryan," she said hesitantly, taking her seat on the bed beside him, "Cousin Clotilde and the others have come from Thornfell. There is . . . nothing left and they had to

241

come to New Orleans or . . . starve. They are my family, Bryan. I could not turn them away."

Bryan nodded, a thoughtful expression coming into his silver-gray eyes at the news. "And you are afraid that I will . . . object?"

"There are . . . six of them, plus Lizzie," she answered in a distressed voice.

"Do you think I would turn any of your family away?" he asked with a gentleness in his voice.

She gazed at her husband with grateful eyes and lovingly touched his cheek with her lips. She felt his fingers tighten their grasp on her hand, and then he sank back onto the pillows.

"My body is . . . weak when I do not wish to be weak," Bryan complained. "And I am tired of being in bed."

The smile brightened Aimée's face and she teasingly responded, "When a gentleman complains, that means he is getting well."

"It might mean that he is tired of having no one to share his bed," Bryan said, a trace of gruffness in his voice. "How long will you continue to sleep on . . . that thing?" he asked, pointing to the chaise across the room.

"Until you are completely well, Bryan," she answered firmly.

"And if I . . . extend an invitation for you to share my bed before then?"

Aimée laughed. "The . . . invitation will be politely declined."

"Would you disobey an . . . order?"

Aimée, seeing that the effort of speaking was tiring him, merely smiled and said, "We will speak of orders later. Now it's important for you to rest. And I need to see about some soup for your dinner, as well as extra food for our guests."

It was almost like Thornfell again, except for the peace of having Bryan with her.

Chapter 26

Anderson and Tink had been pressed into a hurried trip to the market for additional food for dinner, and when they returned, Cousin Clotilde was in the kitchen to help prepare the food. After setting four places in the kitchen for Lizzie and the three children, Aimée carried the rest of the china into the dining room.

"I would have helped Cousin Clotilde in the kitchen, Aimée," Vickie explained, placing the silverware on the dining table, "but for those ferocious dogs. I dare not go near them."

"They won't hurt you, Vickie. They're very gentle most of the time."

"Gentle?" Vickie's voice contained an unbelieving timbre. "With all the growling they did when I walked in? No, Aimée, they're ferocious dogs and I barely managed to escape before they leaped on me."

'I am sorry, Vickie," Aimée apologized. "They've never acted that way before."

When everyone had assembled in the dining room and the food was placed on the table, Vickie glanced at Anderson and Tink with a frown as Clay seated her. "This is a very . . . democratic table, I see."

"Yes," Aimée answered easily. "We work together and share equally—and you and Cousin Clotilde have been much help already. I'm grateful."

"We are grateful that you have such a large heart, Aimée, to take us in," Cousin Clotilde responded.

"Does your . . . husband know that we have descended

243

upon you like this?" Vickie asked. "I wonder if he might not turn us away when he finds out that there are so many Secessionists in the house."

"Bryan knows—and he will not turn you away because you are my family," Aimée replied.

"It must be comforting to be loved that much. You seem to have accomplished quite a lot in a short period of time," Vickie said, glancing knowingly at Aimée's ripening figure. "I was not aware that you were married, Aimée. It must have been quite recent. Although you may not wish to divulge *how* recently."

Aimée felt the sting of her words but forced herself to refrain from giving a biting retort.

Vickie turned to Clay. "It must be difficult for you with your brother fighting for the enemy," she said with sympathy in her voice. "I understand you were in the Confederate Army."

"Bryan and I have always been different, never agreeing on anything as boys." Clay warmed to Vickie's concern. "He was always my father's favorite, while I seemed to have had the giant share of my mother's love."

"Ah, the old tale of Esau and Jacob—'And Isaac loved Esau, but Rebekah loved Jacob,'" Cousin Jorge joined in.

"Your mother was from Virginia, was she not?" Vickie continued, ignoring Cousin Jorge's comment.

"Yes. She would take me on trips home to her family each summer, so it seemed only natural when the war broke out that I would defend her family home. That's when I joined the Army of Northern Virginia. Bryan had already volunteered with the Massachusetts Company."

By this time Cousin Jorge was engaged in conversation with Anderson, who had been totally ignored by Vickie. Toward the end of the meal the sound of the bell Aimée had placed by Bryan's bed rang imperiously, cutting through the conversation. Aimée stood up, saying, "If you will excuse me, I need to see to Bryan."

"Bryan always *did* demand a lot of attention," Clay said. "You'd better hurry, Aimée, before he shouts an order down the stairs. He's used to being obeyed immediately.'

As Aimée left the dining room, the conversation trailed after her.

"I was quite surprised to learn that Aimée is married to your brother," Vickie said in a low tone.

Clay laughed. "Not half so surprised as I—especially since Bryan vowed he would always remain a bachelor."

"It would be interesting to know how she . . . accomplished it," Vickie purred. "Did he confide in you . . . give a particular reason?"

Aimée shut the door, closing out the rest of the exchange. But her cheeks were flushed with annoyance at Vickie. What if she ferreted out the real reason Bryan had married her? Had Bryan confided in Clay?

"You . . . wanted something, Bryan?" Aimée asked, her voice not quite steady because of the conversation between Clay and Vickie.

"Yes . . . you." He held out his arms and Aimée went to him, feeling a need for his love. "I am a lonely man, Aimée, and I was jealous listening for your voice amid the conversation downstairs. I didn't want to share you with them a minute longer."

"Oh, Bryan," Aimée whispered, hiding her face on his shoulder.

His hands moved down her back and slowly stroked her body with his sensuous fingers, drawing out the feeling of desire.

"You will have to sleep with me tonight, you know. I will not allow you to be apart from me any longer," he said in a husky voice.

"Are you sure that I will not . . . disturb you?" Aimée asked.

"You will disturb me only if you persist in sleeping across the room from me. Shall I order Anderson to remove the chaise from my sight, or will you give in and share my bed?"

"I will . . . give in, if that is what you wish, Bryan," she answered uncertainly.

After Aimée had made a last-minute check on the sleeping arrangements of the others, seeing that enough quilts were available, she came back into the bedroom that she shared with Bryan. He was still awake, watching for her.

"Everyone is settled down for the night," Aimée whispered. "The baby, Charity, has been fretful, but Lizzie has finally gotten her to sleep. Faith and Hope had no such problem—they went to sleep as soon as their heads hit the pillows."

"Faith, Hope, and . . . Charity?" Bryan repeated in an incredulous voice. And then he laughed. "Do you mean we actually have faith, hope, and charity present in this house?"

Shyly turning her back to remove her clothes, Aimée answered, "It is a Southern custom to name little girls after the three gifts. Do you not do the same in the North, Bryan?"

"I am not well versed on what people name little girls," he commented, "either in the North *or* in the South."

There was a silence between them. Bryan continued to watch her as she self-consciously reached for her long-sleeved nightgown.

Breaking the silence, he said, "Do not turn away from me, Aimée. We have no secrets from each other, have we?"

"No . . . no secrets, Bryan—except that I do not wish you to see my spreading figure. My waist is no longer small, and I am afraid I have 'tossed my corset on the armoire,' as you accused me of doing that night long ago."

Bryan laughed. "That saying doesn't apply now, though, does it? You had no chance to grow old and fat as a spinster. And it's not surprising that you are in the shape you are in. No man could resist the temptation to get you with child."

Aimée, not responding to his teasing, blew out the light and climbed into the high-carved bed, beside Bryan.

"You are more beautiful carrying my son, Aimée. Did you imagine that I would think you ugly—that I would no longer desire you?" Bryan asked.

"How are you so sure that I am carrying your son, monsieur? Daughters are born sometimes, too."

"We will have many daughters later, with red-gold hair and turquoise eyes. And you can even name them such names as Faith and Charity, if you wish. But first, we will have a son."

"Is . . . is that an order?" she asked, giggling, nudging her head into his chest. She immediately drew back and asked, "Does your wound hurt, Bryan?"

"Only if I turn suddenly. I will have to be gentle tonight, not only for your sake, but also for mine."

But his lips, starting out gently, became more possessive and more passionate and his words once again turned Aimée to fire.

"You excite me so much, I have forgotten how to be gentle," he whispered.

Aimée was caught up in the tremendous emotion that Bryan had started.

"Sweet, so sweet," he murmured, and then he clasped his lips to hers, shutting out all need for words, since their bodies were in perfect harmony and rhythm with each other . . .

Bryan lay exhausted, breathing heavily, while Aimée curled against him, her hand stroking his cheek. His arms gave her a security, even in the peaceful silence. As the silence stretched into a contented timelessness, his breathing became relaxed and Aimée knew that he had lapsed into sleep.

But Aimée did not sleep. She lay in bed beside her husband and pondered the events since she had first met this strong man who could turn her resolutions upside down, her sorrow into joy. And the throbbing sensation remained with her, reminding her body that she had been conquered anew, loved exquisitely and well.

"Aimée?" the faint voice called to her. "Are you awake?"

"Yes, Bryan. I thought you were asleep. Did I wake you? Perhaps I had better move to the chaise so that you can get your rest."

His hands reached out to stop her. "If you have that idea again, I shall have Anderson use it for firewood. I have reached out too many times for you, not to find you there." His voice was fierce but then it suddenly softened. "Once you accused me of never having known fear—but when you disappeared and I thought I would never see you again, I knew . . . fear for the first time, and it is not an easy thing to live with."

For a moment Aimée felt afraid of their mutual need. Bryan had seemed so strong, never relying on anyone else, yet he had revealed a loneliness and a need for love that he had kept hidden until this confession. What would happen if they were separated again? If he were torn from her?

"Bryan," Aimée called out softly in the darkness, "we will talk tomorrow. Go to sleep, *mon brave*."

Bryan sighed, still holding her in his arms, and soon his gentle breathing in her ear brought a sense of ease to Aimée, who closed her eyes and went to sleep.

Aimée twitched her nose, and when the tickling sensation did not disappear, she put up her hands to remove the teasing object. Her fingers came into contact with Bryan's hand and her eyes flew open. He was leaning over her, teasing her cheek with a strand of her own red-gold hair.

"I was beginning to think a spell had been cast over you, Aimée, and a hundred years would be a little too long to wait for you to wake up."

"Bryan!" Aimée protested. "It must be early. Why are you so impatient to start the day?"

"Because I have decided to get up today."

Aimée sat upright, staring unbelievingly at her husband. "It is far too soon to begin thinking of that," she protested.

"No, it is time to be up and about. At least I shall walk to the chair by the fire . . . where are you going, my love, in your bare feet?" he asked.

"To get Anderson. He will stand no nonsense from you."

Bryan grinned at her, saying, "Well, as long as you are seeking out Anderson, tell him to bring my breakfast in a hurry. I am hungry as a devouring north wind."

Bryan in his convalescence made his presence known in the house as much as the great north wind blowing. Ears pricked to listen to his demands; Anderson stepped to in a military manner; and even the house itself seemed to quake lest it fail in some way to come up to the expectations of Bryan Garrard.

"You see what I mean," Clay confided to Vickie. "It has always been this way. All his life, everyone has stepped lively to give Bryan what he wants."

"Will you have some more cake, Clay?" Vickie asked sweetly. "There's another piece I saved just for you, if you should want it."

"Thank you, no, Vickie—but I appreciate your thoughtfulness. It's not often I am catered to around here."

"You are much too thin, Clay. Someone needs to give *you* lots of attention, especially after being in that horrible prison camp."

Aimée made a grimace and walked on past the salon where Vickie and Clay were sitting and conversing. Increasingly they had sought out each other's company from the rest, and Vickie seemed to be making inroads into Clay's confidence. But Aimée was far too busy to keep her mind on the progressing relationship between the two.

Bryan was recovering and it was now time to begin fulfilling the vow she had made on Christmas Eve in the cathedral.

Up the stairs she went, intent on her purpose, not seeing the man in uniform until his hands reached out as she collided with him.

"Mrs. Garrard," the voice said, "what a pleasant surprise."

Alarmed at the familiar sound of his voice, Aimée stared into the face of Colonel Tilson. She attempted to push herself from his embrace, but he held to her.

"C-Colonel Tilson, I believe?" Aimée's voice was low and pavid. "You have come to . . . visit my husband?"

He made no reply but stared into her turquoise eyes with a searching look. Aimée, caught in his grasp, trembled in mesmerized terror. He made no move to free her.

Only Anderson's approach caused the still tableau

to come alive. Colonel Tilson dropped his arms, freeing Aimée from his hold. "You must be more careful, Mrs. Garrard," he said, pretending to steady her. "The next time I might not be willing to let you go."

The man followed Anderson down the stairs and Aimée stood watching with a vague feeling of uneasiness until the colonel disappeared.

Did he suspect that she had masqueraded as Delphine? His words struck her mind like a warning bell—"I might not be willing to let you go." But even if he suspected, what could he do? Nothing.

Relieved, Aimée continued down the hall, pressing open the door to Bryan's room. He was already asleep, and not wishing to disturb him, she quietly closed the door and tiptoed toward the railless stairs to the attic, her original destination.

The lute in its case was in plain view where Anderson had stored it. In regret, Aimée caressed the marquetry, the delicate design of the instrument, and finally shut it in its case. "Forgive me, Great-great-*grand-mère*, for what I am about to do, but I need the money, and the lute is the only possession that is mine alone to sell."

Aimée left the house through the courtyard, and taking the pony and *calèche*, she headed to the shops near Lafayette Square.

Tying the pony to a hitching post, she stepped across the gutter and walked down the banquette. She looked into each shop window loaded with goods that had been sold by destitute people.

It was the presence of another musical instrument, a handsome rosewood piano glimpsed through the window, that made Aimée select the shop.

When she entered, the shopkeeper was busy with another customer and Aimée hung back, waiting discreetly for the woman to finish her transaction.

"I'm sorry, ma'am, but I got more weddin' rings than I know what to do with," he said to the elderly woman. "And as for your silver spoons, there ain't a market for them anymore. Too bad you couldna' come a little earlier, while 'Silver Spoon' Butler was still here. He'd a taken them off your hands, ready enough."

The man gave forth with a hearty laugh, but the woman, dressed in an old faded muslin, maintained her sad dignity.

"I thank you for your . . . kindness in advising me." The woman rolled the silver again into the portion of an old tablecloth and walked toward the door.

"Try Avalon Priddy's down the street," he called out to her. "Maybe he ain't so overstocked. . . . Now, ma'am, what can I do for such a pretty little lady?"

He glanced appreciatively at Aimée in her subdued beige muslin dress whose prim white collar and cuffs were the only decoration alleviating the plainness. But, unknown to Aimée, the dress acted as a foil for her flaming hair, now caught in the afternoon sun.

The man, temporarily blinded by the invasion of the sun, put up his hand to his eyes, while Aimée opened the case and placed the priceless lute upon the counter.

The proprietor tried not to show his excitement, but as he handled the beautiful old instrument, his hands trembled.

"It is very old," he said, feeling the highly polished wood and the ivory inlay. "It has been in your family for a . . . long time?"

"*Oui*, monsieur. It belonged to my great-great-*grand-mère*, who came from France over a hundred years ago. But the instrument is much older than that."

"A . . . pity that you have to sell it," he said, looking greedily at the lute. "One hundred dollars is all I can offer you. Of course, it is worth far more, but . . ." He shrugged his shoulders and smiled benignly.

Aimée said nothing, but packed up the lute, prepared to leave.

"No, wait. Perhaps we can . . . negotiate. How much do you want for it?"

"I cannot take less than three hundred dollars, monsieur."

"I'll give you two hundred."

Aimée stared at him and said nothing.

"Two hundred and . . . fifty?"

She shook her head, at the same time taking a step nearer the door.

"You drive a hard bargain, ma'am. All right. Just bring it back and let me look at it again—to make sure."

Aimée laid it on the counter and waited while the man again lifted the lute out of its case, turning the instrument over, plucking its strings, until satisfied. He said, "I will get you your three hundred dollars."

Aimée returned to the house and unhitched the pony to place him in the stall. Sagefly and Dark Lightning had been sold and the pony again had the stalls to himself.

Later that day Cousin Clotilde found Aimée in the upper hallway. She looked at her with a questioning expression. "There is a man downstairs with a wagonload of supplies, Aimée. He said you ordered it."

"Oh, yes. I must tell him to bring everything into the kitchen," Aimée said, as if she ordered a wagonload of supplies every day.

The next day other deliveries were made, until the kitchen overflowed. Still, Aimée said nothing to the others about her vow—the vow she made when Bryan lay so ill. But now her prayer had been answered, Bryan was almost completely well, and it was time to fulfill the vow— to build an altar to St. Joseph in the courtyard, as she had promised. She would place the notice in the newspaper and get ready for the city's poor to flock to her gates to feast on the food laid before the altar of the saint who had answered her prayer.

For the next four days Aimée spent every possible moment in the kitchen—baking bread in different sizes and shapes, and cooking the hams and other meat.

"You are very busy, my sweet. Let the others help you," Bryan said. "It will not be good for you to get too tired."

Aimée looked at him, propped up in the ornate Lannuier bed, as if he had always owned it. He had a way of putting his mark on everything. He had been getting up a portion of each day—walking about the bedroom, but so far, he had not come downstairs. Each morning Anderson had helped him shave and get dressed so that he would not feel the invalid, but by the afternoon Bryan was glad to go back to bed to rest.

"If you are worried about . . . the baby, Bryan, you need not be. I am healthy and strong."

"But it is you I am worried about, Aimée. You look very tired. I have been a demanding husband, and with the others in the house, you are doing too much." Bryan frowned and Aimée nervously brushed back the hair from her forehead.

"I promise to rest more . . . in a few days," she said with a reassuring smile.

At the last minute Aimée took Anderson and Tink into her confidence, and they helped her decorate the courtyard and place the small green potted tree on the banquette by the gate, to point the way to the St. Joseph altar.

The day of the feast dawned bright and clear and Aimée dressed quickly before Bryan awoke. She crept out of the bedroom to meet Tink and Anderson in the kitchen.

By midmorning the noise of the people coming through the gate to the courtyard reached the ears of everyone inside the house.

"Aimée, something is happening in the courtyard. The most awful looking people are crowding in. I think you had better send someone for the authorities," Vickie said, looking out the window of the salon.

"Oh, that's all right, Vickie—they're the people who are coming to the St. Joseph altar I have set up for them."

"I . . . I don't understand, Aimée. Have you actually *invited* these people here?"

"Yes, Vickie."

"But why? Why would you do such a thing?"

By this time the salon was filled with Clay, Cousin Jorge, Clotilde, and the two older children—all curious at the happening outside their doors.

"I made a vow to feed the poor, if my . . . prayer was answered."

"You mean all these people are being fed?" Vickie asked, horrified at the idea. "You are wasting all this money, just to feed these people? What does your husband say to this, Aimée? Does *he* know you have lost your mind, spending all of his money?"

When Aimée did not answer, Vickie turned to Clay. "Clay, as his brother, you should go upstairs and tell Major Garrard what is going on. This should be stopped before they trample down everything and ransack the house as well."

"It is not . . . my place, Vickie. I am a guest here, also."

"And they're being very mannerly, Vickie," Cousin Jorge said. "Look out and see. Anderson is attending to that." His voice had risen in excitement. "I do believe I'll go out in the courtyard. Anderson might need some help." Cousin Jorge left the window and walked toward the salon door. "It's almost like Christmastime when I was a boy, when we handed out the baskets and suits of clothes to each slave."

"Hope, don't you dare follow Cousin Jorge," Vickie admonished. "You'd be crushed to death in that crowd outside. Lizzie," she called in her agitated voice, "take the children upstairs and don't let them out of your sight!"

Cousin Clotilde looked at Aimée with tenderness in her eyes. "You are . . . doing this because your husband is getting well. Is it not so, my dear?"

Aimée nodded, and the understanding Clotilde put her arms around her.

The girl left the salon to enter the courtyard, where she saw to the table and the food. Greeting her guests with a calm assurance, Aimée sent Tink and Anderson back and forth into the kitchen for food to replenish the table. The loaves of bread, baked in assorted shapes and sizes, all types of jellies and jams, meat and fruit, were laid on the table before the small statue of St. Joseph, to commemorate the day. The courtyard teemed with people, polite and courteous even in their hunger, who had come to help Aimée celebrate her answered prayer.

When Aimée went to the upstairs bedroom, she saw Bryan standing at the window and watching the strange proceedings, a baffled expression on his face.

"Perhaps you would like to explain . . . what is going on?" he asked in a severe tone.

"It . . . it is St. Joseph's Day, and I have prepared an altar in the courtyard."

"Aimée, I do not understand your . . . customs. You will have to be more explicit with me."

Her eyelids lowered in embarrassment and she could not look at her husband.

"It was a . . . vow I made some time ago, Bryan—something I had to keep on St. Joseph's Day. And today is St. Joseph's Day," she finished lamely.

Bryan forced her chin up with his hand so he could see into her eyes.

'When you veil those turquoise eyes, Aimée, I know you are trying to hide something from me. And I thought there were no secrets between us."

She looked up at him, a startled expression meeting his unsmiling gray eyes, glistening with disappointment.

"I . . . do not wish to hide anything from you, Bryan."

"But you kept it a secret from me, did you not—this altar you have built. And the reasons for it. Why did you do it, Aimée, and why did you not tell me beforehand?"

She could not bear the accusing look in his eyes. The tears touched her lashes and her face became flushed.

"I . . . I made a certain vow, when you were so ill, that if . . . you were made well, I would . . ."

He looked at her incredulously, gradual understanding spreading over his dark face, lifting the stern frown from his brow. He drew her to him, caressing the nape of her neck with his giant hand.

"Do not tell me any more, Aimée. I think I . . . understand." And then he laughed and teasingly held her out from him. "But couldn't you have made a *smaller* vow, instead of feeding the entire city? I have an idea that the price of my getting well is going to be very . . . dear."

"Oh, Bryan, there is no such thing as a *small* vow. You are teasing me, afraid that I have spent all your money, as Vickie has accused. She even asked Clay to come up and get you to put a stop to it."

"How long will your . . . altar last, Aimée?"

"Until . . . all the food is gone, Bryan."

"I'm glad you've arranged it that way instead of having it last until all my *money* is gone," Bryan said in a dry tone.

Chapter 27

That evening the dinner was served in silence. And when it was time to adjourn to the salon, each found an excuse not to stay long after coffee. Vickie became busy with the children; Clay, Anderson, and Cousin Jorge disappeared to the carriage house; and Cousin Clotilde vanished to the kitchen to help Tink and Lizzie clean up after dinner.

Aimée, glad that she did not have to act as hostess for long, banked the fire and went upstairs to sit with Bryan.

"You are free now?" he asked hopefully.

"Yes. Everyone seems to have something important to do this evening. And I am glad to be . . . upstairs."

"It has been a long day for you, has it not, Aimée?"

"Yes, and I am very tired, Bryan," Aimée admitted.

"Then let us both go to bed."

Bryan's recovery was gradual but sure. Each day he was a little stronger than the previous one, until he could take his meals with the rest of the family and the dining room held eight places around the table.

Aimée's eyes shone as Bryan dominated the table with his presence. Clay withdrew, but Cousin Jorge warmed to the big man, asking him questions and listening as he responded.

Impatient to go back to active duty, Bryan poured over the newspapers—keeping up with Grant's assault toward the Yazoo Delta and the activities of the Department of the Gulf, now fighting under General Bank's command.

"We are pleased, Major Garrard, that you are now well enough to join us for dinner," Vickie said, looking at Bryan and then at Clay, as if comparing the two brothers.

"It is my pleasure, Mrs. Brittain. The walls upstairs echoed with your conversations and I have been anxious to join you, instead of facing the four walls. It is good to be downstairs again."

"And I suppose you will be returning to duty very soon?" she questioned.

"Probably within the next week or so," Bryan admitted.

Aimée looked in his direction—alarmed at his answer.

"The Army of the Gulf needs all its men, and I will be joining them as soon as possible."

"For the next siege of Vicksburg, Brother?" Clay asked.

"Now Clay, you know a soldier never divulges his destination," Bryan said in a censuring voice.

"That is true, Clay," Vickie agreed. "You never know when a . . . spy might be listening." Vickie's glance was deliberately directed at Aimée.

"It wouldn't take a spy to ferret out that information, Vickie," Clay countered, seeming not quite certain of the undercurrent in the room. "The newspapers are full of it—of the fighting up the Mississippi, with Grant living off the land. I hear every cow within miles of Vicksburg has been slaughtered to feed the Union Army.

"Please, do we have to talk about the war?" Aimée asked. "Let's go into the salon for coffee. It's a festive time, having Bryan at the table with us, and I do not wish to spoil the evening with talk of war."

"A very good idea, Aimée," Cousin Clotilde said. "And perhaps you will make it even more festive by playing the lute for us."

Aimée, shaking her head, tried to capture Cousin Clotilde's attention, but the woman continued. "I am so curious about the beautiful lute that belonged to the famous first Aimée."

"But the lute has been stored away, Cousin Clotilde.

It would be too much trouble to get it down. P-perhaps another time."

"Anderson will get it for you, Aimée. Besides, I have missed hearing you sing and play lately. Anderson," called Bryan.

"Yes, sir?"

"You put Mrs. Garrard's lute in the attic, did you not?"

"Yes, sir."

"Then will you please get it and bring it to the salon?"

"At once, sir." Anderson started up the stairs and Aimée, still protesting, went into the salon with the others.

"Really, I do not wish to play this evening, Bryan." Aimée's voice was so low that Bryan looked at her, alert to her agitated, quiet tones.

"My dear," Cousin Clotilde said, "if you do not feel like playing, then I withdraw my request for this evening. Having heard so much about the beautiful instrument, I was anxious to hear it—not realizing that you did not feel up to playing. Another time will do just as well," she added, smoothing over the awkward moment.

"I think she wants to be . . . encouraged," Vickie said with a slight sarcastic note.

Aimée sat in the salon, ignoring Vickie's remark and downheartedly waiting for Anderson to return without the lute. His limping steps came down the hallway and stopped at the open door into the salon.

"Excuse me, Major, but the lute is not in the attic," Anderson said, an apologetic look on his face.

"Not in the attic? Are you sure, Anderson?" Bryan asked.

"I am sure, sir. Although I distinctly remember placing it on the table next to the armoire. I have looked all over the attic—even under the dust covers, but the lute has been moved."

'I wonder what could have happened to it," Bryan said, staring at Aimée who was looking down at the ring on her finger.

"If you will excuse me, I don't feel so well," Aimée said. "If . . . there is nothing anyone needs, then I will say *Bonne nuit*."

Aimée fled from the salon, up the stairs, her hands

held up to her flushed face. Why had Cousin Clotilde suggested the musical evening? In time, Bryan would have forgotten that the lute existed, but now that he knew the instrument was missing, he would not let it rest—especially since Anderson had taken charge of it, placing it in the attic.

She had been in the bedroom a few minutes when the door opened and closed.

"Aimée."

She did not turn around, but stood looking out the window, where the wind was blowing leaves across the old brick courtyard.

Bryan's hand touched her arm and Aimée was startled by the bodily contact.

"Turn around, Aimée. I think we have something to discuss."

All was lost. She knew Bryan, and knew he would not let the episode rest until he had heard her full confession.

"Tell me what happened to the lute, Aimée." Bryan said it in such a tone that Aimée became indignant. She faced him and said unflinchingly, "I sold it, Bryan."

He nodded his head gravely and asked, "And when did you sell it?"

"It was mine, Bryan. I do not have to answer your . . . question."

"You do not *have* to answer anything, Aimée, but I have asked you when you sold it, and I expect an answer from my wife—given willingly."

Aimée stared at the rug on the floor and traced the pattern of swirls with her eyes. But knowing she could not stand long against him, she sighed and answered, "I sold it last week."

"You must have had a good reason to sell a family heirloom, Aimée. Will you kindly explain to me this good reason?"

"I . . . I needed the money," she answered lamely.

"And what was so important that you had to take part of your heritage and bargain like a fishwife—which I presume you did?"

The silence grew more embarrassing each moment as Bryan waited for her answer.

"It was for the altar to St. Joseph."

"And you were afraid to ask me for the money for this . . . altar?"

"You do not understand, Bryan. It had to be a . . . sacrifice on my part. I could not ask you for the money."

"Aimée, after that unusual occurrence in the courtyard last week, I have gone to some length to understand your Creole traditions."

"It is not strictly a Creole tradition, Bryan. In fact, it is more prevalent among the Italians in the city—"

Bryan cut her short. "Do not try to confuse me with the various nuances of your religion. I repeat—I have gone to some lengths to understand and be lenient about your Creole traditions, but there are some traditions in my family that you must understand, too. And the most important one is that a wife always obeys her husband and gets his advice before doing anything on her own. Do you understand, Aimée?"

"Even as to . . . how to pray?" Aimée asked haughtily.

Bryan's face took on a stormy look, the scar flashing white against his cheek. He glared fiercely at Aimée, and stepped back from her, as if he dared not touch her in his angry mood. Aimée could see that she had made her husband furious.

"Even that, Aimée. For I advise you to pray hard that your fleecing shopkeeper still has your lute and has not sold it to anyone else!"

The door slammed behind him and the downcast Aimée was left alone with her misery.

The shadows upon the wall moved in distorted images, translating the flickering flames into an erratic dance, leaping high and then low, depending on the amount of wind that blew down the chimney.

Aimée lay in bed. She was tired but unable to sleep. Bryan had not come back after the brief exchange of words, and Aimée, feeling defeated and censured, had blown out the lamp on the table and gone to bed.

The door opened quietly and Aimée quickly closed her eyes so that she would not have to exchange any more words with the immutable Bryan. The sound of his getting undressed filled the room and the bed complained with a slight creak as his full weight extended over a large portion of it.

She waited in silence—hardly daring to move.

"Aimée?" he whispered, but she did not answer.

The hand, moving out to make contact, infused her only with desperation, and steeling herself to think of other things, to forget the rapture of his love, she held her breath, and when there was no response, his hand withdrew. Soon her husband's even breathing told her that he had gone to sleep.

"Aimée, a man can never stay mad at a beautiful woman. So if one is ever incensed with you, *ma petite*, make yourself as beautiful as possible—then he will forget that he was ever mad at you."

Tante Dee Dee's words echoed in Aimée's mind the next morning, and she wondered if her advice included husbands.

Bryan had evidently risen early, so Aimée had the bedroom to herself. She leisurely bathed in the brass tub behind the screen near the fireplace.

Unable to get into her blue dress without lacing the corset, Aimée conceded to the slight discomfort but made certain that it was not laced too tightly. When she looked into the mirror to brush her hair, she saw how the dress accented the color of her eyes, now large and liquid—a doe's eyes except for the color. She swept the red hair upward, leaving two curls hanging gracefully on one side of her long, slender neck.

Satisfied at last with her appearance, Aimée started down the stairs toward the dining room for breakfast.

"Has the major eaten?" Aimée asked Anderson, who was clearing away the dishes from the table.

"Yes ma'am—the others, too. But Major Garrard gave instructions that you be allowed to sleep late this morning, since you were not feeling well last night."

Aimée sipped the hot coffee and buttered a large piece of bread, daintily breaking off part of it to dip into the black coffee.

The noise at the door interrupted her silent musings on

the previous evening. She was still uneasy at Bryan's display of anger, but with the sound of the steps in the hallway, she dismissed the thoughts that had absorbed her off and on since arising.

"Mrs. Garrard, Colonel Tilson is in the salon," Anderson informed Aimée. "He asked first for the major, and then when he learned the major was not at home, he asked if he might see you for a few minutes."

A deep-seated fear crept into her at Anderson's words. What did he want? Why would Colonel Tilson request to see her in Bryan's absence?

"I . . . I will see him, Anderson, but will you—" Aimée hesitated—"will you stay . . . nearby?"

"Certainly, Mrs. Garrard."

It was not often that Anderson revealed any emotion in his face, but Aimée's request caused a fleeting protective expression, quickly suppressed. Seeing this, Aimée felt better.

She walked down the hallway, into the salon, where Colonel Tilson was seated on one of the apricot lampas chairs and was studying the enameled snuffbox on the table. When she came into the room, he immediately stood up, actively taking in her total appearance.

"You . . . wished to see me, Colonel Tilson?" Aimée asked, facing the man.

His eyes examined her hair and then her eyes and finally he smiled an insidious smile, while Aimée quaked before his insolent inspection.

"How nice to see you again. It has been some time since our encounter at the . . . ball."

"The ball?" Aimée questioned nervously. "But we have . . . bumped into each other since the Officers' Ball, Colonel. Upstairs, the day you visited Bryan. But do sit down," Aimée continued, while finding her way to the sofa where she carefully spread the blue dress in a demure manner, glad that the crinolines and corset hid her secret.

The man took a chair opposite her and the smile was replaced by a blossoming anger. His voice, a growl, barely penetrated the air between them.

"You made a fool of me, Delphine . . ."

Aimée's hand swiftly flew to her cheek. "D-Delphine?

I am afraid you are mistaken, monsieur. I am called Aimée."

He gave a harsh laugh, not bothering to acknowledge her protest. "What would Major Garrard say if he knew you had made a contract to be my mistress?"

Aimée was speechless at the colonel's effrontery. She stood up and stammered, "Y-you will please leave this house, Colonel Tilson!"

Instead of leaving, Colonel Tilson stood up and edged toward Aimée, who stepped back until her retreat was stopped by the sofa.

"There are no other eyes like yours in the city. You've had your fun, Aimée, pretending to be someone else, and now I intend to have . . . what was promised me."

She found herself in the man's arms. Grasping her tightly, he whispered in her ear, "The house is waiting for you in the Ramparts—House Number 9. If you do not wish your husband to know of your escapade, you will meet me there this afternoon, Aimée. I am sure you have no wish to be thrown out on the street by your husband. And knowing Bryan Garrard, that's exactly what he would do if I ever talked."

Aimée struggled to remove herself from his grasp, but it was impossible.

"Protest all you wish, my dear. I am determined to have my way."

"Anderson," Aimée called, frantically twisting her face from the colonel's seeking lips.

"You called for me, Mrs. Garrard?"

He limped menacingly toward Colonel Tilson, who quickly released Aimée from his hold.

"Yes, Anderson, P-please show Colonel Tilson out of the house."

Aimée sank onto the sofa, her strength ebbing from the encounter. What was she to do? If she told Bryan of Colonel Tilson's insults, he would more than likely challenge the colonel to a duel, and since he was still weak from his wound and the fever, he would be in danger. No, she could not risk it. She would have to remain silent.

"My, my! What an interesting life you lead, Aimée—

from one man's arms into another's."

Aimée lifted her head from her hands to see Vickie standing in the doorway.

"It . . . is not what you think, Vickie. I had no wish to suffer the colonel's insults."

"Does Bryan know?" Vickie asked.

"No—and I do not wish him to know," Aimée stated firmly.

"Well, I can understand why you would want to keep it a secret. Bryan may begin to wonder just whose baby you are carrying. And there does seem to be a choice—Juba Barnard, John Runefelt, and now this . . . colonel. But you were smart, Aimée, to get someone to marry you in time . It does make it easier for you, doesn't it?"

Aimée felt sick at Vickie's insinuations, but she was too weak to defend herself.

"Nothing has been easy, Vickie. But I doubt you would understand, even if I told you the reason for the colonel's visit. I can only request that you remain silent about . . . what happened this morning."

"Of course, Aimée," Vickie replied silkily. "It would be rather awkward for you, wouldn't it, if Bryan ever found out—"

Aimée, intent on her conversation with Vickie, had not heard Bryan's footsteps. Now he faced her in the doorway to the salon with a questioning look, turning to Vickie and back again to Aimée while waiting for an explanation.

"Oh dear, you *are* in a pickle, aren't you, Aimée? Well, I think if you will excuse me, I will find something else to do. Marital spats are always a little . . . embarrassing to listen to."

Vickie glided out of the room, past Bryan, and disappeared down the hall.

"What was that all about, Aimée?" Bryan demanded.

Her stricken eyes looked up at him in a beseeching manner.

"Do not . . . ask me to explain now, Bryan. I promise I will tell you later."

He nodded, his eyes dwelling on her ripened breasts straining against the soft blue material.

"Are you still upset, little love, at my anger last night?" He reached out tenderly for her, caressing her cheek, before letting his hand glide down her throat to stop at the opening to her dress. "I was an ogre, speaking to you that way. But everything is all right. Your lute is safe. Now you will be able to sing many a lullaby with it, instead of having some stranger enjoy it."

"You . . . bought it back, Bryan?" Aimée asked, ignoring his searching hands.

"Yes—and the old goat made his profit. Next time, Aimée, pray to a saint who will take a few candles in his honor."

His teasing eyes met her startled ones, and before she could react to his annoying comment, Bryan swept her up in his arms and carried her from the salon.

"Bryan," she protested, as he dropped her on the bed in their room.

"You denied me last night, by pretending to be asleep, you little minx," Bryan accused, continuing his lovemaking. "And I am not used to being denied."

"You are . . . devastating my dress, Bryan."

"Then remove it, Aimée, if you wish to preserve it. I am an impatient man."

Chapter 28

All that afternoon Aimée was troubled, thinking of Colonel Tilson and Number 9, Rampart Street. Was he waiting for her—thinking that she would be foolish enough to come? And what would happen when she did not appear? Would he actually tell Bryan of that evening at the Quadroon Ball? Aimée knew that the colonel could make it sound much worse than it actually was. And Bryan was a jealous man. She badly needed advice, but who would listen without condemning her?

Cousin Clotilde's face assumed shape in her mind, and remembering her kindness in past days, Aimée sought her out. Cousin Clotilde was not in the house.

"Tink, have you seen Cousin Clotilde?" Aimée asked in the kitchen.

"She . . . she's out, Mrs. Garrard," Tink answered, as if holding something back.

"Out? Do you know if she will be away long?"

"Until five o'clock. That's the time she usually comes back—in time to help in the kitchen."

The words caused Aimée to frown. "The time she usually comes back." Tink's reticence combined with her answer gave Aimée a moment of quiet reflection. Cousin Clotilde must be leaving the house regularly. But why? And why had she been so secretive?

"Do you know where she has gone, Tink?" The suspicion grew while Aimée waited for a reply.

"I . . . I promised not to tell, Mrs. Garrard."

"Then keep your promise, Tink. I will speak with her later."

But for the rest of the day there was no chance to speak with Cousin Clotilde. She had simply disappeared. Nagging suspicions teased Aimée, making her wonder what the woman could possibly be doing so long away from home.

Could Cousin Clotilde have a job? Surely not. Her family would feel disgraced—as if they could not take care of their own. Far better to suffer genteel poverty than go against the tradition of generations—was that not what Cousin Clotilde had said?

But with each passing block of time, Aimée grew more and more suspicious. She remembered the words that the woman had used when they arrived in New Orleans from Thornfell with only a wagonload of goods. "Everything is gone, Aimée." Would that be sufficient cause for Cousin Clotilde to flout the traditions that she had been so careful to maintain up till now? That had meant so much to her?

It was now almost five o'clock, and still no sign of Clotilde. Aimée went to the kitchen to help Tink with dinner. She was already heaping more wood on the fire in the old black iron range. Using the poker to set the lid back on top, Tink dropped the round cover into place with a slight bang, her cheeks flushed from leaning too close to the fire.

The heat of the stove sent out great waves of warmth and Aimée, after a few minutes, picked up the old paper fan on the table to push some of the stifling air away from her face as she stirred the cooking pot with the other hand. A utilitarian fan, advertising Feesy's Shrimp Bowl down on the levee—a poor man's substitute for the delicate lace fan from Paris that Aimée had been given on her sixteenth birthday.

Her sixteenth birthday—how long ago that seemed. She looked at Tink, wondering about the girl's own sixteenth birthday. Suddenly the girl's name jarred. Tink was not a suitable name for a young woman who was old enough to be thinking of marriage. She should be called by a more proper name.

"Tink," Aimée plunged in without any preliminaries, "do you remember the name your mother gave you? Your . . . proper name?"

Tink seemed startled that Aimée would ask. "I never knew my ma since she died when I was a baby, and I been called 'Tink' ever since I can remember."

Aimée was disappointed with her answer. "But 'Tink' must be a contraction for something else. Think hard, Tink."

The girl screwed up her face, the tiny freckles standing out as she thought hard. Hestitantly she said, "Is there such a name as 'Ka-tink-a'?"

"Yes," Aimée answered, smiling. "It's a beautiful name —and it's logical that someone would shorten it to Tinka or Tink when you were small."

"Well, I ain't absolutely certain that's it, Mrs. Garrard," Tink said, frowning.

Aimée inwardly winced at her language but she did

not correct her. "But wouldn't you rather be called by a more dignified name, now that you are a young lady?"

Tink went on with her work while Aimée set the table in the kitchen.

"People would laugh at me if I started puttin' on airs," Tink said mournfully.

"Major Garrard wouldn't laugh. He would think it a lovely name."

"He . . . would?"

"I'm sure he would, Katinka."

The mention of Bryan seemed to be the determining factor. The girl said the name several times, getting the feel of it on her tongue, tasting the sound, then she smiled. "If you think nobody would laugh . . ."

Aimée, satisfied that Tink would accept her new name, took the empty pail into the courtyard for water. The huge jars stood in the shade—for the fresh water that had to be brought in every few days from the river, to be sweetened with alum and charcoal and allowed to settle. The old well at the back of the courtyard contained brackish water, unfit for anything but taking a bath and washing the laundry in, as was the case with wells all over New Orleans. Aimée dipped the water into the pail, and tugging at the heavy load, she started back toward the kitchen.

The iron gate to the banquette squeaked on its rusty hinge as it announced someone's arrival. Aimée saw Cousin Clotilde approaching, but before she could question her, Cousin Clotilde began her gentle scolding of Aimée.

"Aimée, you have no business carrying such a heavy pail of water. Here, let me take it the rest of the way."

Despite Aimée's protests, Cousin Clotilde took the pail from her, carried it into the kitchen, and set it near the sink. Hurriedly the woman slipped on her apron that had been hanging on the back of the door and began her chores.

The two women eyed each other with a sense of uneasiness. Aimée knew that Cousin Clotilde did not wish to be questioned as to her whereabouts all day, but that did not deter her.

"Cousin Clotilde—"

"Yes, Aimée?"

"I . . . I do not wish to be . . . impertinent, especially when . . ."

Tink walked back into the kitchen and Aimée became occupied, slicing the carrots in silence.

When the girl disappeared again toward the dining room, Cousin Clotilde turned to Aimée and said, "You are wondering where I go each day, are you not?"

Aimée nodded. "Yes. Not because I wish to pry, but because . . ."

"I should have told you long ago, Aimée. I am . . . teaching music pupils."

'But why, Cousin Clotilde? You are part of the family and it is not necessary for you to . . . work."

"Thank you, my dear, but I feel I can no longer live with an empty tradition. There are so many of us that I must contribute something to the expenses. And it is very interesting, Aimée, really, it is—even if my pupils *are* children of the Union families. It seems no one else is able to afford the luxury nowadays."

"Do you . . . go to their houses?"

"Yes."

"And you are sure you want to continue?"

"Yes, my dear." Cousin Clotilde, seeing Tink in the doorway, called gaily out to her. "Well, Tink, our secret is out. Aimée was too suspicious, so I have confessed."

The girl grinned, relieved of the burden of keeping the secret any longer.

"By the way, Cousin Clotilde, we have also made another discovery—one that concerns Tink."

"And what is that?"

"Tell her, Tink," Aimée urged.

"I think my real name is Ka-tink-a, and Mrs. Garrard says it's time I started using it, since it sounds prettier than 'Tink.' "

"What a beautiful name. I like that, Tink—I mean, Katinka," the older woman exclaimed.

And from that time on, with only a few reversions, everyone in the house began calling the young girl "Katinka."

Bryan was now well enough to return to duty with the army and Aimée missed being with her strong, demanding husband for a large portion of the day, especially now that Cousin Clotilde was busy and Clay and Vickie seemed so engrossed in each other.

Aimée spent more time with the children and the shy Hope blossomed under her attention. Aimée gazed down at her own increasing size and she was happy knowing that it would not be too many months before she and Bryan would have a child to love and care for. It was during those times of introspection that Aimée gazed tenderly at Vickie's three little girls.

They went for walks with Lizzie and Katinka, and Hope, slipping her hand into Aimée's, would skip delightedly on the banquette as they made their way to the French Market, where the children would spend their pennies on honey cakes or marzipan from the *marchandes*.

The city had a constant carnival air, a boisterousness that had come with the fortune hunters, opportunists, camp followers, and the cotton merchants—trading, always trading their valuable cotton. They were the new rich, living side by side with the new poor; the rich purchasing, the poor looking, unable to afford anything in the marketplace except a bunch of bananas, the cheapest food in all New Orleans.

It was the afternoon that Vickie had suddenly decided to go with them that Aimée saw the man standing at one of the buying stalls. She had gone a little way from the rest when his shadow loomed at her feet.

"Good afternoon, Mrs. Garrard," Colonel Tilson greeted her, but Aimée, with eyes blazing, refused to return the greeting and turned on her heel to escape. She felt a strong grip on her arm, stopping her escape, and heard a low voice meant only for her say, "I am still waiting, Aimée."

"You will have a long wait, monsieur," Aimée choked, her face flushed. She drew the cloak around her, as if to ward off his advances.

He laughed, and releasing her, he threatened, "You will not escape me forever. Sooner or later you will be mine, whether you wish it or not."

Vickie hurried to Aimée's side as the man disappeared into the crowd.

"Wasn't that the same man as the one who came to the house not long ago—Colonel Tilson?"

"Yes. He is . . . incorrigible."

"What hold does he have over you, Aimée?"

When Aimée did not answer, Vickie slyly asked, "Did you ever tell Bryan of his visit to the house?"

"No, Vickie. I did not wish to bother Bryan, especially since he had been so ill."

"Mother, come quickly—there's a man with a monkey on his shoulder, and he's playing some funny music!"

Aimée, relieved at Faith's interruption, joined the crowd to watch the organ grinder and his pet perform near the coffee house.

A few days later Aimée sat at the dinner table with the family, the encounter with Colonel Tilson in the marketplace still plaguing her mind. She looked at Bryan, so handsome and dark, and could not bear the thought that she might once again be the cause of any injury to him. For his sake she must remain silent about Colonel Tilson.

Bryan looked up from his plate. He caught Aimée's loving gaze and he responded with a caress of his silvergray eyes. They remained locked in each other's eyes until Clay broke the spell, clearing his throat nervously and standing up.

Conversation around him stopped; the room grew still while he captured the attention of everyone at the table. Fingering the black patch, Clay cleared his throat again and said, "I have an . . . announcement to make."

Again there was silence, with everyone waiting for him to continue.

"Vickie and I were married this afternoon. I hope we will have your . . . best wishes."

"Married!" Cousin Jorge exclaimed in amazement.

As Aimée looked around the table, Bryan's face and then Cousin Clotilde's revealed the same astonishment.

"By golly, that *is* a surprise," Cousin Jorge chortled.

"Well, a toast seems to be in order." Cousin Jorge stood up as Clay sat down beside Vickie. "May your lives be filled with love and prosperity and may your shoes never be called upon to know the holes in your stockings!"

"And what do you say, Brother?" Clay asked Bryan, who sat silently at the head of the table. "Will you congratulate me, too?"

For a brief moment a tense air pervaded the room, but when Bryan stood and smiled, it dissipated.

"May you find as much happiness with Vickie as I have found . . . with Aimée."

"Hear! Hear!!" The noise at the table was deafening and the children, who had eaten earlier, stood at the door watching the hearty scene, not certain what was happening.

Clay, seeing them, motioned for them to come in. He took Charity from Lizzie's arms and set her on his lap, while drawing the other two little girls to him.

"It seems, Bryan, you will have to work hard to catch up with me. There are now *four* women in my family."

Vickie, seeing Clay's acceptance of the children, gazed at him with soft, adoring brown eyes. When they turned toward Aimée, they became as black as onyx.

"My dear, we are so happy for you," Cousin Clotilde said, hugging Vickie, while the men, slapping Clay on the back, departed for the library to drink another toast with a stronger brew.

"You have taken on quite a responsibility, Clay, marrying a woman with three children."

Bryan's voice carried into the nursery where Aimée was busy placing the clean sheets on the two cots hastily set up for the two older children, now that they could no longer share their mother's room.

"I trust you are . . . sure of your actions."

"I am, Bryan. Vickie suits me very well. She has a certain . . . sympathy that no one else in this house has shown me."

There was a silence and then Bryan spoke haltingly. "I hope there is a better reason for your marriage than

. . . sympathy, Clay. In the best of circumstances, it is not easy to rear another man's child."

"Maybe we will both have an opportunity to find that out," Clay answered enigmatically.

"And just what do you mean by that snide remark?" Bryan asked gruffly.

Aimée did not wish to hear Clay's reply, but the door was ajar and the two men apparently did not know she was within hearing distance.

'There seems to be a question as to the father of the child Aimée is carrying, according to Vickie. There are at least two other candidates, besides you, Bryan, for the the father—"

Footsteps sounded across the room and a startled exclamation came from Clay before Bryan's voice, low and deadly, erupted. "The child is mine, Clay. Never let me hear you repeat such insinuations while you are staying in this house."

Aimée did not wait to hear the rest. She fled from the nursery out into the hallway, intent only on escaping from the malicious words.

How could Vickie be so cruel? And what perverse pleasure had made Clay repeat the words to Bryan?

Aimée, blinded by her tears, rushed down the hallway, only dimly seeing the disappearing frame of Cousin Clotilde below the stairs.

Trying to control her tremulous sobs until she reached the courtyard where she could cry in peace, Aimée reached out for the railing of the slightly curved stairs that would take her away from the taunting words. But her hand missed the railing and her body, propelled by her urgency to escape, become overbalanced. She pitched forward, rolling down the stairs. Frantically she reached for the railing but her body merely succeeded in gaining momentum until she landed with a sharp thud upon the carpet beyond the stairs.

She could not move. The pain shot through her shoulder and the distorted strands of twisted pale light arching through the leaded glass of the courtyard door concealed the familiarity of the entrance hall. Aimée's eyes deceived her, making the dull gray dress coming toward her into a swishing, shuddering apparition, demanding a penance for a crime she had not committed.

"My baby—you cannot have my baby," Aimée whispered.

"Oh my dear, my poor dear," the anguished voice crooned over her. The dull gray dress flowed over her as the woman bent beside her.

"What was all the racket, Clotilde? What happened?" Bryan's voice demanded from the head of the stairs.

The voluminous folds of the dress that had obscured him from view now moved, leaving a small lopsided sliver of vision upward to the stairs where Bryan stood.

"It is Aimée. She missed her footing and fell down the stairs."

"Oh, my God!" The exclamation was torn from his lips, as Bryan rushed down the stairs, two at a time.

"Bryan," Aimée whispered, "the baby . . ."

His hands reached under her to lift her from the floor, but Clotilde's voice stopped him. "I don't think you should move her, Major. At least, not until a doctor comes."

"Will you get Anderson to hitch the pony to the *calèche*, Clotilde, and go at once for Doctor Floud?"

"Where does he live?"

"Dumaine Street."

Clotilde left to attend to Bryan's request and Bryan, on his knees beside Aimée, removed his coat to place over her. Remaining by her side, he stroked her cheek in an agitated motion.

'Bryan," Aimée said, struggling against the pain in her shoulder, now throbbing acutely.

"Yes, my darling?"

"The baby—you are the father of my baby—no one else . . ."

"Hush, my love. I know." Bryan's voice was strangely gentle and his face devoid of color. But as Aimée watched, Bryan's face took on a hard, angry look, stone-chiseled and frightening to see.

"Anderson and Jorge are leaving at once." Clotilde, with a pillow and blanket in her hand returned to kneel beside Aimée. "Now all we can do is keep her warm and wait until the doctor arrives."

"I think she did it deliberately—to spoil my wedding night."

"Hush, Vickie," Clay's voice sounded. "She'll hear you."

"Well, I don't care if she does."

"Aimée would not deliberately fall down the stairs, Vickie—especially in her condition. She could lose the baby."

"I know. And maybe Aimée knew, too. It would certainly simplify matters, wouldn't it, considering the baby's uncertain parentage."

"Bryan has threatened to throw us out of the house if we insinuate that the baby is not his, so let's keep quiet, Vickie. Knowing Bryan, I am convinced he would do it without a qualm—and we *are* dependent on him for our every morsel."

"You mean you do not have any money of your own, Clay?"

"Not a penny. I put it all in Confederate bonds. We are completely dependent upon Bryan's generosity, and I am afraid if we continue to talk about Aimée, that generosity will dry up in a hurry."

"I . . . I wish you had told me that, Clay, before we were married," Vickie replied sullenly.

The door closed and again Aimée was reminded of the conversation the night before between Clay and her husband.

Chapter 29

"It looks as if your grandfather's famous Lannuier bed is destined to claim one or the other of us at all times."

Bryan, peering from the desk that had been moved into the room for his benefit, watched Aimée as she awakened from sleep.

"It was . . . stupid of me to miss the handrailing," Aimée lamented. "I have gone up and down those stairs at least a thousand times with no mishap until . . . last night. And just when there is so much for me to do, I am put to bed like a naughty child."

"You have only *one* important thing to do, Aimée," Bryan remonstrated. "And that is to take care of the child you are carrying. Doctor Floud said you were fortunate not to have lost the baby last night—so you should not complain about a few days spent in bed to assure your health and the child's."

Bryan put down the pencil and ruler and Aimée, seeing the concentrated frown on his face, was uneasy.

"Aimée—"

She listened, waiting for him to continue.

"Aimée, who is Juba Barnard?"

"Juba?" Aimée repeated, feeling the insidious trap closing about her. "He . . . he was a cousin who was wounded at Shiloh, or Pittsburg Landing, as you call it. He died at Thornfell and is buried in the family plot."

"Then who is John Runefelt?"

The subtle inquisition, the gnawing doubt put in

Bryan's mind by Clay's gossip—Aimée sighed, sensing the force of destiny that was now separating her from Bryan.

"He is a . . . spy, who took Juba's identity."

"And he was also at Thornfell—when you were?"

"Yes."

"Where is he now, Aimée?"

"John is probably in England by now."

"England?" Bryan picked up the blue pencil again, toying with it in his fingers. And Aimée waited for the next question that he would ask.

"Was he on the same British ship from which you were taken?"

"Yes."

Bryan suddenly stood up and paced between the windows before coming to stare down at Aimée from his intimidating height.

"And did John Runefelt plan your rescue so that you could go to England with him?" he asked, a sarcastic tinge to his deep voice.

"Yes."

Murderous anger shook his large frame and he stalked up and down, brushing his hand agitatedly through his blue-black hair.

"God! How could you get mixed up with such a man, Aimée—one who had no qualms about murdering a man for his wife?"

"He was not . . . aware that I was married," Aimée said in a defensive tone, "until I reached the ship."

"Then Vickie might be right, after all. What proof, Aimée, do I have that this child is actually mine—that it doesn't belong to one of your . . . *amours*?"

His words were cruel, designed to hurt.

"Only my word, Bryan." Aimée, fighting back the tears, kept her dignity and answered him quietly.

"Your word!" Bryan snorted. "How am I to accept your word, when you have deceived me from the moment we met?"

Aimée waited unhappily, knowing that Bryan had not finished driving the icy barbs into her heart.

"And what did he suggest, Aimée—this John Runefelt—when he discovered you already had a husband and were with child? Did he propose going through another ceremony with you, making you a bigamist, or were you going to continue as his mistress?"

"I was never his . . . mistress, Bryan. He . . . he said he would see to a . . . divorce, if you were still alive."

She was crushed to Bryan's chest in a passionate, cruel grasp. "No man will take you away from me, Aimée. I told you once that I would never let you go. And regardless of whose child you are carrying, you are *my* wife, and I will never let you forget it!"

She fell against the pillow as he pushed her from him, and sudden, cold fear clutched at her, as Bryan stamped from the room.

Aimée's closed lids could not prevent the tears from escaping, making a wet place on the embroidered pillow case. Her shoulder, merely bruised from the fall, ached in concert with the nagging ache in her back.

She had lost Bryan, and any love he might have had for her. Vickie had seen to that. He was intent on keeping her as a possession—nothing more—a chattel, subjugated to him, without the position of honor and trust a wife normally held.

She was so tired and she ached all over. The tempo of the pain increased, and Aimée, alone, turned her head into the pillow and held tightly to the side of the bed.

Suddenly the rush of liquid drenched her gown and she stared down in horror at the blood seeping through the sheets, the blanket, and the mattress upon the bed, as the ribbons of pain tightened in steady and unrelenting rhythm, until she could remain silent no longer.

The door flung open and Bryan's voice shattered the tiny moans from Aimée's throat.

"I should not have left the engineering plans of the river where a Rebel could see them."

But the words meant nothing to Aimée. She was beyond caring. . . .

Cousin Clotilde sat beside her. The flickering lamp answered the wind hypnotically. Aimée slowly opened her eyes, her dark pupils adjusting to the light in the room. Looking down, she saw the dry, clean sheets and felt the different texture of her gown.

"Cousin Clotilde, did I . . .?" The question was in her voice and the tall, sympathetic woman nodded.

"Yes, Aimée. You lost the baby. I'm so sorry, my dear."

Aimée closed her eyes again, drifting into a tired semisleep. She was bereft, a part of her gone, her child—hers and Bryan's, whether he claimed it or not.

There was a light tap on the door but Aimée did not raise her head from the pillow. Cousin Clotilde left the chair, and the sound of her tiptoeing steps and the slight swish of crinolines sounded in the room; the door opened and closed, and whispered voices outside confided in each other, closing Aimée out.

"I . . . I do not wish to see him," Aimée said in a determined voice.

"But my dear, don't you think . . .?"

"No. I . . . I don't want to see anybody—especially Bryan."

"All right, my dear," Cousin Clotilde said with a sigh. "I cannot force you, although I think you are treating Bryan as if . . ."

Aimée put the pillow over her head to drown out Cousin Clotilde's last words.

When Aimée finally left the room that had encased her like a cocoon, protecting her from the outside world, she was pale and a certain spark had gone out of her turquoise eyes. Her dress now fit her, no longer tight except for the bodice, which still strained against her breasts.

Knowing she could put if off no longer, Aimée went downstairs. She would have to face Bryan sooner or later and it would be easier with the family around. After that day she had been so vehement against seeing him, Bryan had made no further attempt to come into her room.

The house was quiet; there was no sign of anyone but

Cousin Jorge and Hope, who were in the salon playing a quiet game of chess.

"Aimée, how are you, my dear?" Cousin Jorge stood up, jostling the table and causing some of the chess pieces to fall on the floor.

Hope quickly stooped down to pick up the king and pawns, while Cousin Jorge apologized.

"This child, Aimée, was beating me soundly, so it's just as well I knocked the pieces over. She's not kind to her elders at all. She would soon have checkmated me if you had not come into the room."

His blue eyes were twinkling and he reached down to tweak Hope's nose as he talked with Aimée.

"Oh, Cousin Jorge," Hope said in a giggling voice, "I was having a hard time. You were actually winning."

"Well, why didn't you tell me, instead of letting me sit there and worry about the next trap you were going to spring on me?"

The carefree banter between man and child relaxed the tension in Aimée as nothing else would have.

"Where . . . where is everyone?" Aimée asked.

"Clay and Vickie have gone to the convent to see about schooling for Faith and Hope. Clotilde and Tink are doing the marketing. Now, let's see—Faith has gone with Lizzie to take Charity for a walk . . . I guess that's it."

"And . . . and Anderson? Where is he?"

"Why, he is with Bryan, of course," Cousin Jorge replied, surprised at Aimée's question.

"Anderson said he would bring me a present when he comes home," Hope confided.

"Today?" Aimée asked.

"No—when the army gets back from upriver." Hope answered in the tone reserved for grown-ups who asked her foolish questions, and Aimée, recognizing the tone, grew tremulous.

"Bryan is . . . away with the army?"

Cousin Jorge stared at her, trying to hide his surprised expression. "Yes. I thought you knew, Aimée. He left five days ago."

Five days ago—the day she had refused to see him.

Aimée sank onto the sofa, far weaker than she had imagined she would be.

"I have not seen him since . . ." Her voice died and Cousin Jorge made no effort to prompt her.

A gust of wind banged the door open into the courtyard and Hope ran down the hall to secure it.

"Aimée is downstairs, Cousin Clotilde." Hope's voice was childish and shrill with excitement as she greeted Clotilde, who had evidently just come home. "She didn't even know that Bryan had gone away to fight."

"Colonel Garrard to you, Hope. You must not get into the habit of calling him by his given name. And you must remember to preface Aimée's name with 'Cousin.'" Cousin Clotilde's voice was firm as she instructed Hope.

"All right—*Colonel* Garrard," Hope said with a sigh. "But last week he was Major Garrard. What will he be next week, Cousin Clotilde? A general? It seems to me it would be easier just to call him 'Bryan.'"

"When he gives you permission, you may call him 'Uncle Bryan'—but not before."

"Then will I call Aimée 'Tante'?"

"We'll see. Now take the basket and run along to the kitchen with Katinka. I want to go and see Aimée."

The two women met in the hallway.

"Bryan has gone?" Aimée questioned with a distressed countenance.

"Yes, dear. He wanted so much to see you before he left, but he understood how you felt."

"How . . . how was he when he left?"

"Distressed because you were still ill. He did not want to leave you, but he had no choice."

Aimée, stunned at the news of his going, could not bring herself to ask what she most wanted to hear.

Cousin Clotilde hesitated and then continued. "He confessed to me the . . . things he had said to you, and naturally I knew how hurt you would be from such an accusation. I took the . . . liberty of telling him about Vickie's jealousy toward you, so you need not worry that he still questions your . . . fidelity."

Clotilde walked slowly down the hallway with her arm about Aimée's waist.

"He left a letter for you, Aimée. I have it in my room."

Aimée stopped and turned immediately. "May I . . . have it *now*, Cousin Clotilde?"

"Of course, my dear. I'll only be a minute."

Aimée watched her ascending the stairs, willing the woman to hurry. She forced herself to remain at the foot of the stairs instead of following behind Cousin Clotilde, who resembled some gray nun on her way to answer a summons from the Mother Superior.

Oh, Bryan, if I had only known you were leaving. . . . The words did not pass her lips, but they echoed and re-echoed down the gold-and-white hallway where Aimée stood and waited.

"Here you are, my dear."

Aimée forced her hand to reach out casually for the letter, instead of snatching it to her breast. And when it was in her hands, she did not know what to do with it.

"Excuse me, Aimée, and I will go to the kitchen to help Katinka."

"Aimée nodded absentmindedly, still holding the letter in her hand. Slowly she mounted the stairs and walked to the bedroom—hers and Bryan's—and sat down at the desk by the window. She laid the envelope on the desk. Fearful of opening it, she gazed at the strong, bold handwriting of her husband.

It was better not knowing what message the letter contained; for once she opened it, the words could never be erased.

Aimée got up and walked toward the fire, envelope in her hands. Would she have the courage to throw it into the flames? If she never knew what it contained, she could still pretend that he loved her, still desired her as a wife.

But once she opened it . . .

The letters of her name stood out on the white envelope, compelling her with their strength, with the power he had to make her weak and trembling, even by writing her name.

Slowly Aimée tore open the envelope, although her eyes were afraid to look. But the words demanded to be read.

My dear Wife,

I do not ask your forgiveness. It is far too much to hope for—that you would ever forgive me for the vile things I said to you.

Only know that I love you and grieve with you over the loss of *our* son.

In the event I do not return from the fighting, Clay has instructions to rebuild Thornfell for you.

Bryan

The grief tore from Aimée in great sobs. She read the letter over and over so many times that it was no longer necessary to stare down at the shapes of the individual letters. Her tears stained the letter, causing the ink to run in places, but the message was engraved on her aching heart, never to be forgotten. And when her grief had emptied its well of tears, Aimée washed her face and went downstairs to seek news of the fighting toward Port Hudson and Vicksburg. . . .

Chapter 30

"The gunboats seem to be having a hard time, with the shallow waters and the shore batteries sinking so many of them," Cousin Jorge said. "And it says here, Aimée," he continued, glancing at the newspaper, "that they are trying to divert the river to get past Vicksburg. That will be an engineering feat."

"The tinclads and transports are caught in every direction," Clay said, laughing triumphantly. "The Confederates are cutting down trees in front of them and behind them, too, trapping them and making the boats run aground."

"What are 'tinclads,' Papa?" Faith asked, turning to Clay.

He pulled her toward him, teasing at her pigtails, severely plaited to control the unruly brown curls.

"Why, they're like floating tin cans, Faith. The Union Navy has bragged that they draw so little water they can float on a heavy dew."

Faith wrinkled her nose and asked, "But why would the Yankees want to have tin cans in the water?"

"Because they can transport at least two hundred soldiers and land them almost anywhere in the dry season. And they're protected against musket fire by the tin armor. It's just the big guns on the batteries they can't stand up against."

"Is Uncle Bryan on one of these tinclads, Tante Aimée?" Hope asked from across the room.

"I pray not, Hope," Aimée answered with a worried look on her face.

Each day Aimée kept up with the news, sometimes going down to the wharf to talk directly to the wounded soldiers who had been sent downriver to New Orleans.

"Vicksburg is like Gibralter, ma'am," one of the soldiers informed her. "We can't get near her from either upriver or downriver. And Port Hudson has heavy guns up and down the bluffs for miles, and great searchlights mounted to train on each boat trying to slip by. If one finally manages to get past in the cover of a dense fog, it's crippled by a torpedo or it runs aground and sinks."

And so Aimée continued to worry about Bryan and only halfheartedly attended to the daily affairs of the family, until Vickie sought her out one rainy afternoon.

"Aimée, I have a . . . request to make." Vickie, who had avoided Aimée as much as possible after the loss of the baby, looked embarrassed.

"Yes, Vickie?"

"Clay and I would like to live in the carriage house, if you have no objections. Cousin Jorge could move back into the main house and we could furnish it with some of the furniture in the attic . . ."

Vickie paused, waiting for Aimée to make some comment about her proposal.

So Vickie had already been up to the attic, thought Aimée, and had selected some of Tante Dee Dee's furniture that had been stored.

"And the children—what do you wish to do about them, Vickie?" Aimée asked. "Would they move to the carriage house with you?"

"We will leave them in the house for Lizzie to take care of. There isn't that much room in the carriage house, if we use one room for a sitting room for Clay and me, and the other for our bedroom."

"Have you mentioned this to Cousin Jorge?"

"Yes, and he's perfectly willing to move back into the townhouse. He spends most of his time here anyway."

"Well, it's all right with me if you wish to use Tante Dee Dee's furniture for the carriage house."

"Thank you, Aimée," Vickie said, getting up from her chair. "I will find Clay and tell him."

Vickie had finally made her peace with Fréki and Geri. Maintaining a distant truce, the dogs stayed out of her way, allowing her to go back and forth across the courtyard without fear. She now walked toward the carriage house where Clay was waiting for her.

Two strong Irish Channel workers appeared the next day to move the furniture from the attic to the carriage house, and Cousin Jorge moved back into the house—not to the bedroom that Clay and Vickie had vacated, but to the bedroom that Cousin Clotilde and Katinka had shared.

"I think you would enjoy a little more quiet, Cousin Jorge," Aimée explained, "in the far bedroom, rather than the one adjoining the nursery. And Cousin Clotilde and Katinka will be able to supervise the girls more closely if they are next door to them."

"I appreciate your thoughtfulness, Aimée. Children's squabbles are best heard from a distance, not in an ear's throw—when you get to be my age."

Aimée smiled, leaving Cousin Jorge to place his belongings in the far bedroom. She walked downstairs and went to the salon to rest from the morning's activity. She had no more than sat down when a knock sounded at the door.

Katinka, who was in the hallway, said, "I'll get it, Mrs. Garrard," and before Aimée could stand, she was off down the hall to the door. Soon Katinka appeared again.

"Mrs. Garrard, there's a black woman at the door. Said her name is . . . Lisette, and she asks to see you."

Lisette? Lisette was at the door—wanting to see her? What reason could she possibly have, after betraying her? Anger tugged at Aimée's lips, but she managed to conceal it, except for the coldness of her voice.

"I will take care of it, Katinka. Thank you," she said, dismissing the girl.

Strangely, after the initial anger, Aimée felt nothing for Lisette except a mild curiosity about her mission.

The black woman stood on the doorstep, her tignoned head hanging in an attitude of penitence.

"You wanted something, Lisette?"

"Yes, Miss Aimée. I . . . I wondered if you would . . . take me back?"

"Take you back? I could never do that, Lisette, since you are free. Are you looking for a job?"

"Yes, ma'am."

"Why don't you get one of the Union families to hire you?"

"They hates us, Miss Aimée. The Bureau sent me to New York, but I was lucky to get back alive. You never seen such riots in the streets—mobs killin' or beatin' up any Negro in sight."

"Come now, Lisette, you're exaggerating," Aimée said impatiently.

"No'm. It's the God's truth. They had to send the army troops in to stop the fightin'. I ain't exaggeratin'— I'm lucky to be standin' on your doorstep this very minute."

Aimée stared at Lisette, wondering if the woman had told her the truth. True, most of the Unionists did not consider Negroes persons—only property to be taken away from the Confederates. Had General Butler himself not referred to them as "contrabands of war" and placed them in camps to dig ditches and work on the canals? And ordered them shot if they tried to leave camp?

Ironic, was it not, Aimée thought, that by his proclamation, Lincoln had freed only the slaves in the Rebel states, where he actually had no authority, and not in the states sympathetic to the Union. If all men were to be free . . .

"The carriage house is occupied," Aimée said dubiously. "You would have to fix a cot in the attic."

"I wouldn't mind that."

"Then get your things and be here tomorrow morning."

"Yes'm—and *merci*."

"*Eh bien*, Lisette."

Aimée realized that Lisette would be a great help in the house, easing some of the work done by Katinka.

For some time Aimée had wondered what she should do about the girl. Having lost her scrawny, uncared-for, urchin appearance, she had grown into a nice-looking young girl, and were it not for her speech, she could compete with anyone in New Orleans. She seemed to be happy only when Bryan was around, but given the opportunity to better herself, Katinka could easily attract almost any young man coming home from the army. And with Lisette to take over many of the chores, Katinka could be freed from many of the duties that she had taken on.

Aimée smiled as the idea came to her. What if Katinka could go to the convent school each day with Faith and Hope? Even a short time with the Sisters would improve the girl's speech.

"I think you are absolutely insane, Aimée, to waste money on a servant girl," Vickie said.

"But she's not a servant girl, Vickie. It's not her fault that all her people are dead. And she's quite capable of improving herself, if given the opportunity."

"I think it's an excellent idea, Aimée," Cousin Clotilde said, siding with Aimée.

Vickie, more irritable than usual, flounced from the salon, flinging her departing words at Aimée. "Well, *I* think you're making a mistake, and you'll probably live to regret it."

"I think perhaps Vickie is not feeling her best these days," Clotilde said when Vickie had gone. "Her face looks a little peaked. I wonder . . ."

"Do you think she might be *enceinte* already?" Aimée asked.

'I wouldn't be a bit surprised, my dear."

The idea made Aimée envious. The sharp sense of loss over her own child had not disappeared, although she had attempted to keep the ache tucked away inside the darker recesses of her mind. That evening Aimée, hiding her loneliness and unhappiness, took out the lute to play and sing softly when she was alone.

She stroked the lute, twice dear to her now; not only had it belonged to her namesake, but it had been purchased again by her husband.

"Oh, Bryan," she whispered with a sob, feeling pain and loss even in the sound of his name. Wearily she placed the lute in its case on the window seat and climbed into bed, her body protesting its half-wholeness—the denial of her husband's arms about her.

The war accelerated and the land up and down the delta became ravaged from the fighting, the looting, and the burning of fields. Deep scars were left on the land as the invading armies converged, gradually separating the two parts of the Confederacy. The few factories along the way were destroyed, so that the Southern army had to do without shoes. Bushels of golden corn intended to feed the hungry men were burned and rails were dug up and twisted so that they could not be used again unless straightened by factory machinery—machinery that only the North had.

Inch by inch, mile by mile, Grant's army continued across the land—pushing its heavy guns, leaving a trail of devastation behind to mark the way the Army of the Tennessee had taken. Sherman's smaller army marched in a westerly direction to meet Grant, while General Banks, with the Army of the Gulf, besieged Fort Hudson.

One year after Farragut had sailed up the Mississippi to capture New Orleans, the Union gunboats and army transports surged upriver from New Orleans and downriver from Columbus and Memphis—under Porter's flag —to prepare for the Armageddon destined to take place on the bluffs and battlements of the rolling river. The object was to wrest from the Confederates the last stretch of the Mississippi they controlled.

Through it all Aimée waited, her voice crying out for her delta land invaded by the enemy, and her heart praying for her husband, who was one of its destructive invaders.

Chapter 31

*T*he sky was chameleon, changing from sunny, dazzling blue to dark, stormy gray. It was the season of flood waters and hurricanes, of deceptive tropical days, or zephyr breezes changing into unfriendly gales that beat against the shutters and scattered the early-flowering blossoms of bougainvillea and sasanquas. It was a dangerous time to be on the river, a dangerous time to be near the black swampy waters that crisscrossed the land, for there the deadly fever lurked.

The pelicans by the levee flew back and forth, never still, silent oracles of the uneasiness surrounding New Orleans. And Aimée, standing on the wharf, waited in uneasiness for the Union ship to dock, to hear the long expected news from upriver.

It was the hospital ship, the reconverted C.S.S. *Red Rover*, carrying the battle wounded, now tended by the Sisters of the Holy Cross.

As the wounded soldiers were removed from the ship and taken to the waiting horse-drawn ambulances, Aimée searched each face for her husband's features, all the while praying that he would not be among them. After the last man had left the ship, Aimée sat down on the nearest makeshift seat—a hogshead of molasses—and gave in to the weakness caused by the sight of all those torn and maimed bodies, the stench of gangrenous limbs, and the fetid air of the dying and near-dying.

She had not even bothered to ask news. The number of casualties proved the hard, bitter fighting, and the wounded, with their glazed, shocked eyes, needed to forget—not remember.

When her trembling eased, Aimée stood up and forced her feet to follow one after the other until she had reached the gate to the townhouse.

The dogs were barking excitedly in the house and Aimée, opening the door, lifted her head and listened to the faint limping walk coming toward her.

Anderson? Could it be Anderson? Aimée rushed into the house and almost bumped into the man in her haste.

"Anderson, it *is* you," Aimée exclaimed, enthusiastically latching onto his arm and kissing his cheek.

He colored and stood very still, looking at her with a benevolent expression. "It is good to see you, Mrs. Garrard."

"Bryan? Colonel Garrard . . . is here?"

Anderson nodded and smiled, making a motion toward the stairs with his hand.

Aimée ran up the stairs as fast as her crinolines would allow, but when she reached the landing, she stopped, hesitating. Her hair had been blown by the wind, and her beige muslin dress was wrinkled. Why had she not worn a more flattering dress? Why had she not worn a bonnet down to the levee, instead of carrying the old, faded parasol? Then her hair would still be in place.

But it was too late, Bryan was in the bedroom and there was no time to change.

The bedroom door was partially ajar, and with a shyness that enveloped her whole being, Aimée pushed it open wider but could take no more steps into the room.

She stood there, gazing hungrily at the sight of him. With his back to the door, he seemed unaware of her presence. His uniform was dusty and dirty, but even the travel stains could not hide the sagging of those once-proud shoulders.

Her need to see his face overrode her shyness. "Bryan?" The sound was so soft that Aimée could not be sure she had actually spoken.

The shoulders straightened and Bryan slowly turned his body in the direction from which the slight sound had come. His face was haggard and haunted, revealing the harshness of the weeks of constant battle.

A flicker of uncertainty crossed his brow, and then a tautness controlled it as he said her name. "Aimée—"

She stood rooted, without feet to move—only eyes to see his pain. Suddenly she ran to him, flinging herself into his arms.

"Forgive me, forgive me," he said over and over as he held her in his arms, as he kissed her hair, her throat, her hands. "I have lived in agony these past weeks, not knowing whether you would ever want to see me again."

"You are here, Bryan," Aimée assured him in a tremulous voice. "That's all that matters now."

Later Anderson brought the pails of steaming water to empty into the brass tub, and when it was filled, Bryan removed his dusty uniform and eased his large frame into the soapy warm water.

"I have wished for this room, Aimée, many times during the long nights away—for the pleasure of a bath and a comfortable bed." His eyes twinkled in a teasing manner.

"And that is all you wished for, Bryan?" Aimée asked archly.

"One other thing," he added with a sober expression.

'What was . . . that?" she asked eagerly.

"A meal of shrimp and fowl, gumbo and . . . strawberries."

Aimée frowned and answered in a cold voice, "The strawberries are not yet ripe, Bryan. I fear you will be disappointed tonight."

Bryan laughed and held out his strong wet arms to

Aimée, but she shook her head and remained in the chair near the hearth.

"If you refuse to come to me, then I must come to you, Aimée."

He stepped out of the tub in all his nakedness and headed toward her. She quickly snatched the towel to hand to him and turned her blushing face from the maleness of his body.

"Does it embarrass you, my sweet, to see that I already desire you?"

Through the light dress Aimée could feel the hardness, pressing close to her, his body clothed only by the towel.

"I have teased you with my petty wishes, Aimée . . . not the overwhelming, encompassing *need* that was always with me." His voice was suddenly serious, with no trace of teasing. "The need to have you in my arms—the need to feel your soft, enticing body as part of mine."

Bryan continued to caress her, holding her close to him.

"I think you will have to be my heaven tonight, Aimée —for tomorrow, I go back to hell."

"Tomorrow?" Aimée cried out. "You are leaving tomorrow? Oh, Bryan, you can't!"

"I must, Aimée. Those are my orders."

She gazed at him with a stricken expression, and then slowly she pushed back from him. "I must see to your dinner. I know you must be hungry."

"Aimée?"

The voice stopped her at the door.

"Yes, Bryan?"

"I do not wish to share you with anyone for the few hours I have. Tell Anderson that we will have dinner up here tonight—just the two of us."

The old arrogance, the forceful command, were again in his voice.

"Yes, Bryan," Aimée said meekly before disappearing down the hall.

By the intimacy of the fire Bryan and Aimée shared their dinner—the terrapin soup, the turkey fattened on pecans, cauliflower, and apple tarts. But through it all,

Aimée tasted nothing. She could have been eating a poor, unflavored meal of earlier days for all the attention she gave it. But Bryan was hungry and he showed his enjoyment of the special meal Aimée had been so anxious to put before him.

"I have seen men so hungry these past weeks, Aimée, that they have eaten bacon raw, without taking the time to cook it."

He stared down at his own plate of delicacies and added, "I am not sure you should have served me this feast. The transition back to hardtack will be difficult to stomach."

Seeing her worried look, Bryan smiled and said, "Don't be so distressed, my darling. I'm grateful for everything this night offers. And I have no business intruding the privations of war to spoil our time together. I will speak no more about it. . . . Tell me of the news here. What is happening with the family?"

"Faith and Hope are going each day to the convent school," Aimée said, "and so is Katinka."

"Katinka? Going to school?" Bryan laughed. "Is she not too old for school by now?"

"The Sisters say she is a good pupil, Bryan. And she deserves a chance to better herself. With Lisette taking over many of the chores that Katinka did, she has the time."

"Lisette?" He repeated the name in surprise. "Isn't she the servant who betrayed you?"

"Yes, but she is sorry for that—and she needed a job."

Aimée did not give Bryan an opportunity to make any additional comments, but kept up the news. "And I am almost certain that Vickie is . . . *enceinte*."

"What is that? Do you mean she is expecting a baby?"

"Yes, Bryan."

He grinned and said, "What a surprise—Clay to be a father. I had thought I would be the first."

The pain passed over Aimée as a moving shadow and Bryan quickly asked, "And what about Cousins Clotilde and Jorge?"

"She is still teaching her music pupils and Cousin Jorge has begun to write a history of Louisiana."

Anderson brought in the fresh, piping hot coffee and Aimée poured it into the thin porcelain cups while Anderson cleared the remnants of the meal from the table.

"And you, Aimée?" he asked gently, coming to sit beside her on the small sofa.

"I go to market every day and spend time with Vickie's little girls. I go to the wharf often to get news of the—"

She looked at Bryan and stopped. "I'm sorry. We were not going to speak of the war, were we?"

His arm was now around her shoulder and the old sensuous caressing sent a shuddered thrill through her body. Disconcerted, she continued to talk while he slowly numbed any other thought but her desire for him. Aimée frantically searched for other bits of news, but he put his fingers to her lips, silencing her.

Her head lay against his chest, and he stroked the red-gold hair. He found the pins that bound it up and removed them to free the strands to fall in cascaded splendor across his chest.

"Each night I have been away, a golden witch has invaded my dreams, but by morning she always disappeared from my pillow, leaving me desolate. But tonight—tonight, she will not be an elusive thing. She will stay in my arms until I let her go."

Abruptly he got up, walking to the window seat, without saying a word to her. He fingered the lute case before him, and opening the lid, brought the pear-shaped instrument back to Aimée. "Play for me, Aimée."

His voice was suddenly wistful.

"Some nights, on the river, the wind would sing through the trees and I imagined your voice in the courtyard. It was the only thing that could soothe me when I heard the cries of the wounded." Bryan made a grimace. "It seems I cannot even keep my own silence."

Aimée ran her fingers over the strings, making certain they were still in tune, and soon the words of the haunting *chanson* rose above the sound of the lute.

Bryan relaxed, closing his eyes, and the tired, haggard expression of his face softened and disappeared, leaving only the pale mark of the saber cut to mar his handsome face.

He sat in the chair across from her while, with song after song, Aimée wove a magic in the air. All the time, Bryan did not open his eyes. Certain that he had gone to sleep, Aimée stopped and returned the lute to its case.

She met his eyes gazing tenderly at her when she took her place on the sofa, and without taking his eyes from her, he arose from the chair and came to sit beside her.

His kiss, a gentle thing at the beginning, brushed across her lips, and as it did so, her mouth responded, demanding a more ardent exploration.

Crushing her in his strong arms, he was not aware that once again the buttons of his uniform dug into her flesh, until she drew back with a little gasp.

"I am afraid, monsieur, that your gold buttons have come between us."

Bryan laughed and whispered in her ear, "And shall I remedy that, my love?" He stood up, hastily throwing off his coat.

'If you will excuse me, Bryan, I will make sure everything is . . . in order downstairs."

He laid his hand on her arm, forbidding her to go. "No, Aimée. They can do without you for one evening."

When she protested, Bryan looked down from his great height and demanded, "Do I embarrass you by removing my clothes in front of you?" He continued taking off the belt at his waist and lifted his shirt from its restriction.

"You did not appear too embarrassed this afternoon when I stood naked before you. What was there about this afternoon that is different from tonight?"

The gentleness she had glimpsed in him when he was sitting listening to the music was gone, almost as if he were ashamed of its power to stir him, and to counteract it, must once again play the part of the conqueror.

His arrogant teasing made her indignant. "This afternoon, your intent was to take a bath, but tonight . . ."

She stopped.

"Go on and say it, Aimée. What is my intent tonight? Let us remove this shyness of yours, once and for all."

Aimée brushed her hair back from her face. "But it has been so long since—"

"—Since I bedded you? Is that what you were going to say?"

She nodded, her face flushed from his obvious enjoyment of the verbal exchange.

"But you were the one who complained of the clothes between us, Aimée. I am only bowing to your wishes. Do I have to woo you all over again, and make you forget that you married no Creole gentleman who undresses for the night behind his big black umbrella?"

"You are . . . playing a game with me, monsieur." Aimée stared at the floor and nervously clasped her hands together.

"If it is a game, then know that I will be the winner," he said in a husky voice.

"Unbutton my shirt, Aimée," he ordered in a serious voice.

She lifted her head in surprise and the flash of her turquoise eyes stabbed him with their brilliance. "I . . . I am not your valet, Bryan."

He laughed. "I think you will make a very good valet—and I am tired. Do as I say, Aimée."

With trembling hands, she obeyed him, fumbling at the buttons until the white shirt lay open, revealing the dark hairs of his chest. Her hands lingered on his shoulders as she helped him off with his shirt.

"And now my boots." He sat again on the sofa and held out one foot.

In silence Aimée grasped the heel of the boot, tugging at it back and forth, until it loosened and came off in her hands.

"And now, the other one."

The right boot was harder to remove than the left and Aimée, making an intensive effort, jerked hard, and fell backward, with the boot in her hand.

Bryan leaped up to bring her to her feet. "I don't think you will ever take Anderson's place," Bryan commented, his silver-gray eyes teasing her. "But then, Anderson could never take your place either.

"My prim, little Creole wife, if I did not know what

fire lay under that girlish dress with its pristine collar and cuffs, you would have the advantage. But you seem to forget—I have tasted the wild honey many times.

"My men are quite envious of me, Aimée. They have asked if a Secessionist can love as ardently as she hates."

"You have . . . discussed me with your men?" Aimée's eyes turned to dark troubled pools and her face became wan and pale.

"No, my darling. I would never be that insensitive," he said, acting suddenly tired of teasing her. "Come, it's been a long day. I am weary and ready for bed."

Aimée walked toward the screen where the brass tub lay hidden, and reaching up her hands, she attempted to loosen the hooks at the back of her dress. But her hands met Bryan's.

"You have been kind enough to act as my valet, my lady," Bryan said lightly, "so it is only courteous that I act as lady's maid."

"That is not . . . necessary, Bryan."

But her protests went unheeded. He helped her with her crinolines, as he had done many times before, and when she stood protesting, "I have forgotten to get my gown," he said nothing, until her soft white body, framed by long strands of golden hair, emerged from the layers of clothes.

His sudden inhalation made her even more nervous. "You are so beautiful," he said, running his hand down from her breasts to curve around her hips. And before she could voice any objection, he lifted her and carried her toward the bed.

"My gown," she whimpered, but he shook his head. "It would be a sacrilege to hide such beauty. You must let me worship you as you are—a Venus born out of the sea."

He placed her on the bed as if it were an altar and he knelt beside her, drinking in her beauty while the tongues of fire on the hearth leaped up, casting a pale translucence over the room.

Aimée shivered from the cold and Bryan, seeing this, climbed into bed beside her to warm her, drawing her into his demanding arms, pressing her to his body. And she responded, feeling his flesh against hers.

One night of love—that was all she had been allotted by the gods of war and then Bryan would leave her. It was too much to bear, to be left alone and desolate, with no part of him.

"Bryan," she whispered.

"Yes, my darling?" he murmured into her hair.

"Give me . . . your son, tonight. I beg of you . . ."

"Aimée . . ." The hoarse cry was one of triumph, as he turned her body into a willing receptacle, waiting to be shaped to his love.

"Now, Bryan—give me your son now," she begged, and he was upon her, giving her what she desired. She willingly received it, praying that she would be with child because of this night of love.

The knock at the door the next morning awakened them both. "The boat is due to leave in a little over an hour from now, sir."

Anderson's voice cut through the peaceful still morning, bringing a trembling to Aimée, a despair because the night was over.

"I am awake, Anderson," Bryan called out. "I'll be down in time."

But instead of leaving the bed, Bryan reached out for Aimée, who placed a kiss on the dark head leaning over her. Feeling his hands moving down her body, she sensed a prelude that could only end in fulfillment.

"Bryan, there is not enough time. You will have to have breakfast and then get dressed to get to the wharf."

"Do you think I would wish coffee and brioche when there is something more delectable offered me?"

She pushed at him, but he held her arms upward, imprisoning her body with his. "Nothing else has been offered you this morning, except breakfast, Bryan."

He continued his lovemaking, forcing Aimée to feel the same urgency as he felt, but still, she resisted.

"Perhaps you did not conceive last night," he whispered. "And you asked me for a son, if you remember—in fact, you begged me. Shall we . . . deny each other what we want most?"

With a soft, reconciled sigh, Aimée said, "No, Bryan. Do not deny me my son and I shall not deny you your pleasure."

Chapter 32

She should not be sad, Aimée told herself. Had not Bryan been given a day to spend with her, one that had clearly been a gift, when she had not expected it?

But the night with Bryan had poignantly shown her how empty her life had been without him. Now the sense of loss was overwhelming. How much longer was he to remain apart from her?

For the rest of the day Aimée persisted in a pensive state, attending to minor duties in the house and taking a long walk with Charity and Lizzie. The hours dragged by and finally it was time for dinner.

"Well, Bryan clearly showed what he thought of the rest of us," Vickie said at the table.

"*Thought* of us?" Clay said with a biting laugh. "For Bryan, we did not even exist."

"He was here such a short time," Cousin Clotilde defended him with her soothing voice. "It was only natural that Colonel Garrard would want to spend that time with his wife."

"You seem to know a lot, Cousin Clotilde, of what men want." Vickie looked at the spinster with a certain malicious glint. "I am surprised that one in your . . . position is such an expert."

Cousin Clotilde colored at the subtle slur on her unmarried state.

Aimée, indignant at the disrespect shown her cousin, faced Vickie with an angry glare. "I will not have you speak in that manner to Cousin Clotilde at *my* table, Vickie. Take your viciousness out on me, if you must, but leave Cousin Clotilde alone."

Aimée continued to glare at Vickie and added, "It seems that you and Clay are not immune from wanting to be alone at times either. Was that not why you moved into the carriage house?"

"We know when we are not wanted, Aimée," Vickie said in a hurt little girl's voice. "And if Bryan did not depend on Clay to watch over his financial affairs while he is away, we would have moved to a home of our own long ago."

"Please, it is not good for the children to hear quarreling at the table," Cousin Clotilde said, glancing worriedly toward the open door.

Clay and Cousin Jorge looked uncomfortable at the show of tempers, and staring down at their plates, continued to eat in silence. But Cousin Clotilde's gentle admonition had its effect and for the rest of the meal tempers were kept in check.

It was Katinka who provided relief from the strained silence that followed the exchange of words.

"Did you know that pelicans can't cry?" Katinka said.

Cousin Jorge, looking at the girl with his myopic blue eyes, answered, "Where did you learn that, my dear?"

"In . . . in school today. Sister Marie was giving our lesson about the early Indian civilization and what the ancient Indians found when they reached Louisiana . . . and what disappeared with them."

"But not the pelican." Cousin Jorge tried to keep his lips from twitching.

"No. Sister Marie said if they had been good to eat, they would not have survived."

"Why can't the pelican cry, Katinka?" Clay asked.

"Oh, they can at first . . . but not after adolescence. Something happens to their voices and they can barely make a sound when they're grown."

"It's a pity that some adults don't have the gift of the pelican," Aimée reflected aloud.

Vickie looked sharply at her, but Cousin Clotilde hastily turned the conversation back to Katinka.

"Did Sister Marie also tell you the legend that the Indians had about them?"

"Yes, and I think it's beautiful."

"I don't believe I've heard it," Clay said. "Enlighten me, Katinka."

Katinka flushed but looked pleased at the attention. "The old Indian legend says that when there is a famine in the land and the young pelicans cry for food, then the mother pelican tears the feathers from her breast and feeds her babies with her own blood."

"You think that is a beautiful story?" Clay asked with a look of repugnance on his face.

"Yes," Katinka answered seriously. "Because it is a symbol of charity and . . . and self-sacrifice."

With a bitter note in his voice, Clay said, "I fear that all too soon, Katinka, your Indian legend will be alive again."

Aimée stood up and the others followed her into the salon. Clay's comment had a sobering effect on them all, and as Aimée thought of the ravaged land, a vast uneasiness swept over her.

Hard Times Landing—It was the twenty-ninth of April and Grant had marched into Louisiana to meet Porter, who had slipped downriver seventy miles past Vicksburg.

Through canebrakes, swamps, and black lagoons, Grant forged a corduroy road for his troops and guns. Kidnapping one of the local Negroes to serve as guide, Grant and his army reached their rendezvous, and at daybreak the soldiers and the big guns crossed the river, with Porter's gunboats and transports acting as ferries.

The Union Army was now below Vicksburg, on the eastern side of the river, and for the first time the Northerners had the advantage. Vicksburg's rear was ahead of them; there was no water to separate Grant from his objective.

From Port Gibson, Grant pushed on—to Raymond, Jackson, Champion's Hill, and Big Black, until the Union line reached close to the ridges of Vicksburg. On that day, May 17, the message from Washington to abandon this latest campaign and march his army to help General Banks and the Army of the Gulf at Port Hudson was ignored by Grant. It was too late and the two-month siege of Vicksburg began.

At the same time, Banks and his army were engaged in fierce fighting at Port Hudson to prevent the shipping of supplies from the West by the Red River entrance to the Mississippi. If Port Hudson and Vicksburg fell, the South would be broken in half.

The atmosphere in the townhouse was strained. Bryan had been away for over three months and Clay, who held the purse strings, became increasingly stingy with the amount of money allowed Aimée.

"I am afraid, Aimée, that Katinka's tuition will have to come from your household allowance. Personally, I don't understand why you wish to educate her above her station."

Aimée said nothing, knowing that Vickie had influenced him and she would be unable to change his mind with her protests.

She economized on food and clothes, making do with what she had and relying more on the small amount of money that Cousin Clotilde put in the sugar jar each week. Vickie, on the other hand, dressed more and more elegantly each day.

"We are thinking of renting the townhouse several blocks away," Vickie mentioned in the salon one evening as they sat sipping hot coffee despite the warm, humid weather. "It will be available in a few weeks, because the people are unable to pay their taxes. With the baby on its way, Clay does not want me to be climbing those dangerous stairs to the carriage house any longer."

Vickie glanced toward Aimée with a questioning look on her face. But Aimée cast her eyes downward, trying not to show her disappointment that she was not also expecting a child. Despite the night spent with Bryan, Aimée had not conceived.

"Aimée, it's all right, isn't it, if we take the furniture we have been using in the carriage house? That way, we won't have to spend so much money buying furniture."

Bryan's money, Aimée thought bitterly before she answered, but there was nothing she could do about it. "No, Vickie, you may take the furniture with you."

On the day that she and Clay moved, Vickie informed Aimée of Lisette's willingness to go with them. "I hope you will not mind that Lisette has promised to work a few days, helping us to get settled. Lizzie is so busy with the children, and with Cousins Clotilde and Jorge the only other ones living with you, Tink should be sufficient help for you for a while."

"*Katinka*, Vickie. Do not call her 'Tink.' "

Things had not worked out well with Lisette. The old antagonisms were still there. Lisette was always looking to see which way the fair wind was blowing, and it was definitely blowing in Vickie's direction.

When Lisette had not returned after a week, Aimée knew that the black woman had made a decision to stay with Vickie and Clay. Aimée could not afford to pay her anyway, so she did not protest Lisette's defection.

The letter from Vickie was delivered on a Wednesday afternoon, just after Cousin Jorge had left the house to do some research for his book. Cousin Clotilde had not returned from her teaching and Katinka was not due home from the convent for another hour.

Leaving a note for Katinka on the table in the hallway —in case she was delayed—Aimée left the townhouse and walked down the street the few blocks to the house where Vickie and Clay lived.

She used the heavy knocker at the gate but no one came. Knocking even louder, Aimée waited to be admitted, but her second knock went unheeded. Surely they had heard her, since they were expecting her. The gate was unlocked, and finally Aimée, not seeing the waiting carriage in the alleyway, pushed the gate open and walked into the passageway. She called out Vickie's name but the house seemed to be deserted.

"Good afternoon, Aimée," the voice greeted her.

Aimée, startled at the sudden sound of the man's voice, shuddered in recognition, and in an unbelieving voice asked, "What are *you* doing here?"

"Waiting for you, my dear."

"But Vickie . . ." Aimée protested.

"Your sister-in-law is very useful. She is as determined as I am to see your downfall."

"Why are you not . . . with the rest of the army?" Aimée asked, pretending no alarm while frantically trying to think of a way to escape.

"Someone has to remain at headquarters," he said, edging slowly toward her as she backed from him.

"I have waited a long time for you to come to me, Aimée. And this time I will see that you do not escape." Colonel Tilson snatched her roughly into his arms.

"No! Take your hands off me, monsieur!"

His hand closed over her mouth and the next moment she was rudely carried into the alleyway, to be thrown into the carriage. The colonel's arm pinioned her to his side, while the driver sped through the streets. The curtains of the carriage were drawn and Aimée could only guess where she was being taken. A tiny muffled sound was all that came from her mouth. Because of the gag, Aimée's cry for help was too weak to be heard.

It was a dollhouse, with masses of color tumbling about. The delicate scent of roses came to Aimée's attention, even as she was slung, like a sack, over the man's shoulder and taken into the house—the house in the Ramparts that had been waiting for her ever since the night of the Quadroon Ball.

Once inside, the tall heavy man set her down and removed the gag from her mouth. Even as he held her captive, a gentleness came into his voice.

"I hope you will like the house that was purchased for you, Delphine."

Aimée looked sharply at the man. Why had he reverted to calling her Delphine?

"Do not be alarmed, my dear," he said, caressing her shoulder. "I shall be very gentle with you tonight, since you are still so shy with men."

His gentle manner alarmed her far more than his earlier anger.

"Come with me, and I will show you the rest of the house."

Could the man be mad—actually thinking her to be Delphine? Hesitatingly, she was drawn with him while he went from room to room.

"I have a surprise for you here, in the bedroom."

Leading her to the tall armoire that covered the wall space at one end of the room, he swept open the doors to reveal one elegant dress after another. "These are all for you."

A whole wardrobe full of costly dresses—more than she had ever had in her life—with slippers and crinolines and accessories to match. A fortune—money made by speculation—lavished on the house and clothes, for the colonel's own selfish pleasures. Suddenly Aimée was more afraid than ever. He had prepared the house for Delphine, his octoroon mistress, and in his sick, glazed eyes, *she* had become Delphine.

In an instant Aimée saw that to gain time, she must acquiesce to this macabre drama, must play the part of the demure, chaste Delphine until she could find some means of escape. And Aimée prayed that the man would not be too impatient to claim his mistress.

"I would like for you to wear this dress tonight." He took the gossamer green silk from the armoire and laid it carefully across the chair. "But it is too soon to dress for dinner. I will show you the remainder of the house and the garden, and then you must rest."

The house, furnished exquisitely from the auctions of family heirlooms, brought a bitterness to Aimée, but she hid it from the man beside her. Walking outside with him, she entered the walled garden and her breath caught at the beauty.

"I knew you would like it," he said, leading her to the wrought-iron chair near the fountain. A pitcher of cool lemonade waited for them on the table. And as the colonel sat opposite her in the other chair, he said, "You may pour our lemonade now, Delphine. There will be time enough for wine later."

With trembling hands, she picked up the pitcher and poured the contents into the two glasses. In her nervousness one glass overfilled and she gave a start at her clumsiness. Colonel Tilson stood up, wiping the excess from the table with one of the fine embroidered napkins, the napkin that Aimée remembered seeing at Michele's house—a fine old square of linen with an elaborate T in the corner. The recognition of something that had belonged to the Toulouse family etched the pain deeper into Aimée's expressive eyes.

Colonel Tilson reached out and took Aimée's hand, gently kissing it. "My little love, don't be so afraid of me. I would not harm you."

"M-merci, monsieur," Aimée stammered.

He smiled and said softly, "I have wished to hear my name spoken by those sweet lips. Would you say my name now, Delphine?"

She looked puzzled and he laughed. "But of course, you do not know it, do you? It is Titus. Say it, Delphine."

"It is very pleasant here in the garden . . . Titus."

The smile spread across the man's heavy face. "I shall never forget the way you looked just now, Delphine. You have made me very happy."

He sat back, watching her every move, and her embarrassment caused Aimée to lower her eyes and pretend to be absorbed with drinking the glass of lemonade. She held the glass for a long time after it was empty, nervously twisting it in her hand while she pursued her thoughts of escape.

Titus Tilson shifted his empty glass from his hand to the table and also took Aimée's glass and set it on the table.

"You must rest until time to dress for dinner. I mustn't let you become too tired before evening."

Again Aimée was drawn reluctantly to his side and led back into the house. If she were expected to rest, perhaps she could find a way to escape from the bedroom. But that idea was soon crushed when she heard the key turning in the lock. She was a prisoner; the iron grills across the windows precluded escape from that direction.

It was hot in the bedroom and the heat of the afternoon drained Aimée of energy. Her eyelids drooped and she gazed longingly at the comfortable bed. No, she must stay awake to plan her escape. But she could not think, with her body wet from perspiration, with her brain numbed by the desire to sleep. Only for a little while would she rest her head on the pillow. . . .

She sensed his presence before she opened her eyes, felt the mild stroking of her hair and heard the breathing close to her. She must not appear too alarmed, Aimée thought, when she saw him.

Slowly she opened the turquoise eyes and asked in a sleepy voice, "Is it time for dinner, Titus?"

His face was close to hers—too close for comfort, but she resolutely remained calm, though aware of the erratic beating of her heart.

"Yes, Delphine, I came to wake you—but you were so beautiful while you slept that I could not bring myself to disturb you." He leaned over, taking her in his arms, and his mouth, searching for hers, brushed her cheek as she turned her head.

"Please," she said, pushing him away, "I must get dressed."

When the ugly look began creeping across the bloated face, Aimée quickly said, "I want to look beautiful for you, Titus. You . . . have been so kind to give me such beautiful things."

The face relaxed, and again he looked tenderly at Aimée.

"I am glad I chose the green dress for tonight. It will act as a perfect foil for your red-gold hair. Strange, isn't it," he said in a perplexed voice, while holding one curl in his hands, "I somehow remember a girl with turquoise eyes and *black* hair."

He shook the puzzled expression from his face. "Yet it was the fire that always drew me—the fire with the ice. But tonight the fire will consume the ice."

His last words, a mocking threat, were lashing at her, making it difficult to subdue the terror in her heart.

Titus stalked across the room, closed the door, and the key made its familiar sound in the lock.

What am I to do? Aimée asked herself in anguish. Only Vickie was aware of what had happened to her, and Aimée knew better than to expect help from that source.

Would Katinka go in search of her? And not finding her at Vickie's house, would the girl have the least idea where to begin looking in earnest? Cousins Clotilde and Jorge would be worried when she did not return. But by the time she was allowed to leave the Ramparts, the damage would have been done. Colonel Titus Tilson would make sure of that.

With the water from the ewer Aimée bathed her face, and when the last drop had been poured into the basin, she removed her garments and hurriedly sponged herself before Colonel Tilson would have time to return.

The gossamer green silk clung to Aimée like a skin soon to be outgrown. The voluminous skirt accented the tiny waist, and her breasts, not finding enough room in the low-cut bodice, struggled to free themselves from restriction.

I must not lean over, Aimée admonished herself, or I might be in trouble far sooner than I think.

Putting the finishing touches to her hair with the silver brush and comb, she heard the grating sound in the door. It was time for the drama to begin. . . .

He was in full dress uniform, even to the saber hanging at his side—the same blue uniform that Bryan had worn, with identical gold buttons down the front. But the difference between the two men was astounding. Titus Tilson stood before Aimée, his paunchy stomach destroying the fine lines of the coat, his bloated face with puffed eyelids making him a debauched caricature of a soldier, who had wasted his strength on dross.

Bryan's dark eagle face superimposed itself on Colonel Tilson's, but the image was soon gone and Aimée stared at the face of a much older man, seeing the desire for her written in his eyes.

Aimée went through the appropriate movements at dinner, responding to Colonel Tilson's conversation, to his solicitous concern in offering her the best delicacies at the table. He poured the wine into fine stems, filling and refilling his own glass, while Aimée sipped hers, wondering who had prepared such a dinner for them. Someone must have come in while she was asleep that afternoon. But she had heard no one—no one to call out to for help.

The minutes ticked away. The meal was over. Still, Aimée lingered at the table, pretending to finish her wine. Still, she had not thought of a means of escape.

The man held out his hand to her and pulled her to her feet. Woodenly, Aimée walked to the sofa he indicated and sat down, her trembling hands hidden in the voluminous folds of the green silk of her dress.

"Tell me about . . . your life, monsieur," Aimée croaked, hoping to divert his gaze from her low-cut dress.

"I had no life before I met you, Delphine," he answered slowly, his eyes still glued to the figure before him.

"What? No wife, waiting at home? No children to greet your return?" Her attempt at lightness was lost.

The man frowned, as if daring his past to creep into his thoughts at this moment. His hand slid up Aimée's arm and rested against the hollow of her throat where her pulse was beating in fear.

Aimée moved apart from him, but her movement stirred him to action. He crushed her in his strong grasp and his kiss brought a shudder of revulsion to her. And once again the gold buttons of the enemy tortured her flesh, while the cold steel of the saber's sheath lay heavily against her.

"Monsieur, you are wounding me with your uniform," Aimée said sweetly. "Would it not be more . . . comfortable for you also if you removed your coat?"

Colonel Tilson laughed and stood up. "So my little flame is not quite so afraid as I thought. And not so patient either, eh?"

His saber clattered to the floor, followed by the coat, and he was back beside her, impatiently drawing her to him.

"Monsieur, you would not leave such a beautiful coat crumpled on the floor. Let me hang it up for you," Aimée suggested.

"Already the little mistress of the house, taking care of her man," he said indulgently. "But I see your game, Delphine. I know what you are thinking."

Aimée gave him a glittering smile with her even little white teeth while she slowly picked up the coat and felt the saber underneath.

"What am I . . . thinking, Titus?"

"That you will delay my loving you by pretending concern for my coat."

Aimée's languid manner changed at the sudden removal of the saber from its sheath.

"That is exactly what I am doing, Colonel Tilson."

The naked steel glistened in the flickering light as Aimée faced the colonel with his own weapon.

"Put the saber down, Delphine. You will hurt yourself," he said, still not alarmed at her action.

"I am not Delphine," Aimée quietly explained. "I am Aimée, the wife of Colonel Bryan Garrard."

"No," he exploded, standing up. "You are Delphine and you are mine."

"I will never be yours, Colonel Tilson."

He lunged for the saber. Aimée stepped back, horrified at the surging red of the man's face, the rousing fury displayed at her resistance. His swift movement brought him to her; his hands reached to tear the saber from her grasp. But Aimée clung to the sharp-edged steel with a surprising stubborn strength. The spurt of blood from the man's hand caused a bellow of rage that reverberated through the room, and Colonel Tilson, slightly drunk from the excess of dinner wine, shifted his weight and lunged again, jerking the saber from her. The sudden twist of his body caught him off-balance, and before Aimée knew what was happening, the heavy man had fallen, knocking her down with him.

Dazed by the fall, Aimée saw only the spinning of the room, felt the heavy weight of the man's body pinning her to the floor.

Aimée did not know how long she lay there with the man's body a dead weight upon her own. She felt the trickle of the warm blood spreading over her, and in panic she pushed and struggled to get free. The man did not respond to her struggling. He was dead . . . the enemy had fallen on his own sword.

She continued to push and prod until the body moved, and then she slowly extricated herself. She sat up, staring down at the man. Who would believe that it had been an accident? Aimée's only thought was to get away—to escape from the horrible scene before her and return to the safety of her own house on Royal Street.

Chapter 33

She staggered across to the door and fled to the banquette, where the lamplight encircled her in its glow. Out of the light—she must get out of the light to where no one could see her, where no one could see the gossamer green dress stained with blood.

After a few blocks of running, the nagging thought revealed itself to her. Aimée had left her own clothes in the bedroom—clothes that could be used to trace her. She would have to go back for them. She could not afford for anyone to know what had happened that night.

Retracing her steps, Aimée stumbled over the uneven banquette and pushed her way into the house, as the sound of a carriage on the street grew louder.

Titus Tilson was where she had left him, and Aimée, as undeterred as a somnambulist with a goal, walked past the man and into the bedroom where her clothes lay folded in the base of the armoire.

After stripping the stained green dress from her body and kicking off the matching slippers, Aimée pushed the clothes in a bundle toward the back of the armoire and put on her own robin's-egg-blue dress and worn slippers.

Again she was on the banquette. The fog creeping through the city made it imperative for her to get home quickly, before she became hopelessly lost in the thick miasma coming from the river.

Once she came into the Vieux Carré, the streets were

laid out in straight lines and right angles, making it easier for her. Aimée followed along the edge of the shops lining the banquette until she was on Royal Street.

The voices at the corner made her cautious. She must not attract attention. She darted into a darkened doorway and remained until the voices passed by, the laughter a raucous jar upon her nerves.

The pink stucco and brick house rose out of the fog. She was home, safe from the ordeal. The lights were ablaze, and when Aimée entered the house, she was met by an incredulous Katinka, standing in the hall.

"Mrs. Garrard, where have you been? Everybody is out searching for you. They made me stay here in case you came back."

Katinka followed her up the stairs, her anxiety over Aimée's disheveled appearance easy to read in her face.

"Did you not get the note I left you this afternoon, Katinka?" Aimée asked, trying to maintain a calm that she did not feel.

"There . . . there wasn't any note, Mrs. Garrard."

"No note? But I left one for you on the table in the hallway."

"Well, it must have blown off. I didn't see one when I came home. Where did you go?"

Looking at the girl, Aimée said, "I can never speak of what happened tonight, or where I went, Katinka. And you must never tell anyone of my . . . disordered appearance. Will you keep the secret with me, Katinka?"

"Of course," she said. "But you'll have to get those clothes off, while I bring water for a bath. It wouldn't do for anyone else to see you like this."

"Thank you, Katinka."

As soon as the girl had disappeared, Aimée went downstairs to the hall to look for the note. It was wedged behind the table, where the wind had evidently blown it when the door opened. With relief, Aimée took it back upstairs and tore it to shreds. Now no one in the family would ever know that she had gone to Vickie's house. She would manufacture some suitable cover for her long absence by the time the others came home.

Aimée, sitting in the salon, listened for Cousins Clotilde

and Jorge to return. Outwardly she was calm, but at the sound of the opening door, nervousness pervaded her.

"Mrs. Garrard's back home," Katinka's voice assured them. "The note she left for us was blown off the table by the wind."

"Thank the good Lord!" Cousin Jorge's voice responded to the news.

"Where is she now, Katinka?" Cousin Clotilde asked.

"In the salon, waiting for you."

Aimée stood and rushed to Clotilde's side, when she appeared at the door.

"I am so sorry to have caused such concern," Aimée apologized. "I left a note telling you where I would be, but it seems no one saw it."

"Katinka said it was blown off the table," Cousin Jorge cut in, his anxiety slowly ebbing at the explanation.

"Yes, I found it wedged behind the table where it had fallen," Aimée explained.

"Where were you, my dear—to have been away for so long?" The dubious look Cousin Clotilde gave her indicated the woman was not entirely satisfied with what she had heard.

"Michele, my best friend, asked me to go upriver to her cousin's house, to help with the rolling of bandages for the wounded, and it was later than I expected when we returned."

Cousin Clotilde frowned. "Aimée, would that not be considered giving aid to the enemy? As much as I commend you for your actions, I hope you will not get into trouble because of it."

"Then we will have to keep it a secret, Cousin Clotilde."

"Well, no real harm's been done—just a few anxious hours for us, wondering where you were, my dear. We'd better let Clay and Vickie know. Clay might keep on searching for you, if we don't tell them you're safe at home."

Cousin Jorge turned to Clotilde. "Do you remember, Clotilde, when you did nearly the same thing, and Mama was so frantic with worry?"

The next day a puzzled Vickie watched Aimée for

some sign of her abduction, but Aimée, determined that the woman should never know, casually apologized for not being able to visit her the previous afternoon.

"Michele was waiting for me to accompany her, Vickie, but you received my note, explaining that—"

"Note? What note, Aimée?"

"You mean the little boy did not return to you with my answer?"

"No, I saw no note from you."

"And I paid that little rapscallion, too," Aimée added in an exasperated voice. "Well, that cannot be helped now. What is it that you wished to see me about, Vickie?"

Aimée's body obeyed her, not giving any outward sign of the agitation she felt inside as she faced the woman responsible for her traumatic experience.

"It . . . it was not important," a sullen Vickie replied.

All through the day Aimée listened for a knock at the door, listened for the authorities to come to arrest her for the murder of Colonel Titus Tilson. But no one came, except the man with the water wagon.

It was the next day that the news appeared. Cousin Jorge, sitting in the salon, kept shaking his head and repeating, "What a pity! What a pity!"

"Wh—what is it, Cousin Jorge?"

"It is a 'crime of passion'—not suitable for a woman to read, Aimée. These Yankees will print anything in their newspapers," the man said in disgust, folding the paper neatly and putting it on the table beside his chair.

Aimée willed Cousin Jorge to disappear, but he seemed to be in no hurry to remove himself from the salon. He was in an amiable mood and chatted inconsequentially while Aimée, answering in monosyllables, sat eyeing the newspaper and suppressing her urge to hasten the little man's departure.

Finally he got up, saying, "I will be going for my morning walk now. Will you be all right, Aimée, while I am gone?"

Aimée, attempting to hide her relief at his impending departure, answered, "Certainly, Cousin Jorge. Do not worry. I will be busy all morning."

"Bring the dogs inside if you feel uneasy. They would protect you with their lives."

Aimée gave an uneasy laugh. "You sound as if someone intends to harm me, Cousin Jorge, while you are out."

"No, no, my dear. Not at all. It's just that . . . I do not want you to be alone. Perhaps it would be better if I stayed in the house until—"

"By the saints, Cousin Jorge, go for your walk. I will bring the dogs inside, if that will make you feel better."

A self-conscious laugh came from her cousin as he left the room. She heard him upstairs, getting his gloves and cane, and then his steps as he returned to the hall.

"I am leaving now, Aimée."

"Have a nice walk, Cousin Jorge."

He walked down the hall and Aimée heard the side door open and close. She stood up and snatched the newspaper, but before she could begin reading it, she heard the door open again. Cousin Jorge had forgotten something, as usual. Hastily Aimée put the newspaper back in its place and pretended to be rearranging the *objets d'art* on the table.

"I forgot to tell you, Aimée. Clotilde will be a little later than usual."

"Thank you, Cousin Jorge."

Aimée waited until she heard the squeak of the gate before taking up the newspaper again. With trembling hands, she folded the paper to the article on the second page and began reading.

"Army Colonel wounded in crime of passion." *Wounded*! The word struck her with relief. He was not dead, after all.

Aimée's relief was short-lived. If he were not dead and he revealed her name, she could be punished just as severely as if she had murdered him. And the disgrace to Bryan. In despair, Aimée followed the words of the story.

"A Union Army Colonel, whose name is being withheld, was found yesterday in strange circumstances in a house on Rampart Street. The man, wounded by his own saber, identified his assailant as Delphine, his octoroon

315

mistress. The woman, Delphine, is still at large, but the police are acting speedily to apprehend her and bring her to justice for this crime of passion against a Union officer."

Aimée folded the newspaper and returned it to the table.

A brief reprieve—until Colonel Tilson remembered that it was Aimée Saint-Moreau Garrard who was in the house on Rampart Street. How many days would it be before he remembered? How many days of torture would she have to endure before the police came to her gate?

The dogs, whining at the door, were hungry. Aimée let them in, leading them to the kitchen to feed them. Feeling a vast need for consolation, she put her arms around Fréki and Geri and buried her face against their soft, white fur.

Katinka, sensing that Aimée had suffered a frightening experience, became protective toward her. In fact, Katinka became a virago in defense of Aimée. The change from her former accusatory attitude had been so gradual that Aimée was hard pressed to realize just when it had begun.

Could it have started when Katinka entered the convent school? Whenever it had started, the fierce protectiveness was now in full bloom and Katinka watched over Aimée, especially when Vickie was near, as if daring her to harm her.

The girls were now out of school for the summer, but seeing the pleasure that Hope gave to Aimée, Vickie curtailed her visits to Aimée, making Aimée lonelier than ever. During the hot, exhausting days of June Aimée welcomed the close attachment of Katinka while Cousin Clotilde continued her music lessons in the homes of her pupils.

Never leaving the house without the dogs or Katinka to accompany her, Aimée continued to go to the market and to the cathedral. But each time she went out onto the banquette, she was uneasy. No more had been printed in the paper about Colonel Tilson. Aimée could only assume that he was getting well, and that if he had remembered

316

that she had been in the house on Rampart Street, he had chosen not to reveal it. Still, there were times when Aimée awoke during the night from a nightmare that unleashed the terror of that day.

The war news continued to trickle downriver, with the wounded bringing back news of smallpox and fever in the camps and the hundreds of graves being dug along the levee, the only high ground suitable for a burial site. And the horror of the fighting was in the men's voices and in the slump of their shoulders.

"They can't last much longer—they're bein' starved into surrender. No shoes, no clothes, no food . . . and little ammunition."

No trace of animosity toward the enemy remained—only a tiredness and a sickness at so much blood being shed. The feeling of one suffering human being watching death creep up to snare his brother . . . the heartbreak of a futile war—*that* was the message of their voices.

The man with the bandaged head kept saying over and over, "One night we heard the Rebels foraging on the battlefield, and the next day, when we went out under the flag of truce to bring back our dead, the bodies had been stripped of their clothes. Can't say as I blame them, though—the Rebels, that is—I'd a done the same thing if I was half-naked."

The dazed voice started over again, until one of his fellow comrades led him away from the crowd along the levee.

Half-naked—no more colorful kepis, or striped pantaloons—no more brand-new uniforms. How long ago it seemed that the young soldiers in the Delta Rifles had sailed downriver to New Orleans—waiting to be mustered into the army. Their uniforms had been so new that some of the seamstresses had sailed downriver with them, working rapidly to complete the uniforms before they reached port. Aimée remembered the eager, excited look of the young soldiers. Now those who had been left to defend their delta land were ending their days in tatters and starved defeat. Tears brimmed in Aimée's sorrowful eyes. Her own people were dying to defend their land from the enemy, because a man in Washington had said

317

they had no right to secede from a disadvantageous union of states. And yet Bryan, her husband, believed in that union, and for *his* belief, was adding to the suffering of her people.

The siege and the suffering continued through June and the first of July, until on July 4, 1863, Vicksburg raised its flag of starved surrender. The people of the city came out of the caves where they had sought refuge from the enemy shells. And down at Port Hudson, when the Confederates who were holding on with a weakening grip, destitute for shells to shoot and food to eat, heard the news of the fall of Vicksburg, they, too, surrendered. The mighty Mississippi flowed unhindered from its source all the way to the sea. And the Confederacy was now broken in two.

As if to protest the enemy's stronghold upon the water, the winds howled and rains came, soaking the earth and flooding the low places.

For two days and nights it rained without ceasing. And then on the third day, the rains stopped. All during that day ominous gray clouds rolled in from the Gulf toward New Orleans and Lake Pontchartrain—a false lull before the eye of the storm.

Aimée, sitting at the dinner table with Katinka and her two cousins, heard the shutters of the pink townhouse banging and creaking under the strain of the howling wind.

All conversation stopped as the four sat and listened to the increasing belligerency outside. Suddenly a crash brought Aimée to her feet and she rushed to peer out from the fan-shaped glass beside the courtyard door. The blackness revealed nothing to her.

Her thoughts were on the treacherous river, swollen from the two days of constant rain. Oh, Bryan, where are you? Aimée cried to herself. . . . Please let him be safe. The words formed on her lips and she whispered them without knowing she had spoken, but the sound of the wind wiped them out.

"Can you see what caused the crash? Was it one of the trees, Aimée?"

Cousin Jorge stood beside her, also peering into the black darkness.

"It might have been one of the myrtle trees along the carriage drive," she responded. "But I cannot see anything."

Suddenly a tall figure loomed out of the darkness, and for a moment Aimée thought that her prayers had been answered. But it was not Bryan. It was his brother Clay who lurched frantically toward the door. When Aimée unlocked it, the force of the wind ripped it from her hands and it swung hard against the wall.

Clay stepped inside and all three—Aimée, Clay, and Cousin Jorge—pushed the door shut against the penetrating wind.

"Vickie is ill, Aimée," Clay said, his face showing the effects of worry. "And she is asking for Cousin Clotilde."

"What is the matter? Is it the baby?"

"No. Vickie has a fever and she's getting delirious . . . but I fear for the baby if the fever isn't broken soon."

"Then I must go with you at once, Clay." Cousin Clotilde came to stand beside Aimée. "Wait until I get my cape."

"Come, sit down, Clay, while Cousin Clotilde is getting ready," Aimée suggested, but Clay shook his head and remained standing, ill at ease, in the hallway.

"No, I'll wait here. The wind is getting steadily worse. We'll have to hurry if Clotilde doesn't want to be blown away."

"Did you walk?" Aimée asked.

"Yes."

"Then take the pony and *calèche* back with you. It will be easier for both you and Cousin Clotilde, if you ride."

"No, Aimée. There's nowhere to put the pony and carriage for the night. Clotilde will have to manage walking back with me."

"I'll drive you," Cousin Jorge spoke up. "That way, I can return home with the carriage and you won't have to worry about it."

"Thank you, Cousin Jorge," Aimée said soberly to the rotund little man.

Clay did not protest his offer and the little man hurried

to the kitchen for a lantern. Aimée watched while the lantern swung erratically back and forth across the courtyard to the pony stable underneath the carriage house.

"I am ready, Clay." Clotilde with her dark cape about her held a small valise in her hand when she came back into the downstairs hallway.

"Cousin Jorge is hitching the pony to the *calèche* to take you to Vickie. That way, you will not have to walk against the wind."

Clotilde nodded in a mute appreciation toward Aimée, and at the sound of the carriage wheels, Clay opened the door for the woman to hurry outside. Katinka, standing near the newel post of the stairway, came to help Aimée shut the door and they both stood looking out until the carriage, rocking against the wind, proceeded down the carriage drive and disappeared.

They could not have gotten far before the rumble of thunder vied with the wind. The lightning lit up the courtyard and the rains descended rapidly onto the already saturated sod. Water, standing several inches in the courtyard, seeped under the door and Katinka and Aimée hurried to get towels to bundle against the lower edge of the door.

"I just hope the levee holds," Katinka said with a shiver. "Have . . . have you known it to . . . give way, Mrs. Garrard?"

The frightened eyes of Katinka stared at her. "Only once," Aimée replied, and attempting to alleviate the girl's fear, she added, "But the levee has been reinforced—it is not likely to give way."

The towels placed against the door were soon soaked and Aimée replaced them with others, but the barrier was of little use against the determined water.

"Quick, Katinka, we must roll up Grand-père's oriental runner so it will not get soaked."

The two girls stooped and rolled the carpet to the end of the hall, as the water slowly followed.

"I think we should start carrying things upstairs," Aimée said to Katinka.

"Do you expect the downstairs to be . . . flooded?" Katinka asked in alarm.

"Not entirely," Aimée answered matter-of-factly for Katinka's benefit. "But the mud that oozes in with the water can be devastating to the furniture. I remember that when Etienne, my brother, and I came to live here with Grand-père, so much was ruined. And when the water finally subsided, a six-inch level of mud was left on the walls."

Back and forth the two went, carrying the items that could be lifted—the small chairs and tables—and while they worked, the water climbed higher and higher, until the hems of their dresses were soaked and their slippers sloshed noisily in the water.

Fréki and Geri had taken up their wary watch in Aimée's bedroom upstairs, but at the activity, they pranced up and down the upstairs hall like sentinels manning their assigned posts.

"The dogs think we're playing a game," Katinka said above the force of the wind. "And I hope that's all it's going to be."

Aimée smiled at Katinka. "Katinka, do you remember when you first came here? That first night there was a storm. You assured me that I had nothing to fear from the storm—and you were right, the storm did not harm me. Now we seem to have exchanged places, and you're the one who's frightened of the storm."

"Yes'm—but I was scared that night, too. Only I was determined not to show it in front of the major—I mean, the colonel."

"You have been so much help to me, Katinka. I'm glad Bryan found you and brought you home to us."

Katinka's eyes misted and her fierce little voice blurted out, "I'll always be here when you need me, Mrs. Garrad. You and . . . the colonel. It's the only home I've ever known and I won't forget what you've done for me—letting me go to school at the convent.

"When the colonel was shot, I blamed you—but I know now you'd never do anything to harm him, even if he *is* a Union officer."

Aimée and Katinka held on to the gilt chair, and when they had gotten it up the stairs, Katinka asked, "Do you think the colonel will be coming home soon, now that the fighting is over at Port Hudson?"

"I pray so, Katinka. But I hope he's somewhere safe this night. The storm sounds as if it will continue all night and it's always so much worse on the river."

Aimée waded back to the door to look again toward the courtyard. "Cousin Jorge should be getting home soon. He has had enough time to take Clay and Cousin Clotilde and return. I hope the pony is not giving him any trouble. Blackie can be stubborn at times."

"I didn't hear you, Mrs. Garrard. The wind and rain drowned out your voice."

"Cousin Jorge—it's time for him to be home," Aimée shouted.

"Here he comes now," Katinka said. "I can see the lantern."

The light flickered down to the carriage house, but as Aimée stood watching the disappearing light, the angry and devastating wind pierced through the courtyard and produced a holocaust of devastation—uprooting the trees and sending its death force against the carriage house.

"What's happening, Mrs. Garrard?" Katinka screamed in terror—her voice suddenly loud over the quiet that now covered the garden like a shroud, a deadly silence that lay over the courtyard after the death knell of destruction had sounded.

Like a man struggling to hold onto the last bit of rope before crashing down a mountainside, the carriage house gasped and shuddered and then fell apart.

"The carriage house," Aimée cried. "It's giving way!"

The wrought-iron curving steps to the second story fell to the courtyard and the walls crashed into a pile of rubble before her eyes.

Aimée ran outside, with Katinka behind her. The agonized whinny of the pony inside sounded with the collapse of the wooden beams.

"Cousin Jorge! He's in there! Run for help, Katinka— he's trapped in the rubble!"

"Where can I go, Mrs. Garrard?" Katinka asked in a tearful, quivering voice.

"To Father Anthony at the cathedral. He will find help for us."

Katinka obeyed and ran through the water covering the bricks of the court. Her progress was impeded by the wind and she slipped and stumbled, drenching her clothes. But each time she picked herself up to brave the winds and edge toward the gate.

"Cousin Jorge! Cousin Jorge!" Aimée shouted, picking her way through the debris that had once been the carriage house. "Where are you, Cousin Jorge?"

No sound, except the wind, greeted her. No voice to give her direction where the man lay. Aimée, in the darkness, stumbled over a large soft object. It was the pony—the pony, Blackie, that Bryan had given her as a present.

The small flickering light under a deluge of timbers showed her the way to Cousin Jorge. Scrambling carefully under fallen beams that were ready to shift at the merest touch, Aimée came upon the crushed *calèche*, and underneath the *calèche*'s wheel lay Cousin Jorge.

Pushing at the *calèche* in an attempt to move it from the man's body, Aimée succeeded only in bringing another timber down. She would have to wait for help, or both would be crushed.

She knelt beside Cousin Jorge and whispered his name, but there was no answer. She leaned over to listen for a heartbeat. The slight moan coming from the man told Aimée that he was still alive.

She took his plump hand and held it lovingly to her cheek. With a soothing voice, Aimée said, "Katinka has gone for help. Father Anthony will be here soon."

"My legs, Aimée—they're caught under the carriage wheel."

"I know," she said in a broken voice. "I tried to move the carriage, but the rafters are ready to shift at the slightest movement. You . . . you must try to bear the pain for a little while."

As she answered him, the creaking noise of the beams sounded again.

"Leave me, Aimée," the little man whispered. "You're in danger, too, staying in here with me."

"No, Cousin Jorge. I'll wait beside you until help comes."

Aimée looked up at the creaking beams. There had

been barely enough room for her to crawl through without disturbing them, and now she watched warily as, at intervals, the white dust of the stucco poured down upon them from above.

The lantern, lying on its side, was too far away for Aimée to retrieve it. She could smell the kerosene as it slowly leaked out. But the straw had not caught fire. At least they were lucky in that.

The beams continued to groan and shift slightly while Aimée waited for the help Katinka sought.

Cousin Jorge was silent, thankfully unconscious because of the pain. Aimée laid his limp hand back on his chest, while she watched the flame crawl out of the lantern to lick at the spilled kerosene.

Each minute that the man lay trapped under the carriage wheel increased the danger. Where was Katinka? Why did help not come?

Aimée looked at the rotund little man's face, no longer ruddy, but an ashen gray, and she knew she could not leave him, even to call for help. She must rely on Katinka to save them both.

"Aimée! Aimée!" the deep voice across the courtyard frantically shouted over the penetrating wind.

Clay? Had Katinka gone to him instead of to Father Anthony?

"Where are you, Aimée? Answer me!" The voice was demanding, arrogant, and powerful over the storm.

Bryan—it was her husband Bryan calling to her.

"I am here, Bryan—underneath the beams of the carriage house," she answered. But at his approach, she shouted, "No, do not come any closer—the wood is shifting and Cousin Jorge is trapped."

"Come out, Aimée," he ordered.

"No, I must stay with Cousin Jorge . . . until help arrives."

The fire had now flamed up in earnest, catching the straw, and by its terrifying light Aimée saw her husband standing on the other side of the opening.

At once his voice became coaxing and soothing. "I will bring him out, Aimée. But you will have to move from under the beams. Hurry, my darling. The sooner you come out, the sooner I can try to rescue him. Come, Aimée."

Bryan held out his hand toward her and Aimée, listening to the sounds of the shifting timbers, glanced uncertainly toward Cousin Jorge before obeying the crooning command of her husband.

When she was near enough to touch him, Bryan grabbed her, sweeping her swiftly away as the timbers suddenly changed position and crashed on top of the *calèche*. A leaping flame illuminated the courtyard, and Aimée, screaming, tried to escape from Bryan's grasp and return to Cousin Jorge.

"Fréki! Geri! Guard!" He pointed to Aimée and the dogs immediately took up their stances, keeping Aimée from moving toward the carriage house ruins. With one command, the dogs were no longer her friends, but Bryan's animals obeying his orders—orders to guard Aimée and prevent her from leaving the place where he had put her.

Bryan disappeared into the pile of rubble and Aimée watched in horrified fascination for some sign of her husband.

The winds continued and the rains, coming down in torrents, dimmed the flames from the carriage house. Just when Aimée felt she could stand it no longer, Bryan came out, carrying the limp body of Cousin Jorge.

Chapter 34

*B*ryan called to the dogs, and at his command, Aimée was set free to follow him into the house, up the stairs, to the room where he laid the man gently on the bed.

"Is he . . . still alive?" Aimée asked.

"I think so," Bryan replied. "But he needs medical attention." He turned to Aimée and said, "Why were you two alone? Where are the others?"

"Katinka has gone for help and Cousin Clotilde is nursing Vickie, who's ill with fever."

"Is Vickie not staying here?" Bryan questioned, his attention shifting back to the quiet man on the bed.

"No, she and Clay have a house several blocks away."

"Aimée, stay with Cousin Jorge. I'm going back to make sure the flames are not spreading."

"Bryan—"

Her urgent tone of voice halted him.

"Be . . . careful."

He nodded and left the bedroom as the noise of Katinka's return with help sounded at the gate.

Father Anthony came in first. He took one look at the injured man before he spoke to Aimée.

"I just saw Colonel Garrard. The men who came with me are helping him put out what fire is left."

As he spoke, Katinka walked into the room with Doctor Floud beside her. Aimée, with a feeling of relief, left the room with Katinka. Doctor Floud, removing his instruments from his black medicine bag, began to examine his patient as the grandfather clock struck the half-hour. Now the clock struck the hour of nine. During that time, Aimée and Katinka had watched from the upstairs landing, straining to see into the courtyard, to follow the progress of Bryan and the heavily-muscled men putting out the remnants of the fire.

When Doctor Floud came from the room, Aimée asked, "Should . . . should we send word to Cousin Clotilde?"

"I don't think that's necessary, Mrs. Garrard. I have given your cousin something to make him sleep through the rest of the night."

"Will he be all right?" she persisted.

The man's face became cautious—its expression revealed nothing to her, and he hesitated as he replied, "We will have to wait and see. He has suffered a bruised spine as well as injury to his legs, but as to the extent, I am not able to tell this soon."

Aimée at once became more fearful. "Will he . . . be able to . . . walk again?"

"Perhaps," Doctor Floud answered and focused his attention on Aimée and Katinka, whose gowns clung to them in wetness and whose hair hung limply down their backs.

"If you two do not wish to be my patients as well, then I advise you to put on dry clothes immediately."

"Katinka, do as he says. I will wait for Father Anthony." Aimée knew the priest was administering the sacrament to the injured man.

"The city—how flooded is it?" Aimée asked Doctor Floud.

"The same as here." He glanced around at the furniture stacked in the upstairs hallway. "The lower floors of the buildings are standing in water and some of the flimsier buildings have been wrecked by the storm, but we hope the worst is over."

"Yes, we hope the worst is over," Aimée repeated in a parrot tone, her eyes watching the activity in the courtyard. A limping figure came down the carriage drive as she watched—Anderson. The dogs rushed to greet him. In all Aimée's distress *that* was what had been nagging at her—Anderson's absence. But now he was here, safe with Bryan.

Father Anthony closed the door to Cousin Jorge's room. "Is there someone to sit with him, Aimée?" the priest asked, referring to Cousin Jorge.

"Yes. Katinka and I will take turns," Aimée replied.

"Then I will leave with Doctor Floud. Others are waiting for me at the *presbytère*."

"Thank you, Father—for coming and for bringing help."

Aimèe tiptoed into Cousin Jorge's room and peered down at the man, peaceful in his imposed sleep. So near, so near a tragedy. . . .

She was weak now that there was no need to be brave. Her small frame shivered at the nearness of death.

"Aimée—"

The hand touched her arm, and like a startled fawn she moved, colliding with the tall giant figure behind her.

Bryan led her out of the room, down the hall to their bedroom. And when he had closed the door, he stood gazing at her.

Aimée, moving her hand nervously across her hair, gradually became aware of what she must look like—a half-drowned marmoset in her shabby, worn, rain-stained dress. Embarrassment flowed over her, embarrassment that Bryan should return to see her this way. And resentment and shame at being guarded by Fréki and Geri, upon Bryan's orders.

His stern countenance blocked out any semblance of kindness. "Did Doctor Floud not tell you to get out of those wet clothes, Aimée?"

"I . . . I was waiting to thank Father Anthony."

"And did you not speak with him before he left?"

"Yes."

"And still, you did not see to dry clothes."

"Cousin Jorge . . . ."

"Cousin Jorge does not need your attention. Katinka will sit with him the first part of the night—and Anderson the rest."

"No, Bryan, I cannot—"

"Do not argue with me, Aimée. Remove your wet clothes—or shall I do it for you?" His voice became soft and teasing, making Aimée even more indignant at his peremptory manner.

"Your dogs may obey you, Bryan, at your slightest command—but I shall not be so quick just because you have ordered it."

"If you are angry because I made the dogs stand guard over you to keep you from throwing yourself on the pile of burning rubble to cremate yourself, then you will have to be angry." The scar on his cheek stood out as his temper rose. "I am not dead yet, and I will not have you behave like some grieving Hindu widow trying to commit suttee. I do not intend for you to escape me that easily."

Each word drove Aimée to madness. The turquoise eyes flashed and the invective was ready to be hurled at him, but the sudden slump of his shoulders made her ashamed of her behavior.

"Sheath your claws for tonight, Aimée. I am exhausted and have not the strength to battle wits with you. Now do as I say," he added gently, looking at her with his gray eyes, "and get into something dry."

"Bryan, I'm . . . I'm sorry," she managed to say. Aimée's hand reached out to him, but at her touch he winced.

Quickly she looked at the hand that he tried to hide from her. "Bryan, your hand—you've burned your hand."

"Only a minor thing," he said, dismissing his injury.

"You must let me attend to it."

"*Now* who's giving orders?" he asked in a teasing challenge.

Her concern for him showed in her eyes, now contrite for her emotional outburst against him. "I will get the ointment and the bandages."

"After you have changed, Aimée."

She obeyed him and quickly removed her wet clothes. Aimée knew he would not allow her to attend to his hand until she had followed his orders. Wrapping the towel about her, she sat down on the little bench by the brass tub and poured the water from the ewer over her feet. She moistened the precious soap that had cost her an entire dollar, and lathered the slim, small feet thrust over the tub. Again, she poured water over them, until they were clean and free of the dirty water that had crept into the house from the courtyard.

The room was still warm in spite of the cooling storm outside, for the windows had been shut all day against the wind and rain. So, barefooted, Aimée walked across the room to the bed where her nightgown lay.

All the time Bryan watched her, while he, too, removed wet clothes that smelled of charred wood from the burned carriage house.

And when she returned with fresh bandages and the ointment from the adjacent alcove, he had on the thin, dark-blue robe that had hung in one side of the armoire while he was away.

Intent on bandaging his left hand, Aimée took the scissors and split the length of linen before applying the goose grease to the burn.

"Have you had anything to eat, Bryan?" she asked. "You and Anderson?"

"Not since morning," he replied.

"Then I will fix something for you."

"I'll go to the kitchen with you," he announced and walked with her toward the stairs. But as soon as she saw the water on the first floor, she gave an exasperated sound.

Bryan laughed and lifted her in his arms. He carried her through the muddy water and into the kitchen, where he set her on her feet with a noisy splash.

"Bryan—"

Anderson, standing at the stove, gave them an amused glance and continued stirring the cooking pot.

They sat with feet perched on chair rungs above the water—Aimée, Anderson, and Bryan—and Aimée watched while Bryan and Anderson wolfed down their food. When Bryan had finished, still not satisfied, he asked for more, but there was nothing left in the kitchen.

Without thinking, Aimée apologized, saying, "I'm afraid there's no more food in the house, but Cousin Clotilde gets paid tomorrow. Then we can replenish the larder."

At her words, Bryan frowned and asked in a low, dangerous voice, "And your own household money, Aimée? What have you done with it?"

"Vickie is ill and has not been able to see to it." Suddenly she stopped, an embarrassed blush spreading over her cheeks at the words she had blurted out.

"Vickie? I was not aware that I left Vickie in charge of my money."

"I am sorry, Bryan—I did not mean to . . . speak of it."

"Speak of it? My God, Aimée, you mean to tell me you have had to use Clotilde's money to buy food, and you still don't wish to speak of it? How long has this been going on?"

"It's not that bad, Bryan. Katinka's tuition at the convent is being paid from the household money, so we have had to economize, that's all."

Aimèe glanced toward Anderson and back to Bryan—

imploring him with her eyes not to continue the conversation in front of Anderson.

Reading her silent request, Bryan said, "I have no secrets from Anderson. But we might as well leave the conversation until we reach the bedroom."

Bryan lifted Aimée from the chair, even while she protested that her feet were already wet, but unheeding, he carried her through the downstairs hall, up the curving stairway, and into their bedroom where he set her down.

With his unswerving prodding, Bryan finally forced the truth from her—that Vickie had taken over the doling out of money soon after he had come home for that one night and ignored them except Aimée.

"So Vickie and Clay have the use of my money, a house of their own, and Lisette and Lizzie to wait upon them."

The cold, angry words were flung toward her and Aimée, standing by the window, looked out but did not see.

"Cousin Jorge—I must see how he is." She moved from the window toward the door.

"We will both go, Aimée," Bryan said, and walked beside her to the far bedroom where the little man groaned in a troubled sleep.

Katinka sat in a chair beside the bed, and the lamp flickering in an uneasy sputter mirrored the uneasiness in Aimée's heart. Seeing that there was nothing to do for him but let him rest, Aimée backed away from the bed. Bryan, taking her by the arm, propelled her from the room.

Her eyes swept over him until they rested on his large bare feet. "Bryan, your feet are still dirty," Aimée announced. In turn, her own were subjected to his careful scrutiny.

"So are yours, Aimée. Shall I perform the foot washing?" His eyes were amused and she quickly answered, "Only on your own. I can take care of mine, myself."

He laughed and wiped his feet on the damp towel and threw off the dark blue robe that had clothed him. He wore nothing underneath and Aimée, mesmerized by his

331

strong, arrogant, naked body, watched as he climbed into bed and pulled the sheet over him. His silver-gray eyes watched her expectantly while she attended to the last-minute rituals before retiring. With a clean towel, Aimèe briskly rubbed her hair before brushing the tangles from the long strands. She began to plait it in one long plait, until Bryan's voice stopped her.

"No, Aimée—leave your hair loose tonight."

With no defiance showing in her eyes, she loosened it from the beginning plait and reached over to blow out the lamp.

"You are not with child, Aimée?" Bryan asked as she lay beside him.

"No, Bryan, I am not with child," she answered him, the disappointment apparent in her voice.

"Then let us see if we can remedy that."

He took her in his arms and she responded to his need . . .

Later that night Aimée slipped out of bed and walked down the hallway toward Cousin Jorge's room. The dogs, asleep on the landing, raised their heads at her passing, and then settled down again to sleep.

Katinka dozed in the chair. The slight pressure on her shoulder caused her to awake, but Aimée, putting her finger to her lips, shunned any exchange of words. Silently Katinka stood up and Aimée switched places with her, while Katinka went to bed.

It was not long before the door opened to reveal Anderson, who had come to relieve Katinka.

"Mrs. Garrard, I am to sit with him," he protested, but Aimée shook her head and walked back to the door with him.

"No, Anderson," she whispered. "You and . . . and Colonel Garrard have had a tiring journey. Go back to bed."

At his hesitation, the thought struck her—"Anderson, do you even *have* a bed?"

"Well, not exactly. I was in the carriage house before."

"Do you mind the cot in the nursery—just for tonight?" she asked, trying to hide the smile that lurked near her lips at the image of the taciturn Anderson in the children's nursery.

"It might be appropriate, Mrs. Garrard." His eyes twinkled, and in an attempt at lightness, he said, "I will probably sleep like a baby tonight, regardless of my surroundings." Then his face sobered. "You are certain that you do not wish me to sit with him?"

"Certain, Anderson. Now go to bed."

Aimée closed the door and settled down to watch over the gentle little man who was getting restless now that the effect of the morphine was beginning to wear off.

"Aimée? Are we still . . . waiting for help?"

The weak voice saddened her. Was he in such pain that he did not know he had been rescued?

"No, Cousin Jorge," she replied gently. "You are safe in bed. Bryan brought you out."

Bryan? He's here?"

"Yes—he and Anderson."

"And Clotilde—where is Clotilde?"

"She's nursing Vickie who has a fever. Don't you remember? You took her and Clay back in the storm."

"Oh, yes," he replied in a vague, confused voice. "The storm—"

"The doctor wants you to rest, Cousin Jorge. Try to go back to sleep," Aimée said in a soothing voice.

"Aimée, I . . . I can't move my legs."

"That's to be expected," she reassured him. "You have bruised your spine and it will take time for you to get well. But you *will* get well."

He seemed to accept her explanation, for soon after, Aimée could hear the endearing little whistle sound that indicated he had gone back to sleep.

Aimée sat in the chair and listened to the wind outside —the wind that had been a violent living thing that night, an ogre waked from its sleep to tread upon the earth and feed upon destruction until, sated, it had quieted its stormy steps and slunk back to its slumber amid the clouds and mountain peaks, leaving only an echo of its footsteps as a reminder.

All around her the sounds gentled, and toward morning the quietness lulled Aimée until she, too, was drawn into the forgetfulness of dreams. As she dreamed, strong arms enfolded her and lifted her from the chair.

"No, do not touch me, monsieur," she said in a cringing, sleepy voice.

"Aimée, it's Bryan. Do not be alarmed, my darling."

With a sigh, she relaxed. The soft pillow cushioned her head and her limbs, cramped from sitting up, stretched in luxury under the cover that had been pulled up to her chin. The giant hand stroked her cheek, and at its gentle touch, she turned and nestled her face in its warmth.

Chapter 35

The man who visited Cousin Jorge early that afternoon showed the effects of the stormy night—not only in his rumpled clothes but in his red-rimmed eyes.

"The city is still staggering under the blow of the storm," the doctor informed Aimée as he followed her up the stairs. "Looking at the blue sky with not a trace of cloud, it is hard to imagine what the city has been through in the past twenty-four hours."

"And the levee? Is it still holding?" she asked.

"Yes, but the water level is dangerously high—and it has not stopped rising. A bad thing, with the fever spreading and the soldiers bringing smallpox and heaven knows what else into the city."

It was not an optimistic picture and it thoroughly depressed Aimée.

"How did our patient sleep last night?"

"Cousin Jorge woke several times. He was concerned because he could not move his legs, Doctor Floud."

"I am not surprised," the tired man answered.

Word had been sent to Clotilde that morning of the accident to Cousin Jorge, but Clotilde, afraid that she would bring back the fever to the weakened man, remained with Vickie.

Bryan, having no qualms about the fever, had gone to see Clay to bring him to account for the stewardship of his money, and returning to the townhouse, he sought out Aimée.

"Get dressed in a nicer dress, Aimée," he said, observing the faded blue muslin that she was wearing. "We are going to the bank."

"Will this dress not do, Bryan?" she asked in a small voice.

"No, Aimée. It's old and faded and I do not wish my wife to appear as if she is some poor, unloved relation. Do as I say and put on something elegant."

Something elegant—the only elegant dresses she had seen lately were the ones hanging in the armoire in the house on Rampart Street, which she had tried to erase from her mind.

Seeing her hesitation, he said, "Surely you have *something* else you can put on, Aimée."

She would not let him know that she had nothing nicer to wear. Thinking to make an excuse not to go with him, Aimée said, "Katinka and I are planning to . . . scrub the mud from the walls and the floor. Do you mind if I don't go with you?"

"Yes, Aimee, I mind. Now go upstairs and get dressed."

For some time Aimée, standing before the open doors of the armoire, stared at the meager assortment of patched and faded summer dresses.

"Here, let me." Coming up behind her, Bryan thrust her aside and pulled each of the four dresses out, took one glance, and threw each one on the floor in disgust.

"Bryan, my clothes," Aimée protested, stooping to pick up the dresses he had heartlessly discarded.

"Leave them where they are, Aimée. They're not worth the effort of picking them up."

He stamped from the room and Aimée, hurt at his actions, smoothed the carefully laundered dresses and hung them again in the armoire. Only her anger kept back the tears.

Why was it that everything she did seemed to inflame her husband? She had taken care of the dresses as best she could, mending them and facing the hems when they became short from constant washing. And he had looked at her as if it was her fault they were not new and colorful. Did Bryan not realize that the money he had left for her could be stretched only so far—especially since Katinka's tuition took up a large part of it?

Bryan had gone from the townhouse without her, so she and Katinka started on the chore that faced them— that of removing the muddy residue of the storm from the floors and walls. Her mind was devoted to the task, for Anderson sat with Cousin Jorge.

Katinka and Aimée, their skirts bundled up, were down on their hands and knees scrubbing in the hall toward the salon when Bryan returned. He was not alone. With him were two hefty black women who were immediately put to work in Aimèe's and Katinka's places.

Bryan took Aimée by the hand and led her up the stairs, his former anger dissipated. When they reached the room, he held on to her hands, looking at them for a long time before he spoke.

"Aimée, this war has been hard on you. And many times I have . . . added to your problems. It was my own thoughtlessness that left you in this poverty-stricken condition. I was not aware that Clay would let a woman's vindictiveness sway him. Now money matters are out of his hands and Clay is the one who has been placed on an allowance. And when you need additional money beyond your usual household expenses, you have only to go to Mr. Villay at the bank."

"Thank you, Bryan," she answered, touched by his concern for her. "And is it all right for Katinka to continue her . . . lessons with the Sisters?"

"If that is what you wish, Aimée."

Her shyness with him that moment overwhelmed her

and she turned her head to look out the window. She did not wish him to see how his kindness had affected her.

"One other thing, Aimée—Cousin Jorge will have a nurse to sit with him at night until he is better. There will be no need for you to sit up with him."

"Oh, but Bryan, that is too much. I don't mind."

He came to her and placed his hands on her shoulders. "But *I* mind, Aimée. I mind not having my wife in bed beside me when I need her."

It was a sentence imposed upon her—sleeping each night beside him—trying to hide from him the nightmares that had troubled her ever since that night in the house on the Ramparts. Sometimes she woke, crying out in the night. It had not mattered before. She was far enough away from the others not to be heard. But with Bryan again sharing her bed, she would not be able to keep it a secret if she should cry out. Sitting with Cousin Jorge for part of the night had been a good excuse, but now Bryan had taken that away.

He had also taken away the offending dresses from the armoire and replaced them with new dresses of his own choosing, made of crepe, tulle, silk, and muslin.

"Bryan, let me keep the old dresses, too. I cannot do some of the chores dressed in such finery." She pointed to the pale blue silk dress interwoven with ribbons that lay across the bed, waiting for her.

"No, Aimée. I never want to see them again, to be reminded of the stinginess of my brother and his wife, and my own stupidity." His tone was angry. "The dresses are fit only for scrubbing floors. And you will not be doing such menial work again."

Aimée, dressed in her camisole and crinolines, stood on tiptoe and kissed Bryan on the cheek.

"Thank you for being so generous to. . . . to Katinka and Cousin Clotilde and me. They love their new dresses, too, Bryan."

He lifted her off her feet for a moment, holding her against him, demanding a deeper kiss. Then he set her down with a swat on her backside.

"Hurry and finish dressing, my little temptress, or I might forget that I promised to take you for a drive this afternoon."

Aimée quickly donned the blue dress and tied the matching bonnetlike *fanchon* over her hair. Bryan appreciatively took in her elegant appearance and then his eyes rested on her face. "I hope the fresh air will bring the bloom back into your cheeks. Your labors in the sickroom have made you much too pale."

That night her sleep was troubled, and when morning came, she awoke to find Bryan leaning over her, studying her face.

"Won't you tell me what is troubling you, Aimée?"

She had tried to remain awake as long as possible, but she had finally succumbed to sleep, and the nightmare had visited her again.

She vaguely remembered Bryan holding her in his arms and comforting her during the night. "I . . . had a nightmare, Bryan—a silly thing."

"This is not the first time, my love, that you have cried out in your sleep. And the nightmare is always the same, isn't it?"

Alarmed, Aimée asked, "Did I . . . say anything in my sleep?"

"You rambled, Aimée, about blood and a sword and . . . running away so that no one could find out—"

"I am sorry, Bryan. Maybe it would be better if I . . . moved into the room next to Katinka for a while. Then your sleep wouldn't be disturbed."

"The nightmares do not disturb *me* as much as they disturb *you*. No, you'll stay here with me. And when you feel like telling me what is troubling you, I will listen."

Her trembling began and there was a trapped, wild look in the depths of her turquoise eyes. Another night of talking in her sleep and Bryan would guess.

Bryan took her in his arms and whispered, "Let me help you, my darling. Tell me what has hurt you and caused such fear."

With a sob, Aimèe cried, "I . . . I can't. I can't ever tell you, Bryan."

"Don't you trust me, Aimée?"

She held to him in her sobbing and the strong arms comforted her. But if Bryan ever found out, there would be no comforting arms, no endearing words to her, only condemnation . . . and a sword.

Bryan's time at home was temporary, for General Banks had been ordered to invade Texas. With Napoleon III's puppet emperor, Archduke Maximillian, now on the throne in Mexico and fifty thousand of France's best troops at his side—troops sympathetic to the Confederate cause—the Federals were uneasy.

Bryan and Anderson sat in the bedroom with Cousin Jorge—discussing the departure of the Army of the Gulf for Texas. Aimée, bringing in Cousin Jorge's lunch tray, overheard the last part of the conversation.

". . . The main necessity is to destroy the routes for supplies from Mexico," Anderson was saying.

"Will you have the necessary men and equipment to occupy such a vast border?" Cousin Jorge asked.

"No, Jorge," Bryan replied. "Even if the entire Army of the Gulf remained, there would still not be enough men. And as to the danger of the French troops leaving Mexico to aid the Confederate Army, I think Archduke Maximillian will need those fifty thousand troops belonging to Napoleon III to keep him in power as puppet emperor. I do not believe they will have time to fight another war on the side."

"Will you have to go to Texas, Bryan?" Aimée asked.

"Yes, Aimée, but not until the first of September," Bryan replied, getting up from his chair to leave the room with Anderson.

"Don't worry, my dear," Cousin Jorge said, seeing Aimée's sad face, when the two men had gone.

"But he has been in so much fighting already, Cousin Jorge. One day, he will not be so lucky."

"Now, now, Aimee—don't use up all your worry even before he leaves."

She gave a little laugh and changed the subject. "How

are you feeling, Cousin Jorge?"

He sat up against a mass of pillows. His face had regained its natural color and his blue eyes twinkled. "I moved my toes this morning, Aimée. And Anderson said that is great progress."

"You will be walking again soon," Aimée stated, delighted at the news.

Clotilde was now at home again, since Vickie had recovered from the fever. Cousin Jorge, much improved, did not need constant attention, so Clotilde resumed her teaching, and with Anderson in the bedroom with the little man at night, the special nurse was no longer needed.

The workers had almost completed the reconstruction of the carriage house. The same curved wrought-iron steps had been used, but the large oleander that had stood beside them, shading them for so many years, was now gone, leaving a bare area.

"What's missing, Aimée?" Bryan asked, staring at the carriage house. "Why does it look different?"

"It's the oleander tree, Bryan—the one that shaded the steps."

"Yes, the one you hid behind one summer evening not so long ago," he teased.

"I was *not* hiding, Bryan. If you remember, it was a *hot* night and I had come out into the garden for fresh air."

"But you were so quiet that night. I would never have known you were there if it had not been for the dogs.

"Even then," Bryan continued, thinking back to the earlier time, "my feelings for you were fierce and possessive."

Aimée found herself suddenly crushed in his arms. "Do not ever give me reason to be jealous, Aimée. That night I could not stand the thought that any other man had loved you. And that was before I had made you mine. Now that I am bound to you in a tighter bond, my feelings are even stronger. I think I would kill any man who so much as touched you."

His words, instead of bringing joy to her, brought

sorrow. They still rang in her ears later that day as she sat on the window seat and mended Bryan's shirt by the rapidly fading afternoon light.

"Have you heard the news about Colonel Tilson?"

Aimée dropped the scissors in her nervousness over Bryan's question. Forcing her voice to remain normal as she retrieved the scissors, she asked, "Wh-what news?"

"The man evidently became enamored of a young octoroon girl, and he formed a liaison with her. She stabbed him one night with his own sword, and escaped from the house in the Ramparts before the police could catch her."

"How serious . . . was the wound? Is the colonel going to be all right?"

"It was serious enough for him to require medical leave. But he was back on duty today for the first time since it happened. . . . Aimée, are you feeling all right?" Bryan asked, showing concern for her ashen appearance.

"I . . . I have not felt well for the past few days."

"Let's hope you are not coming down with the fever. You have done too much, Aimée—watching over Jorge as well as seeing to the running of the house. You must rest more. Is that understood?"

"Yes, Bryan." Her voice was meek and tired.

"I am not used to such meekness from you, Aimée. I know something must indeed be wrong when you do not argue with me."

Aimée had spent many a sleepless night beside her husband—restless and determined to hide from him any evidence of her recurring nightmares. The sleepless nights were beginning to tell on her. Purple smudges under her eyes served as warning signals and the little catnaps during the day only underlined her need for a deeper sleep.

How much longer would she be able to keep from Bryan what had happened in the house on Rampart Street?

Chapter 36

With the coming of Jou-Jou, the black woman, Aimée's days took on another dimension.

The plump dark-skinned woman with the fine red silk tignon on her head and the frizzled hen under her arm appeared at the door one morning—ready to take over the running of the house.

"The beeg man, your husband, hire me, madame, so we have come, *ma petite poule,* and me."

Aimée stared unbelievingly at the woman, who flashed a large white-toothed smile in her direction. Bryan had said nothing to her about hiring the woman, yet here she was, waiting to enter.

"I will . . . get my husband," Aimée said uncertainly.

"Eet is not *necessaire*, madame. He already geeve me the instructions. I take care of you, *ma petite*, while he is away. And theese one," she said, pointing to the frizzle-feathered chicken, "she know what to do, too. She eat up all the conjure someone throw in your path."

"Bryan, there is a woman downstairs by the name of Jou-Jou. She is already in the kitchen, fixing lunch. Did you . . . did you hire her, Bryan?" Aimée asked.

"Yes, Aimée," he admitted. "Since you no longer have Lisette, I decided you needed help in the house—especially since when I leave again, Anderson will no longer be here to help with Cousin Jorge. With Clotilde teaching and Katinka going back to her lessons soon, you will need someone in the house with you."

Bryan was with the first contingent of troops that left New Orleans early in September. From the beginning, the boats ran into trouble, Aimée learned later. After more than half the boats were lost, the troops, disheartened, did not even land at Sabine Pass, as intended. So plans to reach Houston, the rail center a hundred miles away, were abandoned and the four thousand men and officers returned to New Orleans.

Again Bryan and Anderson accompanied General Banks, who personally led the expedition to Brazos Island at the mouth of the Rio Grand. On the morning of October 26 Aimée, with the rest of the spectators along the levee, saw them off. Bands were playing, and the sky was a cloudless blue as the transports disappeared from sight.

Aimée walked back alone, stopping off at the French Market before going on to Royal Street. There had been nothing to tempt her appetite at the market, so she walked on toward the townhouse. Cousin Jorge, with his two canes by his side, sat in a chair in the courtyard. The morning sun played upon the old bricks at his feet, and shielding her eyes from the glare, Aimée came to sit by the edge of the old fountain.

"They have left?" Cousin Jorge asked.

"Yes. Oh, Cousin Jorge," Aimée said with a tremor in her voice, "when will all the fighting end?"

"Only when one side becomes too tired and hungry, Aimée—when there are no more shells to shoot, or shoes to wear, or bits of bread to eat."

"The . . . Union Army today was dressed in new uniforms and polished boots. And no one left for battle looking hungry. It's only our own thin Confederate soldiers who are brought to prison in rags and looking as if they have not had a decent meal in months. . . . Have you heard, Cousin Jorge, that the Union has refused to exchange any more prisoners, even though their own men are suffering from it?"

Cousin Jorge nodded in affirmation. "War strategy is very cruel, Aimée. The Federals know that we have used up our supply of men and boys—and if prisoners were exchanged, our own coming back home would soon be fighting again. The Union has vast resources to draw from. The government in Washington can allow its own men to remain in prison for the rest of the war. It does not need them as much as we need ours."

"But don't they realize," Aimée argued, "that mothers in the North grieve over their sons dying in prison camps just as much as mothers in the South?"

"Probably. Just as they know when they pass through our land—destroying crops and burning everything else—that some of their own men will starve with the rest. Such is the price of war."

The raucous noise coming from the kitchen interrupted the conversation.

"Fréki! Geri! You leave *ma pauvre poule* alone! I sweep you out of the house for zat!"

The door opened and the two dogs bounded into the courtyard—chased out of the house by Jou-Jou and her broom.

Cousin Jorge chuckled. "Pretty soon those dogs will get the message to leave that frizzle-feathered chicken alone."

Bryan had not been away for too many days when Lisette, appearing at the door, asked for Clotilde. Vickie's time had come.

Lizzie brought Charity to spend the day at Aimée's, and later in the afternoon, when Faith and Hope came home from school, they, too, were sent to the house on Royal Street.

"Is my mother . . . going to die?" Hope asked Aimée.

"Of course not, Hope," Aimée assured her and prayed for the child's sake that she was telling the truth.

Faith, older than Hope by a year, said in a confidential manner, "Mother is having a *baby*, Hope. Don't you remember when Charity was born, we were sent off for the day just like this? I wonder if we will have a baby brother or a baby sister?"

The two children, dashing out into the courtyard, took their excited chatter with them.

Lizzie raised her eyebrows and commented, "That Faith—she knows everything."

Aimée kept the children entertained, sat with them while they had an early supper, and fixed the cots in the nursery for them to sleep on.

It was twilight and Lizzie had already put Charity to bed for the night when the news came from Clotilde. Vickie had delivered a baby boy.

"We have a little brother! We have a little brother!" the two girls chanted as they jumped up and down.

"You also have a little sister that you're gonna wake up if you can't be quiet," Lizzie scolded.

"I want to see my baby brother," Faith said.

"Me, too," Hope agreed, and looking toward Aimée, asked, "Do you think we could go and see him just for a little while?"

Aimée smiled. "Yes. I'll walk with you, and then, when we've seen the baby, we'll all come back here to spend the night."

"Our little brother, too?" Hope asked.

"No, silly," Faith answered. "He's too little. He'll have to stay at our house."

Aimée took the children by the hand and together they walked down the banquette toward the house that Vickie and Clay were renting. It would be the first time that Aimée had set foot in the house since the episode with Colonel Tilson.

"Are you cold, Tante Aimée?" Hope asked.

Was her shiver that noticeable? Aimée smiled down at Hope. "The air is getting cool now that the sun has gone down."

"Maybe you'd like to skip with us, to keep warm."

Faith again admonished her younger sister. "Grownups don't skip, Hope. It's not dignified."

"Why don't we all walk a little faster? We'll stay warm and get there sooner, too," Aimée suggested.

Faith pushed open the gate when they arrived, and then stopped, waiting for Aimée and Hope to catch up. The children, suddenly shy, clung to Aimée and waited for her to take the lead and open the door into the house.

Should she go in without knocking? The awkwardness was swallowed up at Clay's sudden appearance. His happy face told her that all was well. Swooping up the girls in his arms, he said, "Well, how do you like having a baby brother?"

Faith, speechless for once, waited for Hope to answer.

"We . . . won't know until we see him," she replied.

Clay laughed and set them down. "I'll get him. Just sit down and be very quiet and I'll bring your little brother out."

The baby, wrapped in a soft blanket, was carried tenderly in Clay's arms. He sat down in a chair and pushed back the blanket for the girls to look.

Aimée watched from across the room—not breaking into the family scene as the girls pressed against Clay, watching the baby.

"He's . . . awful little," Hope said.

"So were you, Hope, when you were his age," Clay informed her.

"Will he sleep long?" Faith asked.

"I hope so," Clay said, and then as if suddenly realizing that Aimée had remained apart from them, he said, "Aimée, would you like to see him, too?"

"Y-yes," she stammered, crossing the room to look at the sleeping child. She stared down at the small bundle and her heart turned over. He looked so much like Bryan —exactly as she had imagined her own baby would look—and her arms ached to held him.

"Clay, may I . . . hold him?" she asked.

He stood up and waited for Aimée to take the baby. "Perhaps you could take him into the bedroom. I think he's going to wake up."

Aimée gathered the small, squirming, whimpering baby in her arms and began to walk carefully toward the bedroom, her head averted so that Clay could not see her emotional state.

He should be mine—Bryan's and mine, she thought fiercely. She paused before the bedroom door and the baby opened his eyes—eyes shaped like Bryan's—and Aimée could hardly bear to give him up to his mother.

Vickie, looking tired but triumphant, met Aimée's glance with a superior look.

"He's . . . he's beautiful, Vickie," Aimée said, trying to blink back the tears from her turquoise eyes.

Vickie held out her arms for him and said, "Yes. Clay thinks he is, too—and he's so proud that I have given him a son."

The baby began crying and Vickie put him to her breast. Aimée stumbled out of the room and went back to the two little girls.

"We will go now, Clay," Aimée said, "and Katinka will see that the girls get to school tomorrow morning."

"Thank you, Aimée, for keeping them tonight," Clay said, opening the door for them.

On the way back Aimée was very quiet, but Faith and Hope, busy with their own conversation, did not seem to notice her withdrawal—until Hope looked up at Aimée.

"Are babies like kittens, Tante Aimée—with their eyes closed until they're a certain age?"

"No, darling. They can open their eyes even the first day. In fact, your baby brother opened his eyes when I carried him back to your mother."

"What . . . color were they?" Hope asked.

"Why, they were . . . blue, I think. Yes," Aimée said more certainly, "because all babies have blue eyes when they're first born."

"Did I have blue eyes, too, Tante Aimée, when I was born?" the brown-eyed Faith asked, suddenly interested.

"Yes, but they changed—probably when you were just a few weeks old."

"Will our baby brother's eyes change too?"

"That's hard to tell, Faith. Your mother has brown eyes —and I'm not sure what color eyes your . . . papa has."

"*My* papa had blue eyes," Hope said defensively.

"She's talking about Clay, Hope," her sister said in disgust. "He's our papa now."

Aimée thought of the baby, so like Bryan, and as she opened the gate from the banquette, her arms ached. Why could not the baby have been hers to love and cherish?

The weather had made the second expedition of Banks' Army of the Gulf into another fiasco, and although they landed at Brazos Island, the force was too small to hold it, so Bryan was back in New Orleans in time for Christmas.

Through the festivities of Christmas Eve Aimée remained subdued, her desire for a child of her own unrequited. Bryan watched her as she held Clay and Vickie's infant son, and when Aimée looked up to meet Bryan's eyes, her hurt was visible in her expression.

Aimée had brought down the porcelain crêche from the attic to the salon as she had on that Christmas Eve the year before, but this time, Christmas did not go unobserved. There were presents for everyone. Faith and Hope's excited chatter, joined in by Charity, filled the air in the salon, and when Clay and his family finally departed for their own house, they took with them the holiday air that only children can create, leaving an emptiness in Aimée's heart, and an emptiness in her arms.

Cousin Jorge and Bryan sat in a corner of the salon and talked, while Aimée joined Clotilde and Katinka in taking the sweets, empty plates, and cups back to the kitchen for Jou-Jou.

Seeing Tante Dee Dee's old black cloak hanging in the kitchen, Aimée impulsively put it on and slipped out of the house to hurry to the cathedral. No one would miss her for the short time she would be away to light her candles and pray.

One by one, the silent worshippers got up and left the cathedral, but Aimee remained, kneeling and praying, all sense of time forgotten, until a hand touched her shoulder. Raising her tear-stained face, Aimée saw the troubled gray eyes of her husband staring down at her. He said nothing, but lifted her gently to her feet and kept his hand at her elbow until he had guided her onto the street.

Only then did he speak. "You should not have come alone at such a late hour," he admonished. "Why didn't you ask someone to come with you?"

"E-everyone was busy, Bryan. And I did not mind coming alone."

"But I worry about you, Aimée, when you disappear like this without telling me where you are going. The next time I want you to have someone with you."

"Yes, Bryan."

The wind whistled and an occasional star showed itself through the frame of clouds in the heavens as they walked back toward the townhouse. The streets were almost deserted; only an occasional half-empty trolley car passed by.

"I am disappointed that you were not at home to receive your Christmas present, Aimée."

"But you have already given me the beautiful necklace, Bryan," she said, feeling underneath her cloak for the aquamarine stone that lay nestled between her breasts.

"That was not the only one," he said. "There is another waiting for you."

"Another one? Wh-what is it?"

"You will have to wait until we get home to see it," he teased.

"Couldn't you give me . . . a hint?" she asked, her curiosity aroused.

He laughed. "It goes with the carriage house."

"An oleander tree," she guessed immediately.

Again Bryan laughed. "Would you like another guess? That wasn't even close."

Perplexed, Aimée repeated, "It goes with the carriage house . . . could it be a carriage—to replace the *calèche*?"

"Partly."

"And a . . . a pony to go with it?" she asked excitedly.

"Well, you're getting close. It isn't a pony, but it *is* something that pulls the carriage."

"A horse?"

"Partly."

"Partly? You mean . . . *two* horses?"

Aimèe's tears were forgotten as she rushed down the carriage drive and through the courtyard. The sound of whinnying horses greeted her, but as she rushed to open the door, a hand caught her from behind.

"Don't be so impulsive, my love. The horses are high-spirited and could easily trample you in their nervousness."

He held her back while he carefully called to the horses. As he talked soothingly to them, he opened the gate to the stalls.

They were beautiful chestnuts, and when Aimèe had examined them from the distance that Bryan would allow, she broke loose from her husband and climbed up into the magnificent carriage. She ran her fingers along the velvet-cushioned seats and spread her crinolines like some high-born lady out for her evening drive.

By the flickering lantern light Aimèe's hair shone in sparkling glints and her turquoise eyes, bright with excitement, gave an exotic sweep to her fine-boned face.

"I think I shall spend the night here in the carriage. It's so magnificent."

Bryan opened the carriage door and in an amused voice he said, "Come out, Aimèe."

"No, Bryan. I want to sit here for a little longer."

Sounding exasperated at her stubbornness, Bryan said, "It's cold, Aimee. It's time to go into the house." Then he added, "And you know what happens to girls that remain in carriages after midnight . . ."

"Do I?" she teased.

"Yes," he said, suddenly lunging for her and succeeding in bringing her down from her perch in the carriage. She clung to him to keep from falling and looking down from his great height, Bryan explained, "Their dresses turn to rags and their coachmen into mice."

"Only in fairy tales, monsieur," she replied haughtily, but the rest of her response was interrupted by his lips on hers.

Bryan did not let her go, but carried her back to the house.

"Aimée, whose cloak are you wearing?" he asked, noticing the somber dark material draped around her.

"It's Tante Dee Dee's old cloak that I found in the kitchen."

"Don't you have anything else to wear?"

"I . . . can't seem to keep a cloak of my own, Bryan."

"We'll have to get one in a lighter color for you when the shops open again. Maybe another blue one," he said, setting her down in their bedroom.

"No, Bryan, not . . . another blue one," she said fiercely.

"No? Why not?"

"It has unpleasant memories for me."

"I see. Because of the note that came with it, Aimée?"

His eyes were guarded, almost as if she had in some way hurt him by the rejection.

Hastily she answered, "Not that. It is because . . . the woman you were with . . . that night, was wearing one like it."

"What woman, Aimée? And of what night are you speaking?"

"Don't pretend you have forgotten, Bryan. The woman in the *calèche* with you—two nights after I went to Thornfell."

He stared at her without saying anything. Then slowly the words came. "Where were you, Aimée, when you saw us?"

How could she answer him without giving herself away even more than she had already?

He took her by the shoulders and stared sternly down at her. "Answer me, Aimée. Where were you?"

"Across the street," she replied, lowering her eyelids and gazing at the floor.

She heard the sudden expiration of breath. "God! Aimée, you mean to tell me you let *that* keep you from coming back to me? Seeing me with this other woman?"

"I . . . did not intend coming back, Bryan. I only wanted to see . . ."

She stood trapped, but he did not seem to notice.

"Did you think I had forgotten you that easily?"

Aimée, not trusting her voice, made a slight nodding motion, without speaking.

"Aimée," he murmured in a broken, hoarse voice. She felt his warm breath on her neck and the tightening of his hands drawing her close to him. . . .

Chapter 37

*I*n New Orleans for the next two months the war in the West seemed to have been forgotten. General Banks spent most of his time promoting his candidate, Michael Hahn, for military governor of Louisiana.

To Aimée, it was a strange situation. The Confederate capital had been moved from Opelousas to Shreveport, but the southeastern parishes, with the city of New Orleans, would now be governed by the man elected by the Unionists.

St. Bernard, Plaquemines, Jefferson, St. Charles, St. James, St. John, Ascension, Assumption, Terre Bonne, Lafourche, St. Mary, St. Martin, and Orleans—these were the parishes under the rule of the enemy. It was a state divided . . . a state with two governors but only one legislature, and that one in Shreveport, doing what it could to raise troops and supplies for the Confederates and to feed the starving widows and children within its boundaries.

But the people of New Orleans, long starved not only for bread but for their Carnival parades, their Mystick Krewe of Comus *tableaux* and their elegant *bals masqués*, came alive again with the torchlight parades and glittery trappings of the political campaign.

Election Day came and General Banks' man won. In one of the best-loved traditions of old New Orleans, General and Mrs. Banks announced that they would celebrate the victory with an elegant *bal masqué* at the New Opera House.

Old Carnival costumes, dominos, and masks were dug

out from shopkeepers' chests and refurbished for those who had been invited to attend the masquerade that February night.

Shortly before the election Bryan had asked, "Aimée, do you have a Carnival costume?"

"No, Bryan. I was never allowed to participate in the the celebration in the streets. It was far too rowdy—but we were allowed to watch from the balconies."

Bryan smiled. "Yes, I had forgotten how carefully you young Creole girls were brought up. And did you never attend a masked ball during Carnival?"

"No, Bryan, the war came just when I was old enough. But Tante Dee Dee attended, and she had some beautiful masks. I believe they are still in the attic, packed away in some forgotten trunk."

"Well, find one to wear, Aimée. We will be going to General Banks' *bal masqué* in honor of the new governor. He is so sure of winning that he's already terming the ball a 'victory celebration.'"

"I would . . . rather stay home, Bryan."

"But you cannot, Aimée. Much as you dislike the idea of a Union military governor, you will have to go with me. I am expected to attend."

Slowly she said the words. "And I do not have a . . . choice?"

"No, Aimée, I will not allow you to stay at home. You are to go with me."

And so it was for this reason that Aimée angrily spent most of one afternoon searching for the headdresses, the masks, the ball gowns, and costumes of another generation—searching for the most flagrant costume she could find.

In her search she came across the turquoise-and-silver silk costume that looked as if it belonged in a seraglio. The silken face veil—the *yashmak*—was attached to the turban headpiece of satin, feathers, and jewels. Surely Tante Dee Dee had never worn such a costume—and yet . . .

Thinking of her namesake, Aimée decided that it would be appropriate to wear it, for had not her life been arranged in the same high-handed manner as her ancestor's, with her own feelings regarded not at all? Even the pointed, curled shoes were there—and the more Aimée thought of Bryan's demanding arrogance, the more determined she was to appear in the costume. Bryan would not allow her to remain at the ball for long when he saw it.

Now, if she could find something for Katinka to wear. The girl had never attended a ball, and although Aimée knew that she herself would not be staying long, it would give Katinka much pleasure to attend.

"Is it all right if Katinka goes to the *bal masqué*, Bryan? Do you think you can get a ticket for her?"

"Can she even dance, Aimée?" Bryan asked in an amused manner.

"Of course she can, Bryan. She has learned many of the arts since attending the convent school."

"Dancing with a nun can be far different from dancing with a man, Aimée."

"Oh, Bryan, you *know* the nuns do not dance. But once a week the dancing master comes to the convent, so that the girls will not lack . . . the social graces."

"And for her escort—whom shall I get? Anderson?"

She ignored his remark and looked at him sweetly. "There must be a suitable young officer whom you can persuade."

He stared at her and finally capitulated. "When you look at me like that, Aimée, I cannot refuse you. Yes, I shall find her a . . . suitable escort."

Aimée, satisfied, looked through the trunks until she found a pretty costume for Katinka to wear.

On the night of the ball Aimée stared with distaste at the blue velvet cloak that Bryan had brought home with him. She had not wanted another blue one to remind her of those heartbreaking days, but he had bought it anyway, though he had not bothered to give her any explanation for the woman in the *calèche*. But at least the cloak would hide the costume until it was too late for Bryan to do anything about it . . . except take her home.

The young cavalry officer was downstairs waiting to

act as escort for Katinka, and Katinka, so excited over this, her first ball, could hardly get dressed in her costume.

Jou-Jou presided over them both, giving approval to Katinka's costume, while mumbling under her breath about Aimée's.

"Zat cos-yume, madame, is liable to cause . . . much trouble. I feel thees in my bones."

"No one will recognize me, Jou-Jou. My hair and my face will both be covered."

"And what deed your husband say about thees cos-yume?"

"He has not seen it," Aimée admitted.

The curled, pointed shoes were the only things visible under the blue cloak as Aimée went downstairs. Her husband and the young lieutenant were both dressed in dominos, but had not yet donned their half-masks.

"Aimée, may I present Lieutenant Steiker. My wife, Mrs. Garrard."

"Katinka will be down soon," Aimée explained to the young man after the introductions. The three waited for the girl, and as they waited, Bryan said, "Aimée, will you take off your cloak and show me your costume?"

She drew the cloak closer to her and replied, "It is to be . . . a surprise, Bryan. If you see it before the ball—oh, here is Katinka now," she cried, relieved at the girl's appearance at that moment.

Katinka was dressed in a Marie Antoinette blue satin gown. The elaborate white wig hid her blond hair and the beauty patch on her face drew attention to her sparkling, excited eyes. The lieutenant gazed long at the girl, and Aimée, seeing his interested look, felt as proud as any mother launching her own daughter into society.

The carriage and horses were waiting, with the hired driver sitting on the box, and Aimée, filling in the awkward silence inside the carriage, chattered determinedly about the weather, the ball, and other totally mundane things that came to mind, until they had reached the Opera House.

When the carriage drew up to the doors, the men put on their half-masks and Katinka rummaged in her reticule for the white satin jeweled mask. Aimée, whose hair was hidden by the turban, quickly attached the *yashmak*, which veiled her face from view.

Guards, checking the invitations, allowed them to pass, and Aimée and Katinka left the men for the ladies' room to remove their cloaks.

Before they could return to Bryan and the lieutenant, both were swept up into the crowd and Aimée found herself separated from Katinka and propelled onto the ballroom floor. Despite her protests, she was forced to dance with an unknown admirer, while her eyes searched for some sign of Bryan.

"You have escaped from some harem, my lady?" the polite voice inquired.

"Yes and my . . . my master will not be pleased that you have spirited me away from him."

The man laughed. "I would like to spirit you farther away from him than this. Dare I risk it?"

"No, monsieur. He is a very jealous man and I fear for your life if you should try it."

"That is the story of my life," he said sadly. "Always a jealous lover or husband in the background."

The hall, more crowded now, received a new wave of dancers, and Aimée, unable to fight the surge of people, was again pressed into waiting arms and forced to dance with yet another stranger.

Where was Katinka? Had she found her escort? Aimée did not see her anywhere, but when the voice sounded in her ear, all thought of Katinka was forgotten. Cold fear clutched at her at the sound of the dreaded voice.

"So we meet again, Delphine." The tall masked man in the black domino stared down at her and he laughed when he felt her tremble. For a moment only the presence of people close to her kept her from screaming in fright.

"Aren't you going to ask after my health, Delphine? Especially after running me through with the sword?" Colonel Tilson asked.

"I . . . I did not do it, monsieur. You stumbled on your own sword," she whispered frantically.

Angry hands snatched her from the man's arms and her turban slipped—almost falling from her head at the sudden action.

"What are you doing in such a costume, Aimée?" the furious voice of her husband demanded. "Every curve of your body is exposed to view."

Her relief at his rescue was soon forgotten.

"And it does not please you, master?" she asked in a too-sweet voice.

His teeth gnashed in growing fury. "If you don't want to be spanked in front of all these people, you'd better not try my patience further."

She was dragged along with him until he had removed her from the crowd and taken her through a dimly-lit corridor and up steps to a higher landing.

"You will change costumes with Katinka," he said, shoving her into one of the small supper rooms.

"But why, Bryan? If you object to the costume, shouldn't you take me home?"

"You would like that, wouldn't you, Aimée? But no, Katinka will wear it instead. I do not intend leaving, Aimée. Neither do I intend for you to keep on such an exotic costume."

"But will you not object to Katinka's wearing it?" she asked.

"Katinka does not have your . . . voluptuous curves, so it will not look the same on her. You are not to leave this room. Do you understand, Aimée?"

"Yes, Bryan." All the fight had momentarily gone out of her and her mind returned to the fright of seeing Colonel Tilson.

The door opened once more and Katinka was thrust into the room with Aimée.

"C-colonel Garrard said we are to change costumes." Katinka was breathless as she spoke, and Aimée, re-calling Bryan's manner, became angry again.

Aimée stamped her foot in disgust. "He thinks I am his slave to do his bidding, yet he becomes furious when I dress like one." Aimée leaned over to remove the clank-ing gold bracelet from around her ankle, and then she stopped, asking Katinka, "Do you *mind* switching cos-tumes, Katinka?"

"N-not if that is what Colonel Garrard wants."

Katinka hurriedly removed the wig and the dress, while

Aimée fretted. "There's not even a mirror in here. How does he expect us to dress and undress and be . . . be presentable when we finish?"

But Katinka did not answer. She did as she was told, stepping into the exotic costume and adjusting the turban on her blond head.

"Your wig isn't straight, Mrs. Garrard," Katinka said when Aimée had finally exchanged everything.

"Who cares?" she answered, but Katinka, with a few motions, adjusted it correctly for her.

When they came out of the room, Katinka, looking frightened, and Aimée, defeated, faced Bryan, who insolently looked them up and down.

"One moment," he said, stopping them. He walked to Katinka and removed the fake beauty spot from her cheek.

"Your beauty spot, madame," he said, pressing it onto Aimée's right cheek.

In fury Aimée's hand reached out toward him but he quickly caught the clenched fist while threatening in a low voice, "I would not advise you to retaliate."

Lieutenant Steiker, waiting in the shadows at the foot of the stairs, seemed confused at the switch. "I hope you don't mind, Lieutenant, that you have a harem girl instead of a queen?"

"N-no, sir," he stammered, gazing at Katinka, whose slow blush spread over her face at his continued staring.

"Put on your mask, Aimée. We will rejoin the others in the ballroom."

"I . . . must have left it in the room where we dressed," Aimée replied.

"Wait here and I will get it for you," Bryan said, turning to retrace his steps up the stairs and leaving her with Katinka and Lieutenant Steiker.

"It is not necessary for you to wait with me, Lieutenant. Please take Katinka in to dance and I will come later—with Colonel Garrard," Aimée urged.

The young man hesitated. "I should not leave you alone in the dimly lit hall, Mrs. Garrard."

She impatiently waved him on. "My husband is only a few steps away. Now go and enjoy the music."

Obeying Aimée, he departed with Katinka at his side.

The quietness of the hall suddenly disturbed her. She felt alone, far apart from the people and the music, as if she were in another world, invisible, while the merriment went on about her. Here in the corridor at the base of the stairs there were no shimmering chandeliers, no brilliances of light to catch the sparkle of the costume she was now wearing, And her petulant behavior in wearing the harem costume to irk Bryan now seemed childish.

He was angry with her and with good cause. She had not behaved like an obedient, subdued wife. Her headstrong tendencies had again plunged her into trouble, and from Bryan's actions, Aimée suspected that she had not heard the last of his displeasure.

Her husband's anger, combined with seeing Colonel Tilson again, had unnerved her, and when the tall man in the domino touched her arm, she was startled.

"Your mask, Aimée."

She almost laughed in relief. The shadows of the deep-red velvet curtains and the unidentified scuffling sounds farther down the corridor had stirred her imagination with ghosts of dark deeds and intrigue, and it was because of this that she walked closer to her husband—to feel the aura of his strength and protection.

The man lying on the floor next to the open French windows came into sight as Aimée and Bryan turned the corner.

Her husband rushed to the man and Aimée, remembering the recent sound of scuffling along the corridor, stiffened in alarm.

"Bryan, is it . . .?"

"It's Lieutenant Steiker, Aimée. He seems to have fallen and hit his head."

Aimée looked at the open French windows and her anxiety for Katinka was immediate.

"Katinka—where is Katinka?" Aimée asked, while Bryan helped the man to his feet.

"Abducted," Lieutenant Steiker said, still in a daze. "He . . . hit me and took Katinka with him."

The costume! The harem costume that she had been wearing a few minutes before, when she had danced with

Colonel Tilson. And in the dimly-lit hall no one would have guessed that someone other than Aimée was wearing it!

"Who hit you?" Bryan asked in an imperious voice.

"A tall man in a black domino—"

"Aimée, stay with Ward. He'll see you home," Bryan said, waving his hand toward Lieutenant Steiker. "I will get help to look for Katinka."

Bryan, with his giant steps, rapidly disappeared, and Aimée, her heart churning, remained with the young cavalry officer, who leaned against the wall and felt the back of his head where he had been hit.

It was Colonel Tilson, of course, who had abducted Katinka—thinking she was Aimée. And only Aimée knew where he would take her—to the house on Rampart Street. She could not tell Bryan. Neither could she tell the dazed lieutenant before her; for he would be no match for the broad heavyset man. Only Anderson could help her. And she had to get to him quickly.

"Can you walk to the carriage?" Aimée asked.

"I . . . think so," the man replied.

"Hold on to my arm," she suggested when his gait proved to be unsteady.

Together they walked down the steps, bypassing the ballroom and the sound of music. The carriage, drawn up to one of the hitching posts down the street, was unattended. The driver was occupying himself elsewhere, probably in a game of craps.

Aimée pushed the young man into the carriage, closed the door, and then climbed upon the box. Soon she had started the horses down the street and toward her own house, toward Anderson, who would help her.

When confronted by Aimée, Anderson did not waste time but quickly went to his room for his pistols. Luckily Clotilde and Cousin Jorge had gone to bed and it was Jou-Jou who took over, caring for Lieutenant Steiker, while Aimée climbed inside the carriage and Anderson mounted the box and headed for Number 9, Rampart Street.

The carriage slowed long enough to pick up the liveried driver who, having missed it, had started walking toward

360

the townhouse in search of it. Anderson remained on the box with him after he had taken over the reins, and urging the horses on, they moved toward their destination.

The carriage stopped; Anderson stepped down from the high box and the driver spoke sharply to the impatient horses that wanted to continue on their way. Aimée peered out the carriage window and saw the flickering light inside the house that Colonel Tilson had purchased for his mistress.

Please let him be in time. Please do not let Katinka be hurt.

While Aimée sat, listening, waiting, and praying, there was no sound from the little house, until the door opened and a sobbing Katinka, clinging to Anderson, came out.

Aimée opened the carriage door to receive the sobbing girl, and when she was in, Anderson stepped up also, closed the door, and leaning his head out the window, said to the driver, "You may take us home now."

Katinka, continuing to emit sobs off and on, clung to Anderson and he was gentle with her, his arms holding her in a comforting embrace against him. He held his handkerchief for her while she blew her nose, and when they had approached the drive into the courtyard, it was Anderson who gave instructions to the driver to wait for him.

"You are all right, Katinka. Stop your crying," he said in a grave voice, "and go with Mrs. Garrard."

Katinka shared a room with Cousin Clotilde, and the older woman awakened at the noise that greeted her.

"My dear," Cousin Clotilde said, sitting up when the lamp was lit, "what has happened? What is the matter?"

"Katinka had an unpleasant experience. She was abducted from the ball," explained Aimée.

"But Silas saved me," Katinka finished.

Silas? Who was that? Could it be . . . Anderson?

"Anderson?" Clotilde said. "Anderson saved you?"

Katinka nodded and began to remove the silver-and-turquoise turban. Clotilde, her eyes peering sleepily, first at Katinka, then at Aimée, seemed confused. "I thought,

Aimée, that Katinka was wearing the blue gown when she left."

Aimée looked at the woman with the long single plait down her back and replied, "She was. But Bryan made us change costumes. Will you . . . take care of her, Cousin Clotilde? Anderson is waiting to see me downstairs."

"Yes, my dear. And don't worry—I'll put her to bed." Clotilde's soothing words to the girl started before Aimée closed the door.

There was no way that Aimée could get word to Bryan that Katinka was safe. She would just have to wait for him to come home.

What would she tell Bryan when he returned? That she knew *who* had abducted Katinka and *where* he had taken her because it was not Katinka at all that the man thought he was kidnapping? And that she had known where to find her because she had been taken there previously by Colonel Tilson?

No, she could never reveal this to him. Bryan would shoot Colonel Tilson and she would lose Bryan's love forever.

"We put the young *homme* to bed," Jou-Jou said. "The beeg lump on his *tête* verree bad. Zat leetle cos-yume, it bring beeg trouble, *non*?" she said, noticing the satin gown into which Aimee had changed.

"Yes, big trouble," Aimée admitted, passing on to find Anderson.

He was waiting for her at the courtyard door.

"Anderson, you know Katinka was taken by mistake? That . . . that I was supposed to have been the one abducted?"

"Yes, Mrs. Garrard, I know."

"Are you . . . going to tell Colonel Garrard where you found Katinka?"

"No, I gave my word."

"Your word? To . . . to whom?"

"To Colonel Tilson."

"But why?"

"To protect you, ma'am. He threatened to have you arrested for . . . stabbing him."

"Anderson, what are we going to do?" she asked, her

362

grief apparent in her eyes and entire body. "It was an accident, but when Bryan learns that I was the one who directed you to Rampart Street—"

"You knew nothing about it, Mrs. Garrard. You were here . . . taking care of Lieutenant Steiker. I was the one to find Katinka."

"What will you tell Bryan?"

"I will think of a . . . suitable story."

"Do you think Bry—Colonel Garrard will believe you?"

"He will have no reason to doubt my story. I have never . . . lied to him before."

The limping man closed the door and left a guilty Aimée staring after him in the dark.

So now she had caused a breach between Bryan and his trusted Anderson. What else would she destroy before she had finished?

Chapter 38

Bryan must have accepted the story that Anderson told him about Katinka's rescue. But Aimée was not to know. Bryan did not discuss it with her and she was too frightened to ask him.

Yet he did not appear entirely satisfied and at times Aimée felt his questioning eyes following her—almost as if he were trying to fathom a puzzle with an important piece missing.

The surprising thing to her was that Bryan made no further remark concerning her choice of costume for the ball. She was so certain that she would come under fire for it, but like the explanation concerning Katinka, it, too, was never mentioned.

Except for his acid remark when he returned the next day with the new cloak that she had left in the ladies' closet that night, no one would ever have known that they had attended the *bal masqué*.

"Why do you have such a penchant for leaving cloaks behind, Aimée? If you are ever involved in a crime, you will be convicted by a cloak you left at the scene."

With a startled movement, Aimée lifted her head to gaze into Bryan's sober gray eyes. Then he laughed and Aimée slowly relaxed.

The Union headquarters became active, preparing for the conference to take place between Banks and General Sherman. Another Western campaign was being planned, but no one knew where.

"The Red River—it has to be the Red River," Cousin Jorge said to Aimée one afternoon as he sat in the garden courtyard. "That's the only way the supplies are getting through to our Army. The stopping of the supply route and the capture of Shreveport—those are the two important objectives now."

Aimée nodded and sighed. "If Shreveport were captured, then the entire state would be under Union domination, wouldn't it?"

"Yes, I'm afraid so, Aimée. When a capital surrenders, it does something to the people. It's too bad Lee didn't keep on marching and take Washington while he had the chance."

Cousin Jorge's surmise was correct and the Red River campaign began in March. Again Bryan and Anderson left New Orleans by transport, but this time Bryan would not let Aimée see them off. Their good-byes were said the evening before, and by dawn Bryan had gone, leaving Aimée in the care of Jou-Jou and the dogs.

"The dogs are to sleep in the bedroom while I am away," Bryan had insisted.

"I did not think you . . . liked them to be in this part of the house, Bryan."

"That is true when I am here, Aimée, to protect you. But while I am away, it is a different matter."

"Do you have any idea how long you will be gone?"

"It depends upon the amount of resistance we encounter."

"Bryan, you *will* be careful, won't you?"

"Do I hear a trace of concern for me, Aimée?" he asked, holding her close.

"You have been lucky so far," she said, not answering his question. Her fingers touched his cheek where the scar began and she added, "Except for the scar." A moment later she said impulsively, "Bryan, how did you get it? The scar, I mean. Was it a very . . . dreadful battle?"

"It would not interest you, Aimée, and I have no desire to recall the episode. Now hush and let me love you—"

His lips trailed across her hair, across her cheek, searching for her mouth. Finding it in the darkness, he became possessive, parting her lips with increasing ardor, and Aimée, knowing that she would be separated from him by the morrow, let him have his way without protest. . . .

Defeated—routed—driven back to Alexandria. By April, the Red River campaign was a disaster and Banks with his Army of the Gulf returned to New Orleans.

Bryan was safe, and her people still not totally defeated—Aimée had gotten her wish.

But Bryan was hard to live with for some time after the campaign. He paced up and down and swore under his breath. His pride as a soldier had taken a severe beating, not from the Confederates, who fought hard and well, but from the behavior of his own army and navy, and the civilian speculators and carpetbaggers who had tagged along, looting and stripping the land.

"Aimée, we were defeated—not by bullets and guns, but by *greed*," he said disgustedly. "Porter's men left their boats and stamped every bale of cotton they could find as navy prizes to be confiscated—and the army commandeered every wagon and rolling vehicle they could get their hands on to carry what was farther inland from the river. As soon as we neared a plantation or cotton field, a third of the army dropped out to loot. And many of the officers were no better than the privates. The speculators even *hired* men to pick the cotton left in the fields. Is it any wonder such an undisciplined army was defeated—or that the gunboats, loaded down with their prizes, could barely escape through the low lying river?

"I am not proud of the Army of the Gulf at this moment, Aimée. They seem to have forgotton why this war is being fought."

Aimée said nothing, for the picture that Bryan had stirred in her mind brought fresh pain. Her Louisiana country was being systematically stripped. But its people were still not defeated, and for this, she was grateful.

Despite having Bryan at home, despite his passionate lovemaking, Aimée remained barren. The plump laughing son of Vickie and Clay, with his gurgling cooing and trusting silver-gray eyes staring into hers, wrenched her heart, and when she had to give up little Lee Beauregard Garrard from her arms, Aimée would feel an unreconcilable ache.

"It's too bad you lost your own child, Aimée," Vickie said, removing the baby from Aimée's arms one May afternoon. "And no sign of another on the way."

It was too much—this persistent calling of attention to her childless state. Aimée bit her lip and choked back the tears that were waiting for a chance to flow. Vickie handed the baby to the waiting Lisette and climbed into the carriage that headed out the driveway toward the street.

"Zat woman, she verree bad," Jou-Jou muttered while watching the carriage disappear. "Some day, I feex her."

Vickie or Lisette? To which was Jou-Jou referring? Without comment, Aimée rushed up the stairs so that Jou-Jou would not see the tears that, despite her efforts, promised to flow.

Giving full vent to the hurt that was within her, Aimée cried and her face, pink and blotched, gave evidence of her weeping.

There was a knock on the door and guiltily, Aimée sat up from the bed. "Yes?" she called.

"Madame, I bring nice hot water for ze bath. Make you feel better to have good long soak before husband come home."

Jou-Jou came into the room with a kettle of hot water and poured it into the brass tub. Aimée averted her head to hide her tears from Jou-Jou, who went back and forth until the tub was filled.

"You are too good to me, Jou-Jou." Aimée, forgetting to hide her tear-blotched face, looked at the woman who was now helping her undress.

"Madame have no need to be sad. She have beeg plump laughing babee, too, by me by."

Aimée smiled, touched that Jou-Jou had guessed the reason for her tears and was trying to reassure her.

When Jou-Jou left her, Aimée relaxed in the tub, hidden from the rest of the room by the screen. When the door opened again, Aimée said, "Jou-Jou, hand me the towel, please. I'm ready to get out."

The steps came closer and the towel was held out for her. Aimée arose from the tub and reached for the waiting towel.

"You are very beautiful, Aimée," the voice said.

Startled, she gazed up into Bryan's amused eyes and quickly sank back into the tub.

"What maidenly modesty," Bryan said with a laugh. "Shall I turn my back, Aimée?"

His teasing taunted her and with effort she responded in a cool manner. "Only if you wish, Bryan. It matters not . . . to me."

"Then I think I shall take advantage of the view." Still his eyes were amused and Aimée, determined that he would not disconcert her, arose slowly and gracefully from the tub, with her hand extended for his help. Her hair, damp at the ends, curled in wet tendrils and lay over one shoulder, covering one breast and leaving the other exposed.

Bryan wrapped the towel about her and lifted the heavy gold-red strands that she now shook to freedom with a toss of her head.

"Thank you, Bryan," she said, dismissing him with one look from her cold turquoise eyes.

Her icy look was immediately doused by the slow-burning flame that had taken hold of Bryan.

"A thank you, my man, and be off with you. Do you think you can get rid of me that easily, Aimée?" There was a touch of anger in his voice that had not been present earlier.

"Please, Bryan, I do not feel like arguing. I . . . I want to get dressed."

Her face, still slightly pink from crying, was caught between his hands and he suddenly asked, "Why have you been crying, Aimée?"

Aimée sighed. "Can I not hide *anything* from you, Bryan?"

"You have hidden *much* from me, Aimée. Do not deny it. And one day I shall demand total honesty."

Then his voice softened as he caressed her cheek with his finger, running it under her chin and down to the hollow of her throat. "But it's only sufficient for today that you tell me the reason for your tears."

In the silence Bryan waited for her answer.

"I . . . I was feeling sorry for myself," she admitted.

"Go on, explain."

"Vickie was here with Lee Beauregard . . ."

Suddenly she clung to him, leaning her head against his chest and sobbing, "Oh Bryan, why can I not have a child? Vickie has given Clay a son. Why cannot I give *you* a son?"

His voice, gentle and low, responded, "You will give me a son—in time—Aimée. Don't worry so, my darling. Besides, I'm not in such a rush to share you with anyone else. I would rather have you to myself for a while longer."

"You—you're only saying that to make me feel better."

"No, Aimée, I speak the truth."

"But what if I . . . can *never* have a child?" Aimée whispered in a fearful tone.

"God, Aimée, if you cannot be happy being my wife, if you are so obsessed with having a child in the house, then we will go to the orphanage tomorrow and pick one out to bring home. Heaven knows there are enough children in that place for you to find one that suits you."

"But I don't want just *any* child, Bryan," Aimée protested. "I want *your* child."

His sudden irritation and movement caused the towel to drop to the floor.

"No, Aimée, do not bother to pick up the towel. If that is how you feel—weeping until you can have a child —then we are wasting time standing here. . . . Get in bed, Aimée."

"Bryan—"

"Do as I say, Aimée." His voice—rough, distant, commanding—intimidated her. Naked and afraid, she walked across the room and, obeying him, she slipped into bed, with her heart pounding. All gentleness was gone and in its place was an anger—a cold, smoldering anger that demanded expiation. He had never been this way before.

"No, Bryan—not like this. I don't want . . . your son like this."

Aimée's protest went unheeded. His deliberate, cold-blooded, loveless actions made her shrink from him, but she could not escape. Methodically he worked, making her body respond to his demands and against her will the wave of desire roared over her until she was no longer aware of her tears of protest—only aware of a vast degradation under her husband's hands, making her want him as she had never desired him before.

Abruptly his hands jerked away and he sat up on the side of the bed, brushing his shiny black hair from his forehead. His voice was unsteady when he finally spoke. "You drive me to madness, Aimée. But you can stop your quaking. I will not . . . hurt you anymore."

Aimée, more brokenhearted than ever, contained her sobs until the closing of the door told her that Bryan had dressed and left her—left her to taste her tears of bitterness.

Chapter 39

*I*n her sadness Aimée found comfort in Katinka. The girl's accomplishments at the convent gave her a mute satisfaction. She was older than the other girls, but in the short time she had studied with the Sisters, Katinka had done well. But now Katinka's time at the convent had come to an end. The term was over.

What was to become of her, now that she was of marriageable age?

Aimée was disappointed that Katinka had given no encouragement by smile or gesture to Lieutenant Steiker when he had called several times after the *bal masqué* to inquire after her health.

But then Aimée remembered her own reactions to Prosper Gautier and she did not press Katinka to respond against her will. She would just have to find someone else in whom Katinka would show an interest. And so Aimée persuaded Bryan to bring home a young officer occasionally to dine with them. But Katinka did not show the interest Aimée had hoped for. She was far friendlier to Anderson than to any newcomer at the table.

This gradual change—this clinging to Anderson after his rescue of her—did not bode well for the girl, Aimée thought.

"Bryan, I do not like this new dependence that Katinka has on Anderson. Do you think you could speak with him—ask him not to encourage it? Every day they are together. She goes with him to market, she sits in the garden with him. I realize that they have been close in the past, but Katinka is a child no longer."

"I will speak with him about it, Aimée—although I think you're making too much of it."

"Too much? When she won't even *look* at any of the young men you bring home for dinner? She is an accomplished young lady now, speaking French, doing lovely embroidery, and her mind is quick. She's really quite clever and I have hopes that one day soon she will make an advantageous marriage to someone who will appreciate her."

"And you think that Anderson does not appreciate her?" His amusement danced in his eyes.

"Of course he does, Bryan. But you know what I mean. Anderson is . . . more like a father. Katinka needs a husband."

Bryan laughed. "Your matchmaking so far has not gone well, has it, Aimée?"

"Not yet," she answered, forcing herself to smile. "But there is always tomorrow. . . ."

At the start of dinner Bryan was still amused. And Aimée looked from Bryan to Anderson and then to Katinka, trying to get some indication that Bryan had kept his promise and spoken with Anderson. But their faces told her nothing.

The only face plainly showing any excitement was that of Cousin Jorge, who sat happily at the table, with his two canes propped by the side of his chair. He had continued to improve gradually, yet Aimée knew he would never regain his full health. But his writing had given him a sense of purpose, and staying busy each day with it, he had not complained about the slowness with which he now moved.

"How far along, Cousin Jorge, are you in your history of Louisiana?" Aimée asked while passing the bread to Bryan.

"Still in the Spanish rule, Aimée—with the Vieux Carré in ashes after the fire of 1788."

"The entire Vieux Carré was burned?" Bryan asked.

"Yes, Bryan. It started in Chartres Street, in the house of the military treasurer, Don Nuñez. It seems that a candle fell from the altar and set fire to the draperies."

"And one altar candle caused such devastation?"

"Well, it wouldn't have been so bad except that it was Good Friday and the priests refused to let the alarm bell be rung."

Bryan's voice was unbelieving. "Refused to let the alarm bell ring?"

Cousin Jorge, warming to his subject, continued. "It was the religious law—no bell could be rung on Good Friday."

"How many buildings were destroyed because of this insane law?" questioned Bryan.

"Eight hundred and sixteen buildings were burned to the ground."

"All because some priest would not allow a bell to be rung," Bryan finished in a dry tone.

"Well, it wasn't all a bad thing," Cousin Jorge countered. "No lives were lost, and frankly, some of the buildings were pretty bad. When it was rebuilt, the Vieux Carré was well designed and much more substantial."

"With the exception of one carriage house," Aimée volunteered.

"Yes. Well, sometimes it depends on damage done by winds and gales," Cousin Jorge admitted, "but the majority of the buildings were built to last for generations."

"Like Thornfell," Clotilde said quietly. "It, too, was built to last for generations." At the mention of the beautiful old house, Clotilde showed her sadness at its destruction.

"Wouldn't it be wonderful if—like the Vieux Carré—Thornfell could be rebuilt?" Aimée said, looking at Bryan as she spoke.

"It is not likely, Aimée," Cousin Clotilde commented. "It will be hard enough to pay the taxes we owe on the land itself."

Cousin Jorge coughed and Bryan moved his wine glass closer to his plate.

In the silence that followed, Bryan prompted Anderson. "I believe you have something you wish to tell us—you and Katinka?"

Aimée, wondering what it was that involved Anderson

and Katinka, looked first at Bryan and then at Anderson, who was growing slightly red at the attention thrust upon him.

"Katinka and I plan to be . . . married soon, if no one objects."

Aimée, speechless at the announcement, could not believe what she had heard. Why, Anderson was old enough to be Katinka's father!

The congratulations poured upon Anderson from all sides and Clotilde, sitting next to Katinka, put her arms around the girl and said, "I know you will be very happy, my dear."

During the toasts Aimée sat quietly. She had no words to convey her surprise, no words to tell Bryan how she felt, no suspicion that his obeisance to her request would precipitate such an announcement.

Gradually Aimée became aware of the faces at the table. Katinka was staring at her with such anxiety that Aimée knew she had to do something to alleviate the girl's distress at her silent and stunned behavior.

"I am . . . happy for you, Katinka. Anderson will be proud of you, I know." Then her musical laugh rang through the room. "But such a surprise—I had *no* idea!"

Everyone laughed and the tense mood disappeared. How Aimée got through it, she did not remember. She vaguely recollected going through the motions of drinking a toast, congratulating Anderson, and then, mercifully, it was over and time for bed.

When she reached her bedroom, the teasing began. "And what does this do to your matchmaking, Aimée?"

"Don't speak to me. You . . . you deliberately did it."

"Deliberately did what?" Bryan asked.

"You promised to speak with Anderson about Katinka."

"I did, Aimée—and was as surprised as *you* were."

"But why would Katinka want to marry Anderson in preference to . . . to . . ."

"Anderson is more of a man than most of those young, conceited pups I have been bringing to the house at your instigation, Aimée. And Katinka, if you remember, was taken off the street. She doesn't even know her last name.

373

As far as Anderson's age is concerned, he's only two years older than I am."

"But . . . but Katinka is a . . . baby, compared to him."

"She's far older than her years and behaves with more propriety than you do many times. No, I think they will be quite compatible."

"What did you say, Bryan?"

"I said I think they will be quite compatible."

"No—the other."

His scowl was devastating as he said, "Katinka would have more propriety than to wear a costume she knew would make her husband furious."

"I . . . wondered when you were going to bring that up," Aimée said in a small voice.

"Did you think I could ignore it—knowing that whoever kidnapped Katinka thought he had kidnapped you?"

Suddenly he grabbed her wrist. "Aimée, is John Runefelt back in New Orleans? Is he the one who thought he was taking you away from me?"

"No. Let me go, Bryan."

"I will *not* let you go, Aimée. And I am warning you— I will not have anyone trying to take you away from me again."

Impulsively Aimée said, "Then give your warning to Vickie—not to me."

Still holding her by the wrist, Bryan pulled her closer. "What did you mean by that, Aimée?"

"Nothing, Bryan. Just . . . leave me alone," she pleaded.

Bryan released her wrist and walked toward the window. He stood for some time in a pensive mood and Aimée, afraid that she had said too much, quietly went about her nightly ceremony of getting ready for bed.

Sometime later Bryan blew out the lamp, and crawling into bed, pulled the mosquito netting close. He lay on his side of the bed and made no attempt to take her in his arms. He had not done so since the night of bitter tears. . . .

The buzzing in her ears announced the presence of a mosquito. And the heat was stifling. Impatiently Aimée swatted at the mosquito, but after a moment of silence, it returned to pester her.

Finally she got up, put on her robe, and walked downstairs. The slight breeze was blowing the myrtle trees and Aimée, hot and unhappy, pushed open the door and wandered into the garden near the carriage house.

The moon filtering through the trees gave its stippled halo to the dolphin at the fountain. Emotions of past days also filtered through Aimée's mind, much like the stray moonbeams that came into the garden, hopping and skipping from brick to fountain to water jar.

Aimée had almost given herself away tonight by mentioning Vickie's name. And now she sensed that Bryan would be alert to each unguarded slip until he had pieced together what she was attempting to hide from him.

What had Anderson told him on the night that Katinka had been abducted? What story had satisfied Bryan at least long enough to remain silent until now?

"Aimée—" The hand touched her hesitantly. "What is the matter? Can you not sleep?"

"It is so hot, Bryan. And I was restless. I . . . did not want to wake you."

"Is it the heat, Aimée, or is it your unhappiness that has kept you awake?"

When she did not reply, he spoke again. "I am sorry that things have not gone well between us. I had hoped that we would have resolved our differences by this time."

"It is difficult, is it not, when we are on such opposite sides?"

"That does not make it insurmountable, Aimée. Love can bring happiness, if people forget their differences. If love is strong enough, then the disagreements can be put in proper perspective. It need not destroy their lives. Do you remember, Aimée, the time I first found you asleep in the garden?"

"Yes," she said in a faraway voice.

"I had never seen anyone so beautiful as you were that day—when you lay asleep by the fountain, with your flaming hair dazzling my eyes in the sunlight. I could not resist touching you. I could not resist holding you in my arms even for that brief moment, and even then I knew that our lives were destined to be intertwined. But you opposed me and you have continued to oppose me.

"Aimée, when will you come to me as a loving wife—without defiance—without fighting me? Will your enmity toward me last as long as this war, because I am the enemy? What must I do to win your love—to get you to love me?"

"Win my love? Have I not signed an oath to cease giving aid to my people so that I might remain with you? Have I not honored my marriage vows—those vows that were forced upon me?"

"I will admit that our marriage took place far sooner than I had planned—and to you, under the circumstances, it would seem forced," he admitted.

"You *planned* to marry me, Bryan, before the accident?"

"Yes, Aimée. From the moment you threw the tray of food in my face, I planned for you to become my wife. But it was to have been a gradual courtship, one in which I hoped to gain your love. But circumstances forced a premature action. And to make matters worse, I had to compete with a dead lover—always a hard thing to do. For a dead man makes no mistakes. He is perfect from the time he goes into the grave. Only his good qualities are remembered, while the living keep on making mistakes."

"I did not . . . love Prosper Gautier, Bryan. My *grand-père* was the one who wished me to be betrothed to him."

"So all this time he has not been my rival, even though you remember his grave with flowers?"

"No, Bryan."

"And what of John Runefelt? Do you love him, Aimée?"

"I think of John as a . . . friend. We shared a common goal. It was what brought us together."

"And Juba?"

Why was he doing this to her—bringing up each name, as he had on the night she had lost the baby? Did he need to be reassured that they were not his rivals . . . that he was the only one who mattered? Did he want to make her admit that she could not live without him? And yet, he might reject her when he found out about . . . the other. No, she would not admit that each day bound her to him more than the day before.

"Juba saw his dead sister in me. She had inherited the red hair and the turquoise eyes also from our earlier ancestor."

"The Aimée that Vickie hated so?"

"Yes."

"Aimée," Bryan asked while stroking her hair, "why did you say that my warning should have gone to Vickie? Has she done anything to harm you?"

"I did not mean to speak of her, Bryan. Please do not ask me."

Aimée held her breath and waited for Bryan's reply.

"All right. I will not push you into confiding in me tonight. But you know that it is between us—your refusing to give me complete trust. One day, Aimée . . ." His voice trailed as she suddenly turned to him, a premonition of heartbreak spreading over her.

"Hold me close, Bryan—I am . . . frightened."

She found herself in his arms and being carried—not back to the main house but to the carriage house.

"Bryan, where are you taking me?"

"To the carriage house . . . where the memories are pleasant."

"But Jou-Jou. She is asleep in the other room. We will wake her."

"Not if you are silent. Do not protest, Aimée. Let me love you as I did that day when I took you from the garden."

The moon illuminated their path and gave brightness to the curving iron of the steps. There was no need for candle or lamp within the room itself, for the light penetrated through the shuttered windows, casting its slanting glow upon the entwined figures.

"My darling," he said and his voice caused her to tremble.

Time rolled back swiftly and the layers of misunderstanding were stripped away as first love was rededicated. And Aimée, who had unknowingly erased from her mind all painful thoughts of the actions that had brought her to that first experience, now knowingly erased the events that had separated her from Bryan after the return of her memory. His tenderness, his sweet consideration brushed away her hesitancy and became a healing balm on the wounds left from his previous abrupt treatment. And at the height of their passion, Aimée saw for the first time what her life with Bryan could be—could be if fate would allow it—could be if the impasse with Titus Tilson could be resolved without bloodshed.

Aimée became afraid of what she had to lose. Possessing a brief vision of the vast, encompassing love that was possible, she now became aware of the brittleness of the steps upon which she trod.

With the sun's early rays, Bryan aroused Aimée, and together they left the carriage house for their own room. On the way through the garden Bryan stooped down and selected a budding coral flower, still fresh with dew. He put it lovingly into Aimée's hair, and in her white gown, with her bare feet gliding soundlessly over the worn bricks, she resembled Aurora heralding the light of the day.

"I suppose Katinka and Anderson will wish to move to the carriage house," Aimée whispered.

Bryan grinned. "And do you think they will find the same pleasure awaiting them?"

Aimée, looking tenderly at Bryan, answered, "I hope so, Bryan."

The languorous, loving feeling was rudely taken away by the melee in the courtyard shortly after Bryan had gone. Jou-Jou's voice rose loudly and Aimée, who had been singing to herself in the bedroom, went to see what was causing such a blasphemy of sound. She still had the flower in her hair, still felt the vitality of Bryan's arms about her, and so she was annoyed at the disturbance— this interruption of her dreams.

"Jou-Jou, what is happening?" Aimée asked.

"Zat Lisette—she try to leave wicked *gris-gris* at your door. But we feex her—I shake my broom and throw salt after her. She not come again."

Aimée frowned and Jou-Jou hastened to comfort her.

"But not to worry, madame. *Gris-gris* have no power over you. *Ma petite poule* see to zat. Frizzle feathers verree strong magic."

The next day an angry Vickie greeted Aimée. "I have come to complain about your woman, Jou-Jou."

"Why, Vickie? What has Jou-Jou done?"

"She has made Lisette ill—ill with fear."

"Fear?"

"Yes. Lisette came to your house yesterday on an errand for me, but the woman, Jou-Jou, pointed the broom at her and threw salt in her path, and she has been shaking ever since."

"What was the errand, Vickie?"

"That . . . is not important at the moment. What is important is Jou-Jou's behavior."

Aimée smiled. "And of course the frizzle-feathered chicken didn't help either."

"This is no laughing matter, Aimée. You know how superstitious they all are. Lisette can't even take care of the children because her mind is still on her terrible experience."

"I thought Lizzie was the children's nursemaid," Aimée said.

"Lizzie is now doing the housecleaning. Lisette is so much better with the children, or was, until yesterday."

"And what do you expect me to do about it, Vickie?"

"Warn Jou-Jou that I will not tolerate her spells. It's up to you, Aimée, to see that she does not bother Lisette. There are . . . some things that Bryan could be told, if I decided—"

"Are you threatening me, Vickie?"

"I am only warning you—keep Jou-Jou and her tricks away from Lisette or I shall have to go to Bryan to tell him . . . certain interesting facts."

For the first time in the conversation Aimée became angry. "And when he learns your underhanded part in it, do you think he will reward you?" Aimée bit her lip as soon as she had said it.

Vickie smiled a gloating smile. "So, you *did* come to the house that afternoon. I wondered about that."

Suddenly she leaned toward Aimée. "Were you the one who stabbed Colonel Tilson, Aimée? Was it you, not the octoroon, Delphine?"

"I do not know what you are talking about, Vickie."

"If it was, you are in deep trouble. Not only with Bryan, but with the law." Vickie stared at her and then resumed talking. "And if Bryan learns of it. . . . They say Colonel Tilson is an expert with the sword. And Bryan—well, we know from the scar on his face that he is not the best swordsman in the world. Anderson would not finish his fight for him this time, as he did before."

"Do you know . . . how Bryan got the scar?" Aimée asked.

"It was Clay who did it. Hasn't Bryan told you?"

Dumbfounded, Aimée could only shake her head.

"They faced each other in battle and Bryan was a coward. He refused to fight."

"And Clay slashed him across his cheek when Bryan refused to kill his own brother?"

"Clay was surrounded by the enemy. It was either fight or be killed."

"Was that . . . the battle in which Clay lost his left eye?" Aimee asked.

"No, that happened later—in prison camp. A guard did it after Clay had complained about the food. But we're getting off the subject. Be warned, Aimée—tell your woman to stop terrorizing Lisette or I shall go to Bryan."

Vickie stood up and flounced from the salon. Aimée did not walk to the door with her but let her find her own way out.

Chapter 40

Aimée was in the garden when the wrought-iron gate creaked, indicating someone else had come into the courtyard. Could Bryan have returned so early in the day? Aimée moved so that she could get a better view.

The dark-haired girl in shabby clothes walked slowly down the carriage drive, and as she approached the courtyard door, she hesitated.

Aimée, still hidden from sight, continued to stare at the girl. She looked familiar and yet . . .

"Michele!" Aimée's voice was incredulous as she recognized the friend she had not seen for so long.

"Aimée?" Michele, tilting her head to one side, let her hand drop from the brass knocker and turned in the direction from which the voice had come.

Aimée went rapidly toward her, and Michele ran the few steps to meet her. They hugged each other and began talking at the same time until, laughing, Aimée stood back to get a better look at her friend and said, "Oh, how glad I am to see you. But we cannot talk at once. Tell me— when did you get here? And what is the news with you and your family?"

The dark velvet eyes lost their sparkle and became clouded with sorrow. "Papa is . . . dead, Aimée, and Maman . . . it would be better if she were, too," admitted Michele. "She is like a child, not accepting Papa's death. She sits all day in her chair and watches the road for Papa—" Michele's voice broke.

Feeling her heartache, Aimée led Michele into the

house, and they were silent while Aimée fixed chocolate for them to drink. "Have you eaten, Michele?" Aimée asked.

She shook her head. "I . . . came to see you as soon as I left my valise at Cousin Antoinette's."

"Then you are here just for a visit?" Aimée inquired, taking the biscuits from the cupboard.

"My fiancé is a prisoner in the Customs House, Aimée. And I have had word that he is ill."

"Your fiancé? I did not know. What is his name, Michele?"

The girl paused and brushed her hair back nervously before answering. "Jean—Jean Brisot."

The name evoked memories for Aimée . . . of a tall, dark, laughing man who had called on her so often, who had killed Prosper in a duel.

"I love him, Aimée. And I had to come to New Orleans to try to see him. If he is ill, I must try to help him—to see that he receives the right medicine and . . . and enough food."

Aimée looked at the girl who was far too thin herself. "But will you be allowed to see him, Michele?"

"I must see him—even if I have to sneak into the prison. Aimée, you will help me, won't you?" Michele asked, her voice full of anguish.

"Michele, I am . . . being watched," Aimée replied. "I gave my promise that I would do nothing to help my people. And if I go back on my word . . ."

"Your word—to the Yankees?" Michele made a face. "I took the eagle oath to get into New Orleans, but I have no intention of abiding by it. I would perjure myself a thousand times to keep Jean from dying in a Yankee prison."

"Perhaps we can think of something," Aimée said, worried that Michele would soon be in trouble with the authorities, yet concerned for the man in prison.

When Michele had eaten the ham and biscuits, she got up to go.

"I will walk part way with you, Michele, but first, let me go upstairs for . . . something."

The dress that Michele was wearing had been patched

many times and Aimée, knowing that she would probably have no better ones, hurriedly selected a dress from her armoire to give to her friend.

"I cannot take your dress," Michele protested when Aimée brought it downstairs.

"Do you wish Jean to see you in the one you have on?" Aimée asked sharply.

Michele shook her head and smiled at her. "I will . . . return it to you later. I always did have too much pride. But it is for Jean, not for me, that I wish to look pretty."

They walked down the banquette together, and after five blocks Aimée turned around to retrace her steps to the townhouse.

Her heart was heavy. What if it were Bryan who lay in prison, sick? Would she not do what Michele was doing—beg for help to get him the proper medicine and food? She wanted to help Michele and Jean, and yet, she had given her promise to supply no aid. Tears filled Aimée's eyes. What was she to do? Her head ached and she could not think. She should not have walked so far with Michele.

The banquette was crowded with a sudden rush of people and Aimée, feeling dizzy, stumbled in the swirling crowd. Strong hands righted her, and before she realized what had happened, she found herself lifted into a waiting carriage. The blue uniform beside her was blurred.

She laid her head against the seat, grateful that Bryan had rescued her from the crowd. There was a silence, except for the clopping of horses' hooves against the cobblestones.

Finally Aimée opened her eyes, expecting to see Bryan beside her, with his deep scar-shaped frown. But it was not Bryan who sat in the carriage with her . . . . What had she done in her weakness? Why had she not recognized this man at once and cried out against him when he had lifted her into the carriage?

"Well, my dear, it has been a long wait. I am delighted that you have decided to come with me without protest."

Colonel Tilson—and she was in his carriage. She was being taken—where? Surely not to the house in the

Ramparts. Anderson knew of its existence and Titus Tilson could not hope to keep her there for long.

But evidently the man had other plans in mind; for the carriage abruptly turned in the streets and headed north, out of the city.

"You will not regret coming with me, Aimée. I am a rich man now, and can afford to give you your heart's desire. You have only to ask, and I will grant your every wish."

Her heart's desire? Her every wish? How foolish he was to think that he could ever do that.

"Let me go, Colonel Tilson. Please—let me go." Her voice was weak.

He gave a hearty, unpleasant laugh. "Let you go? When all I have thought about is you—your hair, your eyes, your sweet, young breasts? I have dreamed each night of you in my arms and this time I will not be thwarted. No, you are mine now and you will not escape from me so easily."

"You know . . . I hate you," Aimée warned in a quivering voice. "Why would you want me against my will? Doesn't it matter to you that I . . . belong to Bryan—and always will, no matter what . . . happens?"

"It will make it all the sweeter—to take his prized possession."

Remembering his clammy, moist hands on her throat, his sensuous lips seeking hers, Aimée panicked and a scream escaped from her throat.

Titus Tilson turned his body toward Aimée and he no longer offered her her heart's desire. His hand reached out and slapped her across the face and his voice rasped, "Be quiet, Aimée. You are disturbing the horses."

She shrank back in the corner of the carriage and felt her cheek with her hand. Her skin was on fire. To be slapped like a servant—she hated him for it, but the weakness she felt on the banquette was still with her and she had no way of escaping for the moment.

On into the countryside the carriage traveled. One hour —two? Only vaguely aware of the scenery outside the carriage, Aimée sat, her brain refusing to function to tell her what to do.

"I am glad you have chosen to refrain from hysterics, Aimée." Titus Tilson's rough, raspy voice broke through the silence and then took on a softer note. "You will not regret coming with me. I will make you swoon with love far better than that cold husband of yours, Aimée."

"Do you think you could ever take Bryan's place?" she snapped. "Ever send me into the same rapture I feel in his arms?" Aimée sneered at the man in disgust. "And if you . . . take me, you will have to tell me when you have finished, for I daresay I will feel *nothing*."

"You are brave, Aimée, to talk to me this way. But if you think to destroy my ardor for you, then you are wrong. I shall enjoy . . . subduing you to my will, and no amount of struggling or tears will save you."

His voice had lost its soft tone and again he was threatening. "My body still bears the marks you put there," he continued, "and before this day is ended, I shall have my revenge. For it will be *your* body that bears the marks this time."

The silence grew while Aimée shivered. She did not know what was the matter with her—this feeling of weakness, her body suddenly cold, the throbbing in her head.

Finally the carriage turned down a long oak-lined drive, a dark, shadowed drive. Overhead the gnarled, leafy limbs of the massive moss-covered oaks shut out the sunlight.

A plantation—deserted—yet the fields were planted and green. Another of Colonel Tilson's speculations, a means of getting rich from the spoils of war?

Who would think to look for her here? And who would wish to look for her? Bryan? When he realized what had happened to her? No, he would not want her anymore. Now he could wash his hands of her without a qualm, without a twinge of conscience. He would feel no responsibility- for her welfare after Colonel Titus Tilson had finished with her.

The carriage stopped at the porte cochère, and Aimée sat quietly, looking at the decaying old mansion. Paint was peeling from its sides and two of the tall round columns across the gallery were leaning at an angle.

"This is . . . your house?" Aimée asked.

Colonel Tilson, pushing himself from the tall seat, hopped down and tied the reins to the hitching post. "Yes, my dear, it's my house. One day I shall renovate it if I decide to keep you here."

"But your wife in the North," Aimée protested.

"Shall remain in the North. It's too bad I will be unable to marry you, but that will not matter with me."

He lifted her from the carriage and she stood unsteadily on the ground beside him.

"Do you think Bryan would permit you to keep me here?"

The colonel laughed. "Bryan Garrard is a proud man. He would have nothing to do with soiled goods. After today he will make no fuss to have you returned to him. No, Aimée, you are mine, and you might as well become used to the idea."

With his hand on her arm, he guided her toward the house, up the steps, and across the gallery. The glass on each side of the door was shattered and the wooden door, warped and peeling, was easily pushed open.

Dust and heat rose up to greet her in the once elegant hallway. A lizard scuttled across the floor, leaving its trail imprinted in the dust.

The faded strains of music echoed down the stairs and Aimée gave a start at the haunting sound—a memory stored far back in her mind. But then she remembered what it was—the wind bells attached to a swinging branch outside, nothing else.

Like a pilgrim visiting some ancient shrine, she went from room to room, scarcely aware of the man following her. She touched the broken vase in the niche near the stairs, and then her feet carried her into the library. The mildewed book had fallen from the shelf and now lay desecrated, its leather binding chewed away by some wild creature. And the voices—dim at first—grew louder until they crescendoed in her ears. She covered her ears with her hands, but the shrieking, haunting voices continued. "Aimée, look around you. You will be mistress of all this."

"My dear, are you all right?"

The colonel's voice went unheeded. She continued to

walk from room to room, gleaning the memories of Dresden. Into the dining room . . . the tables laden with food. Up the stairs she ran, to the bedroom she had shared that night with Michele . . . the rice powder and crushed rose petals . . . "Come, Felicité, Vincent, and Bastile." And then to the ballroom—the waltz, her crinolines swirling round and round, faster and faster, her feet lifted from the floor by the Viennese waltz—one, two, three— swirling, swirling, and so dizzy, until the room spun like a globe and her head so light, her mouth filled with cotton, and her body on fire—

Chapter 41

The faded red velvet draperies hanging in tatters caught the sunlight pouring through the windows. Aimée lay on the ballroom floor and from this position she could see the intricate pattern of the plaster on the ceiling. Her only movement was to trace with her eyes the shape of the cracked rosettes in the garland surrounding each chandelier.

There was an uneasy quiet in the room while she struggled to orient herself to what had happened.

Dresden—she was back at Dresden. But now it belonged to Titus Tilson. Funny that she had not recognized it at once, even in its decay. But perhaps it was not so surprising, since she had never approached it before by the land side—only by the river.

And Colonel Tilson? Where was he? Why had he left her in the ballroom—alone, on the floor?

The sound of footsteps on the groaning stairs forced

her to sit up quickly, but her head reeled from the swift change of position. She reached out her arms to steady herself, but her head still spun and her arms were weak.

"Katinka?"

The blond-haired girl stood before her, holding a glass of wine. "Here, drink this, Mrs. Garrard. It will make you feel better."

Aimée's hands trembled, and seeing this, Katinka stooped and held the goblet to her lips. The wine was vinegary and Aimée, after one sip, refused another. Pushing the glass from her lips, she asked, "How . . . did you get here, Katinka?"

"We came up the river—Colonel Garrard and I."

"Bryan? He's here, too?"

"Yes."

"But how did you know where to find me?"

"Colonel Garrard went to the tax office—to find out the location of Colonel Tilson's other property, when there was no sign of you in his house on Rampart Street. He had Silas stay to keep a lookout there, while we came on to Dresden."

"But how did Bryan know it was Colonel Tilson?"

Katinka hesitated, and then with a guilty expression, she ventured, "Silas told him. I . . . hope you're not angry with him."

"Anderson made no promise to me, Katinka. It was Colonel Tilson who insisted he keep silent."

"Are you feeling better now?" Katinka asked.

"Yes," Aimée replied, and with the help of Katinka, she rose to her feet.

Aimée gazed around her, seeing the ballroom in all its decay. She did not want to remain any longer. She wanted to escape the memories that boxed her in—in this house that had once smelled of beeswax and delicate aromas of food, but now held odors of dust and mildew and nesting mice.

"I need fresh air, Katinka. I am so hot," Aimée said, holding her hand to her forehead, "Help me out to the gallery, please."

The troubled look spread over Katinka's face. "No,

Mrs. Garrard. The colonel said you were to be kept inside until . . ."

Aimée saw the frustration and the effort to disguise it. Katinka was hiding something from her.

"Bryan—where is he? And where is Colonel Tilson?"

Katinka did not answer and Aimée started toward the stairs.

"I'll get you a chair to sit on, Mrs. Garrard. You mustn't go outside."

But the willful Aimée pushed back Katinka's restraining hand and walked unsteadily down the stairs.

Katinka followed her as Aimée crossed the long narrow hallway on the first floor and went out onto the front gallery that stretched the width of the house.

"Please, Mrs. Garrard. The colonel does not want you to see . . ."

Aimée paused between the old columns, and her eyes searched for Bryan. There, on the lawn beyond the magnolia tree, she saw him. The flash of steel was magnified in the sunlight as Bryan matched blows with Titus Tilson.

"No—Oh, Katinka, stop them. They mustn't fight."

"It's . . . too late, Mrs. Garrard."

In her mind Aimée heard Vickie's voice. "Colonel Tilson is an expert with the sword."

She wrung her hands in distress—wrung her hands and prayed for Bryan, that he would not be killed by the broad, heavyset man he now faced.

Aimée shielded her eyes from the glaring sun, and she followed every movement—not wanting to see, yet not daring to take her eyes from the battle before her.

Thrust and parry—back and forth. Colonel Tilson lunged for Bryan, but Bryan stepped aside and the thrust was impotent.

A relieved sigh came from Aimée's lips at the action.

The swish of steel cutting through the air alternated with the blunt sound of blade against blade. This was no friendly exhibition of prowess for the benefit of spectators. It was a death fight between two men. And the clash of blades and the heaves of the two giants indicated the fury of the fighting.

The agony was more than she could bear and at the

next thrust by Colonel Tilson, Aimée in her fright screamed her husband's name. "Bryan!"

The sound pierced the late afternoon and for one split second Bryan's attention was diverted from his opponent. Colonel Tilson took that moment to draw blood. Bryan stumbled and fell to the ground, and in the horror of watching the red stain widen on Bryan's arm, Aimée realized what she had done. She moved as if she would go to him, but Katinka stopped her.

Bryan was now up and facing his opponent again. Aimée put her hand to her mouth to prevent another sound from escaping her lips.

If Bryan died, it would be her fault. She must not utter another sound.

They were evenly matched in size, the two men fighting upon the turf in the late afternoon light. And Aimée, her body weak and her heart faint, clung to the pillared column and continued to watch from the distance.

In and out of the trees the sun came—its rays blinding her for a moment before its brilliance receded into the cover of the oaks. And then, in a sudden burst, the golden orb of light broke through and hung suspended from the heavens by its threads of gold.

Against the blinding light, Aimée could not distinguish one man from the other. Her eyes watered in protest, in being forced to compete against the sun. But still, she faced the fight, seeing little until one man fell to the ground and did not get up—one man in blue uniform, but which?

She could not look. She could not watch while the victor walked toward her. Afraid to lift her head, Aimée gazed at the dusty military boots as they trod up the steps and onto the gallery. They stopped before her and a voice spoke gently.

"I will take you home now. Come, Aimée."

She clutched at the hand that was held out to her.

"Bryan," she whispered, and flung herself into his arms.

He stroked her hair and quieted her sobs. "Hush, Aimée. It's all right."

"Your arm—are you in pain, Bryan?"

He shook his head. "It's only a nick, Aimée. But I am glad you were quiet for the rest of the time. Your scream didn't help me keep my mind on what I was doing."

"I am sorry. Did you . . . kill him, Bryan?"

"No, he is alive, although he deserved to die for the pain he has caused you."

The men from the boat came from the landing and Bryan, with Aimée beside him, gave instructions for the colonel to be moved.

Aimée stared down at the man who had harassed her for such a long time. She no longer felt the sick, cold fear. His power over her was gone.

Seeing her, the man on the ground moaned, "Delphine —I did it for *you,* Delphine."

He reached out for her, but Aimée shrank against Bryan.

"I will always love you, Delphine," he said. Then his hand fell to his side and his eyes closed.

Chapter 42

A week later Aimée sat in the garden of the townhouse. Despite the heat, her body shivered.

"Aimée, will you . . . forgive me?" A contrite Vickie stood before her in the garden.

"Yes, Vickie. I forgive you."

"I am glad, Aimée. And I hope that we can be friends, especially since we are married to brothers. Clay is . . . beholden to Bryan for many things. It would be difficult for Clay if you and I continued to be . . . unfriendly to each other."

Vickie was still with Aimée when Clotilde appeared. "Have you taken your quinine for today?" the woman asked Aimée.

"Yes, Cousin Clotilde. The bitter taste has reminded me all afternoon. I hope Doctor Floud will not force me to take it much longer."

"You look much better, my dear. But you gave us such a scare. We thought you had yellow fever for certain. What a relief when we realized it was malaria instead. Although the chills and fever have taken their toll, you are lucky to have nothing worse."

Yes, Aimée thought, extremely lucky.

"Have you heard how Colonel Tilson is, Cousin Clotilde?" Aimée asked.

"He is slowly improving. I have heard that he has resigned from the army and will be leaving New Orleans for good as soon as he is able to travel."

And Bryan? What would happen to him? Would he be forced to resign from the army because of the duel? And would he also leave New Orleans?

After Clotilde had gone into the house, Bryan came into the garden. He seemed surprised to find Vickie sitting beside the convalescing Aimée.

With the start of another chill, Aimée began to shake and her teeth chattered. Vickie, with a solicitous air, placed the shawl around Aimée's shoulders, and looking up at Bryan, she said, "Poor dear—she is having another chill. I think you should take her inside, Bryan."

Bryan lifted Aimée in his arms and headed for the house. "Will you come in, too, Vickie?" Aimée asked, but Vickie, walking beside them, declined.

"No, Aimée. I will go home now. But I'll be back tomorrow to see about you."

Once inside the house, Bryan asked, "Have you two buried the hatchet?"

"I . . . hope so, Bryan," Aimée replied between shudders.

Gradually she got her strength back, and between visits

from Vickie and Michele, Aimée had no chance to be lonely.

One afternoon when Michele was sitting with her, Aimée asked, "Have you been able to see Jean?"

"No—but I have been able to smuggle some medicine to him. He has seen me through the slit of the window near the banquette, but there seems to be no way that I can get inside. The Customs House guards its prisoners too well," she added bitterly.

"Have you applied for a pass, Michele?"

"Yes, but so many women have used such a variety of excuses to get inside that the guards are now hardened to any request—especially since some of the prisoners escaped not long ago." Michele laughed. "Can you imagine a prisoner dressed in women's clothes—mincing his way past the guards? That's what happened the last time someone escape."

Aimée smiled. "It would be hard for Jean to pretend to be a woman. His height alone would give him away."

"I shall think of something," Michele said determinedly. "Even if I have to seduce the head of the guards."

"Michele!"

"Oh, fiddle, Aimée! Don't sound so shocked."

At the sight of Bryan coming toward them, their conversation about Jean stopped.

"Good afternoon, Michele," Bryan said before leaning over to kiss Aimée.

"Good afternoon, Colonel."

Michele's voice was low and provocative and Aimée, turning quickly toward Michele, caught the speculative look on Michele's face.

Bryan smiled and sank down in the chair opposite them. His eyes remained on Michele for an instant longer than Aimée liked. Was Michele trying to flirt with Bryan?

"What have you two been doing this afternoon?" Bryan asked, now looking at Aimée.

"Waiting for you, Colonel," Michele said before Aimée had a chance to answer, "to take us for an afternoon drive."

The amused look remained in Bryan's gray eyes.

"Do you have any particular drive in mind?"

Aimée felt superfluous as Bryan and Michele continued their exchange.

"Any place that you would like to take us. I am sure your choice will be excellent."

"Aimée? Do you feel up to it?" Bryan inquired.

"Of course, Bryan. We . . . we will get our parasols and be ready soon." She rose from the chair. "Michele, are you coming?"

Michele smiled and followed Aimée.

If she had said no, would Bryan still have gone, taking Michele and leaving her at home? Aimée was jealous. Michele was up to something. Was she planning to use Bryan for her own purposes? Aimée inwardly chastised herself. No, she would not allow such disturbing thoughts to invade her mind. But wasn't Michele used to getting her way—except with Etienne?

"Your husband is very handsome—even if he *is* a Yankee," Michele commented.

Aimée agreed and walked into the house.

The ride was uneventful, except for the meeting of two of Bryan's fellow officers on the river road. In the shade of the huge oaks Bryan stopped the carriage and Aimée watched while Michele did her best to captivate the two young officers on horseback. One was Lieutenant Steiker, who had accompanied Katinka to the ill-fated *bal masqué*. Aimée could see that he had easily succumbed to Michele's charm.

"What does Lieutenant Steiker do, Colonel Garrard?" Michele wanted to know on their way back to town.

"He's on duty at the Customs House," Bryan replied, "when he is not in the field."

A satisfied look crept into Michele's face. Poor Lieutenant Steiker would not know what had hit him, thought Aimée, with Michele determined to pursue her course to get inside the Customs House.

Through the slow death throes of the Confederacy, New Orleans remained much the same. Union shipping and trading went on as usual. The burnt-out land yielded few crops, but food shipped from the Midwest was plentiful for those who could afford to buy it. If it were not for the Free Market twice a week, when the poor were given food, many would have starved to death.

One by one, the Confederate ports closed—Mobile, Charleston—occupied by Union forces, until Wilmington was the only open port in the Confederacy. There was little fighting going on except between opposing armies in the Carolinas and Virginia, and the Army of the Gulf remained in New Orleans, occupying the city and enjoying its varied offerings.

While the Union soldiers filled their time with gambling, drinking, and going to the theater, the Confederate prisoners in the Customs House waited and hoped for deliverance. And among them was Jean Brisot.

Everywhere, Aimée and Michele were seen together. She was happy to share her clothes with Michele, but viewing her friend's flirtatious behavior, Aimée began to wonder if she had forgotten her reason for coming to New Orleans.

Lieutenant Steiker was a frequent visitor in the house on Royal Street, and often he would escort Michele when they went to the theater or on long drives around the south shore of Lake Pontchartrain.

The day after they had attended the theater together, Aimée and Michele sat in the salon of the townhouse. Michele was restless, hopping up to finger an object on the table, and then flitting to a chair to sit for a moment before getting up again.

Michele looked up and caught Aimée's gaze on her.

"What is wrong, Michele? Why are you so restless?"

"I . . . don't know, Aimée. I think perhaps I need to . . . go to confession.

Aimée nodded. She, too, had not been to confession for a long time. "Would you like to go now?" she asked.

Michele, glancing swiftly at the clock, shook her head. "Not quite yet. A little later, I think. Do you suppose we could . . . take the carriage and go for a short drive later?"

Michele was almost childish in her request. Indulging her, Aimée agreed.

An hour later they drove along the street to St. Louis

Cathedral. Michele appeared to be unusually nervous, even more so than she had been earlier in the day. But she asked to take over the reins of the horses, and as they came to the cathedral, she drew the carriage into the alleyway.

"Why are you stopping here, Michele?" Aimée asked, puzzled that she had not stopped in the square facing the cathedral.

"You will soon see," the girl whispered. Alarmed, Aimée looked in the same direction as Michele. At the side door of the cathedral lingered a tall priest in his traditional black robe. Stepping from the shadows made by the portico, the priest hurried out to them.

Jean—it was Jean Brisot, dressed in the priest's robes.

It happened so quickly. Jean was in the carriage beside them and Michele slapped the reins so that the horses started off. Michele forced the animals into a steady pace, not fast enough to attract attention. Passing by the people lining the banquettes, Jean slid to the floor in the shadows of the carriage. No one would think it out of the ordinary that the two girls were going for their afternoon ride.

When they had reached the edge of the city, the horses were put to a gallop and Michele kept up the pace on the shell road while Jean struggled up from the floor to find a more comfortable seat. Even that small exertion left him breathing heavily. He was still a sick man.

Aimée, unknowingly, had provided his means of escape. If it were discovered, who would believe that she had known nothing of Michele's plans? Would Bryan believe her? It was doubtful. She could have cried out, but seeing the sick man, she knew she would not betray him.

From time to time Michele glanced back in the direction of the city. So far, no one had followed them on the road, and the bayou was deserted. They soon reached an uninhabited part of the shore not far from where Aimée had once hidden her boat in a willow copse. The cypress knees jutted from the water, and there between the cypress, hidden under a camouflage of reeds, was another boat.

"I am sorry, Aimée, to involve you," Michele said, speaking to her for the first time since leaving New Orleans, "but I had to do it."

Michele kissed her on the cheek, and helping Jean from the carriage, she partially supported him as they struggled toward the boat.

Aimée did not wait any longer. She turned the carriage and began the trip back. And then she stopped. She saw the cloud of dust swirling in her direction. With a certainty, Aimée knew that Jean had been missed and that they had been followed after all.

"If you are ever caught, aiding the enemy—"

She could not face going back to the Castle. There was no alternative but to escape with Michele and Jean—if they were not already out of reach.

Aimée headed back toward the shoreline. She stopped the horses and jumped from the carriage. Wading into the water, Aimée called, "Michele, wait—I'm coming with you."

But Michele, seeing the soldiers in sight, continued rowing away from the shore. . . .

Chapter 43

Aimée sat in the dingy prison cell. Her one consolation was that she was in the Customs House, not the Castle.

It had been a long week and during that time Bryan had not come. Her clothes and other necessary articles that she was allowed to have had been left by Katinka.

She sat, letting her hand fall on the strings of the lute. It had been brought that day, and Aimée was surprised that she had been permitted to keep it.

"Hey, beautiful," a male voice called from another cell. "Play us the 'Bonnie Blue Flag'—and we'll all join in."

But Aimée put the lute aside and played no more. She looked at the wall, where the last prisoner had marked off the days. She had counted them—eighty-one days in all—and the scratching of the last days was barely visible, as if the hand that had etched the marks into the stone had gradually become weaker with the passage of time. Eighty-one days. Would she also have to resort to marks on the wall to keep account of the passing time? Already she had forgotten the day of the week. Soon it would not matter at all.

Aimée slept, ate the meager meals brought to her twice a day, and played the lute. There was nothing else to do. She was not even fortunate enough to have a cell with a slitted window looking out onto the banquette.

Aimée had offered no defense. She could not say that she had been duped by her best friend into supplying the horses and carriage for Jean Brisot's escape. And the soldier had sworn that she was attempting to escape also. It was considered justice that she take Jean Brisot's place in prison, although they had to isolate her from the other prisoners. She could not be placed in the same cell with the men.

Aimée lay on the cot in the corner of the cell and closed her eyes. She heard the footsteps down the hall, and when they paused at her cell door, her eyes flew open. The man quickly moved on.

"Bryan?" Aimée called. There was no answer. The man had gone.

At periodic intervals someone came to check on the state of her health. It was surprising that the white pallor was all that proclaimed her stay in the Customs House—that and the days etched upon the walls. If Aimée had counted correctly, it was April, 1865.

She was now almost twenty-one years old. For four years she had witnessed the terrible slaughter, the ravages of army fighting against army, with her land and her people paying the price of war—Etienne, Grand-père,

Juba. She, too, had paid the price.

The Rebel yell came from one of the prison cells, cutting through her thoughts with an enthusiasm never heard in the jail section of the Customs House. It was taken up by others all the way down the long row of cells— that indescribable, terrifying combination of sounds dredged from some ancestral war cry of the Scottish Highlands.

What was happening? Why all the noise? And then she heard the celebration in the streets.

"What is going on?" Aimée cried out.

"The war is over," the man in the next cell shouted back. "Lee has surrendered."

The war was over. They were defeated. Yet there was as much celebration among the Confederate prisoners as the Unionists on the streets. But could they be blamed? They would soon be free. They could go home.

Three days later the prisoners were taken from their cells. Aimée heard the key in the giant lock at her door. A guard called to her. "There is someone waiting for you, Mrs. Garrard. You are to come with me."

"Am I . . . free?" she asked.

"Yes, Mrs. Garrard, you are free."

Aimée, walking beside the guard, could not keep up. Her knees trembled and her steps lagged. The guard slowed his pace to fit hers until they had climbed the stairs and were in a small room on the main floor. The exercise had winded her and she rested in the straight-backed chair. Aimée smiled and touched the chair. For so long she had had the cot to sit on—nothing else.

The inner door opened and Bryan stood before her. He made no move to kiss her, but stared at her coldly.

"You have heard the news?" he asked.

"Yes, Bryan. We are defeated."

A look of anger crossed his face but he continued. "Vickie is here with some fresh clothes, Aimée. You will need to . . . change before I take you home."

Aimée did not trust her voice to acknowledge the information. She sat in the chair as if he had not spoken, and she waited for Vickie. Bryan closed the door and was gone.

It was Vickie who maintained a degree of normalcy as the carriage containing the three of them swung down Royal Street to the pink stucco and brick townhouse.

The yellow dress that Vickie had brought her to wear did nothing for her. And her skin, so white with the unhealthy pallor, seemed almost transparent, stretched across her fragile bones. Aimée had lost weight, but that was to be expected. Luckily she had not developed the fever or smallpox.

"Oh, my dear, my dear." Cousin Clotilde hugged her and then fumbled for her handkerchief that she had tucked into the bosom of her dress. Cousin Jorge, Katinka, and Anderson were also there to greet her. But Bryan stood aloof, apart from the joyful reunion.

Later that night Aimée stood at the window in the bedroom. It was hard being in the same house with Bryan —and even harder to share the same bedroom.

Bryan's voice sounded in her ear. "You must not be bitter, Aimée. Your Confederacy could never have won. You know that—I am only surprised that your army was able to hold on for so long. Accept your defeat, Aimée. The fighting is over."

"And you, Bryan? What do you plan to do now that you are the victor?"

"I still have a month left to serve in the army, and when that time is up, I will not reenlist. I have not decided yet . . . whether to take you back to Boston with me, or not."

Not decided? Did that mean he would leave without her? Now that the war was over, she was to be discarded along with his uniform, his army rations, and his regulations?

Aimée could stand it no longer. She would not beg him to take her with him. She fled from the room—fled, not knowing in which direction she went. The muffled sound of someone calling her followed her footsteps down the banquette.

The streets, the banquettes, overflowed with jubilant faces. It was wrong—this celebration of defeat and death.

The streets should have been draped in black; the people should have been mourning the dead and the cause that was lost.

Aimée shrank from the boisterous noise surrounding her, the laughter, the taunting voices of the victor. She fled to the cathedral, but she had brought nothing with her to cover her head, so she stopped at the door.

The hand closed around her arm. Her husband Bryan towered over her. "You should not be on the streets alone, Aimée. I will wait for you."

"I cannot go in, Bryan. I . . . I brought nothing to cover my head."

He reached into his pocket and pulled from it a white linen handkerchief. "Will this do?" he asked.

Gratefully she accepted the handkerchief and hurried into the cathedral.

On the way home Bryan acted as if Aimée had not fled from him. His voice was even when he spoke.

"Aimée, I have decided to rebuild Thornfell for you. I have been thinking for a long time that New Orleans is not a healthy place for you to live."

Aimée blinked back the sudden tears. So he had made up his mind. She was to stay in Louisiana.

"Does that not make you happy, Aimée—to know that you will have your childhood home restored?"

Happy? Where could she be happy—without Bryan?

"Thank you, Bryan," she said, utterly bereft. "That is . . . kind of you."

He looked at her in a puzzled manner. "If it pleases you, then why the tears?"

"I am . . . tired, Bryan. So much has happened today."

He seemed to accept her explanation and his hand under her elbow gave her additional support.

"Some type of temporary quarters will need to be built first," he said, continuing his plans aloud, "the workers hired, the materials ordered. Do you think Clotilde will be happy, having her musical garden again?"

"She has missed it, Bryan. It meant so much to her."

Within the week Bryan and Cousin Jorge left for Thornfell. Katinka and Anderson, who had been married while

Aimée was in prison, moved from the carriage house to be with Aimée and Clotilde while the two men were away. Bryan had taken the dogs with him. Before, when he had left, Bryan had always made sure that Fréki and Geri had stayed behind to protect her. Now it did not matter. There was a wide breach between them that would not heal, even though she shared his bed.

At the same time another breach occurred and the promise of healing a divided nation was shattered. Lincoln had been assassinated and the country was in turmoil.

"Punish the seceding states" became the cry of the radicals. Had the South not been punished enough by having its land ravaged and its young men slain? Must it now suffer the additional humiliation of being governed by scalawags, carpetbaggers, and former slaves? To Aimée, that would be the final insult and punishment.

Bryan and Cousin Jorge made trips back and forth to Thornfell, but Bryan, sensing Aimée's reluctance to hear about the rebuilding, said little to her about it.

He was still away on the afternoon that Aimée, carrying flowers for Tante Dee Dee and Prosper Gautier, walked to the St. Louis Cemetery.

With the Gautier family removed from Dresden, there was no one but Aimée to remember the flowers on special days for Prosper's grave, so once again she began taking the weekly bouquets to decorate the graves.

It was getting late, the twilight hour. A deepening lavender threaded its dye into the paler blue skein of the sky. Aimée placed her flowers and hurried to the gate, the shadows creeping stealthily between the mausoleums.

The tall figure waited outside the gate—Bryan.

"Katinka said you were at the cemetery, so I came to walk home with you."

"When did you get back?" Aimée inquired politely.

"About an hour ago."

He was not in uniform. Officially, he was no longer in the army, although Anderson still called him "Colonel Garrard." In civilian clothes he looked just as much a giant as he had in army blue, but somehow he did not look so menacing.

"You brought flowers for your aunt's grave?" he inquired.

"Yes, and for Prosper's grave also—since there is no one left in his family."

The softness in Bryan's face disappeared and the jaw muscle jumped as he clamped his teeth together.

They walked in silence for a while, until Bryan said, "I am glad to see that you are looking healthier."

"Thank you, Bryan."

And then the silence trod with them.

There was an awkwardness between them, a politeness, as if each had to be careful not to display true feelings to the other, and when they had reached the townhouse, Aimée was glad. Now she would be busy helping Jou-Jou with supper, and for a while she would not have to listen to Bryan and Cousin Jorge discuss Thornfell and its restoration.

"You have a visitor, Aimée," Cousin Clotilde said to her. "He's waiting in the salon."

"Who is it, Cousin Clotilde?" Aimée asked.

"It's John—John Runefelt."

"John? He's here—in New Orleans?" The smile burst from Aimée's lips, and without a glance toward Bryan, she rushed toward the salon, leaving Cousin Clotilde and Bryan in the downstairs hall.

The man stood by the window, but at the sound of her entrance, he turned to face her. His skin was tawny from the sun, and his body strong and lean.

"John," she said, holding out her hand to greet him. "When did you get back?"

"Yesterday, Aimée. I . . . hope you don't mind my coming to see you?"

"Mind? I should have been very sad if you had not, John. But sit down," she urged, "and tell me what has happened since our . . . experience on the ship."

"I escaped that night into Nassau, Aimée, and waited for the British ship to make port. Several days later we sailed for England, but you know as well as I do that my mission—to get England to recognize us—was not successful."

His eyes lingered on her as their conversation waned.

"And your husband—he was not fatally wounded?"

The voice from the doorway answered John's question. "No, I was not fatally wounded, as you can see," Bryan said in a frigid voice.

"John—my husband, Bryan Garrard," she said quickly. "Bryan, this is . . . John Runefelt."

Aimée feared that Bryan was going to be rude. His face flushed and the anger was apparent in his eyes.

"And now that you are home, what do you plan to do, Mr. Runefelt?" Bryan asked, his voice stressing each word.

"I am in no hurry to decide," John answered, looking Bryan squarely in the eye. "Since I have been away for so long, I shall spend some time in New Orleans before going anywhere else."

Then John turned back to Aimée. "I . . . am glad, Aimée, that everything is well with you." He started for the door and Aimée protested.

"You are not leaving, are you—so soon after you have come? Cousin Clotilde and Jorge will want to see you. Please stay for dinner, John."

But John shook his head. "Clotilde, Jorge, and I have already visited. I only stayed long enough to see . . . if you were all right."

"You won't change your mind?" Aimée asked impulsively.

"Mr. Runefelt has already declined your invitation, Aimée," Bryan interrupted. "I expect he has . . . appointments elsewhere."

John smiled. "Yes, I should not delay any longer. Good-bye, Aimée." He then nodded his head toward Bryan. "Colonel Garrard."

"No longer *Colonel*, I'm afraid," Bryan corrected him. "I am a civilian now."

When Aimée had seen John to the door, she went upstairs to the bedroom to change for dinner. Surprisingly, Bryan was ahead of her—standing at the foot of the bed and waiting.

In an imperious voice he said, "Tomorrow, you and Jou-Jou are to be ready to return to Thornfell with me."

"But I thought the house was not finished."

"It isn't. You will have to made do with the overseer's cottage that has been completed."

"But why, Bryan? Why not wait—"

Not letting her finish, he said, "There is a rumor of a cholera outbreak."

"There is *always* a rumor of a cholera outbreak or a yellow fever epidemic in New Orleans, Bryan," she countered. "Are you . . . certain that is the reason?"

"Why do you question my motives, Aimée?" His voice was severe, but Aimée did not quake at its angry tone. "Have I not the right to decide where my wife is to be —regardless of the reason?"

"It seems that you did not . . . decide until John Runefelt appeared," Aimée said tauntingly.

"And what does it matter *when* I made up my mind? Sufficient to say that I have decided."

Her feet lifted from the floor as Bryan crushed her to him. "Do you think I am going to leave you here in New Orleans for John Runefelt to woo you—or for you to mourn over the dead each day with your bouquets of flowers? No, Aimée, there is just so much a husband will allow. And I will *not* allow you to stay here."

And so it was on the following day that Aimée and Jou-Jou packed their belongings, and with the frizzle-feathered chicken, the dogs, and Aimée's lute, climbed into the waiting carriage to head for Thornfell.

Aimée was sullen and said little on the way. Not only was Bryan planning to remove her from New Orleans for good—he was also making sure that she saw no more of John.

If he actually believed that a cholera outbreak had started, Bryan would have insisted that everyone else in the house come with them. But no, he was only taking her, to punish her for John's return to New Orleans.

Well, she would see about that. . . .

The voice beside her was threatening. "Your eyes have given you away, my dear. I do not know what mischief you are planning, but know that it will be properly dealt with. I suggest you find a more suitable expression for an obedient wife."

She gazed at him in astonishment. Could he read her very thoughts?

Chapter 44

The carriage traveled on, up the shell road, until they had reached Lake Pontchartrain and the ferry.

Aimée and Jou-Jou got out of the carriage and Bryan led the nervous horses across the chained planks, onto the ferry.

For once, Aimée was glad that Bryan had insisted she bring her cloak. The wind whipped over the lake and the sudden chill penetrated the cotton of her dress. Jou-Jou helped her into the wrap and Aimée tied the ribbons to keep it from being blown off into the lake. If she lost this one, too . . . .

In the middle of the lake the water looked much more intimidating than it had at its narrow neck close to Lake Borgne, where she had rowed across on her trips from Thornfell to New Orleans. Here, the waves lapped against the sides of the ferry in increasing ferocity, and at its constant movement, Aimée became nauseated as she had in the freight car of the train that night when she had hidden from the guards.

"Madame is seasick, *n'est-ce pas?*" Jou-Jou whispered close to her.

"A little," Aimée admitted, but only to Jou-Jou.

When they reached the northern shore, Aimée was glad to get back on land again. Her queasiness subsided soon after they left the ferry.

But fresh problems occurred, delaying their journey. It began to rain, and the yellow-dirt road became a clogged mire the horses had to strain against.

Thankful for the isinglass across the windows, Aimée huddled in a corner and tried to keep dry. The dogs lay curled at her feet and pretended to sleep while watching Jou-Jou's pet chicken with a practiced eye. But Jou-Jou, protective as usual, kept the coop close to her, and with her dark looks dared the dogs to harm her *petite poule*.

At last they were at Thornfell. The carriage pulled off from the main road and turned down the long avenue of trees. Despite the weather, despite her reason for being brought, Aimée was at Thornfell and her heart quickened because of it. She anxiously looked for the house across the rolling meadow, but the land was covered with weeds and jungle growth so unkempt looking that it was difficult to see the house over it. It was still a shell and Aimée received some small satisfaction from this, knowing that until it was finished, Bryan would be near.

Not too soon—please don't let the house be completed too soon.

Sheds and other buildings dotted the outlying area, and passing near them, the carriage, pulled by the matching horses, went on until they had come to a rise in the land, near the site of the old sugar house. There, upon a slight knoll, stood the overseer's cottage, which would be her home until the big house was completed.

It was a modest house. The cypress boards, still new, had not yet taken on the weathered gray they would eventually be colored. It had a small porch where one could sit and fan oneself in the hot weather . . . and the stone chimney gave indication that they would not be cold during the winter months.

Where had Bryan gotten the stones, Aimée wondered? Had they been the ballast from some ship that had come to New Orleans? She made a mental promise to look for a stone that had not been used. She would right the error in the family cemetery as soon as she could. Juba deserved his own name on his grave.

While Jou-Jou started the fire, Bryan unloaded the carriage, bringing in the trunks that had been lashed to the back of the vehicle. After Aimée brought in the food they had packed, she removed her wet outer garments and spread them before the fire to dry. She hugged herself near the hearth, slowly turning from side to side and back to front, until the slight dampness of her camisole and crinolines disappeared.

Bryan, returning from feeding and stabling the horses, asked, "Have you looked over the cottage yet, Aimée?"

"No, Bryan. I went into the room where the trunks are to get dry clothes, but I could not unlock the trunk."

He stared at her and grinned. His arm drew her to him. "Come with me and I'll open it for you."

"You're wet, Bryan. Don't hold me so closely," she protested. "I have already roasted myself like a hen on a spit to get dry, and I don't wish to start over."

But Bryan held her even closer and ran his hand up the curve of her throat to her cheek. "Your cheeks are flushed from the heat, Aimée—a very appetizing picture. Is your blood warm, too?"

She avoided him as he leaned his head toward her. Bryan laughed again and released her, saying, "I can wait until tonight to find out. A fire kindled must be nurtured to full flame, and we have too much to do at the moment to tend to the fires, do we not, my pet?"

Aimée changed clothes, ignoring her husband, for she was still peeved at his domineering manner. When she went into the kitchen, Jou-Jou already had the gumbo steaming.

"Zat husband of yours will be verree hongry, so I feex nice beeg pot of gombo."

While the gumbo was cooking over the fire, Aimée wandered over the cottage. There was one main room with a double fireplace that backed into the kitchen. Sparsely furnished with crude furniture that was far different from the elegant, sophisticated artistry of the French cabinet-makers, the cottage was nevertheless built to take hard wear—and in the bedroom adjoining the main keeping room, the dried moss mattress lay over the roped bed. How many times Aimée had watched the moss gatherers turning their moss with pitchforks so it would dry evenly in the sun. And now she would be sleeping on such a mattress instead of the downy, soft feather mattress that she was so used to. An example of Bryan's New England thrift? Would he furnish Thornfell in the same manner, with no regard for comfort, since he would not be sharing it with her? Only Cousin Jorge and Clotilde. . . .

On the back of the porch was a room just large enough for a bed—the typical visiting parson's room, self-contained, with its own entrance from the back. And it was in here that Jou-Jou would sleep. No priest or traveling parson was likely to come their way anytime soon.

For all her reluctance in coming, Aimée had to admit her eagerness to explore the land again, to travel over the countryside and become reacquainted with the sugarcane fields, the bayou where the old bull alligator bellowed and the pelican zealously surveyed his domain.

It was a strange dual feeling that night, sharing everything with Bryan, yet knowing that one day Bryan would not be there with her.

Aimée lay on the stuffed mattress of moss and listened to the rain outside. In Bryan's arms she was warm and comfortable, and the eeriness of the dreary, silent night, punctuated only by the drops of rain, held no fright for her.

"Are you still angry with me, Aimée, that I brought you with me?"

She hesitated before replying. "It was your . . . arrogant manner, Bryan. I had no say about whether I came or not. No choice—only to obey you."

"And is this why you were planning your revenge on the way—because I gave you no choice? Will you continually try to run away from me?"

What could she say without giving away her feelings, her desolation at knowing that he was to leave her? "I . . . was not planning revenge, Bryan," she stated simply.

"I do not believe you, Aimée. I have seen that look before. If I remember correctly, you went around for days before the ill-fated ball, determined to find a costume that would assure my taking you home immediately. But I shall be on watch in the coming days, you may be sure, even as you ply me with that deceptively innocent look. I warn you, Aimée, I shall be on guard against you this time."

"If it is so unpleasant for you to have me here, then why did you not leave me in New Orleans?" she teased.

"Did I say that it would be unpleasant, Aimée? No, you have misunderstood me. And remember—I gave you no choice whether to stay or come . . . just as I give you no choice now to deny me."

His lips came down upon hers, preventing any sound. Slowly he made love to her and the roped slats creaked under his weight.

"Bryan, the noise," she protested, remembering Jou-Jou in the back room.

"Must you always object to the sound of my love-making, Aimée?" He sat up, frowning, and climbed out of bed from the side nearest the door. Pulling her to her feet, he slung the mattress over his shoulders and disappeared into the keeping room. Moments later he returned. A startled Aimée, uncomprehending, stood in the same place where he had deposited her. But she found herself jerked along with him toward the hearth where the fire had settled down into glowing embers.

Bryan had moved the mattress to the floor by the hearth, where there would be no telltale sounds. He proceeded to push her gently onto the mattress. His hands, insistent and impatient, removed her gown, and her body took on the strange glow of the fire—warm and enticing.

"Ze love-birds verree lazy thees morning, *ma petite poule*," Jou-Jou said, kneeling by the hearth and poking at the fire.

Aimée quickly felt for her gown that lay on the floor beside her.

"Jou-Jou," Bryan called out, sitting up and rubbing his back. "Is there some magic potion you can make to get a wife to share a noisy bed with her husband? My back protests this sleeping on the floor."

410

Jou-Jou chuckled, "Eet not take much magic, monsieur. Jou-Jou just feex creak, so rope bed not sing."

Chapter 45

The workers swarmed over Thornfell, raising timbers, stone, and columns, mixing the mortar, and the sound of hammers made a pinging noise over the landscape. Bryan was amidst it all—talking, watching, and consulting the plans he had drawn.

While the work went on, the steady stream of returning Confederate soldiers passed by—some on wagons, but most of them on foot, so many maimed and scarred and cadaverous. Aimée opened the larder to them and handed out bread and provisions. She kept a cooking pot filled with gumbo, and while Bryan was at the big house, she dispensed food and coffee to the hungry hordes that traveled along the Pontchartrain shore from the battle-fields, hospitals, and Northern prison camps to their homes in western Louisiana.

"Aimée, have you had a St. Joseph's altar again?" Bryan asked, looking at the rapidly dwindling supplies. "I'm sure the workers have not eaten this much."

"There have been . . . some visitors, Bryan, each day. And they were . . . hungry."

Aimée was surprised that Bryan said nothing more after that. He kept his mind attuned to the steady completion of the house and the clearing of the fields for planting, and this allowed Aimée to work on her project.

In the shed she labored on the stone that she had purloined from the stockpile—worked on it amidst the few

411

other stones left unused, for it was too heavy to lift to take elsewhere. It was painstaking, etching Juba's name into the hard rock, but now it was almost finished and she was pleased that she could remove the false marker from his grave.

But how to get the stone to the cemetery—that was her dilemma. Aimée and Jou-Jou had cleared the fenced-in plot of its weeds and dug up wildflowers along the bayou to plant. What a pity that there were no headstones for her own *maman* and *papa*, lost in the flood. Perhaps later she would see to some suitable marker for them. She would have ample time through the years alone.

Aimée glanced down at the finished lettering, proud of her handiwork. Covering the stone with the old piece of cloth, she left the shed and walked back to the cottage. Tomorrow she would borrow one of the low wagons and ask a worker to lift it for her.

The next day Bryan left early and Aimée, impatient to see Juba's headstone in place, finished her morning chores, mended Bryan's shirts and gave them to Jou-Jou to wash. She set the table for the midday meal and helped Jou-Jou prepare it. When Bryan had eaten his meal, Aimée was eager. The rest of the afternoon was now her own.

She walked toward the shed, ready to see the stone in place, but when she opened the door, emptiness greeted her. Every single stone was gone.

The workers, they must have taken them to the house. But no, they couldn't use Juba's headstone—the one she had worked so painstakingly on. Aimée rushed from the shed to find Bryan to stop the workers from setting it into the cement, from ruining her hours of careful labor.

"Bryan," Aimée called above the noise of the roof workers, "where are the stones that were left in the shed?"

"Why, they were used this morning, Aimée, to finish the fireplace."

"But one was Juba's headstone, Bryan. I must have it back."

"It's far too late, Aimée," he answered, frowning. "You will have to find something else to use," he advised.

"But the lettering, Bryan—I spent so many hours carefully chiseling Juba's name. Did the workers not see the letters?"

"You know, Aimée, that the majority of the men can't read. To them, it meant nothing. They were merely following instructions in bringing the rest of the stones from the shed."

Aimée sank to the steps and her frustrated tears flowed vigorously. "I worked . . . so hard," she managed to say, "and for nothing."

"I am sorry, Aimée. You should have told me and then I would have seen that the workers left it alone. But now there is nothing anyone can do about it."

Aimée stared at her husband, so unmoved by the tragedy that had occurred. Standing up, she tore away from his restraining arm and ran from him, with her tears of frustration and disappointment choking her.

Not long after that Bryan went into New Orleans for additional supplies.

"Make a list of what you need, Aimée, and I will have it brought back for you," Bryan said.

"Am I not going with you?" Aimée asked.

"No, it takes too long in the carriage. I'll ride one of the horses and will be back by evening. I'll leave my pistol with you, Aimée, if it will make you feel safer, although the foreman will be listening out for you."

"I am not afraid, Bryan," Aimée replied fiercely, drawing herself up to her full height. "It's just that I . . . miss Katinka and Cousin Clotilde."

"They will be here soon enough. Now, get to your list—and you might consult Jou-Jou."

Aimée, indignant that she was not to be allowed to go with him, sat down to begin her list. She had no writing paper, for it was still scarce. She went to her trunk and secured an old envelope, one from a letter that she had kept after she and Prosper had become betrothed.

She looked down at Prosper's florid writing, the embellished letters of her name and the smaller letters in which his own name was written in the top left-hand corner of the envelope. The sight meant nothing to her.

Prosper's writing did not have the power to cause her heart to beat rapidly, as did the dark and bold writing of Bryan. She would never give up a scrap of paper that Bryan had put to words.

Impish mischief glowed in her eyes as she began her list. At the top she wrote, "1 headstone for Juba Barnard," and underneath it, the articles she and Jou-Jou needed. When she had finished, Aimée left it on the table for Bryan.

It was still dark when Bryan awoke her the next morning. Jou-Jou, knowing he wanted to get an early start, already had the coffee brewing, and the aroma reached the bedroom where Aimée lay on the roped bed beside Bryan.

"Out of bed, Wife, and see to your husband." Bryan gave her a playful smack with his hand and Aimée stretched sleepily and climbed out of bed. She went into the kitchen to bring back the hot water for Bryan to use in shaving, and when he had finished, his breakfast was ready.

He sat at the table and ate the slice of ham and warm bread, and drank the steaming hot coffee.

"Are you not going to eat, Aimée?"

"I am not hungry this early, Bryan."

She would not tell him that for the past several days, the sight of food had been repugnant to her.

"Your list, Aimée, where is it?" he asked, getting up from the table.

She leaned over, picked it up from beneath the sugar jar, and gave it to Bryan. As soon as he had it in his hands, she became busy, removing the dishes from the table.

She saw Bryan staring down at the florid writing and she said, "On the other side, Bryan. I had to use an old envelope for the list."

Frowning, he turned it over and out of the corner of her eye she observed him as he read. Suddenly he crushed the list in his hand and Aimée scooted for the kitchen with the dishes.

The door closed and Aimée knew that Bryan had gone.

He had gone in a fit of temper, forgetting to show her where he had put the pistol.

What would Bryan have said if instead of writing "1 headstone for Juba," she had written "the *cassette* of baby clothes"? Would he have gone away angry then? She thought of the tiny garments that she had so lovingly made for her first child. She had despaired of ever using them, but now there was a chance . . . if nothing prevented her from having this child.

The headstrong feeling that had made Aimée write such a request was now gone. She was sorry for her impetuosity, for it had not been Bryan's fault that the men had taken the stone. She had not gotten permission from Bryan to use it, and she would always be reminded of her foolish secrecy, for now that the excess mortar had been cleaned from the fireplace, the chiseled letters were in plain view. Thinking about it, Aimée saw the humor in the situation. Not many fireplaces could boast a tombstone for a cornerstone. And on cold nights, when she sat by the fire, she would be reminded of those hours of work that had gone for naught. Suddenly she laughed and dismissed it from her mind.

While Bryan was away that day, the hammers did not sound so busy and Aimée suspected that the workers were not quite so industrious.

The afternoon passed slowly and the workers left for the day. Only the foreman and his cook remained on the plantation. He was responsible for the house, and while it was going up, he never left the premises. But now the house was silent in that strange twilight that hovered between light and darkness.

Aimée sat in the summerhouse and stroked the lute while she sang softly. It was good to be alive. Soon it would be completely dark—time for Bryan to be home, and past time for Aimée to get back to the cottage. She shivered despite the cloak around her, shuddered at the sudden lowering of the temperature and the quickening uneasy silence of the land now under a widening shield of shadows. Blackness stalked the familiar blades of grass and moss-covered oaks in the distance, until they, too, took on a menacing primeval energy, forcing her mind back to earlier times of danger, when she had been the hunted. The happy feeling vanished and her song left her lips.

Aimée stood up, breathing in the danger as some wild creature in a forest glade, her head tilted, listening, her feet ready to flee as soon as the danger had been identified, as soon as the path it would take became known to her.

And then she saw the source of her disquiet—a mass of humanity, black and white, ragged and menacing even from a distance. No returning heroes, these, but scum and scourge of the already torn land—jayhawkers—deserters and outlaws, come to loot and take and kill. And Aimée was alone.

They saw her standing by the summerhouse poised for flight, and they came toward her, cutting off her path back to the cottage. No time to warn Jou-Jou or the foreman—no time to search for Bryan's pistol. She was alone, with only Thornfell to save her from their hands.

Into the unfinished house she fled as the excited voices advanced. The stairs to the second floor were temporary ones, and one misstep would plunge her into the waiting darkness of the cellar below. Aimée hesitated but an instant—just long enough to hear the front door open—and then she lifted her skirts to struggle up the stairs. Her foot slipped and she fell. She clutched the tread until she could right herself—a close call—and then she continued up the steps while the hooting sounded directly below her.

"She's up the steps," a voice called. "Follow her."

"In this blackness?" another voice sounded. "I'll break my neck, climbin' those steps in the dark."

"Wait—here's something. Make a torch and then we can flush her out."

The light flickered below the stairs and Aimée ran along the upstairs hallway until she had come to the even more rickety pieces of board forming the steps to the attic. She paused, knowing that if she fell this time, she would fall two flights—to her death.

Was the secret room finished enough to hide her?

Aimée looked back and the torch came nearer. They were coming for her and Aimée knew her only safety was in getting to the secret room and sealing herself in.

She pressed the panel in the darkness, but it would not move. And the voices and the light kept getting nearer. Had Bryan changed the location of the secret panel? Had he not rebuilt Thornfell as it was before?

Aimée sank to her knees and frantically pressed her hands against the unbudging wood. At one last effort, the panel opened and she rolled into the small room's enveloping blackness as the light flared a few feet away.

"Where did she disappear to?" a rough voice called out. "She was here just a minute ago."

"Well, she couldn't have come down the steps. I'd a seen 'er," another male voice answered. "She has to be up there somewhere, hidin', 'cause here's the cape she was wearin'."

"We'll burn 'er out, that's what we'll do. She'll have to come out then."

"Not if she's a witch. They say witches don't burn."

"What's the matter with you? Just because she's disappeared into thin air don't mean she's a witch."

"Well, is she up there? Have you seen 'er?"

"No, but I ain't seen 'er fly off the roof on a broom, neither. Here, ya want the cape she was wearin'?"

"No—better leave it be. Might cause a heap o' bad luck, takin' a witch's cape."

"Told ya she warn't a witch, Cougar. How many times do I have to tell ya, 'fore ya get it through your thick skull?"

The sound of dogs barking in the distance combined with the slamming of doors and the receding of voices, and Aimée clamped hard on the finger in her mouth to avoid crying out. Would they leave anything at all? Would they burn the house down? When Bryan returned, what would he find after the jayhawkers had had their fun?

The wind rose, carrying away the night noises, and Aimée, cold and shivering, finally gave way to the frozen, drowzy numbness that diffused her body . . . .

The noise of the creaking steps penetrated her drowsiness. Were the jayhawkers again coming to look for her? Had they tired of their looting, and were they now looking for the diversion that had been denied them earlier?

The steps hesitated and started again. With a dawning terror, Aimée waited in her hiding place in the darkness.

The sound stopped at the secret panel. Feet shifted and walked on past. Doors opened and closed. Then the steps were back and Aimée, listening from the thin partition of wood separating her from them, heard the man's breathing, and her own breath came in quicker gasps as she cringed into a tighter ball from the terror waiting on the other side of the panel.

The wood scraped and moved, and a slit of light told Aimée the man had found the secret panel. A hand brushed across her skirt and suddenly gripped her arm. Aimée screamed.

"Aimée, it's all right. Don't scream. You're safe."

"Bryan, Bryan." She was in his arms and sobbing her terror. And Bryan stood, stroking her hair and speaking gently to her.

"They're gone. It's all right. You don't have to be afraid anymore.

Over and over until the message reached her, Bryan repeated the words, and when Aimée finally stopped her clinging, finally pushed away from him, he led her down the steps and out onto the gallery, where Aimée could see the sun peeking over the horizon.

"When did you . . . get back?" Aimée asked.

"Hours ago," he replied. "I have been searching for you all this time along the bayou, but I found only Jou-Jou with her pet chicken. The house was the last place I thought to look. And when I saw your cloak, I knew you had been there. But I didn't believe you could have gotten up the makeshift steps to the secret room . . . . It was very dangerous, Aimée, for you to try it. Yet I cannot fuss, because it saved you. But one false turn and I hate to think what would have happened."

"Did they . . . take much, Bryan?"

"They cleaned us out as far as the food goes, and they took some of the furniture and clothes."

"And Fréki and Geri?"

"They're all right, but they were locked in one of the sheds by the cook. I will have to speak with him about that. They were no protection to you because of it."

For the rest of the day Jou-Jou's eyes were wide and staring, and every so often she went to the front porch of the cottage to peer at the vista, almost as if she were expecting the jayhawkers to come back momentarily. By late afternoon the yard was strewn with strange objects and a few frizzle feathers, proof that Jou-Jou had cast a spell to keep danger from the door.

Chapter 46

The pace quickened; Thornfell was finished and each day brought wagons of furniture—strong sturdy pieces with good lines.

Aimée began to watch for the wagons, wondering what they would bring next. And she excitedly saw the loaded vehicles appear, the goods carried into the house, and the empty wagons disappear down the avenue of trees.

One day in the early afternoon Aimée sat by the window in the overseer's cottage. Working on the quilt from the scraps of cloth in one of the trunks, she heard the rumble of yet another wagon as it came up the road and stopped before the main house. She continued with her sewing until Bryan came into the keeping room.

"Aimée, the piece of furniture from the townhouse has come. You will need to tell the men where you want it placed, for it's too heavy to move if you change your mind. Can you come to show them? They're taking it up the steps now."

Aimée quickly set down her sewing, smoothed her hair, and walked with Bryan to the main house. While she climbed the stairs to the second floor, she wondered which piece Bryan meant—which piece had been brought from the house in New Orleans.

"It's in the master bedroom." Bryan urged her on down the hall to the large bedroom. Standing in the middle of the high-ceilinged room was the carved Lannuier bed—the one that had belonged to Grand-père, the one Aimée had shared with Bryan.

Aimée's eyes shone as she ran her hand along the carved wood. "Against the wall, Bryan, don't you think? Opposite the windows, where it can catch the breeze in summer."

He nodded and the men moved the bed to the place she had designated, and then they left.

Bryan watched Aimée patting the soft feather mattress and tracing the carved pattern of the headboard with her slim long fingers. Unaware that she was being closely observed, she sat upon the bed, and then rolled onto the feather mattress, drinking in its softness with her body, feeling the difference between it and the stuffed moss mattress of the past weeks.

"This bed has pleasurable memories for us both, does it not, Aimée?"

Aimée nodded her head happily and then she became aware of her husband very close to her.

"Shall we try it out now, Aimée, to see if it still holds the same magic?"

Scandalized at his suggestion, Aimée stammered, "In . . . in broad daylight, Bryan?"

He laughed and said, "Who is to know, Aimée? Certainly not Jou-Jou. She is too far away to hear the creaking. The workers are in the fields. We could be the only two in the entire world right now. And we have the afternoon to ourselves."

He leaned over and brushed his lips across her throat while his hands unbuttoned the top of her dress.

"You are . . . seducing me, Bryan," she protested, feeling the familiar longing for his body upon hers. "I should be finishing my sewing while it is still light."

"Forget your sewing, Aimée," he whispered, nibbling at her ear. "There are more important ways to spend an afternoon."

Aimée sighed and relaxed, knowing that Bryan would not be content with just a kiss. . . .

"Bryan," Aimée said, still lying in his arms, "when we move into the house, who will occupy the overseer's cottage?"

"Anderson and Katinka," he replied.

"What about Vickie and Clay? Will they be here at Thornfell, too?"

"No, Aimée. It will be better for you to live apart from Vickie. They will probably visit occasionally—I can't help that, since they are part of the family—but Clay will soon take his brood to another plantation farther upriver from New Orleans."

"Which plantation, Bryan?"

"I . . . had hoped you would not ask, Aimée, but I suppose you would find out eventually. It's Dresden."

The startled, bruised look appeared in Aimée's eyes. "Dresden?" she repeated. And her mind turned again to the horror of the day when she thought Colonel Tilson had killed Bryan. She saw the house as it had been that afternoon, a ghost of the past, when the blinding brilliant light of the sun prevented her from seeing clearly what was happening.

"I realize it is not . . . pleasant for you knowing that Vickie will be mistress there, knowing that if the war had not come, you would be the one enjoying its elegance with your . . . husband, Prosper Gautier."

Bryan looked away from her, acting as if he expected no answer, yet waiting.

"I love Thornfell," Aimée said simply.

His tensed arms relaxed and he said, "Then you do not mind that Vickie and Clay will have Dresden as their home?"

"No, Bryan. I hope they will find happiness and contentment there. It is a good place . . . for children."

Aimée lay silently, wondering if now would be a good time to tell Bryan about the baby . . . that Thornfell would be an even finer place for children than Dresden.

"Bryan, there is . . . something I wish to tell you."

There was no answer. "Bryan?" Aimée softly called, but still there was no sound except her husband's steady low breathing. Bryan had gone to sleep.

In two days' time Katinka, Anderson, Clotilde, and Cousin Jorge arrived, and Aimée waited on the gallery for them to appear down the road. When the carriage came into sight, she walked down the winding curved steps. She was in the yard when the carriage slowed and stopped.

Everyone talked at once, no one really hearing what the others were saying, but it was a joyful reunion. Anxious to see the house, they came inside and Aimée proudly showed them through and helped Cousin Jorge and Clotilde get settled.

Soon, amid the conversation, Aimée missed Katinka and Anderson.

"Bryan, where did Anderson and Katinka go?" Aimée asked when she did not see them anywhere.

"They have gone on to the overseer's cottage. Katinka is not feeling well these days."

Before she could ask him about Katinka, Cousin Clotilde claimed Aimée's attention. "My dear, what is the writing on the stone in the fireplace?"

"It's Juba's headstone, Cousin Clotilde," Aimée answered.

"What?" Her reply had shocked Clotilde.

"It's a long story, Cousin Clotilde—a suitable one to be told by the fire on a cold, windy evening." Aimée glanced up at Bryan and her brilliant smile lit up her face. Bryan, surprised, returned the smile, with an added twinkle in his eyes.

"That reminds me of a strange story I heard when I was a boy. It seems there was this young free man of color by the name of Gabriel. . . ." Cousin Jorge was home.

The idyllic life did not last long. Aimée had hoped that perhaps by this time Bryan would have changed his mind—would stay at Thornfell—but he had not forgotten his original decision.

A week after the others had arrived, Bryan packed his trunk. "Aimée, I have stayed at Thornfell much too long. There are things in Boston waiting for me to do."

So he had not changed his mind after all. He was planning to leave her as he had said he would. Their life together at Thornfell had made no difference to him. Trying not to show her dreadful disappointment, her voice croaked, "And when will you leave, Bryan?"

"Tomorrow, for New Orleans. And then the next day for Boston by ship."

Aimée whispered, "Do you need me to help you pack?"

"No, Aimée. I am almost finished. There is nothing left to do except for Anderson to take me to the ferry tomorrow," he explained, "and bring the carriage back, since you will need it here."

Aimée nodded, and not trusting her eyes to behave, left the room and found the path to the cemetery, where tears were not looked on askance.

For days she had tried to find an opportunity to tell him about the child. But now it was too late. Bryan would probably think she was attempting to hold him by the oldest of women's tricks. Would he ever come back? Would he ever know he had a son? Or that his wife would grieve for him until her dying day?

Aimée sat on the little bench under the myrtle tree, sat and thought of her life and the change that had come into it. She was back where she had started at Thornfell— but it could never be the same. Too much had happened in between.

"Aimée, it's too cold for you to be sitting out here. And it's almost time for dinner. Come inside." Her husband Bryan stood over her, his dark hair gleaming in the late afternoon sun. She drank in his tallness, his fierceness, and traced with her eyes the scar upon his cheek— memorizing for the years ahead when she would no longer see his stern gray eyes gazing down at her, no longer feel his arms about her. And she silently mourned for herself and her child.

The next day he was gone. From the gallery, Aimée

watched the cloud of yellow dust swirling about the carriage and she silently said good-bye to him forever.

One month passed, and then part of another, and still, Aimée's heart had not become used to the ache. She lay in the Lannuier bed at night, alone, with her hand outstretched to the empty place beside her. If she could only forget him—forget the feel of his hands upon her body. Remembering took too great a toll. She must learn to forget.

But how could she forget, with the fluttered movements of his child within her body to remind her? The flutterings grew stronger and more noticeable each day, and to give her child growing room, Aimée now tossed her corset on the armoire. She had a suspicion that Katinka would soon be doing the same.

The smiles of Jou-Jou and Katinka, Cousins Clotilde and Jorge, and Anderson told her they had fathomed her secret.

"Jou-Jou knew beeg, fat, laughing babee come soon," the black woman said with a chuckle.

The vast kitchen in the big house had become Jou-Jou's proud domain, and she ruled over it with a despot's hand. The chicken coop for her pet hen now sat on a table, high enough out of reach of the dogs, and as Jou-Jou went about her work, she talked to the frizzle-feathered chicken in her strange Creole patois.

"Madame meeses her husband, zat is for sure," Jou-Jou commented, looking toward the chicken coop.

Aimée, sitting in a chair near the stove, glanced up from the almost finished quilt to stare at the woman, who was lifting the lid of the iron range. So they had all noticed, even though she had tried to conceal it.

"What thees place needs is a leetle excitement," Jou-Jou added, "to take madame's mind off her loneliness. Not much, mind you—just a leetle."

Clotilde, walking into the kitchen with the letter in her hand, said, "Oh, there you are, Aimée. I wondered where you were."

"Have you been looking for me, Cousin Clotilde?" Aimée asked.

"Yes, my dear. I have just been handed this letter from Vickie, and the man is waiting for a reply. Vickie wants to know if she and the children might come for a visit. It's taking longer than they expected for Dresden to be completed, and the townhouse has been leased to someone else. Clay will be upriver, seeing to the house, and he does not wish Vickie and the four children to be by themselves in New Orleans. Will it be all right, Aimée, if they come to Thornfell?"

"There is . . . plenty of room, Cousin Clotilde. Tell Vickie she may come."

"Thank you, my dear. You are very . . . understanding."

When Cousin Clotilde had left the kitchen, Jou-Jou rolled her eyes and mumbled, "Deed you hear zat, *ma petite poule*? I ask for leetle excitement, and *le bon Dieu*, he send beeg trouble."

Cousin Jorge met the ferry the following day and brought back Vickie and the children by carriage. Their baggage came later, along with Lisette and Lizzie.

It was Juba's absence at the table that made the difference from the old days—that and the addition of little Lee Beauregard in the nursery. He was a chubby, angelic-looking child, but his tantrums belied his sweet looks.

"Clay says he looks and acts just like Bryan did," Vickie lamented. "He constantly demands attention, and he has everybody waiting on him hand and foot. Of course, the girls have spoiled him miserably," she added. "But Clay is resigned to it. He says his punishment on earth is to have a child who reminds him constantly of his brother."

Lee Beauregard smiled and reached out to grab the toy that Charity had. She gave it up to him without protest and Vickie said, "You see what I mean?"

Lisette came to take the two children upstairs for their naps and Vickie and Aimée sat in the salon alone. Aimée, aware of Vickie's sympathetic look, waited for her to speak.

"Bryan has been away a long time, hasn't he?" Vickie asked.

"Yes, a long time, Vickie."

"Let's see, it must be almost two months now, since we saw him off."

"You went to the wharf with him?" Aimée asked in surprise.

"Well, he had come to tell us good-bye, you see, and Clay thought it was the brotherly thing to do to accompany him to the ship. . . . Aimée, what will you do if Bryan never comes back?"

The words hurt. Had she not turned the same question over and over in her mind during the past two months? But even now, Aimée was not prepared to answer.

"What do you mean, Vickie?" she asked. Had Bryan told Clay that he had gone for good?

"I had not intended telling you, but when a man goes off with another woman and leaves his wife behind, it makes you wonder whether he's planning to return."

Aimée, knowing that Vickie was waiting for her next question, could not help herself. She asked it anyway.

"What . . . what woman, Vickie?"

"Oh, I don't know the woman's name, Aimée. But Bryan was very solicitous toward her, helping her board the ship. She was beautiful—and she was wearing a blue velvet cloak, much like the one you have."

The woman in the *calèche*—the same one she had seen Bryan with before.

When Aimée remained silent, Vickie continued. "But your life is not over—John Runefelt is still in New Orleans. I am sure that he would . . . welcome you if you should decide to leave Thornfell."

"Vickie, you seem to forget that I am married to Bryan—and will soon have his child," she said angrily. "Do not even suggest such a thing." She stood up. "If you will excuse me, I feel the need of fresh air."

She went past the coat rack in the hallway—shunning the blue velvet cloak that hung there, and on down the winding steps toward the cemetery, to the bench under the myrtle tree.

It was warmer than she had expected and she sat for a long time, thinking of what Vickie had told her. Vickie had seemed sympathetic, but could she trust her

426

again? No, she would not let Vickie's words disturb her so. The woman might have been just another passenger, someone Bryan knew who was going in the same direction. She would have to think that, or be torn apart. And Aimée, her heart heavy with sadness, left the cemetery.

Approaching the house, she saw Hope and Cousin Jorge sitting on the gallery. The man's steady, warm voice floated resonantly through the quiet afternoon air as Hope pressed close to him and listened to the words he read from the book in his lap.

"If I ascend to heaven, thou art there! . . . If I take the wings of the morning and flee to the uttermost parts of the sea, even there thy right hand shall hold me . . ."

Bryan! Bryan! Aimée could not escape him. Everywhere she looked, he was there. His will had become her will, his desire, her desire. She was a part of him and could not escape. "If I take the wings of the morning and flee . . ." No, she could never escape him.

Chapter 47

The sugarcane fields hummed again with the songs and chants of the workers. There were no slaves on the plantation, only paid workers, and the cane stalks grew tall and thick, while the cotton on the higher ground bloomed and set its green bolls to burst forth in strands of white in the fall.

Vickie had traveled on to Dresden with the children, taking Lizzie and Lisette with her. Jou-Jou still complained about Lisette but her grumblings were less now that the memory of the visit was slowly fading.

Clotilde's musical garden, gradually assuming shape under her hands, held exotic plants—trumpet vines and thimble bells—and the woman, digging in the soft, fertile earth was happy. Cousin Jorge, content to spend long hours writing his history, consulted his notes and arranged them in proper sequence.

Yet, with all the activity, the land was uneasy. There was an uncertainty that gripped it, while politicians argued over its future. Stripped of the franchise, no longer able to have a voice in the very life that affected them, the men returning from war to the land were burdened with poverty, hard work, and quadrupled taxes. Yet they had no voice to protest. They merely endured.

"Cousin Jorge, how did you manage to keep up the taxes on the land?" Aimée asked.

With a nervous cough, he replied, "I couldn't, Aimée. If it had not been for Bryan, we would have lost Thornfell long ago. And now that he has bought it from me, since I could not afford to keep it, he is kind to allow Clotilde and me to live here. . . . We owe Bryan a lot, Aimée."

Once started, Cousin Jorge kept talking. "He has been away longer than I expected. Has he written when he plans to return?"

"No, Cousin Jorge."

"Even though Anderson is doing an excellent job as overseer, Bryan needs to be here," he said uneasily. "Men work better when they know the owner is watching them. And Bryan has a firm hand. Other men will obey a man like that."

Not only men, Aimée thought. A woman, too.

She sat in the summerhouse. In the warmth of the sun Aimée had become drowsy, and the lute slipped through her fingers. She was dreaming again, back in the old brick courtyard, and she felt the caressing fingers push her hair from her face. She smiled as she had that afternoon so long ago, and she heard the same deep voice repeating the words.

"The temptation is too great—to see if you are actually real, or merely a desire of the imagination. . . ."

Aimée struggled to open her eyes and, still in a dream

state, she felt rather than saw the man bending over her. When her eyes fluttered open, she saw his face, saw his silver-gray eyes staring down at her like translucent chalcedony.

"Bryan?" she whispered, not certain that she was fully awake. "Bryan," she repeated more certainly, and finally she shrieked his name. Standing on tiptoe, with her arms outstretched, she hungrily covered his face with kisses, and he stood, submitting to her joyous greeting.

"If I had known I was going to get such a homecoming, I would have gotten here sooner." And then he was the one covering her lips with his own.

But she struggled to speak. "Did you say—homecoming? Are you planning to . . . stay?"

"Aimée, what is this?" he asked, puzzled at the tears streaming from her turquoise eyes. "You act as if you never expected to see me again."

"Oh Bryan," she gasped, "I thought you had left for good."

Her words stunned him.

"But why, Aimée? How could you have gotten such an idea?"

"You told me . . . you had not decided whether to take me to Boston with you—"

"And you thought that when I left, I was planning to stay without you?"

"Yes."

Bryan angrily clenched his fist and said something unintelligible under his breath. Then he explained in a gentle tone. "At the time, Aimée, I was struggling to decide where we would both live. My property, my interests were in the North, yet I knew you loved this Louisiana and would not be happy anywhere else."

He stared down at her ripening figure, the rounded stomach that could not be hidden. "It seems that we have much to talk about—many misunderstandings to clear up. And it also appears you neglected to tell me something very important before I left."

"I am at last a . . . fat Creole wife." Aimée made a *moue* and giggled amid her tears.

He gathered her in his arms and laughed. "I thought a

Creole wife had to have at least *twelve* children before she became fat. Shall we find out, Aimée?" he asked tenderly.

Before she could answer, Bryan swatted at a mosquito lighting on his neck. "These damned mosquitoes have made a meal off me all day. The weather has been stifling, and the river is supposed to reach flood level in two more days. No wonder you were surprised to see me back, Aimée. Any man with a grain of sense would leave this deadly, pestilent place and never come back."

At the alarmed look in her eyes, his voice softened. "Yet there is a treacherous beauty about this land that seduces me into its web. And a certain fat little Creole wife," he added, before taking her into the house.

Jou-Jou stood in the doorway of the kitchen and she laughed in glee when she saw Bryan. "Madame verree happy with beeg husband home, *n'est-ce pas?*"

"Yes, Jou-Jou. I'm very happy," Aimée admitted, her eyes shining.

When the woman had disappeared, singing, back into the kitchen, Bryan said, "Aimée, can't you get Jou-Jou to wear her shoes when she is cooking?"

"She . . . puts them on long enough to serve the food, Bryan. I haven't the heart to make her wear them in the hot kitchen."

Jou-Jou outdid herself in preparing the evening meal. And when she served it, Aimée looked down to make sure that she was wearing her shoes. Relieved, Aimée lifted her eyes and met Bryan's. With an amused glint, he acknowledged her obvious relief.

"What is the news in the North, Bryan?" Cousin Jorge asked, spreading butter on his hot popover.

Aimée heard the long, slow expiration of breath before her husband answered. "General Butler has been elected to Congress, Jorge."

The little rotund man immediately laid down his butter knife, and in a worried voice asked, "Do you think he will do . . . harm to the South?"

Bryan hesitated. "I have heard that he has already allied himself with the radicals and advocates punishment for the secessionist states. And I fear that there are many of like mind in Washington."

"That does not augur well for Louisiana, does it?" Jorge said, almost to himself.

"No—there is much hate to be stamped out before we can become one nation again. . . . But that's enough bad news. Tell me what has been happening here. I rode over the fields with Anderson this afternoon and he has filled me in on the crops—but what about you? What is the family news?"

Cousin Clotilde answered, "Vickie and the children were here for several weeks, before going on to Dresden."

Bryan frowned and, seeing it, Aimée explained, "The house was not ready, Bryan, and they had given up the townhouse. So while Clay went to Dresden to check on repairs, the . . . others came here."

"And your garden, Clotilde? How is it?" Bryan asked, turning back to Clotilde.

"It's thriving, Bryan. Thank you. There is a new variety of lily I have heard about, so I have written to inquire about it. It's called 'Alba,' or 'Morning Song.' "

The evening was strewn with bits of news and silences. The four sat in the salon and Aimée was conscious of Bryan's every movement. He eyed the mantel, as if impatiently waiting for a certain hour to appear on the face of the clock, and when the hands approached it, he stood up. Claiming Aimée with his arm, he said good night to Clotilde and Jorge.

Together they walked up the stairs to the bedroom, and Aimée, conscious of the long absence of her husband, was suddenly shy.

It was hot in the bedroom, but relief came with the breeze that drifted across the meadow and Aimée, having discarded her long-sleeved gowns for the sheer, sleeveless ones more suitable for the weather, was comfortable.

The lights were out, but Bryan stood by the window instead of coming to bed. There was something on his mind, bothering him, Aimée could tell.

During the last weeks of Bryan's absence Aimée continually thought of the woman Vickie had seen board the ship with Bryan. Did he love her, and was that why he was so restless? Because he had decided to put duty first and come back to Thornfell? Or had he merely come back to ask for his freedom? And finding Aimée with child, changed his mind?

A cold terror swept over Aimée and she was still shaking when Bryan climbed into bed. "Are you having a chill, Aimée?"

"N-no, Bryan. I don't know why but I am suddenly cold."

"Then you would never have survived a winter in the North. It's a good thing that you have remained at Thornfell."

He kissed her lightly and then turned over to go to sleep.

Bryan had not wanted to make love to her. Bereft of his caresses, Aimée lay on her side of the bed—wanting to reach out to him, yet not daring to do so. He had rejected her.

He was in a foul mood the next morning. Nothing pleased him. And Aimée, sad-eyed from lack of sleep, had lost the sparkle of the previous day.

"I will be going into New Orleans tomorrow, Aimée," Bryan informed her. "I should have transacted my business when I arrived, but I was anxious to see . . . Thornfell again."

"May I go with you, Bryan?"

"No. It is healthier for you to stay here, Aimée. If you need something, write it down and I will see to it."

"Bryan, I must see Father Anthony. I must go to . . . confession," she replied stubbornly.

Suddenly he laughed. "And what sins will you confess, Aimée? That you used three lumps of sugar in your coffee this morning instead of two?"

She looked guiltily at him. Did he notice *everything*?

The next day the carriage was brought out and Aimée, with Bryan's reluctant permission, went with him into the city.

"You do not have to go so slowly on my account, Bryan," Aimée said, noticing the slow pace of the horses.

"Perhaps not, but since I am anxious that nothing happen to the child, I shall continue the same pace."

Aimée was quiet, saying little to Bryan even after they had reached the ferry.

The city was still the same, except that there were fewer people in residence. It was always that way, Aimée remembered. During the peak months for the fever much of the population fled to the healthier shores of the lake, or to the islands in the Gulf.

The carriage drew up before the cathedral and Bryan, helping her out of it, said, "I will wait for you, Aimée."

"But you have your own affairs to attend to, Bryan. I . . . I can meet you later . . . somewhere."

"No, Aimée. When you are finished, I shall take you to the St. Charles Hotel. There, you will be able to rest while I am busy for the afternoon."

"But I was . . . also planning to go to the St. Louis Cemetery, Bryan."

"Then we will go when I have finished my business transactions."

Would he not let her out of his sight, except when he shut her up in the hotel for the afternoon? Would she not be allowed any freedom at all, even to go to the townhouse?

For Aimée the rest of the day was a disaster. Bryan, in his overbearing manner, had shackled her to him. He had kept her from going to the townhouse on Royal Street because it was closed up. He had ordered the food for her without consulting her wishes, and he had told her when to rest and when to get up. Aimée, feeling hemmed in after living the past months as she pleased, had not been able to take one step without him. Bryan had seen to that, and now, as they were proceeding home at a miserably slow pace, the storm clouds collided over the lake and emptied upon the carriage.

When they reached Thornfell, Bryan continued to treat her as if she were an invalid, making her get into bed immediately, while Jou-Jou, who was already overworked, fixed a tray of food for her and brought it upstairs.

Aimée sat upright in bed, reading a book by the lamplight.

"You should be asleep," Bryan admonished when he came into the bedroom and found her awake.

433

"But I am not sleepy, Bryan. I slept too long this afternoon."

"When the light is out, you will get sleepy," he said, and he blew out the lamp, leaving Aimée in the middle of a sentence. Vexed, she dropped the book on the floor with a thud.

"I hope our child will not have your temper, Aimée," Bryan admonished.

She gave a gasp. "And what a pity if he should inherit your overbearing manner," she retaliated, hurling the words at him.

Bryan chuckled and Aimée, even angrier at his laugh, pulled up the cover with a jerk and lay staring at the ceiling. Bryan promptly went to sleep, but Aimée watched the shadows on the ceiling for a long time.

It was to Katinka that Aimée turned for solace. The next day she sought her out in the overseer's cottage. The girl sat on the porch and stitched delicately and precisely, as the nuns had taught her, while Aimée paced restlessly up and down.

"Is . . . anything the matter, Mrs. Garrard?" Katinka asked.

"Oh, why are men so overbearing, Katinka? Ever since Bryan got here, he has told me what I must do and what I mustn't do. This morning I was helping Jou-Jou change the linen, and when I walked down the stairs with the bundle, he took it from me and gave Jou-Jou a tongue-lashing for allowing me to carry it—even though she had a much larger load. I can't lift a finger when he's around."

"He is . . . concerned for you in your condition, Mrs. Garrard."

"Not for me, Katinka," she corrected. "Only for the baby. I don't seem to matter."

"Now you know that isn't true, Mrs. Garrard. He loves you."

"No, Katinka. He loves . . . someone else. Vickie saw him with her on board the ship. He took her to Boston with him. And . . . and one night I myself saw him with the same woman."

Katinka's eyes showed distress at Aimée's revelation.

"I . . . am sure there is some mistake."

"There is no mistake. Bryan admitted being with the woman," Aimée said, her voice trailing to a minute whisper.

She sat down and watching Katinka, she asked, "Is Anderson happy—knowing that he is to be a father?"

The look on Katinka's face changed rapidly. "Yes. He is very pleased."

Katinka had a soft, faraway contentment, and Aimée, realizing the girl was lost in her own reverie, stood up and murmured an excuse to leave. In her frustration she had revealed far too much to the girl anyway.

Walking back, Aimée noticed the remnants of clouds piecing themselves together in the sky. The wind began to blow and the sudden gust of air ruffled the landscape, causing the moss in the old oak trees to sway gently. All afternoon the wind teased the low-hanging tattered shreds of gray, until by evening the whole earth seemed to be in motion.

At dinner the lamplight flickered and the high winds, rising, became a steady moan. Doors banged suddenly shut and the rocking chairs upon the gallery moved back and forth, pushed by ghostly hands.

Bryan left the table to go over accounting books with Anderson, and Aimée walked to the front door with him. Peering into the darkness, she watched the increasing clouds as they passed over the moon. Like drifts of snow geese hurrying home, they went—a constant procession.

"It looks as if we are in for a storm tonight," Cousin Jorge said at her elbow.

"Yes—the wind is up from this afternoon. But at least it hasn't started raining yet."

One of the chairs blew over on the gallery and Aimée quickly closed the front door against the wind.

"I think I will go on upstairs, Cousin Jorge. Tell Cousin Clotilde good night for me, please."

"I will, my dear. And I hope you have pleasant dreams."

She was in bed by the time Bryan came home. His clothes were wet, and with his frowning face and burning eyes, he resembled Lucifer awakened by the storm.

Aimée guiltily put down her book and slid under the cover, but Bryan came over and commanded, "Aimée, do not go to sleep. There is something that must be settled between us before I can sleep."

She slowly propped herself up on the pillows and stared at him with widened eyes. What had she done now to put him in such a temper?

She waited for him to remove his wet clothes, and when he had stripped, he wrapped himself in the towel and came to sit beside her on the bed. His broad, massive chest, still slightly damp, was at her eye level, and as he began to speak, she watched his chest move in and out with each breath.

"Aimée, look at me when I am speaking to you."

She promptly lifted her head higher until she met his disapproving eyes.

"Do you actually *believe* that I took a woman with me when I left New Orleans for Boston?"

Shame swept over her. Katinka must have repeated to Anderson what she had said that day. And now it had gotten back to Bryan.

But why should she be the one to feel guilty or ashamed? The blaze apeared in her eyes as she answered him.

"Yes, Bryan. And . . . you were seen."

"Who saw me, Aimée?"

"Vickie," she said.

"So again we have Vickie to thank for this . . . misunderstanding."

"But you forget, Bryan. I *also* saw you with the same woman—that night in the *calèche*. And you did not deny it then, Bryan. There is no need to deny it now."

Chapter 48

"Do you know who the woman was that Vickie saw?"

"No—and . . . and I do not wish to know," Aimée replied, turning her head from him.

She felt his hand capture her chin and turn it so that she faced him again. He brushed the tear from her cheek and in a voice that had lost its anger he said, "She was the wife of Major Jennings. They were *both* returning to Boston, Aimée. We happened to be sailing at the same time, that is all."

Aimée lifted her eyelashes and stared at him as he continued. "That night when you saw her in the *calèche* I was taking her home because her husband had asked me to do so. He was on late duty, Aimée. I took her home and returned straight to the townhouse."

"But the cloak . . ." The hurt was still in her voice.

"I bought one like it for you, Aimée, because I liked the color. And I thought at the time how much prettier it would look on you."

He held her against his bare chest and caressed her hair as he spoke. "But I made a mistake, didn't I? I should never have bought something that another woman already had."

Bryan leaned down and tenderly planted a kiss on each cheek where the tears had made a path.

"But if there is . . . no one else, why have you been so . . . distant with me, Bryan?" Her hand moved to his chest and his body shook.

"I do not *dare* make love to you, Aimée. It was my fault

437

before, when you lost the baby. I should have protected you more and watched over you. . . . But know that I will do everything in my power to keep from hurting you this time," he said fiercely, "even to . . . denying myself."

He blew out the lamp and, removing the towel, he climbed into bed beside her, taking her in his arms.

"I am sorry that you have been so unsure of my love. The first time I saw you, standing so defensive and proud, with the vast hurt showing in those beautiful turquoise eyes, I felt a pull that I had never felt before. And it puzzled me, because I thought you were still a child.

"But then that first night when I realized you were not a child but a young woman, I knew we were destined to be together—and I was even surer when you threw the tray in my face.

"But you didn't seem to know, Aimée, that one day you would be mine. You continually eluded me, continually goaded me, and you have fought me all the way, never trusting me. If it had not been for Anderson, I would never have gotten to Dresden in time to rescue you. You should have confided in me, Aimée," he admonished.

"What would you have done, Bryan, if you *had* been too . . . late?" Aimée asked timidly. She waited for Bryan's answer.

"That would have been Tilson's sin, not yours. I would not have held you accountable. What I could not forgive, Aimée, was your running away with Michele after you had helped your Rebel escape from the Customs House."

"Would you believe me, Bryan, if I told you that I did not know Michele's plans?"

"But you were caught trying to leave with her, Aimée. That was the important thing. You gave no thought to how I would feel, knowing my wife had left me for the second time. There is a part of you that has always remained distant, an elusive thing I could never capture, never touch. And each time when I thought I had made some progress in getting you to love me, something would separate us. One day, Aimée, I will *make* you love me."

"I have . . . always loved you, Bryan," she said softly.

"What did you say, Aimée?"

She pressed her face against his shoulder and repeated, "I have always loved you."

His laugh of exuberance filled the air. He crushed her in his arms, and then as if remembering the child, he relaxed his hold. "Do you mean to tell me that all this time you kept it a secret, never letting me be sure? Lord, I was driven mad with jealousy. Everywhere I turned, there were men who loved you—who wanted you, as I want you now."

She felt his lips sliding from her throat to the cleft between her breasts, leaving a trail of fire.

Abruptly he sat up, and hearing him stumble out of bed in the darkness, Aimée asked, "Bryan, where are you going?"

"To the bayou, Aimée—anywhere to cool off."

"But you can't, Bryan—the alligator . . ."

"Then I will stand in the rain. You don't know what you have done to me this night."

She was listening to her name, whispered in her ear. "Aimée—Aimée, it's time to get up."

She was happy. Even asleep, she was happy. There was something that had happened—was it the night before? What was it to make her feel this joy?

"Aimée, the things from Boston have arrived. Get up."

"Bryan?" she mumbled drowsily.

The sheet was pulled from her, and losing its warmth, she crouched and hugged the pillow in her arms.

"You took away my dreams," she complained in a drowsy voice.

"I only took away your cover," the voice corrected her. "Hurry and get dressed."

But she lay on the bed without moving.

She felt the kiss and immediately Aimée opened her eyes. She stared up at Bryan.

"For a moment I forgot the magic formula to break the spell," he said, teasing her.

She sat up, brushing her hair back. "What time is it?"

"Ten o'clock. I let you sleep later than usual, but the morning is half over, Aimée. I can't wait all day for you."

"What things have arrived from Boston?" she asked, recalling the words.

"That I will not tell you. You will have to see for yourself. And you can't until you're dressed."

The water in the ewer was still cool and Aimée felt refreshed after using it on her face and hands.

Hurriedly she dressed while Bryan waited. She started toward the kitchen, but he pulled her in the opposite direction.

"I'm hungry, Bryan," she protested, but he shook his head.

"Jou-Jou will fix you a mammoth-sized breakfast when we get back. You can wait a few minutes, can't you?"

"I . . . suppose so."

She walked with him out the door and down past the colonnaded summerhouse. "How far is it, Bryan?" she asked.

"Not much farther," he replied mysteriously. Then they were at the cemetery. He pushed open the gate and stood aside for her to enter.

"It's in here?" she asked.

"Yes—do you see it?"

Aimée searched the bench, the myrtle tree, and finally the graves. Then she saw it.

The white marble headstone with urns on both sides sat magnificently in the middle of the cemetery. And with a master's hand the name Juba Barnard was inscribed.

"It's . . . beautiful, Bryan," Aimée managed to say. "But I did not really intend for you . . ."

"What? Do you mean you make a habit of putting things on lists that you don't actually want?"

"I *did* want it, Bryan, but—" She stopped. Then, looking up at him, she said, "Thank you, Bryan."

Together they walked back to the house.

"There is another item that came this morning. It is a piece of furniture. But it is not for you. It's for Clotilde."

"And where is it, Bryan?"

"In the salon."

"My dear, have you seen it?" Clotilde's eyes were glowing. "My piano—my beautiful piano." The woman walked over to the polished rosewood and stared at it as if it might vanish before her eyes.

"In the evenings after dinner we will have our music. You can play your lute, Aimée, and I will play my piano, and together we will all sing."

"But there is one song that is contraband in this house, Clotilde," Bryan warned.

"Which one, Bryan?" Clotilde asked.

" 'Bonnie Blue Flag,' " Bryan answered. He stared at Aimée and said, "A certain young lady sang it defiantly in the streets of New Orleans, and it caused me no end of trouble."

All three laughed and Aimée left the room in search of Jou-Jou and breakfast.

Aimée, with her rapidly increasing size, became uncomfortable with her burden. Her steps were slow and cumbersome and she was not permitted to go up and down the stairs alone. Bryan had made that clear to everyone in the house.

"Babee come soon, or madame pop like ripe persimmon," Jou-Jou observed.

"But I don't think it's time yet, Jou-Jou," Aimée replied, fanning herself vigorously.

"For leetle madame's sake, it better be soon. Babee have whole world outside to grow in. Why he want to stay cramped in lettle space so long?"

The next day after Jou-Jou had made her pronouncement, Aimée felt different—as if something were getting ready to happen. And as the day progressed, the small twinge of vague pain widened until there was no doubt. Her child had decided to be born.

"Jou-Jou, I think you had better get Cousin Clotilde for me," Aimée said, clutching the side of the bed.

Jou-Jou's eyes widened and she grinned. "So babee listen to Jou-Jou. Anxious to see thees beeg world."

Clotilde came in immediately, giving instructions to Jou-Jou about hot water and linens, and sending for Bryan, who was in the fields with Anderson, supervising the workers.

As the sudden pain widened and lengthened, Aimée,

grasping Clotilde's hand, heard Bryan's voice commanding, "Jou-Jou, if you intend to stay in here, put your shoes on —and take those frizzled feathers off the floor."

When the pain had gone, Aimée looked up to see Bryan's face, pale and strained, looking down into her own, watching her.

"Aimée," he whispered in a hoarse voice, "is it . . . bad?"

"It will be all right, Bryan," she said, trying to reassure him because of his worried look.

"It has just started, Bryan," Clotilde said. "And will take a long time. Why don't you join Jorge in the salon?"

"And leave my wife, while she bears my son—or daughter? No, Clotilde, I will stay with Aimée."

He sat down near the bed and Aimée reached out her hand toward him. He took it in his giant one and kissed it. But then she closed down hard on his fingers as another contraction began. She held to him, biting her lip, and when Aimée relaxed, Bryan wiped the perspiration from his own face.

Jou-Jou, coming back into the room with the kettle, wore her shoes, but she ignored the frizzled feathers on the floor, and there they remained.

"Monsieur make it hard for leetle madame," Jou-Jou mumbled. "While he stay, she make no sound . . . so worried for monsieur. Hard on leetle madame not to make sound when beeg, fat babee trying to be born."

Bryan, startled at the black woman's words, looked from Aimée to Clotilde with a questioning in his gray eyes.

Clotilde, seeing it, nodded and said softly, "Yes, Bryan. Jou-Jou's right. I think it would be better for Aimée if you left."

Reluctantly Bryan leaned over and kissed her. "I won't be far away, Aimée." And then he was excluded from the room and the door was shut in his face.

Katinka came, and as the minutes and hours ticked by monotonously, Aimée slept for a brief time until another contraction would awake her. Voices sounded off and on at the door and once Aimée feebly heard Bryan's voice. "My God, Clotilde, how much more can she stand? It's been *hours*."

It was growing dark and the lamp was lit. The pacing up and down the hall continued.

"Bryan? Is Bryan outside?" Aimée asked.

"Yes, my dear. We tried to get him out of the house for a while, but he refuses to go. He's taking this very hard," Clotilde answered.

"Poor Bryan," Aimée murmured.

Clotilde brushed back the limp, wet hair from Aimée's forehead and bathed her face in the cool water. Gently, as she had so many times before, she continued her ministrations, changing the linen on the bed, watching Aimée, and showing sympathy and confidence that all would be well.

Jou-Jou went back and forth to the kitchen, while Katinka sat quietly in the corner of the room, her hands busy with the sewing of tiny garments that would be worn soon by her own child. Occasionally she took Clotilde's place for a time at Aimée's side.

The pacing outside stopped, and Aimée was aware of its cessation only when she heard the sound of the carriage outside. Someone came up the steps. There was a knock on the door to the bedroom, and when it was answered, the tall, heavy-jowled man walked in—Doctor Floud.

"Well, my dear, how are you feeling?" he asked Aimée, taking his place beside the bed and watching her as the hard contraction came and went.

Breathing hard, Aimée attempted to answer and her voice came out in a tiny whisper. ". . . So tired."

The man's voice penetrated the room. "You are progressing quite normally," he said as if surprised. "From the message your husband sent me, I thought . . . well, never mind what I thought."

He took her hand and the spasm began again. "Help your child to be born, Mrs. Garrard. Use your muscles to push down—now."

But Aimée had gotten to the point where her body was not to be told what to do. Without instruction, it acted on its own. The waves came faster and faster, with no respite in between.

Something was thrust into her mouth and a voice commanded, "Bite down on this."

On and on came the pain, while she bit down with a moan, and her hands gripped hard the strong, sure ones of the man beside her. Her body, feeling as if it were being torn apart, gave up its burden and she screamed.

Seconds later the wail sounded—the sound of her baby. It was over. Her child had been born. Aimée could sleep. . . .

The light came into the window—the fresh bright light of a new day. Somewhere Aimée heard a baby crying. She opened her eyes, seeing the shadow—a man slumped in the chair beside her.

Doctor Floud? Was he still here? But no, it was Bryan.

She gingerly moved her body and looked down at the flatness that greeted her. At her movement Bryan stirred and opened his eyes. "Aimée?"

"Bryan—no one has told me. Did I have . . . ?"

"You had our son, Aimée." He smiled at her. "You were so exhausted that you promptly went to sleep without seeing him. Jou-Jou has him in the next room. Would you like to see him now?"

"Yes, please."

The baby lay in Jou-Jou's arms, and Aimée, anxious to see the child, held out her own arms for him. The flaming red-gold hair was the first thing she saw. In alarm she looked at Bryan and back again at the child. "You *did* say a son?"

"It's a boy, Aimée, make no mistake. Only he has inherited your temper, as I feared," he said, grinning at her.

"But I wanted him to . . . look like you," she said, holding the wailing baby close to her.

"Babee not care how he look—only how he feel. Veree hongry waiting for madame to rest. Now he say he longer wait," Jou-Jou cut in.

A slow blush crept across her face and Aimée put him to her breast, as Bryan watched every movement. The wail ceased and the baby suckled vigorously.

Bryan touched the tiny clasped hand of the baby, and the child instinctively curled his fingers around one giant finger, while he continued with his breakfast.

He *is* beautiful, isn't he, Bryan?" Aimée asked.

"Yes, my darling, he *is* beautiful." His voice was filled
with emotion. "Thank you, Aimée—for my son." He
gently removed his finger from the baby's grasp and kissed
Aimée on the top of her head. He swung from her toward
the window, as if he wanted no witness to the deep emotion that showed from his silver-gray eyes.

Epilogue

The child grew strong—this child of the golden flaming
hair and the silver-gray eyes. And as Aimée looked down
at her sleeping baby, a sense of awe swept over her.

A son—a man-child to take the place of those slain on
the battlefield. He would be a child of the land, following
in Bryan's footsteps, learning the ways of the bayou and
the delta, of the cotton and sugarcane.

"He's asleep, Aimée. He no longer needs your attention," Bryan said in his gruff, loving voice. "Come back
to bed."

Aimée carefully closed the mosquito netting over the
cradle and obeyed her husband.

"He is outgrowing the cradle, Bryan. We will soon have
to get a larger crib for him."

"We will speak of that tomorrow, Aimée. Right now
you have a jealous husband to assuage. I do not mind
sharing you with him when it's necessary. But at this moment *I* am the one who needs you."

Aimée lay happily in Bryan's arms. She delicately traced
the scar across his cheek—the scar that would always re-

mind her of the scar on the land, the breach that even now had not healed. But her uneasiness was forgotten as Bryan's hands caressed her body, stirred the love and desire within her to new heights. She clung to him, urging him to love her. Her hands caressed his flesh—her flesh now—for they were one.

"Aimée," Bryan whispered in wonder, and his kisses covered her eyes, her throat, her cheeks, her breasts, and she was clothed in his love.

"I love you, Bryan," she whispered, and he tightened his arms about her, as if he would never let her go.

"My love—so sweet . . ."

Aimée, silent with her thoughts, still basked in Bryan's love. And the voices of the past returned to remind her. "What does a young girl know of love, Aimée, until her husband teaches her?" Grand-père's words so long ago at Dresden took on new meaning. And it was her husband Bryan who had taught her well. Yet she had fought him—had been afraid of him, because he was the enemy.

When she had first loved him, the love had been mixed with pain, with divided loyalties. But amid the pain, there had been no other. Neither Prosper Gautier, nor John Runefelt, nor even gentle Juba—it had always been Bryan, Bryan.

Aimée remembered that day Bryan had come home to Thornfell. And his protective voice later when they had walked over the meadow at Thornfell. The words sounded again in her ears.

"The days of the carpetbaggers and the radicals are numbered, Aimée. There will not always be this division of hate and misunderstanding. Together, Aimée, we will meld the best of the North and the best of the South. Our children will be the new strong generation, shaped by adversity and a heritage of tears, but destined for greatness."

Aimée thought of her sleeping child—the son with the flaming hair and the silver-gray eyes.

Bryan's hand reached for her and she willingly came into the comfort of his arms.

The pigeons emitted soft coos as they settled down for the night. Darkness spread quietly over the cane fields and wrapped the earth in velvet shadows, while the old brown pelican flew toward the lagoon, his silent voice an oracle of hope for the ravaged land.

From Fawcett Gold Medal . . .

Great Adventures in Reading

Fiction

MAJORCA by Sam Dodson	1-3740-6	$1.75
DEFIANT DESIRE by Kaye Wilson Klem	1-3741-4	$1.75
WRATH OF THE LION by Jack Higgins	1-3739-2	$1.50
THE FLORIAN SIGNET by Harriet Esmond	1-3743-0	$1.50

Non-Fiction

PAVEMENT PRINCESSES by Kathy Woods	1-3742-2	$1.50

Puzzle

MORE PUZZLE FUN by L. H. Longley-Cook	1-3744-9	$1.25